COME
CLEAN

I would like to give thanks and acknowledgement to an awful lot of people who have had a hand in helping me write this book. First and foremost, to the many Straight Inc. survivors who shared their experiences with me, including Jeanie, Jennifer, Scott, Wesley, Kelly and Alicia, as well as all of those who live on in my own recollections from my own family's time with the programme. To Melissa Davies and Catherine Somers for their twin tales. To Justin Somper for being a creative inspiration. To David Dobson for years of support. To Wallie Ferose for giving me a new place to write. To Gina Paddock for her early encouragement. To my agent at Ed Victor Ltd, Sophie Hicks, for her persistence. To Gillie Russell, Claire Elliot, Jo Williamson, Mary Byrne and everyone at HarperCollins for their enthusiasm and professionalism. And, last but not least, to my parents, my brother and sister, who have all been through so much and still prospered.

COME CLEAN

Terri Paddock

HarperCollins *Children's Books*

To my sister
and all other Straight survivors

First published in Great Britain by HarperCollins *Children's Book*s 2004

HarperCollins *Children's Books* is an imprint of HarperCollins*Publishers* Ltd,
77-85 Fulham Palace Road, Hammersmith, London W6 8JB

The HarperCollins *Children's Books* website address is
www.harpercollinschildrensbooks.co.uk

1

Text copyright © Terri Paddock 2004

Terri Paddock asserts the moral right to be identified
as the author of this work.

ISBN 0 00 717247 8

Printed and bound in England by
Clays Ltd, St Ives plc

PROLOGUE

You, Joshua, had a problem.

Joshua had a problem, many problems; Joshua was problematic – this was what everyone said, as they looked to me, their eyes formed like question marks, curving into pointless concern.

Joshua is a problem, and, God forgive me, I listened, nodded, agreed. Which, by association, must mean I'm a problem too.

CHAPTER ONE

I'm busy in the swimming pool, dreaming of you and me under water, gripping on to each other's chubby wrists, our cheeks big and round with stored breath, our eyes big and round and locked on each other, the chlorine on our skin, bubbles ringing our faces and our feet kicking out behind us. And when I rise reluctantly to the surface, away from the water-mottled laughter, the heartbeat in my head and the hum of trying not to breathe, I'm dry and nowhere near the pool.

I don't hear the alarm or any other sound. On a Sunday there should be bustling about – Dad shouting for Mom to find his tie with the blue stripes, Mom shouting for Dad and everyone to hurry up, the smell of brewing coffee that Dad drinks by the mugful to stay alert during the minister's sermon. There's nothing.

I attempt to pry my eyes open but my lashes have bound themselves together. I rub at my lids. I'm in the rollaway bed again, in your room, looking up at walls and ceiling, blinded windows, bed frame. The clock face looms somewhere on the night stand above my head. 10:47 a.m. We're cutting it fine. I should bolt out of bed immediately, but...

I let my head fall back into its hollow in the pillow and try with all my might to lie very, very still. But the stillness only draws attention to the trouble spots. My head's exploding. My mouth is completely coated in a foul-tasting furry substance, my tongue swollen, glued to my teeth and the roof of my retainer. My muscles ache, my skin feels tight and goosepimply at the same time, the hairs on my arm stand up like the bristles of a brush. Down below, my stomach burbles, daring me to make any sudden moves.

I turn my nose into the pillowcase for comfort. It hasn't been washed since and I can still smell you there. I sink into that smell.

Footsteps pound heavily along the hallway overhead. They're on the stairs, avalanching down. I hold my head as the door swings open, banging hard against its stop at the back. Mom flicks the light switch and the brightness makes me wince.

'Get up.' She's wearing her navy woollen dress and already has her hair combed and sprayed into place, her nose powdered, navy pumps buffed.

I whimper.

'Get up. Now, Justine.'

'Mom, I don't feel so good. I think I might be sick.'

She makes a noise. 'You're not sick. That's not sickness you're feeling and you know it.'

'But Mom, we're not going to church, are we?'

'Suddenly you're too good for praying?'

'We'll be late, you hate ducking in late.'

'We won't be late. Not if you get a move on.'

'But Mom...'

'But Mom nothing. Get up, I said. Do you hear me? Now! Get!'

Her voice has the edge. I prop myself up unsteadily on one elbow.

'We're going to church and then we're going to the mall.

We've got errands to run, lots of errands. We're leaving in ten minutes and I expect you to be dressed and ready.'

She yanks the door to on her way out, my head cracking between the hinges. Ten minutes. I throw back the sheets and swing my feet to the floor, but as soon as I pull myself erect, my stomach lurches. Vomit rises in my throat as I dash to the bathroom.

I crouch over the bowl there. The porcelain's cool, smooth like vanilla ice cream against my cheek, and the nausea subsides.

Delicately, I get to my feet, brush my teeth and retainer, scrub my tongue and splash water on my face, then stagger back into your room to dress. There's no time for a shower or even to venture upstairs to my closet for a decent outfit. The blouse I was wearing last night is soiled with God-knows-what and my pantyhose ruined from a shoeless midnight sprint across the muddied football field. I dump them in the trash can. My tartan skirt's wrinkled but passable and, thankfully, long, and I find an old turtleneck at the back of one of your half-empty drawers.

By the time Mom returns, I've buckled on my Mary Jane shoes and tied my hair back, just avoiding tearing the scalp from my screaming head, and have started rummaging in the medicine cabinet for that blasted Tylenol and where, oh where, has that water glass got to?

Mom gives me the tip to toe once-over and clucks disapprovingly. 'This is how you dress for church nowadays?'

'I only had ten minutes.'

'Where on earth are your pantyhose?'

'They had a run.'

'Every pair? Oh for heaven's sake.' She checks her purse for lipstick, tissues and Tic Tacs as she shows me her back. 'Get your coat, your father's starting the car.'

At last, the Tylenol. I dump two out and pop both down my throat, but still no water glass. I slurp direct from the tap but can't get a good angle, can't sluice my mouth enough. The pills lodge halfway down my gullet, trapped in the furry sludge. I cough, grab my coat and a pair of sunglasses and follow Mom out to the garage where Dad glowers behind the wheel of the Volvo.

As Mom settles into the passenger seat, Dad motions for me to hit the garage door opener. The chain overhead creaks, the garage murk dissipates as the midwinter light crawls in through the widening opening. I don the sunglasses before it can reach my line of vision and try to catch a parental eye through the windshield. Dad's already pulled down his visor and Mom's staring straight ahead to where the lawnmower's stored. Her face is splotched and extra puffy, but her eyes are dry, hard and glassy like marbles.

'Come on, dammit,' Dad grumbles. I scramble into the back seat next to his neatly folded overcoat and buckle up in double-quick time.

Dad eases the car out of the garage, checking his path in the rear-view mirror in case the rose bushes bordering the driveway are in a mind to scratch his paintwork. Once clear, he reaches to the visor for the garage door remote. He clicks, nothing happens. Click, click.

'Goddammit!'

I know he wants to order me to get my ass up and shut that frigging garage, but for some reason he doesn't. He leaps out, the car door hanging open and dives into the garage himself.

I take advantage of the opportunity. 'Mom, look, I'm sorry, really I—'

'Shut up.'

'But—'

She doesn't move her head one inch in my direction. 'Shut up, shut up!'

The garage door begins its descent and Dad shimmies out beneath it just in time, the rubber seal catching the back of his suit jacket and leaving a smear of dirt that he doesn't seem to notice as he climbs back into the car.

This is bad. Worse than the time you and I trapped the neighbour's cat in the mailbox, worse than when we got picked up by the cop for loitering in the Kmart parking lot, worse than when you brought home the report card with two 'D's and I tried to forge Mom's signature, worse even than when we skipped fifth period so Lloyd Taggart could drive us and Cindy round the block in his Dad's Audi, even though he only had a learner's permit and we hadn't even started our semester of Driver's Ed. I shiver and wish I'd gone upstairs for a new pair of pantyhose, wish I'd remembered my gloves.

I start coughing again and swallow hard to force the Tylenol down but the pills won't budge. I cough until my nose runs. 'Dad, please can we stop at the 7-Eleven for a Big Gulp of Diet Coke?'

'You know the rule, Justine. Or have you forgotten that one too?'

'Just some water then.'

'No drinks allowed in the car. Now quiet.'

I lock my jaw to contain the coughs, my nose still dripping like a garden hose. I'd like to ask Mom for one of those tissues of hers, but I make do with the cuff of your old turtleneck.

*

We coast through the neighbourhood. Past Cindy's house with the peeling green shutters, past our old elementary school, past the playground where you knocked your two front teeth out on the jungle gym. At the lights, we right-turn-on-red on to Route 5 and join the stream of Sunday brunch traffic. Dad speeds up and thumps the wheel if the lights threaten to stop him – as they do, one after another.

'Damn timing mechanisms are way off,' he mutters. We switch lanes, manoeuvre round slowpokes and honk at other roadrunners. As we crest one steep hill and then another, my stomach drops away, and I have to cover my mouth with my hand and bite back the bile.

'Dad, I'm gonna be sick. Pull over.'

'You know the rule. Scheduled breaks only.'

'Dad!'

Twisting round now, Mom takes a good look at me. 'I think you'd better stop, Jeff. She's pretty peaked.'

Dad sighs, flicks on his blinker and gestures at other drivers. There are two lanes to cross to the shoulder and I'm not sure we're going to make it. I've flung the door open and am familiarising myself with the gravel before Dad's got the hazards on. Please, please, please. My stomach convulses, jolting my whole body. I feel wetness at my eyes but nothing else is coming up. Cindy told me last night I should puke before I went to bed: hurl, drink two great big glasses of ice-cold water, swallow three Tylenol, then pass out. It didn't work. I wretch dryly a few more times and then get back into the car.

We drive on. Outside, Route 5 slips by – and before long so does the turn-off by Tastee-Freez for the road that leads to the cul-de-sac where our church is.

'Aren't we going to church?'

'We're going to the mall first.'

I consult my Swatch. 'But church starts in fifteen minutes. We'll never make it in time.'

'We'll go to the later service.'

A truck driver behind us leans on his horn, heralding another wave of nausea to crash over me. 'Dad, please pull over again.'

'Not on your life.'

'I'm gonna be sick.'

'You're not going to be sick.'

My stomach rolls, pressing me forward into my knees. 'I am.'

'You're *not* going to be sick.'

I heave again and here comes the long overdue foulness, spilling out into the well behind Mom's seat. It splashes up on to my shoes and the grey leather upholstery.

Mom gasps, 'Dear Lord.'

Our car swerves as Dad's head whips round, the trucker's brakes squeal, and the sudden motion only makes things worse. 'Holy shit!'

I spit to get the lumps and acid burn off my tongue, but then another eruption flecks my loosened locks of hair and my skirt and your turtleneck, spattering on to my shins as it drums on to the floor mat. I grope for something to wipe my mouth and my hand lands on Dad's overcoat. The belt droops into the vomit as I pull the coat to my face.

'What the hell do you think you're doing?' Dad flails at me with his right arm, the car veering into the adjacent lane to the blaring protest of other drivers.

'Sorry.'

'Dear Lord, I'm so ashamed,' wails Mom. 'First Joshua, now

you. What's the matter with you, Justine?' She's got a whole clutch of tissues unpursed now and is dabbing at her eyes.

'Do you see what you're doing to your mother? Did you think about that when you were gallivanting around last night?'

'I wasn't gallivanting.'

'Don't talk back to me, young lady.'

'I wasn't talking back.'

'I'm warning you.'

'Oh, Lord, Justine. How could you?'

'Mom, it was one time, just—'

'Just nothing.'

'I mean—'

'Quiet! I can't bear to hear another word out of your mouth.'

Dad rolls down the front windows to dispel the vomit stink. Mom hates driving with the windows down at any time of year, but despite the cold not even she's going to kick up her usual fuss. She flips her visor down to determine the havoc the wind's wreaking on her hair and shoots me an evil eye care of the vanity mirror.

The wind cyclones through the car, turning my bare legs blue. I try to appear contrite but am pretty busy feeling cold. I fold my arms and cover my lower half with Dad's coat. I would sell my Michael Jackson collection for just one sip of water to get rid of this post-puke taste in my mouth. I slip out my retainer and gross myself by inspecting the bits clinging to it. No question, the thing needs a rinse. I use the lining of Dad's soiled coat to swab it clean, but it still looks too disgusting to insert in my mouth so I stash it in the flip-out ashtray in the door. No one's ever smoked in this car – that's another one of the rules – so it's as hygienic in there as anywhere.

I lean back against the headrest and close my eyes. I'm exhausted. If it weren't so cold, if my head didn't hurt so much and my bangs weren't slapping so ticklishly around my cheeks with the wind, I might be able to doze off. It's good to have the glasses on so Mom and Dad don't know if I do.

As it is, I do drift. I can see myself last night. In the gym bleachers, too morose for words, with Cindy at my side. Beth and Kelly are there too but they aren't my best friend so they don't know what to do and sit there acting awkward, like unnecessary appendages. Cindy isn't too certain what to do either. So she produces a brown paper sack from her backpack, scans the area for teachers, then furtively extracts a can of Milwaukee's Best from the sack and presses it into my hand.

'You need it. Take your mind off all this family shit, just for tonight.' I don't even like the taste of it, but Cindy assures me that if you drink real fast you can hardly taste it at all. What does Cindy know. She also said the Wrigley's Spearmint would mask the smell, she said our parents had better things to do than wait up for me, she said the beer – then the pineapple wine cooler then the rum – would make me feel better. Wrong, wrong, wrong.

When I open my eyes, we're on the interstate. Cars zoom past in the opposite direction, loud as dying insects.

'I thought we were going to the mall,' I shout.

'The one across town,' Dad shouts back.

I close my eyes again and then I must doze, because when I reopen them, we're off the interstate and the wind chill has tapered some. Mom still has her visor down and is eyeballing me through the mirror as she reapplies her lipstick. According to my Swatch, half an hour or thereabouts has passed.

'What's going on?'

'Your dad's lost.' She touches the corner of her lips then applies another coat. 'It's not bad weather for February, is it? What do they say about weather in February, Justine? It'll tell you if you're going to have an early spring? Or is that Groundhog Day? Maybe Groundhog Day is in February? I don't know. Is it? Maybe it is.'

This is the most she's said all morning. 'What do you think, honey?'

Honey? She's talking to me? 'Errr, I don't know, Mom.'

'I never can remember those minor holidays. What's the point in declaring a day a holiday anyway if you're not going to give people time off, I ask you. Justine?'

'Dunno.'

For a millisecond, I think maybe I've actually made it through the worst. Maybe something magical happened when I was napping and now all's forgiven. But then I see Harvey's Shrimp Shack.

You know Harvey's Shrimp Shack, how could you forget? That falling down old barn of a building with a neon sign tacked to the front that flashes 'All You Can Eat Shrimp – $5.97'. The Shrimp Shack is not a chain, it's a one-and-only, but we've passed by it before, too many times. And every time I pass it I wonder, why on earth $5.97, why not $5.95 or a round six bucks? I don't consider the conundrum this time, though, because there's just a single thought spooling through my mind: the Shrimp Shack means one thing and one thing only.

Then a few other thoughts occur to me, too. One, there is no later service than eleven thirty; two, the mall across town closed down a month ago; and three, Dad never gets lost.

CHAPTER TWO

'Where the hell are we going?'

Mom winds down her lipstick, careful not to catch the edge – she must be wearing about 112 coats by now – and she replaces the cap. 'To the mall, of course.'

I swore – said hell to our parents as loud as you please and she didn't bat an eye. I clutch my hands together, squeeze hard till all I can feel is bone. 'What's going on, Mother?'

'After we finish the errands, maybe we can go to that new frozen yoghurt stand. It's a funny concept, isn't it? Frozen yoghurt? I never have liked yoghurt, I imagine there aren't many people who'd claim to be yoghurt fans. Just the thought of it, just the word – yoh-gert. It's a funny sounding word, foreign sounding, rather unpleasant, a funny food. But freeze the stuff, and people can't get enough, you've got a craze on your hands. Amazing. And they do have such inventive flavours, don't they? You'd like that, wouldn't you, Justine? Pay a visit to the frozen yoghurt stand? We can get one of those waffle cones with the sprinkles on top. You'd like that.'

'The yoghurt stand is at the other mall.'

She brushes nonexistent hair out of her eyes and flicks her visor mirror closed so I can't see her face any more. 'I'm sure they'll have one at this mall, too.'

'We're not going to the mall, Mom. You know we're not.' My voice rises. The 7-Eleven slides past our open windows, the Hardee's with the kiddies' playground, the David's Son motorcycle repair shop, the Green Valley block of low-rent town houses. 'Why are you going on about the damn mall?'

'Of course we're going to the mall. We're going to the mall to do some errands.'

'What errands?'

'What errands? Oh, you know, the usual things.'

'I don't know.'

Mom hesitates. 'Well, we've got to go to the dry cleaners for one. And, then there's the, uh, we've got to stop off at JC Penney's because I need some blue thread for my sewing kit. And, well, while we're there we should probably buy you some new pantyhose because you don't appear to have a pair left to cover yourself with. And—'

'Mom, there are no errands.'

'Of course there are, why else would we be going to the mall?'

'Stop it!' I snap, trying desperately to retrace the route in my head, in case it comes to that. 'That mall closed down over a month ago. There is no Penney's, no yoghurt stand. They're all shut.' Cindy will have to steal her sister's car or get Lloyd to drive. And she'll need directions. You get on to the interstate heading north, I'll say. Then how far do you go? What exit do you take? Is it a left or a right after the lights? How many miles do you drive? How many minutes? Look for the Shrimp Shack, the Shrimp Shack's the marker.

Our mother's pint-sized head moves about in juttery starts the way it does, like a bird. Tilting from side to side, bobbing down

18

repeatedly as she inspects her lap, her cuticles, the contents of her purse. Peck, peck.

'Mom. Where are we going?'

She punches Dad in the arm. 'Jeff, why don't you say something? Am I the only one here?' She punches him harder. 'Jeff, say something dammit!'

Our mother swears this time. Our mother *never* swears.

Maybe I should jump. How bad could it hurt after all? We can't be going more than 35 mph. I will my hand to the door, my fingers glance the handle. Just yank then tuck and dive, like a gymnastic exercise that Mr Zarrow or Ms Loy or whoever taught us in PE class, nothing more. I screw up my eyes and squint at the tarmac, whizzing by. It's hard, black, gravelly. No.

Dad slams the blinker and turns into that road. There's no reason to say or do anything now. I cast about frantically for a road sign, but can't locate one. Why don't I ever know the names of roads? Warehouses flank us on either side. Strictly business trade. Look for the warehouses, I'll say, there's the Caterpillar tractor warehouse, the Billy's Printing Supplies warehouse, the Dutch Tulips warehouse. Half a dozen others, all locked up, Sunday-quiet and stacked full of bulbs, books or heavy farm equipment. All corrugated iron and identical from the outside except for the choice of potted shrubbery, the executives' initials on the VIP parking spaces, the company logos.

Only one warehouse is logo-free. It's even more nondescript than the rest. This is where we're going. Of course it is. No logos, no shrubbery, no signs, no initialled spaces. But it is open for business. There's a smattering of cars in the front lot and I can see lights and the manned reception desk through the glass of the double doors. Dad eases into an empty space a few yards from the entrance, kills the engine and leaves the keys dangling in the ignition. The fob – in the shape of a miniature, but perfectly formed, set of dentures – knocks against the steering column.

My knuckles are white and taut, my veins braided like blue-coloured macramé beneath the surface of my skin.

Dad lumbers out of the car. 'I'll go and tell them we're here.'

Mom keeps nodding even after he's gone and out of sight. She fishes in her purse for Tic Tacs: I can hear mints clattering against plastic.

'What's going on, Mom? Tell me. Please.'

'It is cold, isn't it? I think we ought to roll the windows up now, don't you? I just hate driving with the windows down.' She leans over and notches the key enough to power the internal electrics then presses fingers on the automatic up-buttons for all four windows. The planes of glass hum until we're sealed in.

'That's better, isn't it? I think so, too.'

'Why are we here?'

'Tic Tac, Justine?' She rattles the box.

Laughter springs up within me even as my eyes wobble. I unfasten my seat belt. 'This is no time for mints, Mom. Listen, I know I was bad last night, but it was just once. I was – was... stupid. I promise, Mom. It'll never happen again. Can we go home now? Please.'

'Oh. That's right, you're thirsty. You don't want a mint, you want some water. How silly of me. Let me go get you a glass.'

'Are you listening to me, Mom?'

'Certainly, Justine. Mommy'll bring you some nice cold water.'

She snatches the dentured key ring and darts into the building after Dad. Probably I should make a run for it then and there.

But, like our parents, I'm not thinking clearly. We all need a chance to come to our senses.

By the time they return with another woman – and without any water – I've thumped all the car locks down. Our father realises this when he tries to open my door.

'Open the door, Justine.'

I pretend I'm stone. Like when we were little and used to play statues.

'I said, open the door.' Ferociously, he jiggles the outer handle. 'Helen, the keys. Where are the keys?'

Our mother delves back into her handbag. The bag is on the small side and it's a big ring of keys, but they appear to have gone missing nonetheless. Her hands tremble, like my own. One by one, she removes the familiar purse contents and places them on the kerb. When the purse is empty, Dad seizes it from her, rips the lining pockets inside out, tips the whole thing upside down and shakes it, lint and stray pennies go flying.

Then Mom discovers the keys in her coat pocket.

Dad brandishes the dentures fob like a mad prison warden. The keys for the Volvo jingle heavily against those for the house, which domino the ones for the practice, the spare set for Mom's VW and the little skeleton one for the cabinet where he stashes the Novocaine and other anaesthetics. 'We've got the keys, Justine.'

'I can see that, Dad,' I holler.

Still I don't open the door. Dad marches to the driver's door and inserts the appropriate key in the lock. The button pops up. He grins triumphantly, but I pound the button back down quicker than he can lift the handle. His grin turns to grimace. After a few

21

more tries, me punching the button down each time, he scurries round to the passenger side. I'm there before him too and we rerun the same routine.

'Helen, get the spare keys.'

Mom stands, flummoxed, with her purse disembowelled all over the pavement.

'Where are the spares, Helen?'

'In the key cabinet, Jeff. At *home*.'

Dad removes his tie and circles the car a few more times, until he's panting. That's when the other woman steps in.

She places her hand on his elbow. 'I don't think that's necessary, Mr Ziegler.' She's pretending to talk to our dad, but her eyes are trained on me so I glare straight back. 'Justine knows she can't stay in there for ever. She'll come out when she's ready.'

I grit my teeth. I'm not sure whether or not I'm scared shitless or angry as hell. I bead up my eyes and fix them on her. Her own eyes – small, grey and widely set – hold my gaze. She's nearly as tall as Dad and there's too much of her body, too tall, too wide, too much. Around her neck hang two cords. At the end of one is a discus of keys, fobless and even more crowded than Dad's; at the end of the other, a whistle.

I recognise this woman. Her name is… Hilary, I think. I'm pretty sure she's the director of this place, the big cheese. I don't know her last name – they never use last names – but I know her. She sat in on my sibling interview soon after you were admitted. Your intake, that's what they called it. Barely uttered a word then, just watched me like she's watching me now. I didn't like her. Didn't like her then, don't like her now. I would say hate, but Mom told us never to say you hate on first impressions. Hate's a thing that needs time to grow.

22

Ten minutes pass, maybe less, maybe more. I press the spot on my forehead just above the bridge of my nose until I glimpse stars. Twenty minutes. I unbutton my coat. Thirty minutes. There's no air in here. Forty minutes. The smell from the vomit is horrible. Forty-five minutes. The smell's overpowering, it flavours the air. I pinch my nose and take short, sharp, shallow breaths so I don't have to taste the wretched stuff all over again. Fifty minutes, it must be fifty minutes. I consult my Swatch for the 2,367th time. I'm hyperventilating, my head is ratta-tat-tatting. I may pass out. If I pass out, they'll get me.

What would you do in this situation?

An hour later, I open my door and puke at Hilary's feet. She doesn't move, just blows her whistle until four new feet bound into my field of vision.

'Very good, Justine. Now you can accompany us inside of your own accord or Mark and Leroy can assist you.'

I raise my eyes to Mark and Leroy who are standing, stony-faced, legs apart, arms folded, shoulders swelling. They should be visiting college football recruiters, and arguing with our dad about who's likely to make it to next year's Rose Bowl, not witnessing me wring my guts out.

'Your choice. What's it going to be?'

CHAPTER THREE

A week late, dragging along an uninvited guest. That's how we arrive in this world. It's that time of day where people don't know whether to call it night-time or morning and Mom's been in labour for going on ten years. She alternates between a shade of puce and a white so white you could lose her on the gurney if you crossed your eyes. The doctor shouts at Mom to push and she pushes and pushes and pushes.

'I can see the head!' bullhorns the doctor. Then, in a motion that might seem sudden if everyone hadn't been congregating so long round Mom's nether regions, you slide out.

'It's a boy!'

You're holding on to your winky and wailing. Mom throbs in strobe-light fashion, one constant pulse of pain, but still reaches out to draw you to her bosom. 'A boy.' Her lips flutter into a feathery smile.

'Here comes another one!' announces the doctor.

'Another what?'

'Eh?' The doctor's clearly half deaf. How else can his missing that second heartbeat in the first place be explained?

A fresh contraction doubles Mom up as one of the nurses wrenches you from her. And then here comes me, follow-theleadering you right out the trap door, a little soggier, a little quieter, with nothing to hold on to but Mom's umbilical cord, which I let go of pretty swift-like.

That's how we imagine our birth, anyway. We can't say for sure. Mom never told us particulars. When we got to an age of wondering after such things, she'd answer vaguely. 'It was such a long time ago,' she'd say. Or, 'They had me so drugged up, kids, I didn't know who was coming or going.' Or, if maybe we'd been why-ing her for awhile already, she'd just snap, 'Because,' even though it wasn't a 'because' kind of question in the least, or, 'Does it really matter?'

This is what we know for sure: we were born sometime in the morning (5:00 a.m.? 11:52 a.m.?) on 25 August at the University Hospital in Piedmontville, North Carolina, home of the Central State University, where Dad was finishing up his dental degree. You came out first and, seven and a half minutes later, I appeared.

We've never had it confirmed but we strongly suspect Dad was nowhere in the vicinity of the hospital when we made our grand entrance. We figure he arrived later, at a respectable hour, the sun high in the sky. Maybe he's been taking an exam or memorising a textbook or practising with his drills. Or maybe he's late because he's picked Grandma and Grandpa Shirland up from the airport. Grandpa's still alive at this point though already ancient and doddery, gone soft in the head with age. He clings to Grandma's arm and stops to let his heart slow down after the excitement of the doors that whooshed open and closed all by themselves.

Meanwhile, Dad barrels past the nurses' desk unannounced,

his leather soles dog-whistling along the swept salmon-and-lime-speckled tiles. He heads the wrong way, striding purposefully towards geriatrics until some doctor or orderly or whoever it is at the hospital on glad tidings duty recognises him and steers him in the right direction while attempting to share said tidings. Dad listens with one ear and nods his understanding, but all he hears is 'boy' and 'twins'. And his mind adds those two words together in an equation that goes boys + twins = identical = two sons. Because twins mean identical, right, and identical means, if nothing else, same sex. Right?

You'd think they would have taught him otherwise at some point in all that expensive medical education of his. But what do budding orthodontists know? Dad knows twins are identical and boys are little creatures who grow up into men who carry on the Ziegler name. He hauls up at the viewing station and shoulders his way through some other newborn-gawkers to the front of the glass so he can size us up. We've been stashed in the same crib and, to be honest, we're not too impressive. Downright tiny, only five pounds apiece and drowning in hospital regulation cotton. And we're yellow, shrivelled and flaky – overcooked, as Mom used to say – these are things she remembered to tell us. But we're men-to-be. Dad eyes his progenies and, without consulting Mom who's got many days and weeks of drugged-out-ness ahead, he decrees us Joshua and Justin. He tells the nurse or orderly to write it down. And they keep shtoom, do as they're told and write down Joshua and Justin Ziegler.

'How adorable,' coos Grandma who's just caught up, towing Grandpa behind her like a badly hitched trailer.

Then Grandpa judders to a halt and follows Grandma's finger to where it crooks at us through the glass. Just a bundle of baby under a single snowy blanket. He lowers his chin, squints and peers through his Norman Rockwell bifocals. 'Amazing, Jeff,' he says to Dad. 'How on earth did you and Helen manage to have a two-headed baby? Ain't that funny.'

That last bit is true, Grandpa really did say that, or words to that effect. Grandma Shirland has been telling us that story for years and others around the family have been retelling it to their neighbours, their friends, mailmen and each other until it comes full circle back to us and they tell us again like we never heard it before.

And the naming thing was also true, though Dad didn't let that one get round quite so far. I imagine he was pretty disappointed when he realised I didn't have a winky. He tacked an E on to my name on the hospital form, wrote it in himself, a big messy capital letter that didn't match any of the pretty orchid-like penmanship that blossomed across the rest of the page. And I became Justine.

CHAPTER FOUR

The Amazon woman named Hilary repeats the question. 'What drugs have you used?'

'None.'

She sways slightly in her seat, left to right. Hers is one of those office swivel chairs with wheels for feet. All of the chairs in the intake room are woefully mismatched. Four chairs, none the same. Mine's a correct-your-posture ladder back, splintering wood, no cushion. 'You sure about that?'

'Yeah, I'm sure.'

'Alcohol is a drug too.'

'OK, then, alcohol, I've had alcohol.'

Dad grunts. He's lumbered with a forest-green garden chair, plastic and stackable. It's not a piece of furniture that's kind to the spine or accustomed to bulk. Its front two legs splay out beneath Dad as if in pain; he struggles to keep his neck and shoulders straight despite the sag. On the wall above his head hangs a needlepoint godsquad quote: 'Believe in Him' it commands. The rest of the walls are whitewashed, bare except for a few dusty cobwebs that cling to the furthest reaches of the ceiling. The spiders have vanished.

'Anything else?'

'No.'

'You sure about that?'

'Yes.'

A checked, Formica-topped table is shoved up against the wall just behind Hilary. On top of the table sits a pile of papers – some normal-sized and lots of little scraps – and on top of the pile is a clipboard. She picks up the clipboard and taps her pen against the metal clip. I focus on the tabletop. The Formica is yellowed, curling up at the corners like a half-peeled banana.

I'm hungry. And thirsty and tired. But I'm struggling to hold myself together. I saved Mark and Leroy the effort of flexing their muscles. Raised myself up, held my head high, carried myself into this dingy place with as much dignity as possible. I'm still thinking, though, that bruises, broken bones, abrasions or come what may, I might have been better off jumping from the car.

Hilary curls the top pages over the back of her board. 'According to our files, there may have been other substances.'

'I don't know what you're talking about.'

'Marijuana perhaps. Mary Jane, grass, dope, weed, call it what you will.'

That makes me giggle because I never knew marijuana was called Mary Jane which only puts me in mind of my shoes, a girl I knew in kindergarten, and the nougaty candies in the mustard-coloured wrappers we used to love to chew even though they stuck to your teeth for hours on end. That candy business infuriated Dad, who made us floss three times on the spot.

'Something funny?'

'No.'

'So how many times have you smoked marijuana?'

'I haven't.'

29

'Never?'

'Never.'

She checks the page, glances from it to me and back and forth again.

And waits.

I wonder. She couldn't mean that time with you, could she? That doesn't count. I just wanted to know what you and those weirdo friends of yours were doing. I remember it, last summer, how for weeks on end I heard you stirring in the night, watched from my window as you crept out and down the drive to where that trash-heap of a car was idling with its lights off. Where were you going, my Joshua? I had to know.

One night, past twelve, I crept down the stairs and met you at the front door. 'I'm coming too,' I announced.

'No, you're not.'

'I am. Unless you want me to wake Mom and Dad.'

'You wouldn't.'

I opened my mouth as if to scream.

'All right, all right, come if you must.' I followed you outside in my slippers and, by the time we reached the car, my feet were sodden from the puddles formed by Dad's sprinkler system.

I didn't recognise the three other boys in the car. They didn't look much like boys at all. They were older, their features harder, their faces in need of a razor. 'Who the hell is this?' snarled the driver, who had a perm and sideburns resembling cotton balls.

'My sister. She's cool.'

We drove around a lot, stopping occasionally in deserted parking lots. You and your friends nursed a case of beer, smoked and shared a bottle round, even the driver swigged at it. I slouched down on the hump in the back, wedged between you and a chubby guy with an earring. You passed the bottle over me.

Finally, we parked down by the river and you and the driver went for a walk. You didn't say goodbye to me or tell me where you were going, and the other two just kept smoking and talking over my head. I wished I was home, tucked up in bed, fast asleep. After a while, the one in the front rolled another cigarette and offered it back to Chubby. He eyed me suspiciously as he took a long drag, then he jutted his elbow in my ribs and handed it over. I knew it was no Marlboro, I wasn't that stupid. I could tell by the sweet smell, by the way they pressed it up against their lips with their thumb and forefinger and held their breath afterwards, their chests puffed out and faces screwed up in constipated expressions. I could tell but I accepted the thing anyway and tried to do like they did.

That's when you reappeared. You reached in through the open window, whacked me on the back and started me coughing. 'Stop it! Don't do that. You hear me, don't ever do that.' Then you hollered for a while at Chubby and the other guy. What the hell did they think they were doing, you wanted to know, just what the frigging hell.

They drove us home after that and you never let me join you on midnight rides again, no matter how much I threatened to scream – as if I would. I didn't want to come, though, not really.

'Once,' I concede. 'I smoked marijuana once.'

Our mother wags her head despairingly and tears at her hankie. Mom has the only comfortable chair in the room. An armchair that's deep-sea blue and coffee-stained. But it's low slung and she's sunk down into it, engulfed, making her seem even smaller than usual.

31

'And?'

'And what?'

'Any other substances?'

I'm tempted to snap 'no' again but am not in the mood for more backpedalling. 'You tell me.'

'Prescription drugs maybe?'

'Only when they've been prescribed.'

'And other times?'

'Nope.'

Hilary pokes her pen through the hole in the metal clip of her board, where the nail would go if the board was hanging on the wall. 'Your father is a doctor.'

'*He's an orthodontist.*'

'I stock painkillers,' Dad interjects, defensively.

'Painkillers perhaps?' Hilary asks.

Do they think I've been tiptoeing into Dad's office on the weekends? My eyes drift unconsciously to Dad's denture fob which peeks out of the pocket of his jacket, now draped over the arm of the garden chair. All other eyes trail mine. I blush.

'Could I have a glass of water?'

'There's time for that later. Please answer the question.'

'No, I haven't used any of Dad's painkillers.'

'OK then. How about caffeine?'

'Are you serious?'

'Absolutely.'

'Well, I drink Diet Coke but I'm not much for coffee.'

'I mean caffeine pills. Vivarin, No-Doz, that kind of thing.'

'You can get those over the counter.'

'Many things sold over the counter can be abused,' Hilary informs me. 'So, have you used caffeine pills?'

'I still don't think it counts. I was cramming for exams.'

'I'll take that as a yes then. How about solvents?'

'I don't even know what a solvent is.'

'Glue, paint thinner, lighter fluid, aerosol sprays, nail varnish—'

'Be serious.'

'Magic markers?' Her eyebrows hike knowingly.

'That definitely doesn't count! We were just kids, we liked the smell.'

'Mmm-hmm.' She lifts her pen to her mouth and chews on the cap. I'm hungry, tired and so so thirsty. 'Tell me, Justine, why do you use drugs? Do you know?'

'I don't use drugs.'

'Alcohol, then.'

'It was one time.'

'Last night you mean?'

'Yes.'

'OK, assuming last night was the only time you've used alcohol—'

'There's no assuming, last night was the only time.'

'Fine, assuming it was the only time, why don't you tell me why you drank last night?'

'I don't know.' I shrug my shoulders, cross and recross my arms and then my legs. My chair couldn't be less comfortable. 'I was upset, it was there, it was no big deal.'

'No big deal?'

'No.'

'Do you feel guilty when you use?'

'I don't *use*. Would you stop saying *use* that way? It's not like that.'

'Do you feel guilty about last night?'

I address our parents now, beseechingly. 'Yes, yes I do. I feel very guilty. I wish it had never happened. It wasn't worth it. It wasn't even any fun.'

'Interesting,' she nods. 'You were expecting it to be *fun*.'

Dad seizes on Hilary's implication. 'Is that what you wanted, Justine?' he demands. 'A little *fun*?'

Can't they hear anything I'm saying? Don't they understand? I feel like I'm speaking a different language. 'I wasn't expecting anything. I hadn't thought about it enough to expect anything. I'm sorry. Mom, are you listening? I'm sorry.'

Mom slides her eyes away from me, and Hilary lets my apology hang there for a moment, unanswered. Our father shifts in his chair, the green plastic legs creaking beneath him; Hilary wrests back control. 'How much money do you spend to support your habit?'

'I don't have a habit.'

'How much money do you spend on drugs?'

'Nothing.'

'Alcohol included?'

'Alcohol included.'

'Have you ever been to a party?'

'What's wrong with parties?'

'Nothing's wrong with parties *per se*,' she concedes. 'Do you go to them?'

'Not counting my parents' dinner parties or country club socials?'

'Not counting them.'

'No, I'm a complete and utter social outcast. I never get invited anywhere.'

She doesn't appreciate the sarcasm, and neither does Dad,

whose eyes are boring into me like I'm one big, blackened cavity. 'Please answer the question.'

'Yes, I've been to parties.'

'Is there drinking and drug-taking at these parties you go to?'

'Don't know about drugs.'

'But drinking?'

'Yeah, I guess so.'

'What radio station do you listen to, Justine?'

'Q105.'

'The rock station?'

'Yeah.'

There goes the eyebrow again, arching in Dad's direction as she scribbles. 'Have you ever been to a rock concert?'

'Yes, I have, with Josh. And, before you ask, we had our parents' permission, too.'

'What was the last book you read?'

'I suppose you want me to say *On the Road* or *Naked Lunch* or something.'

'Just the truth, thank you.'

'*Great Expectations.*'

'For pleasure or for class?'

'Class.'

'What's the last book you read for pleasure?'

'That would be *On the Road.*'

She smirks.

'Are you going to ask me about movies now?'

'No. Thank you, Justine. That's fine.' Hilary flips to another page on the clipboard. 'Now, if you could answer yes or no to the following questions. Do you ever have difficulty waking up in the morning?'

'Doesn't everyone?'

'Yes or no, please.'

'Yes.'

'Do you often feel that something dreadful is going to happen?'

'Well, I didn't see this coming if that's what you mean.' Mom roots around in her purse with fierce concentration.

'Yes or no,' says Hilary.

'No.'

'Do you ever fear being enclosed in a small place?'

My eyes roam the walls. Where have the spiders gone? Did they escape or did they die and shrivel, plummet to the carpet, their carcasses vacuumed away in a twice-monthly tidy up? 'Someti— Yes.'

'Have your friends ever been in trouble with the law?'

'No.'

'You sure about that?'

'Yes.'

Returning to the pile of papers, Hilary pulls out a wodge of pages belted with a rubber band. One-handed, she rolls the band off and shoots it on to the table.

I pinch the bridge of my nose. Oh, for one lousy glass of water.

As she rifles the pages, the top one breaks loose and flutters to the floor. The thick black frame round the edge identifies it as a Xerox of a smaller piece of paper. The writing on the page within the page is fainter, but there's no mistaking the loops of the 'l's, the circle-dots above the 'i's, the doodles in the margin, the date marked in the top right-hand corner and framed with a box. I haven't had the strength to even look at it, let alone write in it, since before you left, but I still recognise it in an instant.

'That's my journal! What are you doing with my *private* journal?'

Hilary, ignoring me, finds the page she's searching for. 'According to this, your friend... Lloyd, is it? Yes. Lloyd Taggart. He was caught driving without a licence. He was also found to be in possession of a fake ID.'

I lunge for the entry fallen on the floor. 'What the fuck are you doing with my journal?'

'Language!' gasps Mom and Dad hunkers forward, practically growling.

'Do you want to answer the question?' Hilary continues.

'No, I don't actually.'

'Answer the question, Justine!' Dad barks.

I glare at him. *Journal-snatcher.*

I can see it in the way his cheek twitches. I imagine him asking his receptionist, Zoe Micklebaum, to run the book through the photocopier for him. I can see her laughing, saying, you can't run a bound notebook through a photocopier, Dr Ziegler, but cracking the spine and forcing the book roughly down on to the plate of glass all the same. Later at home, she'll complain to her muscle-bound husband, Felix Micklebaum. 'Photocopying little girls' diaries ain't part of my job description,' I hear her saying, 'but ooh the things that pass through that young Justine Ziegler's addled brain.' This is the woman who snorted like a hog when we last saw her. 'Imagine,' she'd said, 'if I ever married your dad, kids, my name'd be Zoe Ziegler. Imagine, ZZ.'

'Was your friend Lloyd in trouble with the law?'

'Technically, I guess so.'

'Yes or no.'

'Yes. But something like that, it doesn't really count.'

'It seems a lot of things don't count as far as you're concerned.' She swivels left, swivels right. The keys on her necklace chain shift noisily in the canyon between her breasts. 'Have you ever run away from home?'

'No.'

'Don't you lie, Justine! Don't you do it!' Our mother's near hysterical.

'I haven't.'

'Yes, you have. That time your father grounded you over the cleaning rota.'

'That doesn't... *we were at the library*.' Three pairs of eyes pin me down, unimpressed. 'We were gone for less than four hours.' Silence. '*We were only eleven*.'

'Yes or no.'

'Good grief. Yes.'

'Do you hide things to cover up your habit?'

'I don't have a habit. No.'

'Do you ever miss school because of your habit?'

'Are you hearing me? I don't have a habit.'

'Fine. For the following questions, please answer Never, Rarely, Occasionally, Often or Always. Do you seek approval from others?'

'Sometimes.'

'Never, Rarely, Occasionally, Often or Always, please.'

'Occasionally.'

'Do you fear criticism?'

'Occasionally.'

'Do you overextend yourself?'

'Occasionally.'

'Do you have a need for perfection?'

'Occasionally.'

'Are you being honest?'

'Occasionally.'

Hilary lifts her pen off the page. 'I'm talking about now. Are you being honest now?'

'Don't I have to answer Never, Rarely or whatever to that?'

Hilary cocks her chin to the side in a wary be-serious way.

'*Yes*, I'm being honest.'

'So everything applies to you, but only occasionally? Does that sound truthful to you?'

'Yup.'

'Yes to which question?'

'Both.'

Hilary sighs. 'Fine. Let's move on.' She locates her place on the clipboard again, pen poised. 'Do you isolate yourself from other people?'

I hear Mom draw in her breath. 'No.'

'Justine, please answer Never, Rarely, Occasionally, Often or Always.'

'I thought we were back to yes/no.'

Hilary swishes her head in slow-mo. 'Never, Rarely, Occasionally, Often or Always.'

'Never.' Mom pushes the air out of her lungs like it was noxious fumes. 'OK, rarely,' I concede.

'Do you fear being rejected or abandoned?'

'Occasionally.'

'Do you find it difficult to express your own emotions?'

'Occasionally.'

'Do you have trouble with intimate relationships?'

'I'm only fifteen. Are you going to make me out be a sex maniac too?'

'Are you?'

'I'm a *virgin*.' I expect her to say, 'Sure about that?' but she doesn't. Mom and Dad appear momentarily relieved.

'Do you respond with anxiety to authority figures?'

'Yes!' I roar, then make sure to add, 'Occasionally.'

'Fine. Now I'd like to ask you a few questions about your relationship with your brother.'

My vertebrae stiffen against the rungs of my ladder back. 'I don't want to talk about him.'

She distributes sympathetic nods to Dad, Mom and me in turn. 'I realise it's a sensitive subject but I think it's necessary.'

'I don't want to talk about Josh.'

'Do you think Joshua is more important than you are?'

'That has nothing to do with anything.'

'I'm not so sure. Did you feel rejected when Joshua started spending more time with his druggie friends than with you?'

'Stop it.'

'How did you feel when he ran away to Florida?'

I imagine you in Miami, tanned and smiling, wearing pastel print shirts and sipping matching cocktails in fluted glasses with umbrellas sticking out of them. How did I feel?

'Stop,' I tell her.

'Did you think that he'd abandoned you?'

I think I say stop again. Stop, stop, stop.

'Were you ever embarrassed by Joshua's actions?'

'Joshua never did anything to hurt or embarrass me.'

'Maybe it's not something he did, maybe it was just the way he was. He did have a certain reputation after all, didn't he?'

'No. I said, I don't want to talk about this.'

'Did you resent Joshua for not letting you help him?'

I fling myself into tantrum mode, just like when we were kids. I scream at the top of my lungs, pound my feet on the floor, slam my hands against the sides of my seat, splinters shooting into my palms like poisoned darts. *'Would you fucking leave Joshua out of this?'*

Mom's crying but I don't allow myself to cry. Dad uncrosses his legs and plants his feet full-sole to the floor. Hilary starts to gather up her papers.

'OK, Justine. Thank you for being so patient. Just one final question. What do you want to get out of life?'

'Right now? Right this minute?'

'Sure.'

'I want to get the hell out of here.'

'Anything else?'

I pause, roll my shoulders. 'I want a 1500 score on my SATs, I want to graduate from high school *magna cum laude*, I want to go to an Ivy League college and fall in love with a future Supreme Court judge and have babies and discover a cure for cancer and do lots and lots of great things. You know, the usual.' Our mother beams and our father makes a comforting chip-off-the-old-block kind of noise. I'm the golden child again, I can feel the weight of my halo resting round my temples and I love it.

Hilary, too, manages a small smile. 'Excellent. Well, we'll see what we can do about that.'

CHAPTER FIVE

Our earliest actual memory, that's something different. I don't know who had our first memory first, or if I really remember it or just think I do because we talked about it so many times. I'm a baby, lying on the sofa, the one with the fruit-basket pattern. Daddy's not in the frame of my memory and neither is Mommy – could be she hadn't followed us home from the hospital yet after her long stay.

What is in the frame is the ceiling: white, stippled and big as life until my hands come windmilling in. They keep doing that, diving in front of my face in their arc to sink themselves in fistfuls into my mouth. I try to fix my gaze on them for a minute but they're moving too fast. And then, shifting my head, I see, beyond the fleshy pad of my palm, I see myself, my whole self. Not two feet away from me, lying on a plate of pears on another cushion on the same sofa, wearing the same romper suit, dripping the same saliva from the same hand. I'm staring at me, except of course it's not me, it's you. I stare at my hand and then I stare at you and I start to cry because I'm kinda scared. Then you up and do the same thing. Wail, wail, gasp. We look at each other, see the other one crying and then we stop, just like that.

Mom discovered this trick later. If you came down with a bug or couldn't sleep, she'd tuck me in the crib with you. And vice versa. The healthy, happy one calming the other down. Sometimes, of course, it backfired and we both got cranky, wide-awake or sick. I remember catching chickenpox off you, for instance, when we were in preschool. Mom had to separate us then because picking each other's scabs was just too irresistible.

CHAPTER SIX

I'm alone in the room now, and oddly calm. 'I'll just take your parents next door for a quick word,' Hilary said as they jangled out of the room. I shut my eyes and hunch my shoulders up to my ears, let them drop, roll my head round on its axis, listen to my neck muscles pop and stir.

All things considered, I think I handled Hilary's interrogation pretty well. Those questions about you were out of line, and I wasn't expecting that part with my diary, but surely that showed Dad in a worse light than it did me. How could he? Snooping around in my private possessions. I blanch at the thought of him inspecting my blushers and strawberry lip gloss, the new grey kohl eyeliner that I haven't quite got the knack of, flipping through my Judy Blume books and my *Seventeen* magazines to see the pages I dog-eared, the words I underlined, rifling through my underwear drawer, his fingers catching on the stray tampons hidden beneath my new bikini briefs with the little silk rose at the front.

The questions were more intense this time round, much more pointed than when I had to come in for the sibling interview, but really the gist was the same. I was nervous then, too, sick to my stomach after the night before with you. Just a precaution, more a formality than anything, that's what they told me at the time. All siblings are interviewed when a person is entered into the programme. And so they asked me some silly questions about parties and drinking and my favourite *General Hospital* characters and then they sent me home.

I switch seats, slipping into our mother's chair, still warm and scented with her perfume, Chanel. When we were little, we'd curl up in Mom's lap and let her read to us or we'd read to her. I liked it best when it was late at night and we were bone tired. I'd shout dibs on the lap then coil up with my feet tucked into the crook behind Mom's knees, my cheek resting on her breast, her ribcage rising and falling like a cloud, and I'd drift off with the sound of you and Dr. Seuss spinning echoes around me.

There were more questions today, more drugs named, a lot more testing and prodding. And I admit I was worried for a while, really worried. But I was myself, I answered honestly, just like I did before and it all came straight in the end.

Right about now, Hilary should be telling Mom and Dad to stop overreacting. Justine? A drug problem? Don't make me laugh. She'd couch it in all that counsellorese, of course, but either way, it's obvious, isn't it? She knows it and now they know it. Maybe it's no bad thing we went through this whole rigmarole, if only so Dad could be proved wrong for once.

I glance at my Swatch, the one you gave me, with the confetti strap. I can't tell for sure whether it's two thirty or three thirty, but I can tell by the position of the minute hand that Hilary's quick word hasn't been very quick at all.

What are they doing next door anyway? I decide to see for myself.

I try the door only it doesn't open, not all the way. It gives about three inches and stops. I peer through the gap to see the chain on the outside. They've locked me in.

Beyond the chain, I can see Hilary chatting with our parents in front of the glass double doors to the parking lot. 'I think you'd better go now,' she says, ushering them out.

They're leaving and I'm locked in this room with crappy chairs and a Formica-topped table.

My calm evaporates. 'Hey!' I scream. '*Hey!!*' So loud it makes my throat hurt. 'Mom, Dad, what are you doing? What the— What the— What are you doing?!'

The double doors are separating, drawing our parents back out into the February day.

'*Hey!!* Don't leave me here. I didn't do anything wrong. Please! *Don't go!*'

Mom's crying again. She turns and bends towards me like a tree blown by a gale, her arms outstretched like hopeful limbs. But Dad has her by the waist and is pulling her towards the Volvo. Frantic, I try to force my arm and leg through the chained gap. If I can just squeeze myself through, if I can just get into our mother's arms, I know I'll be safe. But it's too tight, the chain's too strong. My face is hot and swelling up, too big for the gap.

'Mom, please. I love you Mommy I love you Mommy I love you I promise to be good I promise to be good.'

Mom wails. 'Give my baby a glass of water. She's thirsty, so thirsty, my baby needs her water.'

'Mommmmmm!' I scream until my scream has nowhere else to go and so tails off of its own accord. Our mother watches my scream fade away and part of her seems to disappear with it. Her panting slows and we reach out for each other.

Then her arms drop, in a clunky, bent-elbow motion, like a Barbie's, and her face recomposes itself into something different, something bitter and blameful. She looks at me and doesn't like what she sees. 'Why don't you ever cry, Justine? You *never* cry.'

I touch my cheek in reply but I don't need my finger nor our mother to tell me that my face is hot and swollen but still dry.

Dad drags her off as she starts to howl again, more subdued this time, and her howls fade until the only screaming left is mine.

I call after them, even though I can't see them any more. 'Please don't leave me here, please Daddy.'

I'm stuck between the door and the doorjamb, the metal chain slicing into my neck. I go limp and hang there as Hilary stands, her clipboard still in hand, and watches me from the reception area. Mark and Leroy reappear. Mark – or the one I think is Mark – stands to one side of the door to the intake room. He stomps on my foot like an anchor and grabs me by the arm as Leroy unhooks the chain. They slip me out of the room and Leroy takes hold of my other side. Mark reeks of BO and Leroy's hands are rough like packing boxes. When I struggle against him, my skin chafes. I stop struggling.

'Your parents have asked to leave you here for a three-day evaluation,' Hilary informs me. 'After that, we'll report back to them with our recommendations. Do you understand?'

No, I don't understand, I don't understand at all. This could not possibly be right. 'I'm not a drug addict, I'm not any kind of addict. I don't have a problem.'

'Well, your parents are very worried about you. And frankly, based on your behaviour here this morning, Justine, I think they're justified.'

'But I don't belong here. You can't keep me.'

47

She considers that. 'In fact, we can. Do you understand? We can.'

I shake my head. 'It's not right.'

One of the double doors swings open again and our father strides back into the centre. A wave of relief washes over me. It's OK now. They've changed their minds, come to their senses at last.

Dad walks up to me and he's going to throw his arms round me, he's going to apologise, kiss my burning cheeks and take me home.

'Oh Daddy,' I blubber.

Our father isn't such a bad man really, he loses perspective sometimes, but he's got a heart and soul and mind that tells him what's reasonable and what's not, what's right, what's not.

He approaches then stops abruptly. He hauls something out of his pocket – a handkerchief? One of Mom's Tic Tacs? The denture fob with the keys to the car that has drying vomit in the back seat but who cares because that's the car that's going to take me home and I'll never be nauseous again?

'You forgot your retainer, Justine,' our not-unreasonable father tells me. 'You know better than that. That's expensive orthodontic equipment and you need to treat it with some respect.' He places the retainer in my hand, then makes to leave again.

'Daddy. Please.'

I can see the lines round his eyes, dragging everything down. 'Justine,' he says, 'you must believe me. It's for your own good.' And perhaps he means the retainer or Hilary or this godawful day or all three. Is he being our father or Jeff Ziegler, orthodontist extraordinaire, or someone else entirely? Whoever he is, he spins on his heel and heads for the door. The smear that the garage door bestowed on his suit jacket is the last I see of him. I hope no one tells him about the smear, I hope it sits so long that the grease becomes well and truly ingrained so that even a dry cleaner can't budge it – that stain will be there for ever and his shirt will be ruined. A reminder of this day.

The double doors squeak on their hinges and swing shut and my stomach does something funny at the sound of it. The ground falls away and, though Mark and Leroy's hands are still on me, they feel like feathers. My body is numb.

'Do you understand now?' Hilary repeats. Simultaneously, Leroy and Mark tighten their grip and still I can hardly feel their fingers. 'Do you understand, Justine?'

I nod. My eyelids are dry and rough like the boxes Leroy has been packing and they chafe against my eyeballs.

'Very good, then. Welcome to Come Clean.'

I'm still nodding as my knees buckle and I swoon into blackness and Mark's stinking embrace.

CHAPTER SEVEN

When I come to, I'm in a room smaller than the intake room and it's dark. There are no windows and the only light is eking through beneath the door that I don't even need to touch to know is locked. My tartan skirt has hiked up to expose my legs and the soft skin at the backs of my thighs is sticking to the cracked leatherette cushions of the couch I've been laid out on. I can't breathe. I wonder for a second if my lungs stopped working when I fainted because I'm puffing now like I've been under water: like when you used to dunk me at the swimming pool and I'd get chlorine up my nose and I couldn't breathe, and you'd hold my head under while you chanted Marco Polo Marco Polo, and I couldn't wait to do the same to you once it was my turn. My other vital organs feel as if they stopped and started again too. I'm hot and cold at the same time and my heart is thwacking inside my chest.

I don't know how long I've been in here, hours probably. I try to read my Swatch, my favourite Christmas present last year. I love it, I've always loved everything you gave me. Even though it's near impossible to tell the time because there isn't a second hand and no numbers. You'd tease me by saying I was the ditzy one – spatially retarded in fact – not the watch. Retard, you'd call me, but you'd say it with affection and that's how I'd hear it too. In the dimness, the hands are too fuzzy to discern at all. The room has an undisturbed air about it, like no one but me, twisting in my unconsciousness, has moved in here for quite some time.

My memory is one thing that didn't stop working when I passed out. I know exactly where I am, if not the precise location within the building.

And I know I've got to escape. I try to retrace the route in my head so I can tell Cindy. But what the heck is the name of the road, Justine? Is it right or left off the main drag? And how many miles after Harvey's? I don't know. Cindy will figure it out. She has to. She and Lloyd will find a map and find a way, they'll get me out of here.

I've just got to reach a phone so I can call her. I survey the room, my eyes adjusting to the dark. I can make out forms though colours and textures blur into shadow. There's the couch I'm lying on, about a foot shorter than me, and two folding chairs, leaning up against the wall to the right of the door, and a trash can, wicker maybe, looking empty and skeletal even in the dimness, and framed things on the wall, yet more needlepoint godsquad pronouncements I'm sure. To the left of the sofa where my feet have been dangling is a spindly side table and there's something on it. It's not a phone, though, that's clear. It's smaller, looks like a tube or canister of something. I lean in and squint. No, it's a cup, a plastic cup, but it's tipped over on its side, thanks apparently to a collision with my feet. The tabletop is a pool of liquid, dripping into the carpet. I dab my finger in it. Water, my glass of water.

I remember how thirsty I am. My lips crack with rawness and when I lick them my tongue sticks like it does to my teeth and the underside of my still foul-tasting retainer. I would hock my Michael Jackson collection *and* all my Esprit sweaters for a drink of water.

Why would anybody put a glass of water in a place like that, where a person could so easily reach out and kick it accidentally. It's almost laughable, the sheer stupidity of it. But then it occurs to me. It wasn't a stupid thing, not thoughtless at all. Plenty of thought went into it. They did it on purpose. *She* did it, Hilary.

She did it to spite me. She did it so that when our mom lost the steel in her lip, started feeling guilty later and called up to see how I was adjusting and asked, is my Justine OK, did you give my baby her glass of water? Then Hilary would be able to say with a straight face and clear conscience, 'Of course we did, Mrs Ziegler.' And Mom wouldn't think to ask, 'But did she drink the damn water, or did you, you evil woman, put it somewhere it was certain to get knocked over so she'd never get a drop of it?' Mom wouldn't think to ask that and she'd go to sleep tonight never realising how thirsty I am or how dry my lips are or how I've got nothing to wash down this taste of bile and vomit and betrayal.

There's movement on the other side of the door. Rigid with fear, I listen to the chatter of the key ring on the other side, the scraping of metal on metal as the key's teeth match up with the lock's grooves, then the turning of the mechanisms deep inside and then the click-thud as the bolt snaps back. Should I hide? There's nowhere. Should I pretend to be asleep? Wait behind the door to pounce? Throw the wicker wastepaper basket over her head? Even as I'm asking myself, I'm imagining Hilary twirling the massive ring of keys round her neck like a witch doctor spins a string of skulls, working his spell over each of his victims.

But when the door opens, there's no Hilary. Instead there's a girl. She flips on the lights too suddenly and almost blinds me, but

I can see her through my squinted lids. I don't know her. She's dressed in a billowy red sweat suit and is several inches shorter than me and wider, almost round like a ball, with pale skin and straight red hair, greasy and slicked back into a ponytail twitching high and off-centre atop her head.

Mark and Leroy are back, lingering behind Pony Girl in the hall and they don't enter all the way when she does. She sashays in swinging a Kmart plastic bag which she flings on to the sofa. 'Your clothes,' she says.

'I'm fine in what I'm wearing, thanks.'

'Not regulation.' She tosses her hair and gestures towards the bag again.

I reach into it. There's a green synthetic tunic littered with pink polka dots and a pair of brown corduroy pants. I hate cords at the best of times, the sound they make as you walk, the friction, the ribbons of material rubbing up against one another, leaving funny brush patterns and picking up lint from wherever you sit down. I hate them and these ones are two sizes too big, cheap and nasty to boot. Very cheap, judging by the price tags still attached to them as well as the tunic.

'These aren't my clothes,' I tell Pony Girl.

'Your parents brought them for you.'

Our parents?

I take a step towards her. 'Did they come back? Are they still here?'

'No, they left them here,' she says, her breath stinking in my face. What's that smell? 'They left *them* when they left *you*.'

I rub the bridge of my nose. There's a spot there where, if I close my eyes and press hard enough, it feels like I'm giving my brain a pinch. A little squeeze that rockets pain like prismed light into my thoughts. It hurts most when I use the knuckle of my forefinger, but it only hurts for a second and then sometimes it helps. It makes things clearer.

Like now, like how it's clear to me now that our parents must have had this planned, who knew how far in advance. Maybe weeks, maybe hours. Time enough for Mom to go shopping at Kmart. Perhaps she went this morning while I was still asleep, dreaming of you and swimming – how long ago was that?

I can't fathom it, nor can I fathom how my very own mother could shop for me at Kmart of all places. We *never* shop at Kmart. And how could she pick out quite such an atrocious outfit? I'll look like a tree with the brown pants and the green top – a cherry tree, even, thanks to those hideous pink polka dots. What was she thinking?

But hang on a minute. Perhaps it isn't all bad. There *is* only one change of clothes. You don't give a person just one change of clothes if you expect them to be gone a long while. It *is* only an evaluation, isn't it? After three days I'll be able to go home again and everything will be peachy keen. Maybe I'll only have to stay one day. One change of clothes, one day.

'You can change into them after the strip-search,' the redhead says.

'The *what*?'

'Strip-search. We've got to check you ain't trying to sneak any contraband into the programme.'

'You must be kidding.'

''Fraid not.'

'I don't have any contraband and I'm no way going to take my clothes off to prove it.'

'Sorry, chickie,' she says, not appearing the least bit apologetic. 'Them's the breaks.'

'No way. Uh-uh.'

She reaches out and picks at the hem of your turtleneck. A loose thread dangles and she yanks at it until it breaks, causing the material to bunch up round the stitching at the edge. 'I'm not gonna have to get Mark and Leroy there to restrain you, am I? You wouldn't like it that way, I bet you wouldn't.'

On cue, the two bruisers square their shoulders and bristle threateningly. Around the corners of Leroy's mouth flickers a faint hint of a smile.

My own shoulders slump and I can feel my lower lip start to quiver. I blink and focus on a point on the wall. I can read the needlepoint now: 'The Lord is My Shepherd' it tells me. 'No,' I say.

'Good, it's always so much easier with a little cooperation.' From the back pocket of her sweat pants, Pony Girl unfurls a pair of rubber gloves. Not the surgical kind, skintight and unobtrusive. These are kitchen gloves. Thick and bright yellow, the kind you use when you pick up Brillo pads and scrape the grill after a barbecue or when you want to clean the oven.

Mom used to wear gloves like that, I recall, when we were little. She warned us not to listen to that flimflam about dishwashing liquids that were good for you – no matter what the commercials said, the grease, the suds, the serrated edges of steak knives and the tines of all those grimy forks, those things were bad bad bad for your skin. You had to wear gloves to protect your hands, to keep them young and unlined and so as not to break your nails, especially after you just paid five dollars for a manicure. Mom would kick up a fuss if she couldn't find her kitchen gloves, which she couldn't sometimes if we'd swiped them from their place, under the sink with the Drano and the vacuum bags. We liked to play dress-up with them. You'd pretend they were evening gloves, the elbow-length satiny kind like Audrey Hepburn would wear in those old films you liked to watch.

Mom had gloves like Hepburn's, too, which she wore sometimes when she dolled up in long dresses with short sleeves and went out with Dad, buttoned up tight in one of those tuxedos with the ruffled shirts, for the annual dental association ball. But she kept the real evening gloves stowed in a shoe box at the top of her closet behind some crumbling family photo albums and we couldn't reach them. So we made do with the kitchen gloves – not that she ever thanked us for the substitution.

Pony Girl pulls on her kitchen gloves, bringing me back to attention as she wrestles the cuffs right up to her elbows, the rubber cracking against her funny bone, just like you did when you were pretending to be Audrey Hepburn. No giggling now, though.

'Get undressed,' she demands.

I raise my eyes to Mark and Leroy. That hint of a smile is still break-dancing around Leroy's mouth and it seems to have spread like a yawn to Mark as well. I'd like to rub those smarmy grins off their faces with an eraser the size of a double-decker bus. I've never undressed in front of a boy in my life. Except for you, of course, but that's not the same. Not even Dad has seen me naked since I was maybe six.

Pony Girl follows my gaze and now she's grinning too. 'Feeling shy, are we?' She crosses to the door and kicks it shut, the two fools jumping back just in time to avoid sore noses. 'Right, but remember, they're just on the other side so try anything funny and they'll be in here like *that*.' She tries to snap her fingers but can't with the gloves on so she claps her hands together instead, creating a dull plop of a sound.

I crouch down to unbuckle my Mary Janes. I want to step out

of them gingerly, but my feet have been sweating and, without any hose, my soles have stuck. I pry each shoe off with the toes of my spare foot. Pony Girl's impatient and nags me to 'hurry up already' as she drums her rubberised fingers together. My tartan skirt falls off as soon as I unbutton it at the back. I have to roll your turtleneck up over my head, turning it inside out as I haul it loose. My hair, drawn through the too-tight neck, springs free from the shirt all staticky, like I poked my finger in a socket.

It takes me less than a minute until I'm standing in nothing but my bra and panties, my hands clasped at my belly.

'Underwear too.'

I hesitate and Pony Girl rolls her eyes. 'Underwear too!' she shouts. 'For fuck's sake, don't you people understand English. Howya think a strip-search works?'

I bite my lip and wriggle my arms up behind my back in search of the catch to my bra, but my fingers are shaking and I can't disentangle the hooks from the eyes. I slip my arms out of the straps and twist the clip round to the front. Even seeing it, though, it takes me four attempts to undo both hooks. I slide my panties down next, hustling them past my knees and ankles, and deposit them on to the dusty carpet with the rest of my Sunday not-so best.

'Spread 'em – arms and legs.' It's just like on some TV police show, *Cagney and Lacey* maybe, the one with the lady cops. Except it's longer now, more drawn out, more humiliating – and without clothes, of course.

She starts in my hair, raking roughly through it with her clumsy, kitchen-glove paws, then she pokes in my ears and I'm wondering how how how could I hide any contraband there and what do they mean by contraband anyway, what does it look like and why do they think I would have any? Then the gloves brush against my cheek.

I remember Mom used to get awful mad when she'd go to do the dishes and those kitchen gloves of hers weren't there.

I close my eyes and feel the honeycombed grip of the right palm – or is it the left? – abrading my face. Gripped not for scrubbing faces but for holding on to plates, holding on even when they're wet and slippery.

'Open your mouth.'

And I open my mouth and in slips a sheathed forefinger, probing my gums and my incisors and molars, pushing down my tongue, poking into my tonsils – or not the tonsils, but that dangly doohicky at the back, the cartoony bit they always show flapping about in *Popeye* when Olive Oyl opens her trap big enough to swallow the screen and lets rip with an almighty screecher.

Our mother also hated it when somehow we'd accidentally puncture one of those gloves, though I always reckoned it was more likely to be the fork tines than our little hands that were to blame.

Pony Girl's kitchen-glove thumb is clamped over my nose and I'm inhaling the rubber that smells like balloons and tastes like them, too, this glove in my mouth, tasting like after we've been blowing up birthday balloons all afternoon, like we did for our tenth birthday party when all the kids from school came. And I wonder if this is what a condom smells like and tastes like, and I swear I don't know for myself but I imagine it must be because it's called a rubber too. The finger is out of my mouth and I have somehow managed to avoid throwing up again.

Whatever the cause, if there was a hole in those rubber kitchen gloves, the ones packed away beneath the sink, the corrosive soap and grime could seep right into your bones and it was as bad as not wearing any gloves at all, according to our mother.

Pony Girl's finger is trailing my own spit down my cheek and around my neck and down. And I'm wondering what exactly it is that I've just had in my mouth, just exactly how many strip-searches these gloves have been a party to and just how exactly do they clean them afterwards? And maybe I am going to be sick on second thoughts.

Our mother always wore kitchen gloves. Up until our family got a dishwasher, anyway, which it was our job to load and unload.

Pony Girl's rubberised finger is wet and slipping down my sternum, ringing round my neck and scooping under my armpits where usually I'm ticklish. And I'm thinking if maybe I laugh now she'll stop, if maybe I pretend we're playing a game to see who's the most ticklish, it'll startle her and she won't be able to go on. But she does go on.

Then we got a cleaner too, as well as the dishwasher. The cleaner, she was named Marjorie. She came in twice a week, so Mom didn't even have to wear the kitchen gloves for handling the mop or scouring the countertops or anything.

Pony Girl's finger is snailing down my arm and checking under my fingernails for contraband – what contraband, how small is contraband, how microscopic does contraband come? – and then it's back circling my waist and skidding down my stomach and then...

I am not going to scream or pee or flinch or cry or sneeze or plead – and then it is delving deep into my pubic hair, down and down and beyond.

Our mother still has lovely soft hands.

My eyes are closed.

And Mommy, I swear I'm a virgin.

CHAPTER EIGHT

I have a memory that floats around in the early-time ether. We're two, maybe three. I only retrieved the memory because of something my best friend Cindy Gregory told me in the seventh grade. Cindy had this kooky old aunt named Anastasia who was an astrologer, who told us that everyone was supposed to know the time of day they were born. If you didn't know the exact time, Anastasia said, then you couldn't ever have an accurate astrology reading because you couldn't ever know your precise alignment with the stars. Something like that.

It always bugged me that Mom couldn't remember the time, but we were never big into astrology so on that count, I guess, it wasn't a disaster. But Aunt Anastasia did cause me to recall this other time. We couldn't have been old enough to talk properly, but I remember us talking to each other, like cartoon thoughts bubbling up out of our skulls except only you and me could see them. We could read, too. We were bright young sparks, even if nobody else knew it.

We little Einsteins were with Mommy – because we called her Mommy then – nearing the checkout at the A&P. They have all these candy bars, rolls of mints, bubble gum and cheapo pocket pamphlets displayed around the checkout to distract you, because the cashiers at this A&P are high-school dropouts and the waits are always long.

I'm feeling a whine coming on, I want a Chunky bar. You're bored, too, but easily entertained by the cheapo pamphlets, cardboard that melts in your mouth. You start fingering one that's got a picture of a fierce but friendly looking lion on it. A lion like Aslan out of *The Chronicles of Narnia* – only we wouldn't have known that then because, though we could read, Dad didn't buy us the C.S. Lewis box set until we were nine.

'A – U – G – U – S – T,' you tell me. 'August, that's us.'

'Yes, very good, Joshua, that's Daddy,' Mommy pipes in, getting it wrong as usual. 'What a good boy to remember Daddy's birthday.'

When you shove the corner of Daddy's birthday into your mouth to see what flavour it is, Mommy slaps it out of your hand.

'Tastes *baaaad*.' She tidies it in its rack and leafs through the other cheapo pamphlets, until she finds another, much more boring-looking one that's got a picture of a lady lounging on it. 'Hey, twenty-fifth of August. That's you.'

I curl up my lip.

Mommy doesn't hear. 'Virgo, the Virgin. That's you.'

'What's a virgin?' you ask, disappointed as I am that we can't be something as cool as a lion. Why does Daddy get to be a lion and we've got to be some lazy old bag on a chaise longue?

'Don't like the sound of it.'

'Sounds stupid.' You tear the pamphlet from Mommy's grip and proceed to drool on it in protest.

There's another woman behind us in the line. She titters and coos away. 'They're so cute. Are they twins?'

CHAPTER NINE

The stump-brown Kmart cords are more like three sizes too big. They bunch round my ankles and the only thing that's holding them up is Pony Girl. She's removed her damnable kitchen gloves – never again to be associated with Audrey Hepburn and playing dress-up with you on Indian summer afternoons so sunny and lazy we could see the dust move through the air – and has hooked her fingers through my rear belt loops which she's hitched up high enough almost to touch my shoulder blades. The loose cord material swishes and grumbles between my thighs as she steers me away from the scene of my humiliation. She instructed me to leave all my real clothes, bar my bra and day-old panties, in the room.

She made me hand over my Swatch and even my retainer. Nothing with wire or metal, including no jewellery, no belts, no barrettes. Hair ties were OK, she said, her own ponytail bobbing in evidence, but I didn't have one of those, so my hair stays electrified. I couldn't care less about the barrette or the retainer – good riddance – but the loss of the watch is a blow. Ordinarily, I'd claw at anyone who tried to take it off me, but I'm no longer in a state to protest.

I'm silent and glum as Pony Girl leads me out of there, past

Mark and Leroy who fall in behind us, down a dim, low-ceilinged corridor, past other small empty rooms like the last one and other rooms with closed, signposted doors, and into a large meeting hall. This is the main warehousey part of the building and the height of the room soars accordingly, with tubes of fluorescent light buzzing from the iron rafters up there in the distance. I recognise this room at once. This is where we came for the 'Open Meetings' when you were in the programme. Every Friday night, as if none of us had better things to do on a Friday night, Mom, Dad and I would file into this room with the rest of the parents and siblings and we'd have our one chance to see you, sitting at the front of the room with the rows – boys on one side, girls on the other – of other… inmates, patients, clients? Phasers, that was the term they used.

You'd sit at the front, usually in the back row on the boys' side but sometimes in the first or second or third, I always counted, and you'd stare out at us, the collective families. Every week I'd try to catch your eye. Though we were a much larger mass, I was sure you could sense when I arrived, was certain you knew exactly where I was. But if you did, you never showed it outwardly, never caught my eye, smiled at me, waved, blew me up cartoon bubbles to read your thoughts or made one of our secret hand signals, the three-fingered rub of the nose perhaps, the fanning across the chin or even the Fonzie thumbs up.

Today's phasers are congregated again here, but to one side with a grey concertina partition half unsprung across the middle of the room. They're not in neat parallel corn rows like you were either, though they are still separated from the opposite sex. Their chairs form a sort of ellipse in the middle of the room, boys all arcing on the right, girls mirroring them on the left. The female arc is somewhat shorter than the boys' one, which makes the careful arrangement appear strangely asymmetrical. I scan the boys' section. Left, right, left. Some faces look familiar, but I can't be sure. I know none of them attend JFK High.

Encircling those seated, a smaller number of boys and girls stand straight and Mark-and-Leroy-sentry-like, legs wide, hands tucked into the smalls of their backs. And here again, towering above all heads, seated and standing, in the centre of the group, is Hilary, a young man with slicked-back blond hair and model looks pacing at her side.

As we enter, the phasers are all chanting: '…make a list of all persons we have harmed and make direct amends to them wherever possible.' The model guy nods vigorously then karate chops his right hand into the palm of his left and shouts, 'And Seven!'

Hilary spots me before the group can respond. As she blows her whistle, a couple of the female phasers, startled by the sudden noise, scrunch up their faces and raise their hands as if to cover their ears. But they seem to reconsider mid-action and let their hands settle back into their laps.

'Newcomer arrival!' announces Hilary as Mark and Leroy peel off from behind and Pony Girl propels me through a narrow aisle of chairs, into the centre of the circle.

All eyes are on me, including Mr Model's. He appraises me from the electrified ends of my hair to the tips of my Mary Janes, which are just barely visible beneath the acres of cord. He lingers on my leather-bound toes for a beat or two then lifts the cuff of one pant leg at the back and sighs all weary-like. The sight of my heels pains him.

'She'll need new shoes,' he informs Pony Girl disapprovingly.

'There weren't any shoes in the bag.'

'Whose problem is that?'

Pony Girl's jaw tightens. 'Mine.'

Next, he assesses my chest, looking down at where my cleavage would be showing if I weren't wearing this stupid tunic. 'Did you check out her bra, too? Did you remember about the underwire?'

'Yes,' claims the girl, even though she and I both know that's a lie. She checked a lot of things, too many things, with those kitchen-gloved hands of hers but my bra wasn't one of them. Mr Model ogles my chest, unconvinced, as he should be. Will he grab hold of my boobs and check for himself? Maybe he'll just shoot one of his own hands right up under my shirt and have a grope? Instinctively, I tighten my arms across my chest, shrink back into the crook of Pony Girl's elbow.

'It's imperative not to forget the underwire,' he chastens.

Pony Girl's arm solidifies against me. 'Yes, Dwight, imperative.'

Dwight, his name's Dwight, dismisses her with the wave of a hand. She releases my belt loop and shuttles off to assume a standing position at the back. Beneath the cover of my oversized trousers, I clench and unclench my buttocks, try to jiggle the wedgie she left behind loose, but Hilary snatches up the loop position again before I can.

Dwight turns back to the rest of the group. 'Who of y'all wants to remind us what the rule is on footwear?'

The phasers go mad at the question. They bounce in their seats and wave their arms. At first, their reaction reminds me of Norman Macalister, the brainy sycophant of second grade (and third, fourth, fifth and so on) whose hand would always shoot straight for the ceiling every time the teacher asked the class a question. Couldn't stand for one minute not to be teacher's pet, the little nerd. You hated him.

This lot, though, they make Norman's eager-beaverness look like indifference. As Dwight strides around contemplating who to call on, their gesticulating grows wilder. They're waving in different directions at slightly different speeds but all getting faster and faster and harder, their wrists snapping in the air as they pump their arms up and down, side to side. Elbows fly in neighbour's faces and no one slows. Several brows start to redden and bead with perspiration and still they don't stop. They wave, flap and pump like... like wild birds or I don't know what.

'What the heck are they doing?' I say, to no one in particular, not expecting anyone to hear me over the din anyway. But Dwight hears, fires daggers in my direction, and everyone else hears too, the flapping stopping as suddenly as it started. The phasers stare at me aghast.

'Did someone ask me a question? Did I just hear a fucking question asked *out of turn*? I'm sure I did.' He sucks in air loudly so no one in the room can mistake his astonishment. 'But let's take things in order, shall we?' Dwight points to an exhausted-looking boy in the front row. 'Jim P, tell us the rule on footwear.'

Jim P jumps to his feet. 'Shoes should be used for walking purposes only! No brands or druggie images allowed! No heels allowed! No shoelaces allowed!'

'Thank you, Jim. You may sit down,' and Jim P sits. 'And because a question has been asked, let's deal with that too. Who wants to tell this little *newcomer* –' and he says the word like he meant to say cretin, scumbag or something worse '– what it is ya'll are doing?'

Again the flapping until Dwight points this time to a girl. 'Beth C.'

'Dwight. We are motivating for the privilege of answering your questions!'

'And?'

Beth C hesitates. 'And?'

'And what else?'

'Um, um, a-a-a-and sh-sh-sh-sharing with the group?'

'Yes, and sharing with the group. Thank you, Beth.' She sits down. 'Now, who will explain the rule about talking to superiors which this *person* has so blatantly transgressed?'

Flip, flap, flop. The chairs scuff loudly against the floor as the group motivates. 'Louise.'

'Newcomers must never speak directly to a staff member unless called upon to do so!'

'Thank you, Louise.' Dwight comes to a halt in front of me. 'I think since our new arrival is so very new we'll overlook her error. For the time being.' He pauses dramatically for full effect. 'Hilary, over to you.'

Hilary yanks me forward by the loop and, not expecting it, I nearly lose my balance. 'This is Justine. She's fifteen and was a student at Kennedy High School right here in Carrefort.'

Was a student at Kennedy High. I don't like that one bit. I *am* a student at Kennedy High, I want to shout. I'm a near straight-A student, as a matter of fact, a sophomore, on the honour roll semester after semester, secretary of the student drama society, member of the pep squad and the JV girls' basketball team and pretty damn popular too. *And I don't fucking belong here.*

'Does anybody know Justine?' asks Hilary.

Only one arm flaps in response to this question. It's a big beefy arm playing the piston from the far end of the boys' arc. 'Earl,' calls Hilary. And Earl lumbers to his feet. Very familiar. I'm sure I've seen his face before, but can't quite place where.

'I know her,' reports Earl. 'I got high with her once.'

'Liar!' I shriek and am rewarded with a thump on the back from Hilary and another tug of the belt loop.

'*I did*,' counters Earl. 'We smoked some joints in the back seat of my druggie friend's car.'

Chubby! He's lost the earring, gained a lot of weight but it's him, it's definitely him. So that's how they knew about that time, that one time.

'She came out with us one night with her brother, her *twin* brother.'

Dwight studies me more carefully. '*Joshua Z*,' he realises.

There's a collective drawing-in of breaths. At mention of your name, everybody else examines me anew. Some curious, some confused. They hunt for signs of you in my face, try to decipher your features in mine. Make the connection, make it fit.

'My, my, little Joshua Z's other half,' Dwight tuts.

I don't like the way he says your name, like he's chewing on it or something. And I don't like the way he says 'z' apostrophe 's', 'zeez', like disease without the 'di'.

'Right,' Earl confirms. 'I got high with her and her druggie twin.'

'It wasn't like that,' I say, 'not at all.'

I wait for Hilary to chirp in with 'You sure about that?' but she doesn't utter a word and instead Dwight pronounces, 'It never is.'

'Thank you, Earl,' says Hilary. 'Who'd like to welcome Justine to the programme now?' Flap, flap, flap. 'Emily.'

Emily bolts up from her seat. 'My name's Emily, I'm sixteen and I'm an alcoholic and an addict! Welcome to Come Clean, Justine!

I pray that you'll find the same peace and serenity that I've found through my Higher Power and the programme!'

'Thank you, Emily. Justine, you may sit down.' A sentry totes forward a chair and Hilary pushes me roughly down into it.

Dwight claps his hands together like cymbals. 'Right, phasers, maybe we can get on with our drills now. Where were we, where were we?' Flap, flap. 'Simon G.'

'Dwight, we were on Step Seven!'

'Correct. So, Seven!' And the phasers call out in unison, 'We seek through prayer and communion to improve our contact with our Higher Power and to communicate His will to other addicts!'

'Very good,' says Dwight.

'Very good,' concurs Hilary.

CHAPTER TEN

Pony Girl's name is Gwen. I discover this at the same time I discover that this day isn't going to get any easier. At the end of the drills, it's roll and dole call.

'Roll and dole!' Dwight bellows and for a millisecond I think it's a command. Like when our elementary school teachers – Miss Fawcett, Mrs Wolf, Mr Newhouse or whoever it was used to lead us through fire drills and they would shout out 'Drop and roll!' because that's what we were supposed to do if we ever got engulfed in flames. We'd have to fall to the floor that instant and roll like logs to demonstrate that we could do it without thinking, even in a moment of crisis. We had no real problem dropping and rolling, except sometimes when Wayne Westbrook, before I put him in his place, used to spit in front of you so you couldn't help but roll in the frothing speck of a puddle and get his cooties all over you. Then it was no fun.

But if 'roll and dole' is a command, no one else acts on it too sharpish. The phasers' bottoms stay welded to their seats until Hilary pops off, reappearing with her clipboard which she hands to Dwight. He reels off names. 'Anne A with Lisa M, Andy C with Greg A, Beth D with Jennifer J, Brad with Eric H.' People are moving round me now, girls descending from the standing positions at the back to hook the belt loops of more terrified looking girls at the front.

I'm one of the last names to be called. 'Justine Z with Gwen,' Dwight shouts and here comes the ponytail again, loping towards me and grimacing. As she lifts my belt loop, Dwight plumps a hand on her shoulder. 'I want you to take care of the shoes, Gwen,' he says, lowering his forehead and fixing her with a disappointed look. 'You should know better.'

His and hers mountains of winter coats are piled up en route to the back door and they put me in mind of the ownerless stacks of clothing torn from Jews on their way to the concentration camps, like in that documentary we watched once on PBS. I wish I'd agreed to let Mom sew a name tag into my collar like she used to do when we were little, because mine is just another black woollen coat, a needle in a haystack of black woollen coats and I doubt I'll ever be able to find it again. Gwen makes it clear she doesn't care one bit whether I do or I don't. She hands me a coat from the top of the nearest pile – any old coat, someone else's coat with a button missing and, I discover, pockets made useless by holes the size of fists – and she shuffles me on.

We exit through the back of the building where there's a larger parking lot and a jam of cars and parents and kids being spirited round by belt loops. Gwen steers me towards an oatmeal-coloured four-door sedan and hustles me into the back seat; my head collides with the frame as I manoeuvre my body into place. There's a man at the wheel who I assume is Gwen's dad.

'Buckle up,' he says as we nudge our way into the stream of departing cars.

Gwen ignores him so I do too, but after a second she growls,

71

'Didn't you hear my father? He said *buckle up*!' She stretches across me, whips the seat belt out and over my torso, fastens and tightens it as far as it will go.

About fifteen silent minutes into the drive, Gwen pipes up and orders me to relinquish my shoes and bra. My hands aren't shaking so bad any more so I manage to unhook my bra from the back, but I make sure Gwen's dad isn't peeping before I slip it out via my sleeve. Gwen snatches it and my Mary Janes.

'If you tell anyone about the underwire,' she says as she rolls down her window, 'if you breathe one word, I swear I'll *kill* you.'

I hate it when people say things like that. People just say them like they were commenting on the weather – I'll kill you, I'll murder you, I could just die, I wish I were dead and buried – and they never think. Maybe Gwen does mean it, but I still flinch when she says it and she obviously means something pretty hateful by it because the next thing she does is launch my belongings out through the open window and into the passing traffic.

I can't believe it when she does that and I'm so unprepared, I don't do a thing to prevent it. Too late, I twist and watch as my things recede into the distance. The shoes tumble to the side of the road, one of them landing heel-up in a puddle while the bra seems to float on the car's tailwind for a second and then gets sucked under the muddy wheels of a florist's delivery van. I watch until I can't see any of the items any more and suddenly I'm gripped by sadness. They were the last things, the very last things I had that were my own. I want to slap this Gwen person but then I remember I still have my day-old panties. Kind of gross after thirty-six hours but the thought calms me. I've still got something that's mine.

Throughout this, Gwen's father acts like he doesn't notice anything; his eyes remain glued to the road ahead. I can't imagine our dad wouldn't have something to say on the matter. If only to holler, 'You know the rule, Justine. No littering.'

In the evening's gloom, I can't see the house much when we arrive, except to make out that it's two storeys and the driveway bends up and round to the back. And I'm none too pleased, as I step out with my bare feet, to find the path to the door lined with pebbles. I attempt to tread carefully but Gwen's having none of that. I wince as she trots me across some of the sharper ones.

The dinner table is set. There are sloppy joes, sweet corn and salad, and Gwen's mom, dad and a sulky little sister who eyes me suspiciously. Ten or eleven, I'm guessing. Gwen's dad is thin, dark, weary-looking; her mom has red hair like Gwen's but it's paler and permed into tight frizzy curls. And she's a horrible cook. I've never liked sloppy joes and these are the worst. Too gunky and juicy, soaking up the buns until they turn into nothing but mush that clumps under your fingernails.

I'm so thirsty. The sloppy joes make it worse as they're on the spicy side. I wish I had a frigging glass of water. 'Could I have a glass of water?' I ask Gwen's mom.

'Did anyone say anything to you?' Gwen snaps. 'You're not supposed to say anything until someone says something to you. Got it?'

'I just—'

'Shut up already!'

'It's OK, Gwennie,' the mom interjects, 'I can get her a glass of water, it's no bother.'

'Do you mind, Mother. I'm handling it.'

'But—'

'Milk. There. Drink!' Gwen screeches, slamming a too-full glass on to my place mat so that the milk splashes on to my plate, wrists and the sleeves of my polka-dot tunic. I wipe the back of my wrist dry with my napkin and then everyone watches me as I sip at the milk. It's whole milk and has been sitting out; close to room temperature, it tastes like cream to me. Our family only ever drinks skimmed milk and only ever ice cold and usually only with cereal anyway. I sip some more and the milk curdles on my tongue and makes me even thirstier. I shovel a forkload of sweet corn into my mouth.

Gwen waits until all mouths are full and bulging before announcing, 'Family rap!' Her parents exchange wholeheartedly unenthusiastic looks. 'Whose turn is it?'

'I don't know, Gwennie,' her mom says, lowering a soggy crust from her lips. 'Is it yours?'

'You wish. No, I think it's Dad's actually.'

'Not tonight, Gwen. It's been a long day,' says the dad.

'All the more reason. And it's your turn.'

'Not tonight.'

'Tonight, tomorrow night, *every* night, Dad.'

'Burt, maybe you should make an effort,' urges the mom.

'Hell, whaddya want me to say?'

'Tell us what happened to you today.'

'You don't want to hear about that.'

I have to say, I really don't want to hear about that and it doesn't look much like Mom or little sis do either. But Gwen forges ahead and manages to wheedle an appetite-numbing story out of her father about some small humiliation from his too-long day. From what I can gather, Gwen's dad's a section manager at some manufacturing plant and today he tells his team they can have fifteen extra minutes for lunch because they've been hammering or welding or sawing away so hard, but then the big boss shuffles down at the end of the usual lunch hour and sees these guys hanging about, drinking from their Thermoses and chomping on apples and whatnot, and he says to Gwen's dad, 'Hey, what the effing eff are these guys doing hanging about.' So the big boss overrules Gwen's dad, sends the whole team back to work and docks them five minutes apiece off their next break.

'How did you feel about that, Dad?'

'How do you think I felt?'

'I don't know, you tell me.'

'I felt like an asshole. All my guys think I'm a sorry, good-for-nothing asshole.'

'That's great, Dad, that's really great,' says Gwen, squeezing his knuckles in encouragement. 'Thanks for sharing.'

'Can I watch *Happy Days* tonight?' asks little sis as she pulps the remains of her sloppy joe bun with her fork.

'You know you can't.'

'I wanna watch *Happy Days*. Mom, why can't I watch *Happy Days*?'

'No TV, not while we're in the house,' Gwen reminds her, jerking her thumb in my direction. 'And stop saying that name.'

'It's not fair. I never get to watch any of my shows any more. Dad, it's not fair.'

'Them's the breaks,' declares Gwen.

'I wanna watch *Happy Days*! I wanna watch *Happy Days*!'

'Trish, I'm warning you, you'd better shut up and you'd better stop saying that druggie name or I'm going to report you and you'll hear about it in the next sibling rap.'

'Quiet, Trish,' pleads the mom, all hushed and hurried.

'No TV,' Gwen bangs her knife on her plate like a gavel. 'And you'd better not turn that radio of yours on either. Don't think I don't know when you do that. I can hear it through the wall.'

'It's not fair.'

'Quiet, Trish,' says the mom.

Directly after dinner, Gwen says it's time to get ready for bed. She leads me into the bathroom for my ablutions – one of your all-time favourite words because it sounds like a body sneezing and burping at the same time, you used to say – and I wait for her to leave but she doesn't. She squirts Colgate on her toothbrush, which she sticks in her mouth as she also drops her pants and plops down on the toilet.

'Don't just stand there,' she says through a mouthful of foam, 'we haven't got all night. There's a spare toothbrush on the counter. The blue one.'

The blue one's gnarled and obviously used, but I don't want to risk asking for another. As I lean down to wet the toothbrush beneath the tap, Gwen spits into the basin. I close my eyes and brush.

And I hear Dad reciting the dental care mantra in my head, like he used to do when we were little and he'd stand at the bathroom door to make sure we were doing it right. Up and down, up and down, to the back then to the front then to the back and up and down. Then, don't forget, kids, floss is your friend. You always hated flossing, it made your gums bleed; so sometimes, when Dad wasn't watching, we'd skip that part. But I wish I had some floss now. With so much foulness passing through my mouth today, I could do with a good floss.

Gwen's a brisk brusher – oh how Dad would disapprove – and she gives her face only the most cursory scrub with the washcloth and one pump's worth of hand soap from a sink-side container. I'm hoping she'll beat a quick retreat after that but she doesn't, not even when it's my turn for the toilet.

Our bedroom, which I'm marched into next, is not technically a bedroom because there's no bed. There are two mattresses and a neat stack of sheets and comforters against one wall, but no other furniture to speak of. It's a room as empty as the day you move in. Gwen doesn't even call it a bedroom.

'Inspecting the phaser room!' she bellows as she hands me and my belt loop over to her dad. Then she drops to her knees and rakes through the bare carpet with her fingers. She crawls from one corner of the room to the other tearing into the synthetic weave, poking down the sides by the skirting boards, getting eye level with the windowsills. She checks the door to what I assume is the closet and seems satisfied to find it locked. Turning her attention to the mattresses, she peeks to see what's sandwiched between them (nothing) then lets them plop down on to the floor and leaps on them, one springing step each, like a trampoline. One of the mattresses, the one with the deepest sag in its belly, is kicked into the corner farthest from the door. Next Gwen shakes out each sheet, each frilly comforter, each sad pillow, and tosses them in equal measure on to the separated mattresses. As she makes her way back towards me, her eyes remain on the floor, scanning each step, each inch.

'All clear!' she reports. Her father rolls his eyes and backs away without a good night.

The mattress in the corner is my bed for the evening. Rammed in the corner like that, it makes me feel like a dunce, like I should forget how to spell and sit on my own till teacher calls time, like I should wear a big pointy white cap.

Gwen undresses, twisting off her Velcro-strap sneakers as she yanks down the bottoms of her sweat suit. I avert my eyes from her rolls of blubber, trying not to think how unpopular she must be with the boys, even if it does give me some pleasure. Still, I can't help but notice her nipples which are the size of Franklin Mint special edition silver dollars and wonder how you get nipples like that.

'Get ready for bed,' she orders, stepping into a pair of oversized men's boxer shorts.

'What should I wear?'

'What have you got?'

'Nothing. You know I haven't.'

'Watch it, dirtball, don't you get sassy with me.'

'I—'

She groans then pelts me with a wadded up T-shirt with UNICEF stamped on the front where a pocket would have been. 'Don't get anything on it.'

The T-shirt is too small – I think it must belong to Trish – and the stitching on the label causes the back of my neck to itch, but I squeeze myself into it. Gwen snaps the lights off before I've finished folding up my clothes and the room is darker than I expect it to be. I grope my way towards my dunce's mattress.

'And don't even think about crying,' Gwen hisses from her mattress. 'If there's one thing I can't stand, it's fucking cry babies keeping me up all night.'

I pull the covers up to my chin and try to imagine that I'm in our rollaway, which is similar in its proximity to the floor.

After you left, I found myself sleeping in the rollaway more and more, just like when we were little. I didn't plan to. Grandma came so I gave her my room and Mom made up the couch in the

TV lounge for me. That was the official sleeping arrangement. But I kept tossing and turning out there on the couch, my butt wedging itself into the space between the cushions. About midnight one night, I got up to walk around and passed your door, slightly ajar, the glow from your old Mickey Mouse night-light you never bothered to throw out silhouetting the frame. I kneed the door open, maybe hoping to find you, and there was your room, just as you left it. Except for the rollaway. It was wheeled out from its hiding place beneath your proper bed and jacketed with a sheet now coated in dust. I didn't mind, didn't stop to think twice. I yanked the pillow and bedspread off your bed, crawled into the dust and fell asleep at once.

Mom found me like that in the morning and started bawling all over again. She said I oughtn't be sleeping in your room. Grandma Shirland massaged the small of Mom's back, little circular motions interspersed with pat-pats, calmed her down, changed her mind, bless Grandma. She said if it helped me, what was the harm. 'Trust me,' Grandma Shirland told Mom. 'It's OK.'

But I can't make Gwen's dunce mattress feel the same. The sheets are icy cold, they feel faintly wet and smell of chlorine. I scissor my legs to warm up. It doesn't have much effect and I wish I had some socks. I wish that eternity ago that was this morning I'd taken the time to run upstairs and root out my thickest, warmest pair of black woollen tights. Not that they'd probably still be with me even if I had taken the time. Without my tights or a good pair of ski socks, I'm sure my feet will become frozen little approximations of appendages by morning, like the marbled and immovable chips of Greek statues they display in museums.

My dunce pillow has lumps in funny places and no matter how I plump it, my head feels like an eggshell, fragile and lopsided.

I plunge my nose into the pillow's innards hoping to come up with that smell of you that's lulled me to sleep in the past. I love to sink into that smell. Sorta musky, still fresh nearly and... something. Not a bottled thing, not just a combination of sweat and salt and anti-dandruff shampoo and deodorant. You asked me once, 'How do I smell?' and I leant in and ran my nose across you like a dog would and I thought about it, really tried to capture it but all I could say was, 'Wonderful, you smell wonderful, Josh.'

You pressed me, 'Yes, but what's it like? Describe it.'

I answered, 'You smell like you.'

But the dunce pillow doesn't. It smells of piss, mildew and other people's dead skin cells. There's no way I can drift off to never-never land with my nostrils full of this. There's no way I can sleep at all. I listen as Gwen tosses once, twice, three times. She smoothes her bedspread then punches it away from her. She grumbles and lashes out at someone. 'I know that,' she retorts to the empty room and then her breathing grows heavy, punctuated by an occasional piggy-like snuffle.

I should have peed more. I couldn't let go, not fully, when we were in the bathroom earlier, not with her standing over me like that, toothbrush in hand. But out of nowhere, the need hits me. My bladder's about to burst.

I can hold it, no problem.

I try not to think about it, I count sheep, think of drifting off, think of you floating on a raft in the pool on a summer's day with the sun beating down and the radio playing our favourite Duran Duran songs from the table on the patio.

I listen to Gwen sleep. I don't know how long I listen to her but it feels like a very long time indeed as I tauten my privates, grit my teeth and envisage miles of sandy desert and no swimming pools at all: what a silly idea, no water, no waves, none of that. I count her snuffles – one, three, five, seven. I figure they're at least two to three minutes apart. She hasn't moved in, what, fifteen minutes.

I decide to take a chance.

I creep towards the door, thinking myself weightless while simultaneously trying to gird my bladder. It's working. I always was the best at hide and seek because I could be so quiet. I knew the places you'd gravitate to, sure – under the sink with the Audrey Hepburn rubber gloves, behind the garbage cans in the garage, under the bed in Mom and Dad's room, beneath the tattered tarpaulin shrouding the barbecue out back or under the cushions for the poolside chairs – but that wasn't my real advantage. Though you were the one hiding, I was always the one who had the element of surprise on my side. I'd sneak up behind you, soft like a whisper, and tap you on the shoulder as calm as you please, as if all I hankered for was the time of day, and you'd jump out of your skin, startled and scared and packing your heart back into your chest every time. You're half Indian, you'd tell me, and I'd say, you're half not. And we'd laugh.

I'm at the door. Nothing has stirred and, as long as my pee doesn't splash too loudly, I'm certain I'm in the clear. My fingers close over the doorknob…

And the place erupts.

The doorknob sets off a siren that rips through the house and maybe the whole neighbourhood. Gwen leaps out of sleep like it was last year's fad and lunges for me, screaming, 'Escape, newcomer trying to escape!' With an elbow to the chest, she tussles me to the ground and hefts herself on to my strained bladder. Footsteps come running up the stairs and down the hall, coming from all directions.

Gwen's mom arrives at the door, her robe slouching off one shoulder, her husband out of breath behind her and sulky Trish, looking rather uncharacteristically delighted, weaselling in between them.

I blush. What must I look like to them, what with Gwen on top of me, my body spread-eagled on the floor with nothing but a too-tiny T-shirt and two-day-old panties on to cover up my shame?

'What the hell happened?' wheezes the dad.

'She was trying to escape.'

'No, I wasn't.'

'I caught her red-handed, literally. She thought I was asleep but I wasn't. I caught her.'

'I just needed to go to the bathroom,' I protest.

'A likely story.'

I admit it doesn't seem very likely that I should have to pee, given that I haven't had a single drop of real liquid for the entire day – whole milk notwithstanding. But nevertheless, the need's there and rather urgent. 'It's true.'

'You went before we came to bed.'

'I needed to go again.'

'Stop lying!' screams Gwen and she jounces up and down on my prostrate body for emphasis.

This, as I'm sure Gwen herself comes to agree, is not a smart move, for my bladder, after a valiant effort, finally succumbs to the inevitable – all over both of us.

CHAPTER ELEVEN

We want a baby; we aren't babies ourselves any more so it's time for another one. We realise this for definite one afternoon when we're playing with Christy Crybaby. We're four or thereabouts, I think.

Christy Crybaby 'cries real tears and wets herself too'. She comes with her own bottle that you can fill up straight from the faucet and her own diapers that snap on and off. If you press her tummy, her eyes stream, just like the box says. Her thumb's the same shape as the nipple of the bottle so when you're not feeding her she has something else to suck on.

We love Christy Crybaby, but then doesn't everybody? Christy Crybaby is the most beautiful, most loveable doll ever born. She has blonde-blonde hair that curls up into little baby-doll ringlets, appley cheeks, eyes the colour of the brightest bluest blue in the Crayola box, limbs chubbed out with baby fat and fingers that dimple at the knuckles. Everybody in the whole wide world loves Christy Crybaby. She has an entire row of her own in the KayBee Toy Store and her own TV commercials. The Christmas before, we begged for our very own Christy Crybaby and yowled with glee when we stumbled downstairs before daybreak on Christmas morning and found her perched and glowing blondely atop the other presents that had to stay wrapped to seem half as exciting.

Grandma Shirland elbowed Grandpa Shirland as we tussled to release Christy from her box. 'Do you see? It's Christy, Christy as in Christmas. It's a Christmas baby.'

'That's downright funny all right,' Grandpa pronounced gruffly. Grandpa finds everything funny in an isn't-that-slightly-out-of-the-ordinary way.

Grandma and Grandpa gave us two little stuffed bunny rabbits that year. One for you, one for me. They were very cuddly. We named one Bunny and the other Funny, after Grandpa. Grandma and Grandpa Shirland always gave us one apiece of everything.

'No reason to squabble that way,' said Grandma.

'They never squabble,' Mommy told her. 'They share everything, they like to share.' She said that with pride, I could tell, like that made us different from other kids. We liked being different, though we didn't know many other kids at that point.

So most things we had just the one of. And most times, that was fine. Until there was Christy Crybaby, the most wonderful baby doll ever born.

We're playing in our room one afternoon after Christmas. At night, we take turns sleeping in the big bed versus the rollaway. Sometimes the one in the big bed rolls over and lands accidentally-on-purpose on to the one in the rollaway. That makes us laugh. We both like sleeping in the rollaway because it has a close-to-the-carpet, slumber-party feel about it. That's why we take turns. Once you tried trundling me under the big bed with the mattress, but my face caught on the frame. It hurt real bad but I didn't cry or squeal to Mommy. Scouts honour. You reckoned if I sucked up real tight I woulda fit under. Another time we tried it out on Christy. We mashed her down into the guest mattress, then squeezed her under the big bed. We had the darndest time getting her out. She kept jamming on the big bed's frame coming the other way. When we did finally rescue her, Christie's pretty plastic face was crosshatched from the big bed's box springs.

This afternoon, we're coddling Christy Crybaby, not tormenting her. We're playing nursery maids; we're the maids and the rollaway is the nursery. There are other babies in the nursery – grizzly Teddy Kennedy in the corner, Miss Piggy, Bunny and Funny, Barbie, Skipper and GI Joe. But Christy's the nursery's star baby.

You've already had your turn at changing her and now I'm preparing her feed. 'How's my wittle girl, today? Is my wittle baby feeling huuungry?' I tap the miniature bottle on my wrist, like I've seen them do on a TV hospital show.

'Ooh, Miss Wilmington, I don't know if it's the right temperature.' You're a nursery maid after all and we've named you Miss Wilmington, Wilma Wilmington. Maybe it was Wilma Flintstone I saw testing the formula bottle for Pebbles.

You grab the bottle from my hand, rub it between your hands and sit on it a minute before giving it back. 'That oughtta do it, Miss Betty.'

'Thank you, Miss Wilmington.' Then I say to Christy, inserting the bottle teat into her permanently puckered mouth, 'My wittle baby must be weally huuungry now. Oh yes she is.'

As Christy feeds quietly, you attempt to wrap a Kleenex diaper round the GI Joe that Dad gave you. Only Joe's legs don't open wide enough and he's got a featureless but still noticeable bulge in his crotch that keeps getting in the way and the tissue keeps ripping when you wind it round his waist. You throw him out of the nursery. 'He doesn't even look like a baby,' you grumble. Then you're back at my shoulder, hovering. 'It's my turn now.'

'Nu-uh, you just had her.'

'That was ages ago.'

'Nu-uh. She hasn't even finished her bottle.'

'Close enough, bet she's already peed herself.' You stick a digit down there and pull it out dripping. 'See, she needs changing. Lemme.'

'You been sucking that finger, that's how come it's wet. Bug off.'

You flop back on the mattress, making all the babies jump in their shoe-box cribs, except Teddy Kennedy who's too big for a crib. 'Not fair, we need another baby. We can't both be nurses and mommies to Christie. We need another.'

I tip the bottle out of Christy's mouth. She looks at me silent, kind of accusing-like. 'It would be sorta nice if she burped occasionally or maybe if she said something every once in a while, like Trisha Talk-Talk. Maybe Mommy'll get us Trisha Talk-Talk for our birthday.'

'No, not Trisha Talk-Talk. No good. I want a *real* baby. We need a real one.'

We discuss the traits our new baby should exhibit. It should be a girl, of course, a little baby sister. She should have Christy's hair, eyes and cheeks but her mouth should close and she should be able to cry, though not too much, and say 'Ma-ma'.

By the time our mommy searches us out, we've hatched our plan. I'm holding Christy and you're holding the bottle. 'That's a good girl, drink it all up.'

Mommy cracks the door open and leans into the room with her head and shoulders to see what we're playing. 'Everything OK, kids?'

'Yup.'

She ventures further into the room, a light-bulb-bright smile pasted on. 'You hungry? Need anything?'

'Nope.'

'Oh. OK, then.' She waits, looming Godzilla-like at the edge of the nursery. 'Do you want me to help you feed Christy?'

'No, Mommy, we can do it,' you say petulantly. 'Besides, there's only one Christy Crybaby.'

'I know that, Mister Man.' She wants to reach out and muss your hair but catches herself.

'Mommy,' I chip in, this is part of the plan, 'we need another baby. Please can we have a baby sister now, a real baby?'

'*Please* Mommy, pretty please with cherries on top.'

Mommy's arms are crossed but loose, now she locks them down tight against her tummy. She chews her lip. 'No.'

'But why not? You're no fun.'

Mommy's eyes start to swim. 'I'm afraid not. No.'

'Ahhh, Mommmeeee!' we drag her name out like it had four syllables and, in unison, our cheeks puff and lips jut. 'You can't just say no. How come? We need another baby? Why not?'

'Listen, I...' one solitary tear slips out of the corner of Mommy's eye. 'I'm sorry, but it's just not possible.' She pauses and fills her lungs. 'Your mommy... I – I can't have any more babies. I just can't and that's that.' Her lips are quivering like unset Jell-o. Another tear breaks free and races the first down her cheek. She lifts a hand to wipe it away, but then the tears start pouring like rain out of both eyes.

87

'OK, Mommy,' we tell her as she flees from the room.

Wow. Mommy's crying. This is something we're not overly familiar with, something Grandpa Shirland would undoubtedly declare 'funny'. We don't know what this means. 'Do you think she wets herself too?' I wonder aloud.

You consult your thumb and scrunch up your eyes as you try to picture it. 'Nah, you can't get diapers that big.'

CHAPTER TWELVE

My first full day in the programme begins around five a.m. At least I think it's five a.m. though I can't say for sure and I don't have my Swatch. But it must be awfully early. It's pitch black when Gwen cattleprods me, though I'm only half asleep.

After the events of yesterday and the final humiliation of wetting myself in front of an audience, I lay on my mattress, my thighs still sticky, listening to Gwen snuffling, the house settling, the air cracking, and I tasted the betrayal in my mouth, like onions mixed with chlorine mixed with day-old wine coolers, vomit, Tic Tacs and a thin layer of toothpaste applied with a stranger's toothbrush.

There was a small benefit to wetting myself – I was finally relieved of the panties I'd been wearing for thirty-six-plus hours. They were so sodden and vile it didn't sadden me in the least to step out of them. Even though they were my very last shred of a personal possession. This morning, Gwen unlocks the door to the closet in the corner and brings out fresh underwear. She waves a pair in my face. Hip-hugging granny underpants, they are, and I know they belong to someone else, but they look clean and that's all that matters now. She also shoves into my hands a pair of nursing home regulation slip-on shoes which have seen better days and then some. They're scuffed and stained, fraying round the lip and seams, with heel-less, rubberised soles whose traction grips have worn clean away. But I'm happy for them too and reassured that I won't be questioned about heels or laces or the inappropriateness of my footwear today.

I wait for a new bra from the closet but it doesn't come so my breasts hang loose and floppy beneath my polka-dot tunic. I lock my arms across my chest for fear my nipples, hardened in the early morning chill, will show themselves through the shirt's material. 'Headlights, you've got headlights,' the boys at school, with the exception of you, would squeak in their changeable voices with fingers pointing and jeans swelling in the direction of a particular, unfortunate girl when this would happen. I don't want that to be me, not today.

Gwen hikes the belt loop of my cords – which I'm instructed to wear again, along with my dotted tunic – and proves first thing, make no mistakes, that even with panties the size of an office picnic tablecloth covering your backside, you can still achieve a full wedgie. She pilots me hurriedly through the house, making me wash my face, comb my hair and brush my teeth before breakfast. There's no time for a shower this morning, so I assume we must be running late, though how anyone can be late for anything when it's still pitch black outside, I don't know.

Before we leave the house, just as I'm sliding into the coat that isn't mine, Gwen asks, 'You need a piss or anything?'

I shake my head.

'Sure? Positive?' I shake my head again. 'Ya better be because if I catch you pissing or dumping or yakking up or so much as farting in my car, you're a dead man. I heard what you did in your parents' car and I'm not standing for anything like it so you better be damn sure. You got me?'

I nod and I hear Gwen mutter something like 'disgusting' or 'disgraceful' and that's the last I hear her say to me all day.

In silence, Gwen's dad drives us along the traffic-less roads back to the programme. There are a few other cars parked or idling about the rear parking lot and mini convoys of kids, belt loops, wedgies and hooked fingers straggling towards the building's back door, which is propped open with a splattered paint can.

Gwen rushes me inside, down the hall and into another one of the rooms off the low-ceilinged corridor. This one's the size of my intake room, maybe it is the intake room except the chairs, even the uncomfortable ladder back with the splinters, have disappeared, and instead young girls are scattered around looking rigid and uncertain. Gwen deposits me and I stand with the other girls, none of whom says a word so I don't either. The room fills up as the door opens and closes and more rigid girls are shoehorned in. We're standing shoulder to shoulder like you do in overcrowded elevators, and we all stare straight ahead towards the door.

After half an hour, maybe more, the door sounds again and we draw in our collective breaths and try to shrink smaller. I'm sure that not a single person more can fit in, but this time the door stays open and the girls file out. I'm near the back, one of the last out, and when I emerge into the hallway, a girl I haven't seen before takes over my loop until we're back into the big group room. The fluorescent tube lights buzz busily overhead as before, but the chairs are arranged differently, in clumps this time, all fanning out from a circle in the middle of which stand Dwight and Hilary.

Dwight has donned a preppy look today – yellow polo shirt with collar, pressed khakis and loafers. And his hair's a perfect wave of contrition. Cindy would say he was awesomely droolworthy; Cindy would ask him to dance if this were a dance and he was alone and maybe he didn't look quite so cocky. He can't be too old either. He definitely looks much younger than Hilary with her necklace of keys and her outgrown Farrah Fawcett cut. Hilary must be at least as old as Dad's receptionist, Zoe Micklebaum, thirtysomething if a day.

Dwight and Hilary hold matching clipboards and they consult them as they call attendance. She yells out one name from the boys' list and he yells out one name from the girls' list. As they do so, the body corresponding to whatever name it happens to be leaps up and announces how long they've been off drugs.

'Greg A!' shouts Hilary.

And Greg A jumps up. 'Still here and forty-three days clean!'

'Rachel B!' barks Dwight.

And Rachel's chair nearly topples over in her zeal to declare, 'Still here and sixty-seven days clean!'

'Andy C! Beth D! Brad! Helen F! Mark G! Wendy!'

I race to make conversions in my head, figuring out that, at sixty-seven days, Rachel B has been here for two months and one week. That seems like a long time but some of the others are counting days in their hundreds, two hundreds, four hundreds, six hundreds and that makes me think I must be mistaken about what the numbers mean. I switch my attention to the order of the attendance list instead, which is confusing in and of itself, because the phasers must be listed on those clipboards in alphabetical order by surname but the surnames are never used and initials are used haphazardly, so the order doesn't make much sense to me.

I know with a name like Ziegler that, as usual, I'll be at the end of the list but, with so few alphabetical indicators, I'm still startled when Dwight lets rip with my name. Hearing my name like he says it, cut off without the '-iegler' somehow doesn't sound like my name at all. 'Justine Z!' he says for the second time, clearly perturbed by the extra effort.

I clamber to my feet and manage to form the word 'here' in a small voice before falling back into my chair and hoping it's enough. My heart snags a beat until Dwight moves on.

After roll call, he says it's time to run the Steps and he's taking volunteers. 'Step One!' The group motivates, writhing and flapping for Dwight and Hilary to turn their way until Hilary points to a girl behind me who stands and delivers: 'We admit our powerlessness over addiction and the unmanageability of our lives!' As she sits down, the whole group repeats the line in unison.

There are Seven Steps to the Come Clean programme and we trawl through them all in this fashion once, then Hilary drills us through them again with her whistle, holding up the number of fingers to show which Step she wants us to chant, as she blows to start and finish. We speed successfully through to the end – then she leads us through the Steps again and again and again. The first few run-throughs, I don't say anything because I don't know these Steps, they've nothing to do with me and surely this is the last time I'm going to have to hear them already, so what's the point. But it never is the last time. With each repeat, the volume rises incrementally and I'm beginning to think they're not going to let us stop until we get it one hundred and ten per cent right and loud enough to raise the iron roof. So then I start to move my lips and pretend to join in, like how we used to do in first grade when our teacher Miss Hamlet tried to teach us the Pledge of Allegiance, and by the eighth rendition I'm able to chip in with selected words at the appropriate times like when you hear a new Culture Club song on the radio.

'Powerlessness' I say on cue, 'Higher Power', 'sanity', 'moral inventory', 'amends' and 'addicts'. Finally, after what must be the thirteenth or fourteenth recitation, Hilary lets the whistle drop and swing to a standstill against her ribcage. The phasers catch their breath.

'Right, ya'll,' Dwight calls rousingly as if we've been dawdling all this time, 'let's get this day started!'

CHAPTER THIRTEEN

The morning rap session is first up on the day's agenda. Dwight opens it by asking the group what the Fourth Step means to us. There are no volunteers straightaway, so Dwight singles out a boy called Kenny. He's tall and ultra skinny, like his bones have grown ten times faster than his flesh, and he has a constellation of pimples blinking across his face, including one smack-dab in the centre of his forehead that makes him look like a cyclops out of the Greek myths we used to read in Mrs Mission's English class.

Kenny recites the Fourth Step, once again, for our benefit: 'We admit to our Higher Power, ourselves and each other the exact nature of our wrongdoings.'

'And that means?'

'That means we've got to own up to all the stupid shit we've done.'

'Are you ready to own up to your stupid shit, Kenny?'

'Yes, Dwight.'

'OK, then, we're listening.'

Kenny tells us about how he was real rebellious, how he used to yell at his dad and break curfews and stay out all night and steal his little sister's allowance so he could pay for the gas money to cruise around with his druggie friends so he wouldn't have to go home and deal with his parents and their attempts to ground him.

'Get specific, Ken.'

'Specific?'

'Tell us about a specific past experience.'

So Kenny tells us about one time when he'd committed a real wrongdoing. His dad was away on business, he says, and his mom needed to go out to visit Kenny's grandmom who was sick. Kenny's mom asked Kenny to stay home on a Friday night and baby-sit his little sister. He thought, to hell with that, because he'd already made plans to go out with his druggie friends, so after his mom had kissed his little sister on the forehead and said 'bedtime by nine' and after she'd swung out of the driveway in the station wagon, leaving Kenny with fifteen dollars to order pizza and Cokes and to be generous with a tip on top, Kenny told his little sister it was time for bed even though it was only seven thirty. Then he tucked her in, took the money and went out with his druggie friends anyway. Kenny's mom got home before Kenny did and found his sister cowering in the corner of her bedroom, alone and afraid of the dark. When Kenny staggered in, reeking of beer, his mom shouted at him that he was an abomination and how could he, what was he thinking and wouldn't his father have something to say about this. His mom was hysterical, screaming and crying so much so that the only way to calm her down was to slap her, so he did. Kenny slapped his mom.

I shake my head a notch or two. Automatic-like, not enough for anyone to notice, I hope. But oh, Kenny, that is pretty bad, sufficient to earn at least a good year's worth of room arrest. We would never hit our mother; we never have.

'And how do you feel about that now, Kenny?' Hilary wants to know.

'I'm ashamed,' says Kenny. 'It was wrong.'

'*Really?*' presses Dwight.

'Yes, Dwight, really really, terribly wrong.'

'Is that all?' Hilary queries. 'You sure about that?'

'Yes, Hilary, one hundred per cent sure. I'm ashamed, so ashamed. I made amends to my mom in Talk last week and she said she understood.'

'Did she now?'

'Yes, she did, she really did.'

Dwight shows Kenny his back. 'Comments?' he invites, and the rest of the group motivates.

A girl from the second row jumps up and immediately starts waving her arms around. 'You are so full of shit, Kenny! You're minimising and you know it! You're not coming clean with the half of it. You beat your mom black and blue and you know it!'

'I slapped her,' Kenny maintains.

'You beat her black and blue so you could go out and get stoned with your druggie friends. You abandoned your little sister and you couldn't give a shit whether she got raped or kidnapped or murdered. Just as long as you could get your high. You are so full of shit, Kenny! You need to get honest!'

'I am honest,' Kenny retaliates. 'I'm being honest. It was bad all right, but not that bad. I slapped her and that's it. I made amends.'

Other phasers motivate for the opportunity to tell Kenny that he needs to get honest. 'You son of a bitch, Kenny!' they scream and they call him other names. 'You weasel, Kenny. You asshole, you piece of shit, you motherfucker, you bastard, you fuckwit!' The girl next to me is beside herself. She sprays saliva as she denounces Kenny and I shrink away from her, afraid she might get some on me. Then she spits a huge globule: on purpose, she spits at Kenny. I draw my feet beneath my chair; the spit ball only makes it a few feet across the divide between the girls and boys.

After some time, Dwight commands everyone who has words for Kenny to stand up at once and deliver them. More than half the room seizes the opportunity. They stand and launch into attack mode, shaking their arms and screaming and name-calling and spitting. And Kenny takes it and takes it and takes it. He seems to grow shorter as he does, his pimples blaze redder against his face and I think the cyclops one may explode. His shoulders shake and tears brim in his eyes.

'OK! OK!' Kenny shouts.

Dwight quietens the rest of the group. 'Has Kenny got something to share with us?'

'Yes, OK, OK,' says Kenny. 'I didn't slap my mom.'

'No?' spurs Dwight.

'No, I didn't slap her, I – I punched her, that's what I did.'

'Yes?'

'I punched her so hard,' he falters, 'I punched her so hard that – that she chipped a tooth!'

'Yes? And?'

'And – and she needed stitches. She needed three stitches after I punched her... maybe it was *five*, come to think.'

The group is silent, it takes that in. 'I see,' says Dwight. 'I see.'

Kenny's accusers sit back down, their chests puffed out in satisfaction. 'And how do you feel now, Kenny?' asks Dwight. 'Now that you've admitted the exact nature of your wrongdoing.'

'I'm ashamed, Dwight, very ashamed.' He blinks back his tears, tries to steady his shoulders.

'You should be ashamed, Kenny. You have the right to be ashamed.'

'Thank you, Dwight.'

'That's great,' interjects Hilary. 'Thanks for getting honest, Kenny. Thanks for sharing.'

Kenny steps gingerly back into his chair, looking relieved. His time in the spotlight's over, but more confessions and confrontations follow. We hear about how Melinda cut class to have sex in the afternoon with her druggie boyfriend. We hear about how Roger used to siphon the gas from his dad's BMW and get high off the fumes. We hear about how Suzie P slept with the leader of a street gang because he promised to supply her with free hash for a month. And no matter how awful or quease-inducing the nature of the wrongdoings, somebody else invariably jumps up and tells Melinda or Roger or Suzie P or whoever that they're minimising, they're not being honest, that what they're describing was a walk through the park wearing rose-coloured glasses compared to how it must have really been. Then another stands to accuse and another and another until the whole room is whipped up into renewed frenzy.

So then Melinda owns up to the fact that her druggie boyfriend was six years older than her and on probation and that she cut classes so many times she nearly flunked the tenth grade, in fact she did flunk the tenth grade – twice. And Roger admits that he siphoned gas from all the cars parked on the street where he lived – at least once a month, once a week even. And Suzie P confesses that she had to sleep with the whole gang to cash in on the free hashish offer – and give them blow jobs, and take it up the ass. And there are tears, there are almost always tears.

By the time lunch rolls round, I've lost my appetite.

CHAPTER FOURTEEN

We don't go anywhere to eat. The lunch room as it happens is the rap room. The morning session ends with a few more recitations of the Fourth Step – 'We admit to our Higher Power, ourselves and each other the exact nature of our wrongdoings.' – and even I can mouth it along in full by the final whistle blow. Then Dwight claps his hands, Hilary shrieks, 'Luuunnnnchhh!' and the tightly huddled phasers break into a hive of activity. Someone has me by the belt loop before I can wonder which way to turn and I'm shunted along with the rest.

Chairs are cleared out of the way and, from the back of the rap area, folding tables are unstacked, carried to the centre and formed into one long snake of a banqueting suite stretching the length of the room.

'Straighten it up!' Dwight calls out over the din of squealing furniture, and I'm marched forward with another flank of girls to ensure that the end of each table is flush against the end of the next.

'Sit!'

We scrabble back to the chairs and my faceless human rudder instructs me to pick up two. I try to do as I'm told but the chairs are awkward and heavy and she doesn't leave me enough time to get a proper grip. One of the chairs slips down my side from the shoulder where I've attempted to brace it and I have to bend down and drag it behind me to stop from losing hold completely. The rudder doesn't like this.

'Watch it,' she snarls, 'you can't get anywhere by tripping me.'

Where does she think I'm going to go? There aren't many options so far as I can tell, but the rudder's determined to stop me nevertheless. She kicks one of the chair's trailing legs, causing the body of it to buck and pinch my fingers between plastic and metal. For extra emphasis, she gives my belt loop a zealous tug. When we reach the table, she plonks me down in one chair, lifts the other off me with a yank that rips my thumbnail, and is gone. I still don't get a look at her face.

As in the rap session, the boys and girls are separated but facing each other. The boys' side of the table is much longer than the girls', maybe ten or fifteen bodies more. The boy opposite me is blond like a week-old banana and his bangs hang down into his eyes. His lips are chapped and red, with teeth marks in the dead skin and pinpricks of blood from where he's been biting. He's only a few feet away and I'm afraid he'll be able to tell I'm not wearing a bra. But Banana Boy doesn't glance up so high as my smarting thumb.

Once everyone is seated, Dwight hollers, 'Who here is hungry?'

'We are, Dwight!' the group responds at full volume.

'And who here is thankful for what ya'll are about to receive?'

I scan the length of the bare catwalk of a table but I can't see just what it is we're about to receive.

'We are, Dwight!'

'Who do you have to thank for it?'

'Our Higher Power and our programme!'

'And are you prepared to give thanks?'

'We are, Dwight!'

'Let me hear ya then.'

'We give thanks to our Higher Power and our programme for giving us the sanity and the sustenance to stay clean and healthy and for all that we are about to receive.'

'Eh, what was that ya mumbling?' Dwight cups his hand to his ear like a frail retiree. 'Couldn't hear a word of it.'

The group shouts it out again, word for word, syllable for syllable and my mind fills with images of that old *Oliver Twist* movie where the little English kid works all day for his food and is about to go crazy with hunger if he doesn't get some: '*Please sir may I have some more?*' Are they going to feed us gruel? Will we have to sing for it? Will we have to dance? I'm afraid to dance without a bra on or the lights dimmed or a disco ball sparkling diamond glitter across my cheeks.

Dwight makes us test his hearing once or twice more and then the back door out into the parking lot bangs open and Mark and Leroy and some other thugs hunker in, their arms exploding with brown bags. Dozens and dozens of bags from – am I seeing right? – McDonald's? There's no mistaking the red strip or golden arches.

When we were real little, you hated McDonald's. The clown scared you. It wasn't the blousy yellow suit or the outsized tie or the floppy shoes, you could handle those. It was the shock of scarlet hair. That, I guess, on top of the white face and painted mouth. You said Ronald McDonald reminded you of the Joker from *Batman and Robin* – though I don't recall the Joker having red hair – and the Joker was the bad guy and you didn't like taking food off a bad guy. Besides which, Mom always said not to accept food from strangers and you couldn't get a grown-up much stranger-looking than Ronald McDonald.

There was one thing that changed your mind about McDonald's, one development that made the place, in your opinion, kid-friendly, that made you line up with me and beg Mom and Dad to take us. The Happy Meal. I haven't had one of those pint-size portions since I was in elementary school, but that's the very thing being unpacked from the acreage of McDonald's bagging down at the end of the table – box after brightly coloured box of Happy Meals. A trio of girl helpers grab cardboard trays of drinks and clutches of Happy Meals and distribute them down our side of the table as Mark and Leroy pass down the boys' side doing the same. Napkins, straws and sauces are dumped in handfuls into the centre.

You used to moon over your Happy Meal carton for ages. You'd sit there and let your food go cold while you worked out every maze and puzzle and word play on the game-festooned carrier box, or assembled and tested your Luke Skywalker action figure that came free with every meal.

Such diversions don't seem likely today, though. Not only are there no pens and pencils but, though my Happy Meal box is decorated with winsome pictures of My Little Pony, the free-with-every-meal toy is nowhere to be found.

As more Happy Meals are torn apart around me, I see that, advertising aside, there's not a My Little Pony among them. None of the other phasers seem surprised or disappointed by this short-change. They simply tuck into their limp, already-cold French fries and squashed, sesame-free buns.

I scrounge in the packets on the table for some ketchup. As I reach, my wrist jostles Banana Boy's drink. His lid flies off like it wasn't put on straight in the first place and ice cubes skitter down the table and all over his Happy Meal in a flood of, by the looks of it, Sprite. His burger absorbs a lot of the spillage but, in the millisecond that my hand's suspended there, the Sprite pools on the edge of his side of the table and then cascades lapwards. He springs up from his seat.

'Whoops!' I fumble for napkins to mop up the mess. 'Did I get you?'

Banana Boy acts shell-shocked. He holds his arms out to the side, staring down mutely at himself and his ruined lunch. He doesn't look like he caught it that bad.

'Hey, are you all right?' I ask.

I touch his forearm to get his attention, and he leaps back like I've poked him with a pitchfork. He shakes as his widened eyes move from his arm to me and back again.

'Ohhhhh. Jesus Jesus Jesus.' His and hers guards descend on us from both sides of the table. 'I didn't touch her!'

'What's going on here, Andy?' one of the boy guards asks Banana Boy.

'I didn't touch her, I didn't touch her, I swear!'

'What happened?' one of the girl guards asks me. I explain about the accident, the spilled drink, me trying to make sure he was OK.

'The rule is no physical contact of any kind between male and female phasers,' she informs me.

'Oh.' I turn to Banana Boy, Andy. 'Look, I'm sorry, I didn't mean to—'

'And no conversation of any kind. Except during rap sessions.' The male guards clear away the mess and lead a still mumbling Andy to the far end of the table.

I nibble at the remains of my hamburger and sip at my cup of Fanta. They've taken away my Happy Meal box so I can't study the puzzles or word games or the pictures of My Little Pony. I don't dare glance in any of my neighbouring diners' directions either in case I might spill something again or say something I'm not supposed to. I try to keep my elbows, eyes and hands tight within my own space. I focus on Andy's empty chair.

When everyone's finished eating, one guard passes behind with a jumbo-sized black plastic bag into which all garbage is tossed while another guard follows her handing out scraps of unlined paper and nubs of pencils with the erasers snapped off.

Around me, the others slump over their papers and write furiously. There's an exam-day air about the activity, with lots of kids tenting their words protectively with their hair or shoulders or shielding them with their hands. I feel like I'm in that dream where you turn up for an exam you didn't know about – you haven't prepared, haven't opened the textbook, don't even know what the frigging test is about. And I don't know what this is about, that's for sure. What's expected here? What am I supposed to be writing?

I hear pencil points breaking with the pressure of final punctuated flourishes and several people are already folding their papers over, sharpening the creases with their fingernails. The guards have started at opposite ends of the table to collect the completed works. Perhaps if I just fold my blank sheet up, no one will notice.

But then a girl further down yelps. 'You're not supposed to read it.'

'I'm not reading, I'm looking,' the collector retorts. 'Just a random check. We've got to make sure everybody's actually writing something, don't we?'

Shit.

They're only about half a dozen girls away from me now. I've got to scribble something, quickly. My pencil point tears a hole in my paper with my first stroke, but I manage to scratch out one word before the guard is breathing down my neck. I fold the sheet in half.

'One fold only,' says the guard snatching it from my hand. 'This isn't origami class here.' And my message is dropped with the others into a sack that looks like a pillowcase. I feel like I've just tossed an SOS in a bottle upon the waves. And some hero somewhere, maybe Cindy, maybe Lloyd, maybe Sting from the Police or someone will find it and come rescue me. But I don't hold out much hope. I have a bad feeling about those papers. The other kids are acting weird, like they want to forget they ever knew what a pencil was. There's a shiftiness about them, worse than before lunch. Nobody looks anybody else in the eye, girls or boys.

Maybe the guards are taking our notes away to be analysed by one of those graphologers or graphologists or whatever. I've read about them, these people who can tell everything about you, your deepest darkest secrets, by your handwriting. Maybe that's what the others are so weirded-out about. What new and twisted thing will my penmanship tell Hilary and Dwight about me? Maybe I should've taken a chance and not written anything at all. It's hard to tell any more what's sensible and what's not.

The fact is I did write something.

One word.

Help.

CHAPTER FIFTEEN

Mommy takes us to preschool when we're just-turned four. It's after Labour Day but still feels like summer, hot, sticky and unforgiving. The school is only a few blocks from home and Mommy walks us there. When we cross the road, she steps between us and latches on to our hands, but once we make it to the other side, we flitter free, grab hold of each other and break into a skip. Sometimes we try to outskip each other, measuring who can leap highest or furthest. But mostly we just skip along in unison. If we're really in rhythm, we land on the sidewalk the exact same second, so it reverberates like a single footstep. We can do that sometimes, but not always. One of us is usually thrown off balance as we try to avoid the cracks between the concrete slabs or the congealed blobs of bird shit.

Mommy strides ahead, her long lady-legs swishing back and forth in widened steps. When she reaches another intersection, she brakes on the kerb and waits for us. We giggle and skip and swing our locked arms between us.

'Hurry up, you two.' As she waits for us, Mommy tweaks at the front of her ruffled blouse and billows it against her chest. This is the first time she's worn the blouse since ironing it along with all of Daddy's shirts on Sunday, but its starched creases are already buckling and, along her spine, spots of perspiration are beginning to soak through the cotton weave. 'You'll have air conditioning there,' she sighs. 'Aren't you the lucky ones?'

Aren't we the lucky ones. We skip our way through another block and across one more thoroughfare until we trip into the school yard. Now this is a Grandpa Shirland funny, a scene way out of the ordinary, a scene of utter devastation. There are kids, more kids than we've ever seen before. And there's a top-class playground just begging to be swarmed over – a jungle gym, a bank of swings, a bright red merry-go-round, a revolving gate, two-toned rocking horses on coiled springs and a slide as smooth and shiny as a mirror. Plum pickings. But none of those kids are swarming. Those kids haven't got swarming on their minds. Goodness, no, they're too busy wailing, crying real tears just like Christy Crybaby. Their voices rise and rise, shrieking higher, shriller, louder as they blend into one another. It's not pleasure they're shrieking, either, it's terror.

Three young women wend their way through the chaos. They're dressed in matching white terry-cloth shorts and bubble-gum pink T-shirts with Jack 'N' Jill Playschool scrawled across their chests. They cluck and coax as they move, pausing to stoop and introduce themselves to the hysterical children.

'Hi,' they announce sparkily. 'I'm Lisa.' (Or Ashley or Mary.) 'What's your name?'

Rather than answer, the kids screw up their crimson faces, cling to their mommies and wail louder. There's a boy not two arms' lengths in front of us who has glued himself to his mother and is stamping his feet, and hers in the process, as he screams. Ashley (or Mary or Lisa) keeps talking to him in a level, sweet-as-pie voice, as if this were all perfectly normal.

'We're going to have so much fun today. We've got finger paints and Etch A Sketch inside. And the story lady's coming this afternoon and bringing Kool-Aid.'

The kid ignores every last word. His mom has had enough.

'That's enough now, Harold.'

Harold! How can you blame a kid for crying when he's got a name like Harold? Poor kid. He belts out a whopper, shakes his head and grinds his heels into her toes all at the same time. 'Harold Elliott Weinstein –' Oh heavens. '– I said *that is enough*!' She levers his arms loose from her thigh and transfers him to the playschool woman. 'Now Harold, you go with the nice lady and be good.'

Mary (or Lisa or Ashley) attempts to drag Harold by his wrist towards the school but he's not budging so she scoops him up and carries him. All the while, he's landing kicks and punches into her terry-clothed groin and shoulders and hollering 'Mommy Mommy Mommy.'

Harold's mom flashes him a big smile and waves full-armed as she watches him go. 'Mommy loves you, Harold. Don't you forget, Mommy loves you.' As soon as Harold's made it inside, her smile disappears and her shoulders droop. She presses two fingers to her lips like she needs to keep her mouth in place, and looks down at the thigh of her jeans where the denim has stained darker from Harold's tears or sweat or slobber. That lady must be hot in those jeans.

When she pivots round, she catches sight of us. Mommy's got hold of a hand apiece still, and the three of us are standing like statues, not knowing what to do. The woman's eyes flit from me to you and back again before settling her puzzled gaze on Mommy.

'How on earth do you cope with two?'

As the women commiserate, Mommy loosens her grip and we skip quietly away to the merry-go-round, hoping to get in a few good spins before the bubble-gum brigade notices us.

CHAPTER SIXTEEN

Once back in group formation, we run through the Seven Steps. Again and again and again. Hilary has disappeared so it's Dwight on his own now. He doesn't use a whistle, he just shouts. He's got the voice for it, loud and apparently immune to hoarseness. And Five! And Six! And Seven! And again! And One! And so on.

Near the end of the drills, another female staff member arrives. I know she's staff because she wears a whistle and carries a clipboard. And because there's something different about her too. She doesn't look at all like the girls in the group, though she can't be more than a year or two older than the eldest of us. I can't quite put my finger on it but... She's pretty, that's it, and not just naturally so, she's made up to look pretty. She's got blusher, mascara, a plum lipstick and all manner of make-up and jewellery on and her shoulder-length, light-brown hair is teased up into a coif of moussed curls. She wears figure-hugging, acid-washed jeans, high-top, lace-up Reeboks and a pink top that snuggles in at her trim midriff. I can smell her perfume from here, dime-store Charlie I think.

Charlie Girl hands the clipboard to Dwight and he skims the top page as he continues to conduct us through our Steps. And Three!

I watch the boys watch her. Most of them try not to, they examine their shoes where their shoelaces should have been, but several can't help it and their eyes follow Charlie Girl as she crosses and recrosses the room. I finger my earlobes but Gwen took my earrings – maybe before long the holes will close up. My hair's lank and two days unwashed. I shove a big greasy tuft behind my ear. I feel dirty, ugly, horrible.

The male noses in the room twitch with disappointment when Charlie Girl disappears, but she's back again in a moment, loaded down with fresh supplies and a guard hulking in a pair of bar stools.

The guard dumps the stools at the front and Charlie Girl climbs daintily on to one. Dwight nods at her and hands back the clipboard.

'And Five!' he shouts.

'We make ready to have our Higher Power remove all our character defects and humbly ask him to do so!'

I can see now that, along with the clipboard, Charlie Girl has brought with her a Ping-Pong paddle – though I can't see a table to play on – and a brace of those plastic document wallets that you can hook into ring binders for carrying around any stray un-hole-punchable sheets.

'And Six!'

'We make a list of all persons we have harmed and make direct amends to them wherever possible!'

The plastic wallets appear to be colour-coded. There are four of them, two red, two green, and each has a white label affixed on the front. There's something written on the labels, but Charlie Girl's sitting too far away and at too much of an angle for me to make out the words. What I can make out quite clearly, is that they are full, bulging, and that they seem to be stuffed with unfolded and overly familiar scraps of white paper. Charlie Girl studies her clipboard, peers into one of the red wallets, studies her clipboard again.

'And Seven!!'

'We seek through prayer and communion to improve our contact with our Higher Power and to spread his will to other addicts.'

The group exhales, the drill finished at last. Dwight circles back to where Charlie Girl has stationed herself and the bar stools, and straddles the empty one like he was the Lone Ranger mounting Silver, about to give chase. The stools are drawn back to the mouth of one of the aisles that separates the boys from the girls, where the two staff members can sit without taking their eyes off anyone.

'OK, ya'll, time for the Now rap. Who's got something to share with us?' Dwight's eyes sweep both sides of the group but no one's hand moves. There's no writhing or flapping, no motivating of any kind.

He frowns and Charlie Girl sifts through the slips in one of the red plastic wallets.

'Any volunteers? Anyone?'

Behind me, I hear someone muffle a sob, and from the corner of my eye, I can see the knees of the girl next to me start to quiver, first only slightly then violently as if her bones were made of nothing more solid than Cool Whip.

Charlie Girl whispers something to Dwight. His chin bobs. 'If there are no volunteers, I'll have to call on somebody.' He waits. 'Sure none of ya'll want to speak up?'

The room is still as a painting on a gallery wall.

'Looks like I'll have to then. Now who's it gonna be?' He drums his thigh. He's got short fingers, I notice, like he's missing some knuckle joints or something. 'Who's it gonna be?'

Charlie Girl holds the clipboard up to his line of vision, her pinkie poised over a spot a third of the way down the page. Her nails are painted the same fruity shade as her lipstick.

'How's about...' Dwight surveys the boys' section, his gaze locking intermittently with one trembling boy after another. 'How's about...' He directs his attention to the girls' section, his stare rippling through us like a Mexican wave of dread. '...Emily!' There's a gasp to my right. 'We haven't heard from you in the Now rap for quite a little while, Emily.'

Emily's four chairs down from me. She pushes herself to her feet shakily. She's in profile but I recognise her. She stood up yesterday to welcome me to the programme. Sixteen, that's how old she is. Her face is ashen.

Emily spouts off immediately. 'I'm sorry, honest, I'm sorry...'

'Have you got something to tell us about where you are now, Emily?'

'I'm sorry, Dwight, I'm sorry.'

'No need to apologise to me.'

'I'm sorry, right, but I meant to do it, I really did mean to. It's just that I was so tired, very very tired and it won't happen again, never, I promise.'

'What happened?'

'I fell asleep, Dwight, that's all. I – I fell asleep when I was writing my M.I.'

'Is that all it was?' he bats the indiscretion away in exaggerated aw-shucks fashion.

'Yes, that's all. Really.'

113

'That's all, you say. That's *all*?' No more aw or shucks. 'Hmmm. Tell me, Emily, do you remember the Third Step of our programme?'

'Of course!'

'Recite it for me, will ya.'

'We make a searching and honest moral inventory of ourselves.'

'A searching and honest moral inventory.'

'A searching and honest moral inventory?' Emily repeats in a faint voice.

'What does that mean?'

'What does it mean?'

'Yes, the meaning, what's the meaning of that Step?'

'It means, um, it means we've gotta dig down deep and see what's good about ourselves and what's bad and, uh, what we need to change?'

'OK. And how often are we supposed to make this searching and honest moral inventory?'

'Every day?' Her voice shrinks away, like when you pull a shell away from your ear and realise it wasn't the ocean you heard after all.

'What was that? How often did ya say?'

Emily clears her throat. 'Every day.'

'Does that mean every day except Mondays and Wednesdays?'

She shakes her head.

'Say again?'

'No.'

'Does that mean every day except when you don't feel like it?'

'No.'

'What does it mean, Emily?'

'It means every day, Dwight. Every single day.'

'You betcha. You bet your bottom dollar it means every single day. So then,' he's taunting her, and enjoying it, 'how often is it that you've – what was it? – *fallen asleep* before you completed your M.I.?'

'Just once, Dwight.'

'*Just* once?'

'I mean, once. It was one time.'

'When was that?'

'Last Friday. After the Open Meeting. It was such a long meeting and when I got home, I couldn't keep my eyes open. I tried but I just couldn't.'

'I get ya.' Dwight grunts and sucks a tooth. 'Are you saying then that an Open Meeting justifies your slip? Do you think that maybe on Fridays, after Open Meetings, we should all feel free to take a little vacation from our responsibilities because we're tired? Is that it?'

'No, I—'

'It's an interesting attitude, isn't it? It's like saying, it's OK if I have just this one beer tonight because I'm really pooped, or hey, I'll shoot up just this once because I've had such a tough day. Is that what you think, Emily?'

'No, not at all.'

'What comes of slip-ups like that, Emily?'

'Uh—'

'What happens if we don't complete our Third Step? Do you know, shall I tell ya? If we don't complete our Third Step – even *just once* – then we don't complete our Fourth Step and then we don't complete our Fifth or our Sixth or our Seventh. Our programme falls apart, Emily, and so do we.' Dwight leans forward menacingly. 'And our little lapses become *relapse!*' He slams a fist into his open hand. 'That's what I'm talking about. *Relapse.* Do ya want to relapse, Emily, do ya want to start the programme all over again? I can arrange it, Emily. I can happily arrange that if that's what you want.'

'N-n-no, no, God, no, not at all.'

Dwight settles back on to his stool. 'I'm glad to hear it. So, how are we going to make sure that doesn't happen?' His eyes search the group for an answer. 'I know,' he says, clapping as if a light bulb has flared above his head. I crane my neck back and peer into the rafters. 'I think for the next week, you should write your M.I. not just once but twice a day. And, what the hell, on Friday, after the Open Meeting, you should write it three times. Does that sound good to you?'

'Yes, Dwight,' says Emily meekly. 'That sounds good.'

'You think after that the importance of your M.I. might sink in?'

'Yes, Dwight, definitely. Thank you.'

'Thank *you*, Emily. You've reminded us all of a very valuable lesson.'

Dwight slides his eyes away from Emily like a baseball pitcher checking out the runners on first and third. Her knees bend to retake her seat, she thinks she's sliding into home base now, safe. But Dwight's just winding up for another fast ball.

'What the fuck do ya think you're doing, girlie?' he shouts, his furious face whipping back towards her.

Emily freezes.

'Did I say you could sit down?'

'I thought—'

'You thought wrong is what you thought, missy,' he tells her, clipping each word. 'Let's start again, how 'bout that. Is there anything else you want to share with us about where you are now, Emily? Anything else about how you're working your programme?'

Emily makes a noise in the back of her throat, like she's trying to swallow or cry or something but not succeeding. 'No?'

'No?' He mimics her high-pitched tone.

'I don't think so, Dwight.'

'Wrong again. How very disappointing. I guess you're not feeling so talkative now, not stood up in front of everyone like this. Maybe if we all get up out of our seats and turn our backs to you, it'd get ya over your shyness. Would that help, Emily? Shall we do that?'

Emily shudders in sudden understanding and as she does so, she whips her head round towards where I'm sitting. Her jaw drops, her forehead creases up and her eyes widen to nearly the size of her gaping mouth, from the back of which comes that sound again, that sound like a small rodent or something being strangled. I feel as if I want to start apologising myself, confessing, beating my chest like Tarzan, anything to stop that sound, to wipe that awful expression from her face. But I don't know this girl, I don't know one thing about her except that her name's Emily, she's sixteen and she falls asleep sometimes over her homework. I didn't do anything to her. Did I?

It's not me Emily's gaping at anyway. I can see now how her saucer-shaped eyes are struggling to connect with a spot just beyond me. It's the girl on my left, the one with the Cool Whip knees, who's the target of Emily's shock. The girl's knees are still shaking. She's clamped her hands down on them to stop them from knocking and making her chair squeak, and her flushed face hangs so low that her chin is partially obscured by her shirt collar.

'That's right,' Dwight is saying, 'you've been accused of TBB. You know the rule about talking behind backs, don't you? Surely ya must remember that? We *don't* talk behind people's backs. We don't do it, Emily, because it's cowardly and unkind and, above all, it's dishonest. And what's the bedrock of our programme? The bedrock of the programme is total and complete, upfront honesty. Always.'

Emily's hands, down by her sides, claw at the seams of her khakis.

Dwight smiles coldly. 'Helen C, stand up will you please.' A girl near the back rises, her eyes seething. 'Helen,' says Dwight, 'I think Emily here has something to say to you.'

'No, Dwight, really I...' Emily mumbles.

'Don't ya have something to say to Helen, Emily?'

Her chin wags almost imperceptibly.

'Tell Helen what you have to say. She's listening now. I'm sure Helen would appreciate hearing your opinions. Wouldn't you, Helen?'

'Yes, Dwight,' the girl growls.

'What was it you wanted to say, Emily?' he asks.

She wags her chin again. 'Nothing.'

Dwight leaps from his chair. 'Listen!' he spits, inches from Emily's face. 'I am fed up with your lies! Get *honest*!'

'I – I...'

'What did ya call Helen behind her back? What the fuck did ya call her?'

Emily whispers something.

'What!!'

'A bitch,' she replies, slightly louder.

'Is that all?'

'A stupid bitch.'

'Stop playing games with me, girlie. You know that's not all.'

'A fat stupid bitch.'

'That's right: a fat stupid bitch.' Dwight resumes his perch on the bar stool, composes himself. 'That's not something you should be saying behind a person's back, is it? Not very nice at all.' He examines his fingernails like he's suddenly bored with this line of discussion. 'Now then,' he drawls, picking at a speck of dirt under the nail of his forefinger. 'Say it to her face.'

Emily closes her eyes. A tear runs down her cheek, then another. 'Helen, I called you—' she begins.

'*To. Her. Face.*'

Slowly, she faces Helen who's now hopping with anger in the third row. 'Helen,' says Emily in a low, halting tone, 'I called you a fat stupid bitch.'

No one speaks. Both girls turn back to Dwight, absorbed again with the state of his manicure. They wait. One of the phasers on the boys' side coughs. After a minute or so of silence, of growing redder and redder, Helen pumps her arm in motivation.

'Helen,' Dwight calls at last.

'Can I respond to that?'

'Of course.'

And Helen explodes. 'You fucking bitch! You're calling *me* a fat stupid bitch? You little cunt. *You're* the bitch! You're the fucking bitch! How dare you talk about me behind my back. You don't know what's what. Not one fucking little morsel of what's what. That's how stupid you are. How many grades did you flunk anyway? You and your little pea-sized kindergarten brain. Don't know nothing about nothing. Stupid. Shit for brains. TBB, you don't get no more dumb-ass stupid than that, you stupid, dumb fucking bitch. And who you calling fat? Me? You calling *me* fat? Ha! You don't know fat. You oughta pray they don't ever change that mirror rule, because you put a mirror in front of your sorry ass, and girl, then you'll see fat. You ain't seen nothing like fat until you get a gander at your backside. You dumb stupid-ass motherfucker!'

Helen pauses to gulp air. The veins on the side of her neck bulge.

'OK,' says Dwight. 'That's great, Helen, was there anything else you wanted to say to Emily?'

'Hell yes!' She rants on for what must be another ten or twenty minutes. Once in a while Emily tries to stop crying and pipe in, but then Helen barges forward like she's going over the heads of the girls separating them both just so she can sock Emily in the kisser. Then Emily shuts up, except for those strangling noises that I can still hear despite Helen's high-volume tirade.

'OK,' Dwight says once Helen finally runs out of steam. 'Helen, Emily, I bet you both feel much better for being honest and getting that off your chests. I hope, Emily, you might now be able to remember a little better that TBB rule. Thank you, girls.'

He glances down at the clipboard Charlie Girl has shoved back under his nose then looks up again. 'You may both sit down now.'

Poor Emily nearly collapses into her chair. There are sighs behind me and the girls' side slackens its tensed group muscles. It's the boys' turn now.

CHAPTER SEVENTEEN

'Right. Who else has something Now to share with us? I'm taking volunteers.' No one moves. 'Anyone?' invites Dwight.

Silence. 'OK, guess I gotta pick somebody again.' Charlie Girl refers to the clipboard, then dips into the other red plastic wallet and pulls out a dog-eared slip of paper. We watch as she smoothes out the creases and hands it to Dwight.

Who will it be? The group holds its breath. 'Shaun N,' Dwight calls out.

The other ninety-odd phasers blow out sighs of relief and Shaun N lumbers to his feet. He's a short guy with a square face and short beefy arms that he just manages to cross, high above his chest.

'Anything you want to share with us, Shaun, about where you are with your programme?'

'Nah, I ain't got nothin' to confess.'

'Who said anything about a confession?' Dwight laughs. 'You know better than that. You confess to priests, Shaun. We're all friends here, your fellow addicts. With friends, you share, you don't confess.'

'I got nothin' to share, say, confess, you name it.' .

'Are you copping attitude with me, mister?'

'Just answering the question.'

'OK, how about answering this question – how long have you had home privileges?'

'Two weeks.'

'Getting along OK with your family?'

'Fine.'

'Seeing a lot of your mom and dad? And your little brother... what's his name? Gary?'

'Much as I can.'

'Anybody else?'

'Anybody else what?'

'Are you seeing anybody else at home?'

'Sure, other phasers and stuff.'

'Anybody else? Besides your family and others in the programme?'

'Course not. I know the rule.'

'That's right. The rule is... well, let me ask the group to remind us. Who of y'all knows the rule we're talking about?' Dwight calls on a motivating boy named Gino.

'You're talking about the rule about contact with the outside world,' states Gino.

'That's right. And what's the rule?'

'The rule is that phasers in the programme are to have no contact whatsoever with the outside world, except where authorised and overseen by a staff member.'

'Why's this rule important?'

'So that we aren't corrupted by damaging druggie influences during our recovery.'

'Exactly. So then, who is it that we should avoid most strenuously when applying this rule?'

'Our old-life druggie contacts.'

'Yes, perfect, thank you, Gino.' Dwight returns his attention to Shaun. 'And you're familiar with that rule?' he asks.

'Yep, like I said.'

'You wouldn't do anything to jeopardise your adherence to that rule?'

'No, I wouldn't.'

'Nothing like attempt to make contact with anyone from your former druggie circle?'

Shaun N sticks his chin out defiantly. 'Nope.'

'Someone like a druggie girlfriend maybe?'

'You mean Felicity?'

Arms fly out in all directions. 'What's the matter y'all?' Dwight asks of the entire group, as if he didn't already know. 'Druggie name, druggie name, druggie name!' they chorus.

'Really, Shaun. I didn't think we had to remind you about refraining from using druggie names.'

'I didn't make contact with Fe— with my druggie ex-girlfriend.'

'And you didn't try?'

'No, I didn't.'

'Interesting.' Dwight cocks his head at Shaun N and beetles his brow in puzzlement. 'OK, let's stop beating around the bush. I'm going to give it to ya straight, Shaun. You've been accused of using your little brother to pass messages to this druggie friend of yours.'

Shaun's eyes become slits. 'Did that little twerp tell you that?'

'You know it doesn't matter who reported the incident.'

'Hey, man, if I'm gonna be accused of something, I got a right to know who's dishing the dirt.'

Arms are mobilised again. 'Druggie word, druggie word!!'

'Watch it with the druggie names and words, mister,' warns Dwight, dismounting his bar stool.

'What did I say? Go on tell me,' Shaun goads. 'What did I say?'

'The m-word, Shaun. You know the m-word's banned.'

'That's such bullshit, man.'

The group motivates like tall grasses whipped about by a tornado. From the back of the boys' section, Leroy and two more standing thugs edge forward. 'I'm warning you, mister. Watch it.'

'OK, shit, fine, whatever. The point is, it's not true.'

'What's not true?'

'What you said, the passing messages shit, it didn't happen.'

'Really?'

'Yeah, really.'

'So you never spoke to Gary about this person?'

Shaun mulls that over. 'Well, I…'

'You never asked Gary about her at all?'

Shaun relaces his squat forearms. They remind me of Popeye, his arms. I wonder if Felicity resembles Olive Oyl. I wonder if she's got that dangly thing in the back of *her* throat. 'Not exactly.'

'Not exactly what?'

'I didn't exactly *not* ask Gary about Fe— about my druggie girlfriend.'

'Uh-huh. So what *exactly* did ya do?'

'OK, look, all I did was I asked Gary if he'd seen her.'

'Is that all?' Again with the aw-shucks demeanour.

'Yep, that's it.'

'And why would you care whether or not your brother had seen this… *woman*?'

Shaun shrugs his sailor-man shoulders. 'Dunno. I wanted to make sure she was OK, I guess.'

'Why?'

'Look, we were going out for like three years, we were talking about marriage and shit for when we got older, and then all of a sudden, I'm gone. I can't imagine how she must have taken that. I was worried about her, you know what I'm saying?'

'Ahhhh,' Dwight coos with sarcasm. 'You were worried about your little druggie girlfriend. How admirable.'

'I loved her, man.'

The group motivates. 'Watch the language,' says Dwight.

'I loved her.'

'Uh-huh.' Dwight pauses. 'Of course, whether or not you were just asking after this old flame of yours, you were still breaking one of the rules. You shouldn't have been asking about your druggie contacts at all. You know that, don't ya?'

'Yeah, I know.'

'So that, in and of itself, is gonna cost ya. We're going to have to penalise you for that.'

'OK, OK, whatever.'

Dwight nods absent-mindedly, weighing the crimes and consequences. 'But the thing is, I don't think that is *all*, Shaun. I just don't buy it.' He taps his finger against his temple. He's reeling Shaun in. 'I don't buy that you were just asking about this girl, that you weren't the least bit interested in making contact. Are ya sure you don't want to share a little bit more with us?'

Shaun remains resolute. 'Ain't nothin' more to share.'

'Really?'

'Really.'

Dwight's losing patience. 'I wish I could believe ya, Shaun, I really do. But ya see here, this is my problem. We've got evidence.' He waves above his head the slip of paper Charlie

Girl produced earlier from the red plastic wallet. 'Hard evidence, an eyewitness account. Pretty irrefutable. So what am I gonna do? Take you at your word and ignore the evidence? Is that what ya want me to do? I wish I could, I really do.'

'Do what you like. I'm just telling it like it is.'

'You say that, friend, I hear you say that, but ya know, it doesn't ring true. No, it doesn't. Now part of me, Shaun, can't really blame you. Could be, it's not only the drugs driving you. Fact, I'm sure it isn't. That's not all you've got stacked against you by a long shot. The real problem, it seems to me, is that you're thinking with your dick, that's it. You've been with us... what is it now, Shaun?'

'Seventy-two days.'

'Seventy-two days. You've been seventy-two days without any *pussy*.' Dwight intonates the word just so, for full sleaze value. 'That's tough on a guy, I can accept that. Enforced abstinence, it can drive a guy crazy. You want to get your hands on some skinny-assed pussy and now. Sure ya do.' His tone alters again, loses the slightest pretence of understanding, sympathy, empathy or whatever. 'But my problem, Shaun, is when you lose control, you go too far, you forget your programme and you break the rules. And for what? For a fucking, druggie whore who—'

Shaun charges towards Dwight but the thugs are on him within two feet, pinning his arms behind his back and grinding their heels into the tops of his feet. They don't cover his mouth, though, and Shaun's shouting with both lungs. 'Hey, asshole! Who the hell are you calling a whore?'

'Why, Shaun,' answers Dwight, all proper Southern manners now and mock surprise, 'I'm referring to your druggie girlfriend, of course.'

'Don't you ever call her that!' Shaun screams, struggling against the guards on either side of him. 'Don't you ever! Felicity is no whore!'

The group motivates wildly and Dwight moves right up into Shaun's face. 'That's not what I hear, friend,' his nostrils flare. 'I hear she's slept with every guy in your high school. I hear she gives blow jobs to the entire football team before every game of the season. And to the entire basketball team during basketball season. And to the entire baseball team during baseball season. Hell, she's even licked the balls of the debate team. I hear that druggie whore of yours has got at least twenty strains of VD, some that doctors haven't even heard of yet.'

Shaun's square face is apoplectic. 'I'm warning you, you better shut the fuck up! Shut your fucking mouth, man! Shut up!'

The group flaps and pumps with abandon, their chair legs yelping against the floor. Dwight takes a step back, nodding perfunctorily as he does so. And Leroy and his co-guards pounce. They knee Shaun in the groin. He drops to the floor where they proceed to kick and stomp him in the back, the sides, the legs, the arms. He covers his head with his hands.

'I hate having to restrain you when you get like this, Shaun, but I warned you,' Dwight tells him, cool as a cucumber. 'I warned you not to say that word again.'

CHAPTER EIGHTEEN

We're seven or thereabouts, maybe younger, and on the playground. It's recess. We must be in second grade, I'm guessing. I'm dangling upside down on the jungle gym and you're dangling beside me. Across from and facing us are Hank Wood and Lucy Hamilton. Hank's swinging like mad, his bowl cut turned upside down and swinging with him, a beat behind. Lucy's clutching on to the nearest vertical pole and looking frightened because Hank's swinging is making her side of the jungle gym bounce and she doesn't fancy the idea of falling splat on her head on to the concrete below. What she wants to do is sit up but she doesn't dare because then Hank Wood might think she's a scaredy-cat and that wouldn't do.

Lucy and I are interviewing to become Hank's next girlfriend. It doesn't really mean much being Hank Wood's girlfriend except that you get to give him the Twinkie from your lunch box, he'll hold your hand sometimes when the teacher's not looking and he'll let you call him your boyfriend, for a while anyway. I don't really want Hank Wood as a boyfriend, he's just a silly boy after all and he's not even that cute. His hair is skewy like his mom or barber or whoever dumped a salad bowl on his head all cockeyed before cutting around. But lots of girls, all the most popular ones, have been Hank's girlfriend already. It seems like a sought-after position.

So Lucy Hamilton and I are this week's candidates and you've come along to help me clinch the job. Lucy tells Hank she's very good at math and can help him with his homework, and you pipe in to remind Hank that he's doing all right in math, where he really needs help is in social studies which is my star subject. Lucy says she makes the best chocolate-chip cookies north of the Mason-Dixon line, Hank asks where the Mason-Dixon line is and I start to tell him who cares anyway because I make the best Rice Krispie treats anywhere, except you tell him that yourself before I can get a word in edgewise.

'I sure do like Rice Krispie treats,' Hank Wood says. We have this deal sealed, you can see it in young Hank's hungry eyes.

But before he can confirm it, our negotiations are interrupted. The jungle gym starts to shake something awful, the whole structure jumping and clattering, then the banging and clanging starts, so hard we can feel it in our teeth.

'Is it an earthquake?' squeals Lucy Hamilton. We've always thought Lucy was a dum-dum and this proves it because everybody knows earthquakes only happen in California, which is a long long way away from our hometown in Carrefort, Pennsylvania, which is where we've lived ever since eons ago when Daddy finished dental school in North Carolina, also a long way away.

Earthquakes don't happen in Pennsylvania but Wayne Westbrooks do, and we know he's to blame because we can see him out of the corner of our eyes, swinging a baseball bat at the foundation of the jungle gym.

'Hey girls!' shouts Wayne.

Hank Wood jumps down real quick so as not to be lumped together with a bunch of girls, but Wayne isn't talking to Hank or blockhead Lucy either. He's talking to you and me. Wayne Westbrook loves to pick on us. We swing down to face him, you edging behind me.

'Howya doin' *girlies*?'

'Whaddya want, Wayne?' I ask him.

He stops banging now he's got our attention. 'Yous two are fakes.'

'How's that then?'

'Fake twins. My mom says you ain't real twins at all.'

'Course we are,' I scoff. 'What's your mom know anyhow?'

'My mom knows. She says twins are indentical.'

'You don't even know what that means,' I say, not wanting to admit I'm not one hundred per cent sure either.

'It means you gotta be exactly the same, and you two, you ain't exactly the same.'

'Course we are.' What a stupid thing to say. Don't we dress alike, don't we both like SpaghettiOs and Christy Crybaby (though we're getting kind of big for playing with her) and hate Brussels sprouts and stupid big bullies like Wayne Westbrook? He's as dumb as Lucy Hamilton. Why doesn't she be Wayne's girlfriend and leave my Hank out of it?

'No, you ain't. You ain't indentical, any kid can see that. I mean, he –' and he jabs the end of his bat into your chest, pushing you back a step '– he acts like a girl, all right, but he isn't one really.'

I shove Wayne's bat down. 'Take it back.'

'Take what back?'

'All of it.'

'I ain't taking nothin' back.'

'I'm warning you, Wayne Westbrook. You better take it back or else.'

'Else what? You gonna sic your sissy brother on me?'

Not an option, clearly. I latch on to Hank Wood. 'Or else my boyfriend here's gonna beat you black and blue!'

But even as I'm saying it, Hank is holding both hands up like a shield and backing away. 'I'm not your boyfriend. Uh-uh.'

'I win!' squeals Lucy Hamilton, grabbing hold of Hank's hand.

Wayne Westbrook sniggers. 'What you gonna do n—' he starts to say as I launch myself at his feet, toppling him. Wayne's made the mistake of standing too close to the jungle gym, and though he tries to break his fall with first his bat and then his hand, his head cracks into the lowest metal rung like a home-run ball and then he plummets trap first into the concrete.

The playground's silent as Wayne lies there in a heap. No one has ever brought Wayne Westbrook down before, and certainly not a girl. He's not knocked out, though, just dazed. He drags himself unsteadily to his feet. There's a bright white line across his forehead from where his thick skull made contact with the jungle gym and it's flushing an angry red fast. When he opens his mouth, there's blood, which seems to be streaming from his lower lip. The girls all turn away and the boys grin at the sight of it. I'm going to turn away too but then I notice that Wayne Westbrook is missing some teeth. One of his front ones is gone altogether and a couple others appear distinctly chipped.

I giggle and next thing I know I'm howling, then you start to chuckle, then Hank does and Lucy and soon the whole playground is laughing up a riot at Wayne Westbrook's expense.

I point at Wayne's mouth. 'Ha! You're going to need an

orthodontist, Wayne. And guess whose dad is the only orthodontist in town!'

Wayne Westbrook hightails it into the school building and straight to the nurse's office and we don't see him for the rest of the afternoon. We don't worry about him telling or us getting in trouble because Wayne Westbrook would never admit he got done in by a girl. As far as the school's concerned, Wayne tripped during recess and that's the end of the story. But the kids, they all know different, and you and I never have any trouble from Wayne again.

That doesn't appease us much on the day, though. After school, we race home and track Mommy down in the kitchen.

'We're twins, right Mommy?' you ask.

'Exactly the same,' says I.

'Well...'

'Indentical,' says you.

'Well...' Mommy begins again.

Once she breaks the news to us, the whole sorry truth of it, we escape to our room to sulk and determine to be the same anyway, no matter what anybody else says.

CHAPTER NINETEEN

The Now rap storms on for ever, on and on until it segues into a final drill set and roll and dole call. Into the fourth or fifth hour or so, I become desperate for a pee. I watch other girls squirm in their seats before raising their hands straight up in the air like kindergarteners. Dwight and Charlie Girl ignore these stiffened limbs, but the girls keep them aloft until one of the sentries at the back acknowledges them. I gather this is how you obtain permission for a potty break, but I don't feel confident enough about it to follow suit. What if I gathered wrong, what if Dwight mistakes my timid gesture for motivating, what if he calls on me to confess something or accuse someone or to recite a rule? I don't dare risk it.

I shrink down further into my chair, hoping I can avoid notice. That's when I learn about the Ping-Pong paddle and Charlie Girl's other purpose in the afternoon's session, her purpose in addition to mutely administering the incriminating slips of paper. It's another silent, deadly task. She leaves the shouting and interrogating, scolding, ordering and threatening and so on to Dwight. That way you almost forget about her, you don't hear her and or see her either after a while – not until you feel her, exacting her own little share of torment.

After hours of sitting in the uncomfortable folding chairs, buttocks numbing away to nothing or, worse, shooting with pins and needles, hours of no fresh air and no movement and talk, talk, talk, your eyelids drooping, your shoulders aching and slouching, your backside slumping the way that gravity ordained: that's when Charlie Girl steals away from her ringside stool and begins to tiptoe stealthily amongst us, thunking her paddle with remarkable force across the necks and skulls and shoulders of tired phasers, myself included. Which is how I cotton on to the 'sit up straight at all times' rule.

After hours of all of this and the *Hill Street Blues*-style third degrees, the final exhausting rounds of Step drills come as a relief. And Seven!

'We seek through prayer and communion to improve our contact with our Higher Power and to spread his will to other addicts!' I gladly join in pledging.

As the roll begins, I prepare myself with grim resignation to be reunited with Gwen for another evening, but when Dwight reaches my name, it's not Gwen's name it's coupled with. I'm doled out instead to someone called Moira.

She advances towards me affably enough, even smiling a little. She's tall and skinny, with dark brown hair that's straight, except for at the ends where the split-forked, growing-out tails of a long-ago perm cling on. She reminds me a little bit of my best friend Cindy Gregory, though more unkempt and not as immediately pretty.

I'm tempted to be happy about this change of warder, but not too tempted. Hints of Cindy aside, this Moira person may very well be worse, I tell myself. I don't say a word to her as she hooks my belt loop and steers me out into the darkened parking lot, and into a green station wagon with wood-effect side-panelling.

'Hi, darlin',' greets the father from behind the wheel.

'Hi, Dad,' replies the daughter, ruffling the hair at the scruff of his neck. 'Good day?'

'I've had worse.'

This unexpected affection disarms me but still I don't speak. What if it's a trick? What if I say something and break a rule? I'm only supposed to speak if a higher phaser speaks to me, that's what Gwen said.

I stare out the window. The highway slides by and somewhere out there, soiled and abandoned, lie my favourite shoes. I sniffle.

'First day, huh?' says Moira, startling me from across the station wagon seat.

I bob my head.

'You must be shit-scared, I bet.'

I nod again.

'I know you won't believe it now, but it *will* get better,' says Moira, reaching over to pat my hand. I recoil but not before noticing that the palm of her hand's soft and cushioned, warm to the touch.

Maybe this one's not so bad.

The thought lingers as we pull up to their home, a single storey, white brick affair; and as I meet her mother and father, both lanky and brown-haired like their daughter; and as we sit down to dinner, a steaming vegetable stew with side-chunks of buttered corn bread and tall glasses of – oh, I'm in heaven – water. After filling the glasses, Moira's mom sets an entire pitcher of water, straight from the faucet but with half a tray of ice cubes floating around in it, at the centre of the table for us all to help ourselves.

There's talk round the table as we slurp and dip our chunks of bread into our stew, the motions of a family rap like with Gwen's family but it seems more natural with Moira and her parents and no siblings – Moira, I deduce, is an only child. Just shooting the breeze about Dad's day at the office – advertising I think – and Mom's day at the Hallmark shop where she works three days a week.

Surely this really is a better place.

After dinner, Moira accompanies me to the bathroom, watches me pee, inspects the corners of the furniture-less phaser room, and though they're all the same motions as with Gwen the night before, the pace is gentler somehow.

Once both Mom and Dad kiss Moira good night and tell me to sleep tight, Moira pulls a notebook from her pillowcase and begins to scribble hurriedly. 'This is my Moral Inventory notebook, my M.I., in case you were wondering,' she informs me. I was wondering; I thought that's what it might be but I hadn't asked. I still hadn't spoken, except to say yes or no to a few direct questions over dinner. Would you like some more water, Justine? Yes please!

'You probably remember them talking about it in the Now rap today,' Moira continues, still writing, not looking up from her page as she talks. 'You'll get your own notebook before long. We're supposed to write in our M.I. daily so that we keep our self-awareness high and stay on track. It's the same set formula every day. The way it goes is, you write about a past incident and then say what you did wrong and who you should make amends to and what you've learnt about it. Then you're supposed to write about any present issues. Then you end on a positive note, writing down one good thing that happened to you today. It sounds like a lot of work, I bet, but it's not really. There's a knack to it, once you get the flow of it, you can do it in no time. See!' She lays down her pencil, closes her book and looks up triumphantly. 'I'm finished already. Five minutes, no big deal.'

Before we turn in, Moira asks me if I need to go to the bathroom again and we do. It's lights out soon after that. I try to make myself comfortable in another dunce's mattress, with another person's sheets and pillows that also don't smell like you.

It could be worse, I tell myself, thinking of Gwen. This *is* a better place. Then I hear Moira's voice in the darkness, kindly telling me, 'You can go ahead and cry if you want to, it's OK.'

I hold my tongue.

'Honest, everybody cries after their first day,' she assures me. 'It's like totally natural. And I won't get mad. I mean, it won't keep me awake if that's what you're worried about.'

'Is that what you're worried about?' she asks when I don't answer.

'No. I just don't cry, that's all.'

'What, not ever?'

'No.'

'Are you serious?'

'Yeah.' Maybe I shouldn't be revealing this to her, no matter how nice and normal she seems. Maybe not crying is a bad thing, maybe it's against the rules. *Why don't you ever cry?* Mom said to me, like it was an accusation instead of a question. *You never cry.* 'I don't know why,' I say to Moira, kind of offhand-like. 'I just don't. It's probably faulty tear ducts, something like that, something medical.'

'Huh. I never met a girl who never cried, not in the programme anyway.'

I wait, staring up into the darkness. Moira's dad or mom or whoever has pasted one of those glow-in-the-dark constellations to the ceiling.

'So what are you in here for anyway?'

'I don't know really,' I tell her, and that's the truth.

'You don't know?'

'They say it's just for observation. Three days.' I count the days out on my right hand even though it's under the covers and she can't see it anyway. One. Two. Three. 'That's all.'

'Right.'

'I think it's a mistake. My parents, see, well, they've been kind of whacked recently. They're not thinking straight any more.'

Moira plumps a pillow. 'Sure. But usually there's some big final blowout. What was the straw on the back of your camel?'

'I don't know what you mean.'

'I mean, you must have done something that made your parents say, like, all right, enough is enough. That's when they get the programme involved.'

I think about that night for a minute or two. Cindy and Beth and Kelly and the six-pack of Milwaukee's Best, the low-cal version. I should have never gone out that night. I should have just stayed home. The Presidents didn't even win for God's sake – the Tigers, our rivals from the neighbouring high school whupped us by twenty points. 'I guess that was probably Saturday. There was a home basketball game, and a dance afterwards at my school and, OK, I had some beers and got home pretty late.'

'And?'

'And, that's it.'

Moira doesn't sound like she has total faith in what I'm saying. 'How long have you been using?' she wants to know.

'Using what?'

'Alcohol, speed, dope, grass, whatever.'

'I don't *use*.' God, I loathe that word. 'That was it, Saturday was it.'

Moira snorts and does her best John McEnroe. 'You cannot be serious.'

'I am.'

I can see her silhouette in the half-light as she poles herself on to her elbow as if to look at me, as if she could see my expression. 'You're not shitting me?'

'I'm telling the truth.'

'You mean, you went out for one night of underage drinking and wound up in here?'

'Looks that way.'

The shadow where her head should be sways, the whites of her eyes flashing and floating in the gloom. 'That sucks, man, that really sucks. I mean, there are some kids that don't belong in here for addiction, sure, that's true, we all know that, but you. If that's true—'

'It *is* true.'

'Jesus, that takes the cake. One night out on the razz and boom. That *really* sucks.'

'But it's only for an observation,' I remind her. 'Three days they said.'

'Yeah. Well, that's all right then.'

She flops back on to her pillows and we both lie there, gazing up at the ceiling and all the stars up there and thinking about how much the situation sucks. Moira doesn't say anything else but I've loosened up now, I'm feeling bolder. 'Can I ask you something?'

'Go for it.'

'Are the rap sessions always like that?'

'Like what?'

'Um, all the yelling and – and, I don't know, all that, like they were today.'

'It must seem kinda intense first time out.'

'Kind of.'

'Well, they are pretty much always like that. Dwight and the other staff members – mainly Dwight actually – they scream and holler and shit, but basically it's for people's own good.' She's sprawled out flat now and I can't see her silhouette or the shadow of her face or any movement. 'You know, people come in here with a lot of attitude, a lot of cocky druggie bullshit, and, unfortunately, though it's not always pretty, you've got to break them down, all the way down before you can build them up clean again. That's the thinking.'

'And you believe that?'

Moira doesn't hesitate or if she does I don't detect it. 'Sure, I do.'

'And do they always try to catch you out like that, like with the rules in the rap this afternoon?'

'That happens, yes,' Moira concedes. 'The rules are all there for a reason and they want to make sure you're following them, because if you're not, well maybe there's other stuff you're not doing that you're supposed to be doing. Or like, if you say you're doing them and you're not, maybe there's other stuff you're not being truthful about. They've got a few tricks up their sleeves to check and they'll try to psych you out, push this button, push that button. See if you're being honest and if you're not, they keep at you and keep at you until you get honest. Until you get honest, you can't move on. That's the thinking.'

'Uh-huh. Moira, can I ask another question?'

'Shoot.'

'How do you learn all the rules?'

'Ah well, that's the sixty-four thousand dollar question. And the answer is… I don't know. The answer is, you just do and quick.'

'But how?'

'You know, you kinda absorb them during the rap sessions and from breaking them in the early days. You've probably already figured out a lot of the big ones for yourself.'

'Like no talking behind a person's back? No making contact with druggie friends?'

'Exactly.'

'What else?'

'I can't reel them all off just like that. There are too many. There are rules for just about everything, you know. Dress rules – like no heels or laces on shoes, no belts, no glasses, no brand-name clothes or logos or slogans, no denim, no hairstyling or make-up for girls, no haircuts below the ears for boys. Behaviour rules – no rude gestures, you know, no giving the finger, no speaking to a higher phaser or staff member unless spoken too, no using druggie slang—'

I interrupt her. 'What counts as druggie slang? Everybody seems to swear like bikers.'

'Swearing's OK. It's just certain words with druggie slang connotations that are banned. Things like man—'

I imagine our father and what he would say about the swearing and whether that was OK or not. 'The m-word.'

'That's right. And other words like cool, dude, bitchin', awesome, stuff like that.'

'OK, what are the other rules?'

'Let me see. Well, of course, you've got to motivate for the opportunity to contribute in rap, and you're not allowed to talk to or touch members of the opposite sex – not counting staff or fifth phasers or brothers or dads – or tell anyone outside the programme about what happens inside it and, as I'm sure you've already noticed, if you're a newcomer, you can't go anywhere or do anything unattended. Then there are honesty rules, chain of command rules, lots. Geez, I don't know. There are too many to list. And as far as I'm aware there is no list, no written one, at least I've never seen one. They don't print out study booklets for people to memorise or anything like that. They can't, they'd have to be reprinting them twice a week. They introduce new rules all the time or sometimes they change an old rule if something happens. I don't know, you've just got to try to keep a little section of your brain open to rules and every time you're confronted with a new one you file it away there for safekeeping. That's how you learn them.'

We gaze at the ceiling for a few minutes more. The stick-on stars give us something to look at. It's nice having them up there, like we're camping out beneath the night sky like in Girl Scouts or something, even though I never was a Girl Scout because they wouldn't let you join.

I remember how you begged one year – we were maybe eight or nine – to have a glow-in-the-dark constellation set like Moira's. Dad said he wouldn't pay for you to mess up the paintwork, so you had to save up until you could buy it yourself. We found an inexpensive set in the thrift store, and thought it was an astronomic treasure. But the packet must have been sitting out on its shelf too long because when we got it home, those stars wouldn't stick. They fell off the ceiling – not shooting like a comet or glimmering even so much as a firefly – just falling like stupid, second-hand stickers with no stickiness about them.

I don't feel like a Girl Scout any more. The stars make me sad. 'Moira,' I whisper, as I turn on to my side away from the cosmos, 'did you know my brother? Joshua Ziegler?'

'Yeah,' she says, 'I knew him.'

'Can you tell me… what was it like for him in here?'

Moira sighs then hulks herself back up on to her elbow to face me. There's a shaft of moonlight coming through the window now and one side of her face is illuminated. Her mouth's thin and straight. 'Now see, Justine, this is what I'm talking about. Here's a lesson right here. At this very moment, you're in the process of breaking two rules – talking behind someone's back and using a druggie name.'

'You mean, I can't say my own brother's name?'

'If he were still in the programme, you could, but as it is, no.'

'But Dwight used his name. Yesterday, when I first arrived, he said in front of the group that I was Joshua Z's twin. Everybody heard him.'

'Another lesson. That's a rule you should never forget – rules don't apply to the staff, so don't ever think you can catch them out.'

'But—'

'Listen to me, Justine, leave it alone. You'll do much better if you keep your head low and just do what's expected. Stay smart and your time here will be a lot easier. And hey, don't worry about me. As far as this little conversation goes, and your slips, I won't tell if you won't.'

'Thanks,' I say and mean it. 'And Moira, I won't tell anyone about you using the m-word.'

She chuckles as she flops back down on to her pillow. 'You see, you're learning.'

'Can I ask one more question? The last, I swear.'

'Go for it.'

'What are you in here for?'

'Me?' she asks. 'I belong here, I *am* a druggie. Come Clean was my last chance. If it weren't for the programme, I'd probably be in prison by now. Or dead.'

CHAPTER TWENTY

For the next few days, aside from the night with Moira, no one says much of anything to me so I don't say much of anything either. I watch and listen, and I begin to pick on more of the asinine rules, like Moira predicted I would.

There's the you'll-get-what-you're-given rule which applies to food or clothes or paper or pencils or whatever. There's no physical item in the programme that an individual can claim true ownership of, except for the brief time that it's actually in their hands. Each night I go home to whomever's home I happen to be assigned, with a different coat and, occasionally, mittens – but no scarves, that's another rule, presumably because, given half a chance, we might hang ourselves from the rear-view mirror in our host's car. And each morning I wake up to be given a different set of ill-fitting clothes. By day three, my own unfashionable contribution has been laundered and added to the clothes pool, and my brown cords and cherry-tree tunic begin to make their rounds.

Another rule is the one governing our contact with the host families who lock us in and feed us every night. This is actually a whole set of rules. As a newcomer, you're not really supposed to talk to host relatives except via the phaser whose family it is. You can pose and respond to basic stuff like, 'Can you pass the butter?' 'Here you go.' But you're not supposed to ask anything more personal. You hear a fair amount that's more personal, through the dinner time family raps, but these discussions are driven and monitored by the senior phaser and you only pitch in if and when called upon. I don't contribute to the family raps or any other type of rap, although on the Tuesday I'm sent to a host home where they put up me and two other more advanced newcomer girls on the same night, and those girls are called upon so I see how it works.

Also, the host family isn't allowed to have any newspapers, magazines or books, radios, televisions or Walkmans anywhere we might be able to see, hear or read them. And of course we don't get any of that at the programme facility. Neither we, nor the host families when we're around, are permitted to talk about any news of the day from the outside world or mention the names of any bands or pop songs or TV shows. I'm not exactly sure what the reasoning is for this. Something about these things containing possible druggie influences – though it's hard for me to understand how simply uttering the words *Happy Days* or *Laverne and Shirley* or *Three's Company* is going to influence you to do anything except maybe start humming theme tunes or flicking the Fonzie thumbs up, which is no doubt also against the rules. Further, by not having those songs or shows or magazines or whatever, we limit outside distractions in order for us to concentrate on our recovery.

Then there's the never-speak-out-of-turn rule which, taken to its minutest level, might as well be known as the forget-your-manners rule. During the raps, you're not supposed to speak unless you've, God forbid, been selected for ritual humiliation or unless, if you want to volunteer something, you've motivated idiotically and been called upon. In any other situation, no matter what happens, you keep shtoom. If you tread on someone's toes, you don't excuse yourself; if you mangle your fingers in the springs of your folding chair, you don't yowl 'ouch'; if you fart or belch, you don't grin and go 'whoops'; if you hear someone sneeze, you don't wish them *gesundheit*. You say nothing.

There are some amusing consequences to this particular rule. A diet of fast food lunches plays around with the digestive system and you have to try to keep a straight face when, by the afternoon rap, the occasional lulls are interrupted by bottom burping noises and the air becomes pungent with the stink of such gassy emissions.

'Who cut the cheese?' you'd squeal with delighted disgust if we were back in fifth grade and hanging out in Richie Richardson's tree house with Cindy and Lloyd and Davie Kirchner. 'Whoever smelt it dealt it!' somebody would retort gleefully, noses plugged.

In Come Clean, we try to contain our smiles, lock them away before they do any damage and no one plugs their noses and no one breathes a word.

Sometimes the consequences are not so smellily merry. One morning a girl in the second row sneezes and another girl whispers, automatic-like, 'God bless you'; that afternoon, she's hauled up in the Now rap and confronted for this infraction. Which causes me to wonder if the sneezer couldn't think of anything else to report during the post-meal ratting time.

Because that's another rule. You *always* have to report something when they come round with the pencils and those little slips of paper. Me, I still haven't got the gumption, but as no one

146

much takes any notice of me – I suppose because my being here is only a short-term formality – I just wing it. 'Somebody stole My Little Pony,' I write, or, 'Fanta gives you runs,' or, 'Help please, someone's made a mistake.' A couple of people haven't developed the knack and they get confronted for not being more vigilant, for not reporting on what's happening around them. Some of the smarter ones, I suspect, have learnt to manipulate the system. Probably they report on themselves about things they either think are no big deal or rules they know other people already know they've broken. That way, when and if they get called, they're clear straight away what to own up to. Otherwise, they walk right into Dwight's trap of confessing to the wrong thing and then getting two marks against them, like with Emily.

And you have to confront people, that's a rule, too. If you don't confront often or ferociously enough, you can be confronted yourself.

I watch, listen and learn too about the structure of the programme, the hierarchy of the phasers. It's not too dissimilar to high-school pecking order, though unlike with grades, the phases don't correspond to age in the least. Highest up are the fifth phasers. They're like twelfth graders, the seniors who rule the school. They're the guards, too, the ones who stand at the back of the group, coming forward as necessary, and acting as the extra eyes, ears and fists for the staff members. Supposedly, they're role models for the rest of us, on account of having successfully worked their programmes and nearly completed their Steps to recovery. When the staff decide they're ready, they'll graduate: 'Seven-Stepping' they call it.

Trailing them in rights and responsibilities, all the other phasers are in awe or fear or something of the fifth phasers. The fourth phasers, like high-school juniors, chomping at the bit to take over the reins; the sophomore-ish third phasers, just finding their feet and figuring out how they fit into the scheme of things; the second phasers like freshmen, still a little bit dazed and confused but glad to at last be counted amongst the big boys, high schoolers. And then there are the first phasers, the newcomers. Like me, except not me, because I don't really count. Newcomers are nothing, we're lower than low, worse than middle schoolers or kindergarteners. We have no rights, no privileges, no status. We're so green and ignorant, evil and scheming and whatever else they want to believe that we can't be trusted to be left alone for one single solitary minute.

And so to the belt-looping.

A guard accompanies me everywhere I go, including the places for which the word privacy was invented. And I'm bloated and sore in the gut from constipation because I can't, just won't, couldn't possibly go number two in front of another human being, like we were living in China or some Third World country, like we weren't even civilised. It's painful to be so knotted up inside and painful too because the constant wedgies have left me dry and raw in my privates. I've learnt to walk on the balls of my feet, with buttocks squeezed tight and shoulders splayed to alleviate the worst of the discomfort from the human rudder flapping out behind me.

Belt-looping's irksome, awkward, painful, demeaning, humiliating, embarrassing, but I see why they do it. This is their way of breaking us, or starting to, of putting us in our place.

I watch and listen and it all seems too much. I don't know how I'm ever going to remember everything like Moira says you're supposed to do, but then I tell myself to calm down. I remind myself that I don't really need to learn any of it. I'm not going to be here long enough for there to be any point whatsoever to remembering. I figure out the rules and hierarchies just to pass the time as much as anything. Because if I don't, I'll go crazy with boredom and disgust.

A three-day observation, that's all it is. But who's observing me? As I watch and listen, I can't ascertain any evidence of people observing me, studying, taking notes, passing judgements. I'm never alone, of course, but that's not quite the same. The girls belt-looping me – many of whom I never even catch a glimpse of – act like they'd as soon steer me round as a lawnmower. They're just there, doing what they're told to, nothing more, nothing less. They don't speak to me at all, so how could they be analysing anything?

Each day, I scrutinise the real likely suspects, those who do have the power to analyse and make decisions, the staff members. Are they observing me? Hilary's the programme director, the head honcho, but she only breezes in intermittently throughout the day, her jangling necklace of keys announcing her arrival. Dwight, on the other hand, is always there. Morning raps, afternoon raps, lunch-time reporting, evening roll and dole, he presides over them all like a chieftain. There are other staff members – the silent Charlie Girl, whose name, I discover is Ramona, another guy named Bo with a mullet, a girl named Lois? Lola? Louise? – but they're nigh on interchangeable.

And none of the staff members seem to pay me any attention whatsoever. Not since the day I was admitted. I keep waiting for Dwight to call me a cretin or Hilary to say 'You sure about that?' when I raise my hand to use the bathroom, as I've slowly become accustomed to doing. I hear her chirping the words to other people but never to me.

Obviously, they too have realised how ridiculous this whole exercise has been. Me? A druggie? *Puh-leeze!* They're just waiting until the three days is up so that they can save some face before handing me back to our parents.

That's what I'm expecting to happen on Wednesday, my third full day in the programme. I wait patiently as other phasers are confronted, try to defend themselves then break into tears – there are almost always tears – I wait and train my eyes on the doorway for our parents' entrance. Before long, we're rattling through the final drills of the day.

And Five!

'We make ready to have our Higher Power remove all our character defects and humbly ask Him to do so!'

Then we're into the roll and dole call and of course that makes sense because when Dwight reaches my name – 'Justine Zeeeee!' – he's going to shout out 'Justine Z with Mr and Mrs Ziegler'. But, no, I'm doled out to Gwen instead and yanked into the oatmeal sedan quicker than I can say "scuse me'.

I don't dare ask Gwen what's what, and by Thursday morning, I'm wondering if the crazy counsellors they've got running this place have committed a heinous administrative error and really have forgotten about me completely. All morning I try to catch the eye of Dwight or Hilary or even daft Ramona who traipses in briefly – in ripped jeans and Madonna bustier – to deliver a stack of papers, but I don't connect with any of them. It's like they don't see me at all, like I'm sketched in invisible ink. It reminds me of how you used to retaliate when I did something you didn't like. You'd employ the silent treatment, the so-silent-I-feared-I-went-deaf treatment, until I begged you to stop. Then you'd extract an apology and a quarter towards your next Snickers bar and everything would be hunky-dory.

In this place, I remain invisible. At one point, after a girl named Jennifer J tells us how she was the runner for her druggie science teacher who cooked up crack in the school labs, I even try to motivate for attention. I wave my arm around, snap my wrist, hop up and down in my chair. Admittedly, it's a half-hearted attempt compared to the others, but it's the first time I've done it. I feel foolish so I stop.

Mid-morning, the rap breaks for ten minutes of aerobics. A fifth phaser latches on to me – newcomers can't even reach for their toes on their own – but I make a break for it. Hilary's chatting to another fifth phaser at the far end of the room and I beeline it for her with my oldcomer stumbling behind me.

I stop short in front of Hilary but my guard isn't so quick on the brakes. She careers into me and sends me flying like a domino into Hilary's key-heavy chest. The keys clank loudly. They catch in my hair and claw at my cheek, a skeletal one pokes me straight in the eye.

'Can I help you?' Hilary asks as I rear back, my hand covering the worse affected side of my face.

'Hilary, I tried to stop her—' the fifth phaser starts until Hilary holds a stop sign of a palm to her.

'I'm Justine Ziegler,' I announce, searching for a flicker of recognition in her eyes.

Her eyebrows arch quizzically as she smoothes her keys back down so that their teeth all point once again in the same direction. 'Yes?'

'I got here on Sunday.'

'Of course you did. I admitted you.'

'That's right!' She does know me.

'So?'

'So, now it's Thursday.'

'Is it?' she gasps. 'I'm hopeless with the days of the week. I lose track all the time.'

'Sunday was four days ago. I'm in for an observation, remember? The observation's only meant to be for *three* days. And it's been *four* now.'

'Ahhh, I see.' She bows her head, seemingly sympathetic. 'You must be wondering what's happening.'

'Well. Yeah.'

'You must be wondering when your parents are coming for you.'

I nod. 'Just tell me,' I want to yell. 'When, goddammit, when?'

Her lips part benignly, a little Mona Lisa half-smile. 'They're coming tomorrow, Justine. They'll be at the Open Meeting.'

Tomorrow.

I should argue that really that's not good enough. That a three-day observation period is meant to be limited to, you know, three days. I should tell this stupid, absent-minded woman to stuff it, that I'm not putting up with one more minute let alone another day of this shit. But Hilary charges back to the ring and blows the whistle for the rap to recommence before I can think to articulate any of this, and besides, it is only a day.

I can put up with anything for a day. Tomorrow it'll all be over and tomorrow night I'll be sleeping back in our rollaway bed with Christie Crybaby, Teddy Kennedy and all our old stuffed animals and the scent of you on my pillow.

CHAPTER TWENTY-ONE

We're going on eight and we like to play games. We play all sorts of games, all the time. At school, during PE, our games are super-organised. Our PE teacher Mr Zarrow breaks the class up into groups and teaches us how to play proper sports like softball and soccer and badminton or whatever. Because none of the class is good at score-keeping, those games can lead to disagreements. Then all the boys complain because they don't want to play sports in PE class anyway, not if they've got to have girls on their team when they could be playing in Little League and have their dads come after work to cheer them on.

When the weather's something Mr Zarrow calls 'inclement', he troops us into the gym and we get to play other games which are much more fun and where the scoring is either easy or pointless. We play Tug-of-War, using the half-court line on the basketball court as the marker, and sometimes we play Musical Chairs and even Duck, Duck, Goose, though we prefer not to engage in that pastime because, as we keep trying to tell Mr Zarrow, we're too old for that. We play Red Light, Green Light and Mother May I and Uncle Sam, which I set a record for, being the last one caught five times in a row, which no boy in the class had ever even come close to. By far our favourite gym game, though, is Red Rover.

If we can manage to get on the same team, you stick close to me and whisper the names of the boys we should call. More often than not, I'll call out 'Red Rover, Red Rover, send Davie Kirchner over' because Davie Kirchner is the cutest boy in the third grade and that's plain to see. A lot of boys on the opposing team who are not as cute as Davie, or as popular, will aim for you when they're called over thinking you're the weak link in our chain. They don't break through, not often, because I hold on to your wrist so tight it leaves your arm hair in Chinese-burn knots.

During recess, when we're left to our own devices, the class scatters across the playground for more games. You and I always play together, that's a given, but we move around a lot. Sometimes, we unlock our bikes from the racks on the playground and zoom about in circles disrupting other kids' games. They're brand new Schwinns and super-cool and no one else in our class has bikes like ours, which is how we get our nickname – the Schwinn twins.

Sometimes during recess we like to stay with the girls and jump rope or throw jacks with Day-Glo rubber bouncing balls or play Hopscotch. Melanie Heath is in charge of collecting chalk from the trays in the classroom for us to use for Hopscotch, but she can only ever swipe the nub ends. We eenie-meenie-minie-mo to decide whose turn it is to draw the squares because it's no fun making chalk squares on the concrete pavement when you've only got a little nub to do it with. Nobody's happy when you're the unlucky one, least of all you because your knuckles always end up a bloody pulp. The others aren't happy because you take so long about it and because your squares are ginormously spaced, making hopping from one to the next doubly difficult.

Other times I vote for us to go play with the boys who organise games of Dodge Ball or Kick Ball or Wall Ball – it's always something with a ball with the boys. You're not so keen on these activities because Mr Zarrow isn't around to decide the teams and, if I don't manage to get elected team captain or chief picker, the boys tend to pick you last. You don't like that because you think it's humiliating, but you come along most times anyway because I do so love playing with boys and balls.

In the neighbourhood, when no teachers or parents or other grown-ups are watching, we play other games. We gather at Richie Richardson's house because he's got the biggest yard and we play Hide and Seek or Freedom or any kind of tag you can imagine: Freeze Tag, Home Tag, Hang Tag, Stoop Tag, TV Tag and even Kissing Tag, though it's usually the older kids from round the block who run that one. Whatever the game, there are always stragglers who've strayed too far from base to know when it's over, and one of our very favourite things is climbing up on to the balcony of Richie Richardson's tree house once time is called to shout out at the top of our lungs 'ollie, ollie, otsen free' and make everyone come back to base, though it does cause us to wonder what an ollie is, or an otsen for that matter. If the groups at Richie Richardson's are smaller, sometimes we'll play other games. Often when it's later in the day and the light is fading and we're sure that Richie's parents aren't going to stick a head out the window, we'll gather in the tree house with flashlights and a Coke bottle and we'll play Spin the Bottle or Truth or Dare. Nine times out of ten a kid will choose a dare over a truth, and we'll dare them to do things like pick their neighbour's nose or go lie down in the middle of the road in only their underwear or lick Richie Richardson's big toe or show their boobies to the group.

When it's raining or too cold to play outside at all, even in a tree house, which leaks by the way, we gravitate to the houses of kids with two working parents. Ours is one of those because Mommy has been helping Daddy out with his paperwork at the orthodontic clinic, this being long before he discovered the inimitable administrative skills of Zoe Micklebaum. Lots of times, we'll just sit around watching Scooby Doo but other times we hang out in our room and play Married Couples. If we unleash the rollaway, we've got three beds in total so there's usually enough for you, me and our friends to pair up and get beneath the covers and pretend to do things that married people – not counting mommies and daddies – do. You and I fight about who's going to share the bed with Davie Kirchner, if he's over, until Sheila Marple, my best friend, points out that a married couple must be a boy and girl unless there's an uneven number, which sometimes there is and then you win. It doesn't matter much anyway because we never stay put in the beds for long. Lisa or Davie or whoever will throw a stuffed toy and then a Barbie will sail over our heads and next thing you know the pillows are out and feathers flying, which is always fun, though more difficult to clean up after.

We still like to play on our own a lot too and when we're not Schwinning round the neighbourhood on our bikes – look, no hands! – being cool and making other kids jealous, we stay at home and play card games like Old Maid or Slap Jack, or we play Tick-Tack-Toe, Connect the Dots or the Mad Libs word game. Other times we'll build tents in our room or drag the guest mattress out and prop it up against our dresser and use it as a slide. Or we'll see how far we can get around the house without touching the floor, which is something Mommy hates because we never fail to knock over at least one of her porcelain birds off the bookshelves or leave footprints on her newly waxed coffee table. To placate Mommy, we invent a new game where we walk on the ceiling instead of the furniture. We're able to do that by holding a mirror facing upwards as we traipse around pretending we're fairies. Sometimes we spend hours pretending we're the Wonder Twins off the Superheroes cartoon and we jam our fists together, knuckle to knuckle, like we would if we had those superhero rings of theirs, and we say, 'Wonder Twin powers – activate!' Then you say, 'Shape of… a walrus' or whatever and I say, 'Form of… a bucket of water' or some such, and we foil the baddies' caper.

We like to play dress-up, too, of course. We borrow the rubber kitchen gloves from under the sink and we raid Mommy's jewellery box, her make-up case, and the trunk of old shawls and dresses she keeps in the basement. With your evening gloves, lipstick, pearl clip-on earrings and your Pick-Up Stick cigarette holder, you're the very picture of Audrey Hepburn.

Most days when we play dress-up, it's wonderful and super-fun like that, except one Saturday, a day when we really shouldn't be playing dress-up. We're in our room minding our own business when the door opens and there's Daddy with a load of brown paper bags, just come back from the grocery store. He's about to tell us to help our mother unload the car when he sees what we've been doing. His gaze settles on you, his face turns to thunder and I'm sure it's because of the kitchen gloves which we're not supposed to poke holes in and the jewellery of Mommy's we're never supposed to touch because it's so expensive and the dress which was all folded up neat and ready to go to the Salvation Army.

Daddy drops his bags and marches towards you and he's going to order us to put this stuff away this minute before your mother sees it. But instead he touches your lip, first delicately, and then hard, pressing down and dragging his thumb across your cheek so that your lipstick is one long gash of red.

He looks at his thumb, then at you and then he hauls his hand back and slaps you with all his might across your lipsticked face, causing my own cheek to smart. 'Stop being such a little faggot!' he barks.

You start crying and then so do I and neither of us know what to say. I scurry about picking up the dress-up outfits and pack them away to make it all better again, but Daddy doesn't notice. He's got his finger in your face and I want to tell you to stand back because he might poke your eye out and then you'd be blind as well as having a red handprint on your cheek that looks as permanent as Billy Prophett's birthmark.

'Don't you ever let me catch you made-up like this again. You hear me?'

'Yes, Daddy,' you whimper as you clutch your cheek, tears spilling over the tips of your fingers. And you remove the pearl clip-on earrings one at a time and help me hide Audrey Hepburn away.

CHAPTER TWENTY-TWO

Thursday night, on another mattress in another host home, I dream of you. You're on your bike and Dad's pushing you along, saying, 'Go for it, Joshua,' and I'm trotting along behind, laughing and shouting, 'Josh, you're riding a bike, you're doing it.' Dad lets go of the seat, gives your back a booster shove then you're on your own. You grip the handlebars to stop the wheels from wobbling and for a minute they do, for a minute that bike and you are pure and perpendicular, sailing along like you own the street. You lift your chin up and grin. 'Just, I'm doing it,' you call over your shoulder. But then your elbow jerks, and the wheel beneath you churns. You press back on the pedals, brakes screech, sails collapse, and you're tumbling, face first, face first.

The dream makes me toss and turn. Maybe I even shout out in my sleep, but my host oldcomer doesn't mention it if I do and in the morning the dream's gone. It's vanished in a silver cloud of elation. All day Friday I feel like I'm floating ten feet above the world, soaring high over the heads of Dwight and Hilary, Moira, Gwen, Mark and Leroy, everyone in Come Clean and even myself. I can gaze down and see us all but we're tiny and remote, and I've got that pleasantly numb out-of-body sensation like when you used to play for hours with my hair and my brain would tingle and my arms would go goose-pimply.

All the programme rules, regulations and machinations mean nothing to me. Today I'm leaving. Until then, I just follow along with the motions, not even minding so much. I hardly feel the tugs on my belt loop; I don't wince at the sound of Dwight's roar, his voice is faint, no louder than a mouse's today; and even the half-cold lunch-time burritos from Taco Bell taste delicious.

All's good in the world. I'm going home.

I daydream my way through the drills, the morning rap, the lunch-time tattletelling, the Now rap, confrontations, scuffles, tears. None of it fazes me. I'm imagining my freedom, planning my weekend and what my bed will feel like, what TV shows I'll stay up all night watching, what albums I'll play on my stereo in the wee hours, what shops Cindy and I will be prowling in the mall come tomorrow.

Near the end of the day, when normally there'd be more Step drills followed by roll and dole call, we prepare for the Open Meeting. We unhinge the partition that bisects the main room so that we're left with a wide open space the size of two basketball courts, plus bleachers. At the far end, where the home basket might be, we line our own chairs up in a clump of straight rows, then we fill the visitors' side with facing rows upon rows for the families. There must be three or four hundred chairs to be unfolded and positioned just so. As we lunk furniture and grunt – me with my human rudder that, no, I really don't mind – Dwight jogs up and down the central aisle commanding us to 'Straighten up!' until every last chair is in perfect formation.

Then Hilary toots her whistle and announces it's time for choral practice and everyone begins singing. All the songs are familiar –

combinations of hymns, clappy-happy tunes and easy-listening favourites – but with altered lyrics.

'If you're Clean and you know it, clap your hands!'

Clap, clap.

'If you're Clean and you know it, clap your hands!'

Clap, clap.

'If you're Clean and you know it,

Then your soul will surely show it,

If you're Clean and you know it, clap your hands!'

By the second round, I know the words well enough to sing along and I do, belting out each line. Which is something I'd never do normally because you used to tease me so about my voice – 'Like a cat that's had its tail trod on,' you'd say. But I sing out loud now and it's a pleasure to use my vocal cords again, having spoken so little in the past week. I feel like singing and clapping, dancing too, though on the last I restrict myself to bobbing my knees about. I feel joyous, the joy rushing up through my lungs and my throat and out through my mouth with the music, leaving a sweet taste, like honey, on my tongue. I could sing all night.

I'm going home.

We're still singing an hour later when the two entrances are opened and the families begin to stream in.

'We've lost that druggie feelin'

And it's gone, gone, gone,

Gone for good.'

My eyes are superglued to the doors and I fall behind on the butchered Righteous Brothers lyrics because I'm concentrating so hard. I'm playing Grandma/Not Grandma like we always did at the airport when we were waiting for Grandma and Grandpa Shirland to deplane their flight from Kansas City. We'd be so fitful with anticipation that every time a shadow of a passenger came into view, you'd squeal, 'Grandma!' and then, when it was evident that it wasn't, I'd answer, in disappointed falsetto, 'Not Grandma!' It was always Grandma we watched for because Grandpa was the slowest which meant they were almost without fail the last off the plane anyway. Now I play the same game except I'm on my own and it's Parents/Not Parents.

At last I spot them. They enter through the doors on the left, behind a portly old guy with a cane, and they take their seats on that side of the room, diagonal and far back from where I'm sitting in the back row of the girls' section. Mom has her hair pulled into a bushy bun and she's wearing a long prairie skirt and the forest-green ribbed sweater we bought for her last birthday. We bought it in a medium because it was a hundred per cent cotton and we thought it would shrink, but instead it stretched and stretched, around the waist, the elbows, the cuffs, so that it now hangs gormlessly off her sparrow frame. Dad's wearing a navy sports jacket and a knit tie I don't recognise, dirt-brown and unfashionably wide, and he holds a guiding hand at the small of Mom's back, almost like he's belt-looping her, but protective and kind of gentlemanly, which isn't his customary manner.

Neither of them looks in my direction. Perhaps it's because they're not sure where to find me, but they don't appear to be scanning the crowd for my face either. It causes me to remember those Open Meetings I attended when you were sitting here and I there and I'd desperately be trying to get your attention and you were tuning me out like I didn't exist and, God, that hurt, but now Mom and Dad are there on that side again and they're playing it that way too. Maybe no-eye-contact-during-open-meetings is a rule I haven't sussed out yet.

'Who of ya'll wants to welcome your families to the centre?' cues Dwight once the audience has settled. The group motivates like it couldn't conceive of anything more delightful and we bellow our welcomes.

As the meeting progresses, the format comes back to me. Unlike in the everyday group raps, microphones are used in the Open Meetings because the auditorium and the audience are so large even Dwight's lungs would suffer some wear and tear from shouting to be heard by everyone in every corner of the room. There are four mikes. Two with Dwight and Hilary, one for the phasers and one for the parents, the last of which a Ping-Pong-paddle-less Ramona couriers amongst them.

With the exception of the fifth phasers, stationed around the perimeters and manning the doors, the group members are seated in alphabetical order – by never-again mentioned last names. The parents and siblings, on the other hand, are scattered through their rows higgledy-piggledy, seats claimed on a first come, first served basis. Chaotic.

So the exchange segment of the evening, understandably, is pretty time-consuming. What happens is Dwight or Hilary reads out a name from the roll, that person takes the phaser mike and stands, then their parents stand and wait as Ramona spots them and sprints over to them, like a grim Oprah, to present them with their mike. Then Hilary or Dwight, usually Dwight, passes the decree on the phaser's week's progress, the parents are given a few minutes to react to the news and then the phaser is supposed to react to the parents' reaction. The parents' say can go on for a while because, more often than not, the progress report isn't glowing and that pisses them off, but the phaser's reaction is short, sweet and totally pre-scripted. No matter what the staffers or the parents hurl at them, the only acceptable reply is 'I love you, Mom and Dad', the more plaintive the better.

The roll is alternated between the boys' and girls' sections. The first row of A and B boys are called and then Bo, the mullet-haired staffer, or one of the fifth phasers steps in to baton-pass the mike over the five foot gap between the two sections – because otherwise somebody's fingers might brush somebody else's fingers that they shouldn't be brushing – and then the first row of A and B girls are called. Sweet sixteen Emily, who caught it so bad in the Now rap earlier in the week, is smack dab in the middle of the second girls' row. I'm guessing her name begins with a C: Chapman, Conway, Crawford, Crusoe? Or maybe it's an early D: Davis, Denton, Danvers.

Emily whatever-her-name-is takes the mike with an unsteady hand and Hilary pronounces her fate. 'Emily has committed TBB this week and she has neglected her M.I. As a result, she has been set back to second phase.'

Emily's lip trembles and her hand dangles down to her side, the microphone rasping against her pants, corduroys by the sound of it, maybe my old ones.

'Mom?' prompts Hilary, and Ramona thrusts the other mike in Emily's mom's face.

I don't see a father anywhere although I think there are a couple of tiny tot siblings beside the mom. Their heads aren't visible above the seated row of adults in front of them but I can hear them, huffing, puffing and climbing about on their chairs. The mom leans over to hush them up then pulls a hankie from somewhere and fumbles with the microphone.

'Emily, honey,' she sniffs. 'Try harder, sweetie, you've got to try harder. OK? Please?' She pauses to shush the tiny tots again.

'I know you can do better than this, don't go and get downgraded again. OK? Honey? Please.' Shush, shush. 'You've got to do better. We can't afford this much longer, honey.' Shush. 'Sweetie? Oh, I don't... OK then.'

Ramona nudges her to continue, but the young mother bats the mike away.

Hilary nods at Emily.

'I—' She falters, clears her throat, then lets the words tumble out over each other in double-quick time. 'I love you, Mom. I love you, JuJu and Stevie.' And sits down as hurried as her speech.

Emily's mom starts to sit too, but at the sound of their names and Emily's voice, the faceless tots want to do anything but sit-still-and-do-as-you're-told now.

'Emmy?' one of them bleats. 'Where Emmy, Mama?' And before the mom can stop him, the little tyke with ringlets and romper suit – must be Stevie – toddles out in search of big sis. 'Emmmmmyyyyyyyy!' he screeches, while barrelling up the aisle.

Ramona catches up to him before he reaches the group and, while sis bawls quietly into her hands, Mom drags Stevie and a now whimpering little JuJu out through the double doors.

CHAPTER TWENTY-THREE

Neil, in the third row of the boys' section (Harper? Howard? Huntington?), fares better than Emily. You can tell, even before the mike is within arm's reach of him, that Neil knows what his report is going to be, he knows it's going to be good, real good because he doesn't look the least apprehensive when his name's called. He leaps out of his chair, grabbing the mike before his neighbour Jack F has sat down fully. And when Dwight calls his name, Neil whoops, 'Comin' home!!!!!' with such gusto you know he's been practising. Then he hurdles over the knees of nearby phasers and races down the aisle and into the open arms of his dazed parents. And everybody in the group and in the audience applauds, cheers, shouts, 'Way to go, Neil!' and you'd think Richard Gere had just strode in in his Navy whites and swept Neil off his feet à la *An Officer and a Gentleman*. Some people have tears in their eyes, happy ones.

That's how the momentous leap from first to second phase is marked in the programme, the transition from being a no-status newcomer to becoming a true phaser on the way to recovery. The reverse happens when the roll reaches Shaun N, the guy with the girlfriend named Felicity, in row five.

'This week Shaun has been guilty of dishonesty, copping attitude and attempting to rekindle druggie contacts,' Dwight declares. 'These acts constitute very serious threats to Shaun's programme and, in order to protect Shaun and his recovery, we feel it's necessary to start him over.'

The room falls silent for a beat, reeling from Shaun's misfortune. He's been in Come Clean for, what, seventy-six days now – going on eleven weeks, nearly three months of earning his phaser stripes – and, in the half minute it takes Dwight to articulate those two sentences, all that graft has been erased. Shaun's busted right the way back down to a day-one newcomer.

'Dad, do you want to respond?' says Dwight.

Mr N – Nash? Nelson? Northcott? – is short and stocky like his son and he's wearing a T-shirt, as if it weren't the middle of winter outside, a tight one that shows off his own Popeye arms, muscles rippling as he clenches his fists. He rips the mike from an out-of-breath Ramona and unclenches his free hand long enough to angle a menacing finger at Shaun.

'Boy, you better get your act together. I'm sick and tired of your pussyfooting around. No son of mine is going to go around running wild. I won't have it. I'll leave you in here till you rot if you don't straighten up. You hear me?'

Shaun's mother is a few inches taller than his dad but she acts smaller. Her face is a sheet of white with red splotches painted on her cheeks and neck like a china pattern. She closes her eyes and pretends not to notice when he hands the mike back without asking if she has anything to add.

'Shaun,' says Dwight.

The phaser microphone lies in wait on Shaun's chair. He hasn't touched it. He stands like he did in group the other day, chin thrust out, arms locked high above his chest, resting there like his sternum were a shelf.

'Shaun, it's your turn to respond.'

He acts like he's got all the time in the world, like there weren't five hundred pairs of eyes boring holes into every living-breathing inch of him.

'Shaun, we're not moving on until you respond.'

A minute passes and then another. Somewhere, from the family quarters, a watch tick-tick-ticks: only a Swatch ticks that loudly. I miss my Swatch, the one with the confetti strap, the one you gave me.

'Shaun!'

Shaun N slides his eyes towards Dwight at last, his brows peaked, as if he's just this second heard him. He shrugs, snorts, dives for the mike. 'I love you, Mom,' he autoreplies, then adds, in a tone coated in sarcasm, '*and Dad.*'

As he tosses the mike on, Shaun N kicks out at the chair in front of him, his foot clanging against its metal legs. The fifth phasers on the boys' side close in and David M and the others on either side of Shaun N draw their legs and feet in to clear a route just in case.

Back in the family rows, Shaun's dad is hollering. His voice is more than audible on its own, and when Ramona plants the mike back in front of him, he makes no attempt to adjust his volume. His rage fills the room, the mike whining in protest.

'Boy, you've got no respect! That's your problem, you've never had any respect. Not one ounce.'

Women and children cork their ears.

'I'll show you about respect, boy! You think those chumps up there are gonna give you a hard time? I'll get up there and whip you myself if I hear of any more of your back talk. You hearing me?'

His finger points and shoots like a gun aimed for Shaun's face, right between the eyes.

'Thank you, Dad,' says Hilary with a note of finality.

Shaun's father stays rooted to his spot, fuming and pointing.

'Thank you, Dad,' Hilary repeats in the schoolmarmish voice she usually reserves for phasers. 'Thank you, Dad, you may sit down now.'

The rest of the alphabet trundles along. Two more people 'go home', a few more are promoted and several more still demoted. Finally, the microphone wends its way down my row. It passes through the alphabetical dregs of the boys' section and on to the final female phasers. Jackie W-something – Waverley? Williams? Womble? – cries 'I love you, Mom and Dad' and I focus on our parents who are still not looking at me. I'll leap up and lock eyes with them and I won't mind saying the exact same words. Not because I have to, or because that's the script, it'll be because I mean it and I do. I love you, Mom and Dad; I'm coming home too, for real.

'Thank you, Jackie. You may sit down now,' Hilary says.

Now it's my turn. Jackie W passes the microphone to me, but as I raise it, Bo scoots round and takes it away again, swiftly removes it from my hand like a salt shaker, like that's what was meant to happen all along. Neither Hilary nor Dwight calls my name – Justine Zeeee, the way I hate it – and my turn's gone.

For about a millisecond, I'm disappointed, but then I realise this makes perfect sense. I don't count because I'm not a phaser. Of course. I don't get a turn because there's no need, I'll be going home for real so soon now. So soon.

But first I must endure the rest of this interminable Open Meeting. We're into the testimonials now. Hilary selects two fifth phasers, one boy, one girl, to share their role-model stories of addiction and redemption. Lisa M – Mason? Meadows? Mulcahey? – drones on for at least fifteen, twenty, maybe thirty minutes about how her druggie boyfriend turned her on to hard liquor and getting high and how they used to drive out of town to Lake Eudora and drink, smoke and screw in the back seat, how even after her druggie boyfriend had an accident behind the wheel and killed his best friend who wasn't wearing his seat belt and lost his legs and couldn't walk any more, how even after that all Lisa M wanted to do was get blind drunk and stoned, and so she'd steal her uncle's Buick and drive herself out to Lake Eudora, drink and smoke and fiddle herself in the back seat, until one night she decided to just keep on driving and so she drove straight down I-95 to Miami...

You went to Miami, too. You've got *that* much in common with boring, monotonous Lisa M. It's sunny all the time in Miami and you can wear shorts year-round it's so warm. When I see you in Miami, I see you with your English boyfriend named Jonathan, living in an apartment with bright yellow walls, pastel-coloured throw cushions and a wet bar. I see you happy and tanned, lounging beside your very own swimming pool with two diving boards, one high, one low.

But not Lisa M. She hocked her uncle's Buick, lived on the street until she ran out of money and nearly starved herself to death. She panhandled, spending what little money she collected on bottles of Blue Nun, generic brand vodka and weed, until the police caught her and delivered her back to her parents. Only Lisa M's parents said they couldn't handle her any more so the police dropped her off in the programme instead of at her parents' house and God she was angry. She rebelled and

170

rebelled, denied up and down that she was an addict, but then she saw the light and she succumbed to her Higher Power and now she's on fifth phase and helping others and going back to high school and getting her shit together and isn't she a shining example to us all?

If you're clean and you know it, clap your hands. The whole room applauds politely and some guy in the back, probably Lisa M's dad or maybe the uncle who sacrificed his car to the cause, joins in with an exuberant two-fingered whistle.

Eric, the male fifth phaser, is somewhat briefer. He gave in to peer pressure, started dropping tabs of LSD, became a pusher at his high school, got snagged by an undercover nark, was told he could go to jail or the programme, chose the latter and five hundred and twenty-three days of clean living later he's atoned for his sins, made amends left, right and centre and is now proud to say he's an addict and, thank his Higher Power and the fabulous Come Clean counsellors, recovery is great, it's smooth sailing from here on out. Let go, let God. Amen.

The meeting ends some time later with more announcements and singing. My stomach growls, my eyes burn and my butt's numb from sitting so long. It's late, maybe ten o'clock, maybe later. All I want is Mom and Dad and home, Orville Redenbacher popcorn, Blockbuster videos and my best friend Cindy Gregory. But not yet, not yet. The assembled mass breaks up into more rap sessions. The parents head to their room for the parents' rap, the siblings head to their room for the siblings' rap and we stay where we are, shifting our chairs back into a slapdash ellipse for a final phaser rap. A few newcomers with Talk privileges are peeled away to meet one-on-one, plus chaperone, with their families.

Dwight sets about shouting at the rest of us as Ramona magics a Ping-Pong paddle from somewhere and starts to circulate.

'I am so disappointed in ya'll,' Dwight laments. 'Ya'll know the rules about Open Meetings. Have ya forgotten? Have they slipped your little ole minds? Y'all must present your very best when the families are here, your very very best.'

He reels off our long list of crimes. People yawning, fidgeting, slouching, failing to respond in a swift and humble manner. His litany is punctuated by the thwacks of Ramona slapping phasers' necks and shoulders. No one's slouching now, but the slapping continues.

'Ya'll think we're scared of restraining you in front of your precious parents?' Dwight asks. 'Ya'll better think again. We're not scared, we just don't like to make you look bad. Or should I say any worse, any more pathetic, than you already do.'

Thwack, thwack. It's like she's playing one of those fairground games where the goal is to hammer the head of as many moles as you can.

Dwight crooks his arms on to his hips and scowls. 'I'm downright disgusted with the lot of ya.'

Thwack, thwack.

'Don't ya'll want to be clean?' he asks. Thwack. 'Answer me!'

'Yes, Dwight!' the group choruses.

'Don't ya'll want to maintain your recovery?'

'Yes, Dwight!'

'Huh. That's news because ya'll sure as hell didn't act like it tonight. Now let me see you motivate.'

The phasers start to pump and flap, tentative at first. No one seems to know what they're motivating for. What if they get picked and don't know what to say?

'Harder!' screams Dwight.

Thwack. Ramona slugs away even as the group motivates, but her targets' movements send the paddle off in skewy directions, hitting arms and heads, cheeks and elbows.

'Motivate for your goddamn recovery!!'

The phasers increase their effort, all except for me. I keep my hands in my lap.

'Harder!' Dwight commands, staring straight at me, but I'm still as a statue.

I gaze past his shoulder, past the writhing rows, past the empty audience chairs, straight into the heart of the weekend. I'm going home.

'Harder, harder, harder! Faster, faster, faster!' Thwack, thwack, thwack.

Dwight doesn't call on anybody but continues to egg the group on. Five minutes, ten minutes, who's counting. Only Dwight wears a watch and he's moving too fast to read it, pacing up and down, waving his own limbs about.

The girl next to me, Jackie W, keeps switching arms as they tire, supporting the motivating arm with the spare one. Faces redden, brows drip with sweat, eyes bulge with the strain, necks thicken, a button flies off the shirt of one of the boys and wings through the air, the metal feet of the chairs dig noisily into the floor.

'Harder!' shouts Dwight.

Jackie W tries to switch arms again but instead melts into an exhausted heap, all matted hair and ragged breath, until Ramona descends and thwacks her back into frantic action.

I sit quietly and observe the others as they wear themselves out in the name of recovery. At last, Hilary comes for me. I'm going home.

CHAPTER TWENTY-FOUR

We call Dad 'Dad' now and Mom 'Mom', just like any proper kid should. We can hardly remember how we used to whine and draw out their names into two or three syllables. We're beyond all that kiddie stuff now, we're very nearly nine. Old as that.

We're so near to nine we can feel the new age creeping into our bones like a toothache. Within spitting distance of our birthday, we are. So close we can almost smell the smoke from the candles and the ink on cheques written by aunties, uncles and other distant relations and in the mushy messages scrawled across 'Happy birthday, Grandtwins' cards from Grandma and Grandpa Shirland, who's still alive and thinks it's very funny how big we're getting.

Before we can get any older, though, Dad has to. Dad's a Leo, the right side of the month, so he gets to be a lion, which is much better than being a virgin. We know what virgins are now because Lloyd Taggart told us last year. Lloyd said his big sister Tracey was no longer a virgin; she bled from down there sometimes and he thought maybe that had something to do with it. Lloyd said if you slept with someone of the opposite sex you were no longer a virgin. His parents caught Tracey sleeping with her boyfriend Lance, they yelled like hell and Tracey cried for a week, so Lloyd knew a thing or two about virginity. When he told us, we worried maybe we weren't virgins any more after we played the married couples game, but Lloyd said we were still because we never fell asleep.

So we accept it's our God-given fate to always be funny women who lounge around in togas rather than beautiful lions with manes like starbursts. And what's so great about being a lion anyway? Dad's birthday is exactly five days before ours and, when we were littler, we never could understand how he could be so much bigger when he had less than a week's head start. Course we're older and wiser now.

Annoyingly, unlike us, Dad never drops hints about what presents he wants. So when Mom asks us, this year when we are very nearly nine, what we want to get Dad for his birthday, we're stumped. You suggest a party at Farrell's Ice Cream Parlor where you can buy one big sundae the size of a trough with one hundred scoops of ice cream in it, all different flavours, and fudge on top.

Mom frowns. 'I don't think your dad likes ice cream that much. We need to get him something he would like.'

I can tell you're hurt by the implication. Of course, Farrell's ice-cream trough is something you'd like but wouldn't everyone?

Mom drives us to the mall, drags us everywhere looking for presents. We want to go to the KayBee Toy Store, but Mom directs us instead to the tie counter in Woodward's department store, then to the luggage department, then to men's socks.

She holds up things and says, 'How about this?'

I just want to say yes/fine/whatever, but you won't. You veto one after the other after the other and we go round like that for what must be hours until I take you aside, kick you in the shin and demand to know what you're doing wasting time like this when we could be in the toy store dropping our own birthday hints.

'If it's going to be a gift from us, we should pick it out,' you tell me.

That's pretty rich, if you ask me, considering this is the first year Mom has even asked our opinion on birthday presents for Dad. As I remember it, every year before she simply bought something and signed our names. And to be honest, I don't see why things had to change this year.

I say as much now and you sigh and roll your eyes.

'That's such an eight-year-old thing to say,' you declare, which puts me in a huff. But then you persuade Mom to give us some money to pick out our own present for Dad.

To my astonishment, she hands over a crisp ten dollar bill. And we're off. I now see your grand ruse and stop huffing to congratulate you. 'Yippee! Now we can go to KayBee's.'

You do that sighing thing again and make for the book department instead, marching straight past the kids' corner and into adults. Up and down the aisles you go, until you finally decide that what Dad really wants is a good dictionary. You stand on tippy-toes and pull out the highest one you can reach. It's hardback and as thick as your arm, with a glossy cover striped red, green and blue.

'You think this is something Dad'd like?' you ask me.

'Why not?'

'We've got to be sure. I don't want to get it wrong, I want to get him something he'll really like.'

'Absolutely, I'm sure.'

You take it to the checkout and try to pay but the lady there looks at our crisp new ten dollar bill and says we haven't got enough money. Not to worry, she consoles and finds us another dictionary that's half the size and paperback with a plain brown cover. You're not nearly so pleased with this one and are ready to protest but I shoot you a look that makes you think again. You pay for the dictionary and there isn't enough change to buy a single thing from KayBee's.

The following week when Dad unwraps our present, he smiles vaguely and says, 'Gee, thanks kids.' But later when he thinks we aren't paying attention, we hear him chuckling with Mom and asking if she kept the receipt. We never see hide nor hair of the second-choice dictionary again.

CHAPTER TWENTY-FIVE

I follow jingle-jangling Hilary into the intake room, the place where it all started. Was that only five days ago? Seems like five centuries. Our parents are there already, seated and waiting. They've switched chairs. Mom's perched on the edge of the green garden chair, that doesn't sag in the slightest under her minuscule weight, and Dad lounges in the comfortable, coffee-stained armchair, though somehow the godsquad needlepoint still seems positioned over his head. *Believe in Him.*

I spring towards Mom for a hug, but Hilary conducts me to my seat – the ladder back again – as she retakes the swivel chair and props an elbow on the yellowing Formica of the side table. There's a batch of papers and a clipboard there too and a ball of rubber bands, and suddenly I'm struck by a sickening sense of *déjà vu*. My stomach tightens, my hands flare cold like frostbite.

Calm down, Justine. You're going home.

Hilary clears her throat and begins. She addresses our parents as if I'm not here. No one so much as glances at me. She refers to them, unsettlingly, as Mom and Dad, like the other parents in the group, no Mr or Mrs, no Ziegler, not even a Zeeee.

'Mom and Dad, you brought Justine to the programme on Sunday because you were concerned about some disturbing behaviour of late. At that time, it was, of course, premature to judge whether or not Come Clean was the place best suited to Justine's needs. We agreed to admit your daughter for a short observation period...' *Three days!* I want to yell, *it was only supposed to be three days.* '...during which we hoped to determine Justine's condition and advise on the best course of action. Over the past few days, we've done just that. We now believe, Mom and Dad, that you were quite right to bring Justine here. I regret to inform you that Justine has a very serious dependency and she needs help.'

She could not possibly mean what it sounds like she means, could she? She could not possibly mean, she couldn't possibly, no, she couldn't. I'm going home. *Tonight.*

'With a degree of cooperation, she stands to benefit a great deal from the Come Clean recovery programme. What I'm saying, Mom and Dad—'

'Don't call me that,' snaps Dad. 'I'm not your father.'

'My apologies. I assure you I don't mean any disrespect by it. That's how we refer to all parents here, as you may recall.'

'I recall just fine, but I'm still not your father.'

'Not by blood, of course not. But we're all part of the same family in the programme.'

'Justine is not a part of your programme yet,' Dad answers with a defiance in his voice that I warm to. But I don't like the 'yet', I don't like it at all.

Hilary picks up on that tiny, three-letter word too. 'You're quite right. Justine isn't officially a part of the programme – *yet*. But what I'm trying to tell you...'

I close my eyes and jam my knuckle into the point just between and above my eyes, sending sparks of red and lightning white shooting into the veiled darkness behind my lids.

'…what I'm trying to tell you is that, in our opinion, she should be.' Hilary clears her throat again. 'We're recommending that, for the greater good of Justine and your family, you should leave her here with us, so that she can work her way through the full course of recovery.'

I hear Mom suck in her breath as the floor drops away from me. My stomach plummets down through my legs, past my kneecaps and my shins, out through the soles of my feet, like it does when you're in an elevator that descends too far too fast, except I've never been in an elevator speeding, careering along like this one. She couldn't have said what she just said, she couldn't. The room goes black and I think I must have my eyes closed again, but when I will myself to open them the room is still black, I can't focus because everything remains a dusky, lights-out blur and I've got a bad taste in my mouth. I want to brush my teeth, I want to floss them too and it occurs to me, a crazy thought out of nowhere, that maybe Dad has a twine of dental floss stowed in his pocket for me. I'm about to ask him for it but tell myself not to because I don't need it in here because I'm going home, I'm going home, and I've got an endless supply of dental floss in my medicine cabinet in my bathroom. At home. Daddy, please take me home and let me floss my teeth now.

'For how long?' our father asks and he's not talking about flossing.

'These things are impossible to measure. It depends on Justine. As long as it takes, is the best I can say.'

Our mother has been holding her breath all this time and she exhales loudly now, then tries to breathe again in short swigs, as if she's going to hyperventilate. Dad stares at Hilary and doesn't blink. His lips are sealed together, tight and unmoving, but in profile, I can see his jaw working, like he's grinding his teeth or chewing on his tongue or something, chewing over this suggestion that Hilary has just put forward.

I open my mouth and struggle to find my voice but only air comes out, quick and ragged, as if my lungs were synchronised with our mother's.

'I don't know,' says Dad.

'I can understand your apprehension. What with...' Hilary hunts for the right words. '...with *everything* that's gone before, it must be extremely difficult for you to be faced with this decision again. But let me say this: we firmly believe Justine belongs here. What's more, we think to remove her at this point would be foolhardy and irresponsible – dangerous even. I don't need to tell you how addicts can self-destruct after being discovered.'

'I am *not* an addict!' I stomp my feet as I yell it, trying to find the elevator's brakes and retrieve my guts from the depths.

Hilary unsheathes her ballpoint pen and refers to the top sheet on her clipboard, ticking off something in the margins. 'I should inform you that Justine has already caused a great deal of trouble. On Monday, she instigated a food fight over lunch and physically attacked another phaser.' She glances up from the clipboard and locks eyes with first Mom then Dad before adding, 'A *boy*.'

'No, no, no,' I say, slamming my hands into the splinter-primed sides of my chair. 'I spilled my drink. It was *an accident*, it was—'

'She has also tried to escape on three separate occasions. On her very first night in care, she attempted to sneak out of her host family's home, only to be foiled by the regulation alarm system.'

'That's not true!' My voice is shrill, it doesn't sound like me. It's got a strain in it I don't quite recognise, a strain close to hysteria.

181

I mustn't panic. Calm down, Justine, calm down. Daddy never listens to you if you're not in control. 'It's not true,' I repeat, slower now. 'I needed the bathroom, I just needed to pee.'

'The other two times were right here in the facility, in front of the entire assembled group. On Thursday, during a stretch break, she attempted to break free from her upper-phaser and ram a staff member. Me, as it was,' Hilary sniffs.

'No! No. I was trying to talk to you that's all. Mom, Dad, they wouldn't tell me what was going on, I was only trying to find out what was happening.'

'On the other occasion, Justine hurled a piece of furniture at her oldcomer and again tried to break away.'

I can't even picture that. I never saw the face of the girl who accused me of tripping her when I was only grappling clumsily with the two folding chairs on the way to the lunch table. How can they twist things like this? How can they make something so innocent sound so wrong and premeditated? I lower my shaking head, 'No, no, no. It wasn't like that. None of it.'

'In addition, Justine refuses to participate in any way in group activities and she demonstrates a wilful disregard for the rules – which are there, of course, for her own protection...' Dad huffs and repositions himself in his armchair. '...and she shows a marked hostility towards authority. I don't say any of these things lightly, Mom and Dad...' Dad blinks and repositions himself again. '...they are, I'm sorry to say, irrefutable, having surfaced over many hours and days of close observation.'

'Mom, Dad, listen. None of this is true. This woman hasn't spent a minute with me since you dropped me off last weekend. None of the staff members have, they haven't even noticed I'm here. No one talks to me here, no one; no one's been analysing me—'

For a millisecond, Hilary fixes me and me alone in her sights. 'Do you really think only the staff members have eyes and ears, Justine?' She turns back to our parents as she reaches for the stack on the table. 'As you know, Mom and Dad, Come Clean is a group-help programme. It's based on the principle that kids listen and learn most from their peers. After all, peers are the ones who usually lead teens into drink and drugs; we find peers are also the most effective at leading them out again. Reverse peer pressure, if you will. Our "kids helping kids" ethos is what makes our programme so unique and so successful.'

She holds up a familiar plastic document wallet. It's filled with slips, dozens of little slips of paper, torn not cut, edges fuzzy and jagged as if there were no time or need for something as sensible and orderly as scissors. The floor disappears again and the sour, faintly chlorinated taste blooms stronger and more rancid across my tongue.

'In just five short days we've had a great many reports on Justine from her programme peers. These are kids who don't know her from Adam. They've got no axe to grind with your daughter. But they know the signs and symptoms of addiction intimately and they've recognised them in Justine.'

I push myself forward, desperately try to engage with our parents. 'Mom, Dad, please listen. It's not right, the way she's saying things. You won't believe the things they do to kids in here. The staff members scream all the time, they hit kids, for no reason they hit them, they beat them up and kick them and they humiliate people every day all day, they—'

'She's also prone to dishonesty, of course,' Hilary surmises. 'Addicts have to lie a lot to cover their tracks. Mom and Dad, you

183

can't believe a word Justine says. I'd recommend you don't even listen. It'll only upset you.'

'I'm *not* lying! *I am not an addict!*' The high-pitched strain is back in my voice, I can't shut it up, can't control it any more.

'Lying's the only protection the addict has, especially in the early stages of recovery when they want so much not to have to face up to their problem. They're in a constant state of denial.'

'I'm not in denial, there's nothing to deny. I don't have a problem.'

Hilary swivels back towards me, her head bowed. 'Justine, dear, can't you see what you're doing? You're denying. You're denying all over the place. What is denial if not the act of denying? I've seen so many young people like you. You think you've got all the answers, you're afraid to let go and let anybody help you. But you've got to. It's your only hope.' Her eyes soften; she actually sounds sincere. 'I know it seems hard for you now, impossibly hard, and I can empathise. Really, I know where you're coming from. But it'll get easier. You've got to help us to help you. Work with us, Justine. *It's for your own good.*'

For your own good. Oh Josh, please save me. Does this woman really believe all this garbage she's spouting?

'It's very common in siblings,' Hilary tells our parents. 'We've got many siblings in the programme. Research shows that, if one child suffers from addiction, the likelihood of a brother or sister also exhibiting addictive tendencies increases significantly. We're not sure why exactly this is. Partly, it's due to genetics and partly to the shared environment, particularly if the siblings are close in age and share peer groups. In twins, who already, from birth, display unnaturally high levels of co-dependency, the likelihood that both will share an addictive personality is heightened even more dramatically.'

'Justine and Joshua have always shared *everything*,' our mother sobs and I detect a strange mix of pride and despair in her voice. She unsnaps her handbag and roots around frantically for another Kleenex. Tic Tacs clatter from within.

'Yes,' Hilary confers. 'Unfortunately, addiction is often a part of that "special bond" psychologists do love to harp on about.'

'Hey, whatever Joshua's problem was, it was nothing to do with me.'

'Sure about that, Justine?'

'Hell, yes—'

'Watch your mouth, young lady,' barks Dad.

'Yes, I'm sure about that,' I rephrase. 'Jesus, is that what you really think?'

'Not just what I think, it's a scientific fact,' Hilary replies.

'Bullshit!'

'Justine!'

'Co-dependency is a very serious condition.' She's addressing our parents again. 'I'll grant you that Justine has not developed as severe a physiological addiction to alcohol and drugs as some of the youngsters who've been through the programme, including her brother. Not yet she hasn't anyway. But the likelihood that she will do so is very high. And she has, I'm willing to bet, suffered most of her life from co-dependency, which is an addiction in it's own right.

'Fundamentally, co-dependency is about disordered relationships, it's a disease of lost selfhood. It's about putting so much importance on A.N. Other, that the individual can no longer know or identify their true self. They become subordinated to their need to fulfil the other and their personal boundaries become distorted. Simply stated, it's a case, for the

185

co-dependent, of...' Hilary holds up two fingers of each hand and scratches quotation marks into the air... '"not knowing where I end and you begin".'

She's talking about you and me, Joshua. You and me.

'The sufferer will feel emptiness, shame, fear, anger, confusion and often numbness, particularly when they're withdrawn from the source of their dependency. Does this sound familiar, Mom and Dad? Co-dependency is chronic, it's progressive and very malignant.'

She's saying we're sick, Joshua, that all our life we've been sick for just being who we are. That's what she's saying. Our earliest memory comes flooding back to me. On the sofa with the fruit-basket pattern, when for the first time I see you on a nearby plate of pears and I think you're me, Joshua, which makes me happy, euphorically happy. And she's saying that was sick and diseased, that all the time we spent together, all the years, all the love and secrets were wrong, that's what she's saying. Did they tell you this too? When you came into this place, did they tell you I was part of your sickness? Did they persuade you to cut me out of your body like a tumour?

My stomach feels like it's in the grip of a giant fist that's wringing it to bits. I lean back, steeling myself against the rigid ladder back for support because otherwise I might double over in pain and never ever be able to straighten back up again. Our father chews his tongue, our mother covers her mouth and nose with a man-sized Kleenex as if she might suffocate herself. There's an expression of pure terror in her eyes, like the way Mia Farrow looks in *Rosemary's Baby* when she realises it's the devil himself growing inside her. What foul aberrations did Mom give birth to?

186

'So it starts with co-dependency. And in Justine's case, chances are it'll spiral quickly now into running round with the wrong crowd of teenagers, getting more heavily into alcohol, drugs and finally addiction. You've already witnessed the start of that process. Justine should be thankful she has such vigilant parents as you who were able to catch her before she went too far,' Hilary congratulates, practically winking at our father. 'You don't want to undo any of your good work now, do you?'

'That's crap. Mom, please. You know my friends, you know they're not like that. You know Cindy, you know Beth and Kelly, you know Lloyd. You like them, Mom, remember how much you like them?'

'Are those druggie friends of yours, Justine?' Hilary asks. 'I have to remind you that you're not permitted to use the names of druggie friends.'

Mom half chuckles. 'Oh, I'd hardly call Cindy Gregory a druggie. Cindy's a nice girl. We go to church with her parents.'

Hilary wags her finger in our mother's direction. 'Don't enable her, Mom, please. It doesn't help matters at all.'

'Get them down here,' I suggest. 'Get them all down here, call them whatever you like. They'll testify that—'

'No one's on trial here, Justine.'

'Cindy and Lloyd will tell you I'm no juicer or pothead or whatever.'

'No druggie names,' warns Hilary again as simultaneously Mom says, 'We can't do that, honey.'

'Why not?'

'Honey, we told your friends you'd gone to live for a while with your Grandma Shirland. It's been such a difficult time, you know. Cindy's called just about every day and Lloyd dropped by, some of the other boys and girls have sent cards and such. They all send their love, honey, but we told them to give you some time and space. We said you needed to be on your own and they understood that.'

I imagine my friends, each of their faces flashes before me, I imagine them discussing me in hushed, sympathetic tones. Totally useless, misplaced concern. They don't know where I am, don't know what's happening to me, they aren't coming to my rescue.

'That's quite right,' Hilary concurs. 'Justine needs to break away completely from her past druggie life. She needs the time and space to concentrate on her recovery. Don't you agree, Mom and Dad?'

'Don't listen to her, listen to me, please, I don't belong in here. Take me home, Mommy, Daddy, I promise I'll be good!' No one seems to hear me. Am I really shouting or is it like when the room goes black when I haven't shut my eyes? I swallow and swallow but the bad taste won't go away.

'Justine needs help, Mom and Dad. Can't you give her a chance? I'm sure you don't want to repeat what happened with Joshua. Do you?'

Our mother covers her ears, tears stream down her face. Give me a Tic Tac, Mommy, and make the yucky taste disappear.

Dad's jaw is still, no grinding, no chewing. He nods, more with his eyes than his head. 'If you think it's for the best,' he says.

And I remember the dream I had. You on your bike. 'You should have jumped,' you tell me.

CHAPTER TWENTY-SIX

We're ten years old this very day and we're having a party.

Mom and Dad don't usually let us have a party. They say it's too difficult to round up kids at the end of the summer when some of them haven't come back from school yet or maybe they're on vacation at Rehoboth Beach with their families or visiting their grandparents. This year, they make an exception because we're turning ten and Mom says we'll never move from single digits to double digits again so it's worth commemorating.

We plan and organise and look forward to the big day practically all summer; not even Dad's birthday five days before ours can dampen our spirits. Mom buys up packs of invitations with Tom and Jerry cartoons on the front from the Hallmark shop and helps us fill them in, then she drives us round to every kid's house to hand-deliver them.

Everybody's coming to our big party. Davie Kirchner will be there and Richie Richardson and Beth Jenkins and Billy Prophett and Michael Sanderson and Sheila Marple, of course, my best friend, and Lloyd Taggart and Cindy Gregory and Hank Wood and Lucy Hamilton and Melanie Heath and even Norman Macalister, who you kinda hate because he's the teacher's pet but he's not so bad really, and just about every kid from our class at school. Except Wayne Westbrook. He's not actually in our class any more because he flunked a grade and we didn't invite him anyway.

Grandma and Grandpa Shirland are there too because they're visiting us this summer instead of the other way round. The whole time, practically, Grandpa sits on the back porch, slurps Lipton's Ice Tea through a straw, surveys the commotion around him and declares it right funny. And Grandma, she says she wouldn't miss our tenth birthday for anything and goodness we're getting big. The night before, when she comes to tuck us into bed, she ruffles our hair and lip-smacks slobbery kisses on our foreheads.

Even when there are no friends or parents or grandparents around, she says, you two will always have at least one other person who remembers your birthday. Grandma explains how lucky we are because most people can't say that.

'Trust me,' Grandma whispers as we curl up into her, 'that's a special thing, very special.'

And we feel special because we're almost ten, we're having a party and we're too excited to sleep. Mom says because we've got two digits now we should have two birthday cakes too and she lets us each pick out the one we want. I choose one from the A&P bakery that has miniature Barbie dolls on top, and you decide you want a Baskin Robbins cake made out of Rocky Road ice cream. On each one, Mom writes Happy Birthday in blue icing, followed by our individual names.

We hang streamers, banners and balloons, and Mom and Grandma unpack two trestle tables in the back yard, cover them in *Tom and Jerry* Happy Birthday tablecloths and set out party favours for our friends. It's all absolutely perfect and I don't even get mad when Mom tells me I have to wear a dress: the lacy frock Dad bought me especially.

Kids start to arrive and we're hopping with excitement. They're all dressed up in party outfits, their arms full of presents. They're supposed to bring presents for both of us, but must be that some of them didn't realise or forgot because some only hand one wrapped-up parcel to Grandpa, who's on present duty. Grandpa takes the multicoloured boxes and bags, squints at the labels and then stacks them up in piles on our respective tables.

Everybody rips open their party favour packs and starts tooting their horns, and filling up their water pistols from the garden hose even though Mom shouts and says those toys are for later. My special party dress gets soaked and your shirt gets untucked and you get a grass stain on your new pants.

Dad roasts Oscar Mayer hot dogs on the barbecue, we all wolf them down and before we know it it's time for the cakes. We're wearing our pointed birthday hats and great big grins and everybody sings *Happy Birthday*.

My cake is set down in front of me, ablaze with ten big birthday candles. Mom runs around with a camera, flashbulb sparking and everybody saying 'make a wish, make a wish'. So I squeeze my eyes shut, puff out my cheeks, blow, and I wish we could have a birthday party this wonderful every year.

My best friend Sheila Marple is at my elbow, jostling me and begging me to cut her an extra big slice and could she have one with a Barbie on top. I'm slicing up the cake and serving it on to paper plates that match the *Tom and Jerry* tablecloth when I hear Sheila burst out giggling. I want to know what's so funny, thinking it must be one of the boys has done something dumb like maybe Hank Wood has picked his nose and wiped it on his shirt.

'It's your brother,' says Sheila Marple, 'he's not even half as popular as you. Look, he hardly has any presents at all.'

I look and she's right. The pile of presents on your table is measly and there's hardly anyone jostling for cake around you. You haven't even started to slice yours and two of your candles are still burning. You look like you're about to cry.

Sheila is still laughing but she stops when I pick up that extra large slice of Barbie cake I've cut for her and mash it into her face like they do sometimes on *Tom and Jerry*. Then I abandon my cake and all my presents and come over and help you blow out your candles. I tell you Rocky Road is much more exciting than Barbie and how could I have been so stupid. Everybody has a slice of your Baskin Robbins cake, even though it's beginning to melt already, and they agree. Cindy Gregory tells you it's the best birthday cake she's ever tasted and I decide Cindy's going to become my new best friend.

'Ain't that funny,' observes Grandpa Shirland when he takes a bite. 'It's not really a cake at all.'

CHAPTER TWENTY-SEVEN

It's like arriving all over again. Everything that seemed strange or scary over the past five days now seems terrifying. I'm no longer removed from it, bemused by it, separate. I'm a part of it. I am not going home.

Was it like this for you, Joshua, when you first came here? Did you feel this terror in your belly, like a ball of lead sitting there, so heavy you can hardly move for it? Did you fear for what lay in store for you? Did you feel betrayed, horribly horribly betrayed, and misunderstood and abandoned? Did you feel alone?

Because that's how I feel, Josh. All of those things and most of all, alone. I feel alone, absolutely so. And I am not going home.

In fact, it's so much worse than when I first arrived. Then, as shocked as I was to be here, I really believed it was only for observation. And after an observation, I reasoned, nobody could conclude anything but the truth – that I am *not* a druggie, that *I do not belong here.* I told myself – like Mrs Porter, our sixth grade social studies teacher used to tell us – if you've done nothing wrong, if you're innocent, you have nothing to worry about. I should have known better.

I'm numb at first with the news. I can't close my eyes, can't even blink, but I don't see anything either. There's a point ahead of me, on the ground a few feet ahead and I stare at that. Sometimes it's carpet or linoleum or gravel. I stay fixed on it, and let myself be led around.

I don't remember our parents leaving – though I can still hear Mom crying – or going to a host home or eating dinner, brushing my teeth, peeing in front of anyone or sleeping. And the next day I'm back in the programme and staring at the gouges on the group room's floor. It occurs to me that if I keep my head down maybe nobody will notice me, but my illusion's quickly shattered.

'Still here?' marvels Gwen in mock surprise, stooping down so I can't help but see her even though my eyes are lowered.

'Not so cocky now, I bet. Eh, chickie?'

I don't rise to the bait so she steps on my foot, then steps on it again, grinding down. I'm still wearing the white nursing shoes she gave me earlier in the week and her sneakers leave a new scuff across the toes.

During the morning rap, I pretend I'm somewhere else. Anywhere. I hear the voices, sometimes distant, sometimes raised and angry, sometimes chanting and ricocheting all around me. I'm sitting in the front row of the girls' section and as I gaze ahead at the point on the floor, sometimes legs and feet come into my line of vision. Dwight and Ramona lead today's session.

Dwight's teasing me, too, I'm sure of it. His feet circle closer and closer. He's wearing navy loafers, the cuffs of his jeans brushing the leather shoelaces. Occasionally, he stops cold in his tracks right in front of me and my ears perk up when it sounds like he's about to call my name. Just… a minute, he'll say. Or Just… suppose. Just this or Just that, but never Justine Zee. Not during the morning rap.

It's in the afternoon's Now rap that the gloves come off.

'Tell us why you're here,' he demands of me as I stand shakily, a hundred-odd pairs of eyes scrutinising me.

'I have no idea,' I say. 'I shouldn't be here at all.'

A few people chuckle. 'Of course you shouldn't!' Dwight guffaws. 'But humour me, anyway. Tell me why you *think* you're here.'

I shrug.

'Could it be because you're an addict?'

'I'm not an addict.'

'An alcoholic then, call it what ya want.'

'I'm not an alcoholic, I don't have any addiction.'

'I see. That must mean we professionals here have no idea what we're talking about,' he laughs at that too and the group joins in. 'Folks,' he continues, a shadow falling across his face, 'I'm afraid Justine has got her programme off to a very bad start. Very bad.' He stalls, waiting for someone to guess why. 'She has broken one of the cardinal rules of Come Clean.' Pause. 'Who can tell me what the most important attributes of our group are? Mark G.'

'Honesty!' shouts Mark.

'And?'

'Confidentiality!'

'Honesty and confidentiality, that's right. These things are sacred to the workings of this group. Without honesty and confidentiality, we have no programme. Well, I think it's pretty obvious that Justine Z here is still in denial, that she hasn't yet found the strength to get honest with us or with herself.' Several phasers nod their agreement. 'But what you don't know is that, just five measly days into her programme, Justine breached our confidentiality. *Your* confidentiality.' Dwight points at random individuals. 'Yours and yours and yours.'

Ramona pulls out a tape recorder and hands it to Dwight who punches the play button. Then I hear my own voice, tinnier than I'd hope it would sound but unmistakably mine.

'You won't believe the things they do to kids in here,' I hear myself saying, as I did to our parents last night. 'The staff members scream all the time, they hit kids, for no reason they hit them, they beat them up and kick them and they humiliate people every day all day—'

Dwight switches the machine off and there's murmuring amongst the group.

'Justine Z blabbed,' says Dwight. 'She broke the confidentiality of this group and jeopardised recovery for each and every one of you. Not only that, but she lied about what happens here! She lied to save her own hide. She lied like all addicts do.' He's motioning at me again now.

'Do we scream at you for no reason?' Dwight screams.

'No, Dwight!' the group yells in unified response.

'Can't hear ya.'

'No, Dwight!!' they yell louder.

'Do we beat you for no reason?'

'No, Dwight!'

'Do we kick or hit or scratch you for no reason?'

'No, Dwight!'

'Do we humiliate you for no reason?'

'No, Dwight!'

'Why do we do what we do within these four walls?'

'To help us come clean, Dwight!'

'And what do you want to do?'

'Come clean, Dwight!'

'What was that again?'

'Come clean, Dwight!'

'OK, exactomundo. So that means Justine Z here's not only a tattletale but a liar to boot.' He makes a tutting noise. 'She's disrespected herself, she's disrespected me and the other counsellors here, she's disrespected you and, most importantly, she has disrespected the programme.'

The group is buzzing now, people hopping about in their seats like corn kernels about to pop.

'Why don't you all stand up and tell Justine how you feel about that?'

And they all stand up and they call me names – dirtbag and tattletale, blabbermouth and whistle-blower, shit-stirrer and worse – and they tell me they hate me, that I'm shit, I'm ungrateful and stupid, spiteful, dishonest, hateful, conniving, deceitful and worse. I try to block it out, try not to hear them or see them with their arms waving, their faces red as strawberries, but though I've witnessed such confrontations before, they never sounded so loud, so horrible, so personal as this. I sink back into my chair, lean forward and place my head between my legs, covering my ears and closing my eyes just like when our elementary school teachers – Mrs Wolf or Mr Newhouse or Miss Fawcett or whoever it was – used to make us assume the crash position for a tornado drill. And the storm swirls above me.

Later, I'm doled out to someone named Deirdre for the night, but before she belt-loops me out the door, Dwight drops by my chair.

'This ain't no summer camp now,' he tells me. 'Ya better learn the rules, baby. Fast.' From his jeans pocket, he pulls a stick of Juicy Fruit that's gone all limp and curly. He straightens the gum out, unwraps it, rolls it into his mouth and starts to chew. 'And the first rule you better remember is, never – and I do mean *never* – mess with big brother Dwight here. Never.' He smiles and gives one of my front belt loops an extra zealous tug before he passes me on to Deirdre.

CHAPTER TWENTY-EIGHT

I try to open that part of my mind back up, that little recess where Moira told me to store Come Clean rules and regulations, but now that it's no longer a game, now that it's for real, it's harder to play along somehow. I keep forgetting the stupid rules – half of me doesn't want to comply anyway and the other half is terrified of the consequences if I don't.

I'm regularly hauled up in the Now raps and confronted for misdemeanours: I reached for a lunch-time Happy Meal before being told I could take it; I walked out of step with my belt-looper; I said *gesundheit* to a boy phaser; I indulged my vanity by looking in a car's rear-view mirror; I didn't say thank you to a host father when he passed me a napkin. One day I'm told off for refusing to wear the shirt provided for me by my host family – a shirt I couldn't wear because it was at least three sizes too small – and the next day I'm told off for trying to turn on the boys by wearing a tight shirt that shows off my breasts.

My worst offence, though, is ten times worse than any of those – it's not answering the roll call correctly. Every morning when we first enter the group room, Dwight or Bo or Hilary or whoever calls out your name and you're supposed to jump and proclaim, 'Still here and thirteen (or thirty or three hundred) days clean!'

Only I can't quite bring myself to do that. If I say how many days I've been 'clean', meaning how many days I've been in here, then surely that's as good as admitting that I was once 'unclean'. So every morning, when they call my name, I simply say 'here' or 'still here'. And nearly every afternoon, I'm made to regret it.

One night at Moira's, she implores me to stop being so stubborn. 'Just go along with it a little. Your life will become so much easier if you do. Everybody's will.'

So I try, for Moira's sake. I say what they want me to say at the roll call. When Dwight shouts my name – 'Justine Zeee!' – I shout back. 'Still here,' I say, and however many days it's been, and then I say 'clean' at the end like I'm supposed to but in my mind I substitute 'imprisoned'. That little acquiescence seems to do the trick, and I receive slightly fewer confrontations during the Now raps. There's a price to pay, though. I can't possibly lose track any more of the time passing. Each morning I count off the days, then the weeks and then I'm into counting months.

I also learn to raise my hand to use the bathroom, and sing the songs – 'I'd like to teach the world to be clean' – and echo the appropriate responses at the appropriate times, shower with a see-through plastic curtain and an audience, and write in my Moral Inventory, a glue-bound notebook (wire spirals are against the rules) that follows me around wherever I go. I write stupid things and fast, like Moira taught. Things like, for my past incidents, how when we used to play tag at Richie Richardson's house, you never got to win and I'd like to make amends to you for never letting you win because I've learnt that everybody deserves to win at least once. For my present issues, I write stuff like about my butt being sore from sitting all day or that I'm getting fat – and I am from this shitty fast-food diet – or that my bangs keep falling in my eyes because my hair has grown so long. I usually have to stretch for my something positive postscript because I can't think of anything positive, even if it is all bullshit. So I make do with something like, I'm happy I got a Diet Coke instead of a Fanta or a Sprite or a full-fat Coke with my lunch pack because otherwise I'd leave it blank and be yelled at. I write silly things.

I learn all the Seven Steps off by heart, too. And One! We admit our powerlessness over addiction and the unmanageability of our lives!

Only I never actually admit that. I say the words along with everyone else, but I don't mean them, I'll never mean them. Whenever Dwight stands me up and tries to force me to say them for real, to announce to everyone that I am an addict, I resist. They tell me I'm in denial, and I usually get punished for it but I resist anyway.

Life in the programme falls into a rhythm of talking and eating, belt-looping and shouting, motivating, sleeping and resisting. Each morning we arrive and the newcomers get stuffed into a side room while the oldcomers go off and do their thing. Then we're brought into the group room to find they've rearranged the chairs again, into yet another formation, and they plop us down somewhere totally different from the day before, sitting next to someone new who we're not allowed to speak to or look at too closely. We have roll call, then drills, then the morning rap in which we review one of the Steps and there's a lot of yelling, and arm-waving, confrontations and tears. We break for lunch, must be about half twelve, and we beaver about trying to straighten up, straighten up the tables. We scoff high-in-saturated-fats junk that the fifth phasers picked up from some drive-thru down off the highway and it's all cold, half congealed and sticking to the wrappers by the time it lands in front of us. Then we get handed report slips so we can rat on somebody. Then we re-form into another bizarre chair formation and get yelled at if we don't get it just right. Then it's the Now rap, the slips come back out, people find out what they've been ratted on for and there's a lot of yelling, arm-waving, confrontations and tears. We have some more drills and more drills and more drills. Then it's roll and dole call, we get shunted off into some new girl's eager claws, into her parents' smelly car, then into the host home – where we're not supposed to ask anything and we're supposed to be grateful to have sloppy joes or mac and cheese out of a box for dinner – and then into a bedroom that's not a bedroom because it hasn't got a bed and we're locked in there and God forbid you might need to pee in the middle of the night.

Unless it's a Friday, in which case, everything changes. Every Friday, we have the Open Meeting, when the parents and siblings come to see us, maybe speak to us, almost certainly yell at us and find out how we're doing. On Fridays, the routine changes after the Now rap. We spiff up the room for the Open Meeting, concertina the partition wall back fully and drag out the legions of folding chairs to be arranged in the consistent formation of them facing us, us facing them. Then we sing stupid songs until every last living and breathing relative has filed into the room and taken a seat. The meeting begins, one mike gets passed round amongst us, Ramona sprints around with the parents' mike, Dwight and Hilary announce what we've done or haven't done in the past week, a few lucky phasers get to scream 'Coming home!!!' and make the victory dash across the divide between us-in-here and them-out-there, and the rest of us have to swallow it all and say nothing but 'I love you Mom and Dad'. And there's a lot of yelling, arm-waving, confrontations and tears. Then the parents and the siblings depart for their separate meetings while we have more drills, get told off and Ping-Pong-paddled for all the slouching, yawning, sneezing, stomach grumbling or whatever committed in front of our parents when we were supposed to be presenting our very best behaviour. Finally we have the roll and dole call, get taken home to our hosts as usual except now it's nearly midnight so there's no dinner round the table and we're lucky if we get microwaved SpaghettiOs or Ritz crackers with Cheese Whiz before we're sent off to bed with our bellies still growling.

Those are the days pretty much. My nights have a routine, too. The host home and the oldcomer differ from night to night, they change so much I've lost track of how many houses I've slept in, some grand three-storey affairs in swish neighbourhoods, some little bungalows with no enclosed garage and no central heating or air conditioning. But once we get inside the phaser room, the homes are all much of a muchness – bare white walls, mattresses, locked tight windows and alarmed doors. I listen as the others fall asleep, sometimes it's just me and one oldcomer but other times there's another newcomer or two. The newer newcomers usually cry themselves to sleep and the oldcomers usually cover their heads with their pillows if they do. Some girls snore, some talk in their sleep, some make snuffling noises, like Gwen. One newcomer girl sleepwalks one night and sets the alarm off. The next day in the programme she's stood up in the Now rap and punished with solitary confinement and a one-to-one rap with Dwight for trying to escape, but I know she wasn't trying to escape because I was awake and I saw everything; that girl was like a *Day of the Living Dead* zombie, she didn't know what she was doing. I tell our oldcomer as much but the girl's punishment is meted out anyway and then I get told off the day after in the Now rap for enabling druggie conduct.

I don't sleep much myself and when I do, I have dreams. I dream of you, Josh, in here, and they aren't nice dreams. Sometimes I dream of you and me in the swimming pool, floating on our rafts and sunbathing, the air thick with the smell of tanning lotion and summer. But each morning, before the sun rises, I wake up and panic because I don't know where I am, where you are, what's happening. Later, after a few weeks or more, I start to panic because I don't panic any more because I know all too well.

Occasionally, there are blips in the routine. I come to welcome the blips, even when they're awful sometimes, because they're the only way I can really mark and measure time in here, not like the number of days reeled off each morning, because they're just numbers, melding together into meaninglessness. It's impossible to keep track of the dates or even the days of the week because they're all the same, except for Fridays with the Open Meetings. But the blips I remember, like the really horrific confrontations, the ones that end up in bloody restraints. Or the time when I get so sick from the flu I can't even sit up so I get to go to the infirmary, which is just another room the size of an intake room but with cots where I can lie down all day in peace and quiet and fever. Or when somebody really does try to escape, like the girl who drinks two bottles of shampoo because she reckoned if she got ambulanced to the hospital her friends would come rescue her. Or the newcomer arrivals.

There's a newcomer arrival maybe every week or two. This is Vanessa. She's thirteen and was a student at York County Middle

School. Does anybody know Vanessa? This is Toby S. He's seventeen and was a student at Gunther High School. Does anybody know Toby? This is Bobby G. He's sixteen and was a student at Kelsey High School in Chiverton. Does anybody know Bobby? They check out the group as we check them out; they all look apprehensive, and so they should.

Moments when I have the mike in the Open Meeting punctuate the routine, too. They're so brief and scripted but, as a newcomer, they're the only actual family contact I'm allowed. I keep thinking that if I can just really connect with our parents, they'll realise how much I don't belong here, they'll come to their senses and let me go home.

But Dwight and Hilary never have anything good to report about my progress. 'Justine Z has not cooperated with the group this week ... Justine Z has not earned Talk privileges ... Justine Z has made no progress.' Friday after Friday I watch as our parents' faces become darker and grimmer.

When Ramona hands our mom the parents' microphone, sometimes Mom says, 'We miss you, honey. Come home soon,' but once or twice she starts squalling about how you and me are her only babies and how, please Justine, she can't lose me. And sometimes when she cries so hysterically she can't speak, she surrenders the microphone to Dad and he says, 'Do you see what you're doing to your mother?' Or, 'Pull yourself together Justine, for God's sake!' Or he screams at me to 'Follow the goddamn rules!' Then Bo or Lois or one of the fifth phasers hands me the phaser mike and all I can say is 'I love you Mom and Dad'. After a while, Dad stops coming, or at least not so regularly, and then one week neither of them are there, and the mike bypasses me altogether.

Then I get angry, Josh, I get so angry at them. Why did they put me in here? Why did they put you in here? How could they? They've ruined us, ruined our lives. I think if they do ever come back I might strangle them or spit at them or something or probably I just won't be able to look at them any more, won't be able to look them in the face ever. I remember how I never used to be able to catch your eye when I came to Open Meetings, sitting over there on the outside with you here, and I wonder if you felt the same way then. Maybe even about me.

CHAPTER TWENTY-NINE

The personal confrontations punctuate the days in the programme, too. I get confronted, by Dwight in particular, for all sorts of things, at least once a day. For all the Now misdemeanours in the afternoon and, in the morning Step raps, for things from my past I don't remember, for not getting honest, for minimising. And for you. Morning and afternoon, for you. Though I should be prepared, should know better, oftentimes, I don't even see his attacks coming.

One day during the Now rap, Dwight sifts through the tattle slips with Ramona. I'm praying he doesn't call on me and when he announces the name Francis, I'm relieved, mightily so. I settle back in my chair.

Francis is on the pudgy side, with bushy brown hair and a score of pimples and freckles fighting for space across his nose and cheeks. He's wringing his hands before a word is pronounced.

Dwight tells Francis he's been accused of staring at other boys in the shower.

'Why do ya do that, Francis?' Dwight asks.

'The name is Frank.'

'Frank is it? Trying to act tough, are you?'

'N-no,' Francis mumbles, twisting his fingers into little knotted bundles, not looking the least bit tough.

'Why do ya check out other guys when they're bare-assed naked?'

'I don't.'

'You don't?'

'N-no.'

'Really?'

Ramona hands Dwight a pile of reports.

'I've got boys here say you do. Lots of 'em. Shall we have a little read 'bout what they have to say on the matter?'

'I'd rather you didn't.'

Dwight squeezes his eyes shut and picks out one of the slips of paper like he was choosing a raffle winner. 'Aha.' He reads in silence for a moment, his lips moving. 'Oh my,' he tuts. '"I'd do anything not to have to stay in the same host home as Francis. I don't feel safe in the john, especially not in the shower. I don't want to lean over for the soap."'

He shuffles the slip to the bottom of the pile and picks up another. '"Even when he doesn't look at you straight on, you know what Francis is thinking. He's only pretending not to look. I can feel him sneaking a peek at my reflection in the shower glass."'

And another. '"He was staring at me while he was towelling himself. He was towelling himself off down there for a long time. I'm sure he had a hard-on."' Dwight rereads the slips silently to himself as if he can't quite fathom what they say. Then he taps the pile of evidence. 'What do you have to say to that then, *Frank*?'

Francis has nothing to say to that.

'Are you a homo, is that the way it is?'

Francis doesn't respond.

'D'ya like boys? Do ya swing that way, bat for the other team? Are you an ass bandit, Frank? A butt-fucker? A cocksucker?' Dwight reaches down for his own groin. 'Do you want it, Frank? Is that to your taste, son? Is it dickie-lickin' good? Eh, Frank, *Frankie*?'

'No.'

'No?'

'I'm not gay.'

'I wish that were so, I really do. Do ya know why? Somebody tell me why.'

A few people wave their arms and Roger T stands up and reports: 'Homosexuality is wrong, Dwight.'

Francis doesn't look like you, Josh. Not at all really with his bushy hair and freckles. But I see you standing there in his shoes all the same and have to avert my eyes.

'It is *wrong*,' Dwight repeats. '*Very, very* wrong.' He does a lap around the speakers' circle while that sinks in. 'Tell me, Frankie, how do ya think your parents must have felt when they found out they had a faggot for a son?'

Francis shakes his head.

'I'll tell ya how they felt. I know because they've talked to me about it in the parents' rap. They were absolutely devastated. They didn't know what they'd done wrong. What had they done to deserve a little faggot for a son? And they were so ashamed. Your dad wanted to disown you, he wanted to kick you out on the street. Did ya know that, Frankie?'

Francis shakes his head. His hands are red for wringing.

'But it's your mom I felt really sorry for. My heart went out to her. Did ya even think about how much you'd hurt your momma when you were running around feeling up other guys' balls? Did ya think about her for one single, solitary minute?'

'I never wanted to hurt Mom.'

'I wish I could believe that, too. But let me tell ya, I don't. I reckon you're not being quite honest with us. This is what I think. I think you deliberately set out to do just that. I think you wanted to hurt your parents, real bad, you wanted to punish them. You rebelled in a way you knew would really get to them. That's the worst kind of rebellion, that's so mean and low-down. Despicable. I can't even look at you I'm so disgusted.' Dwight has been up in Frank's face and he backs off now, turning towards the rest of the group. 'Who here wants to tell our little Miss Francis how you feel?'

The group motivates forcefully and people stand up one after another to tell Francis how sickened they are, how disappointed, disgusted, horrified. Homo, they call him, pansy and fudge packer, shirt lifter and girl, queer, turd tickler, brown artist and worse. When they run out of names, Dwight sits them down.

'Does anybody else have anything to say?' he asks.

People search round, puzzled; they've all said their piece and then some.

'Anybody at all? It doesn't seem like we've quite exhausted this matter. Just... a minute now. Let me think. Just... hold on.'

And then he says my name. 'Just-tine Zeeee.'

I don't know what to do.

'Justine Z!' he hollers again.

'Stand up,' the girl to my left hisses.

I get to my feet.

'Thanks so much for joining us, Justine. I figure you must have a lot to add to this here discussion. A lot of first-hand experience to bring to bear. So share with us. What do you think?'

I shrug my shoulders.

'You must have an opinion. Go on, tell Frank over there what you think of his behaviour.'

Francis is still standing. From the group, it's just him and me on our feet, and Dwight buzzing about between us like a wasp trapped in a car, ready to sting. I stop staring at the ground to catch Francis in the eye. He looks as terrified as I feel, as terrified as you must have been. This too, Joshua. They told you that this part of you was sick and diseased, too. Did you believe them? Did they leave any inch of you untouched or untainted?

'It's not wrong, Frank,' I tell him and the group wheezes in disbelief.

'What did you say?' Dwight thunders.

'I said it's not wrong. There's nothing wrong with being gay.' Francis's eyes glisten and his lips part. I think he's about to mouth thank you, but he doesn't and it's best he doesn't – it might turn up in tomorrow's Now rap if he did.

'Sit down, Francis,' Dwight orders. Then he drives the full force of his attention down on me. 'Are you disagreeing with the group, Justine Z? Are you disagreeing with everything that I – that we – have just said?'

'Yes.'

He begins to pace, back and forth, back and forth. 'I'm gonna give ya the benefit of the doubt, Justine. I'm gonna assume that because you're still somewhat new and because your head is still filled up with druggie nonsense from the outside that you're not quite thinking straight yet. And maybe you're feeling a little bit sorry for our Miss Francis over there.' Back and forth, his step quickens as he warms to his subject. 'Well, I'm gonna tell ya something. Your pity is well and truly misplaced. You think your telling Francis that garbage helps him, you think it makes you compassionate? You couldn't be any wronger, you stupid girl. The people who're helping Francis are all these others sitting around you, these phasers here who have the courage to tell him the truth, who know that the only way to help Francis is to get him honest, help him confront his lies and wrongdoings. Do you understand what I'm telling ya?'

He comes in closer. I can see the dried sheen of hair gel – extra-super hold, must be – shimmer briefly in the light. 'Were you or were you not ashamed to have a brother who was a fairy like Francis?'

I shake my head no.

'I didn't hear you. What was that?'

'No, I wasn't ashamed.'

'Well!' he shouts, flinging his arms out. 'That says as much about you as it does about your sorry excuse for a twin.'

Some of the other phasers fidget about in their seats uncomfortably. One person farts and a few others titter nervously. Ramona stills her paddle.

'Leave my brother alone,' I say. I think that's what I say, but I don't seem to say it as loud as I mean to. I'm having trouble using my voice properly.

Dwight carries on as if I haven't spoken. 'Homosexuality is wrong. It says in the Bible it is wrong. Do you read the Bible? It says in the Bible that homosexuality is the devil's work, it's dirty and immoral and ungodly, it caused the destruction of Sodom and Gomorrah.' With each sentence, Dwight's voice swells so that he sounds more and more like one of those fire-and-brimstone preachers Grandpa Shirland would sometimes watch in amusement on a Sunday afternoon. *Ain't that funny...*

'Homosexuality doesn't occur in nature, that's because it's not natural. Those men who practise homosexuality *choose* to do so, they *choose* to behave abnormally. OK, maybe they know not what they do. Maybe they're labouring under a mental disorder. But whichever way you cut it, they are *sick*. And they're visiting their sickness upon the world.' Dwight has his finger in my face, his cuticles scraggly and in need of a clipping; he bites his nails. 'Do ya know about AIDS, Justine? Do ya know what Acquired Immune Deficiency Syndrome is doing to the gays? It's killing them off, it's a disease of the diseased and it's killing them off, one by one by one.'

He withdraws his finger and laughs a coarse laugh. 'Hell, your fudge-packing brother was lucky.'

The room's so silent you could drop a feather and hear it crash; I'm concentrating on controlling my breathing. If I were any kind of a twin, I'd fell this joker, I'd take him down like I took down Wayne Westbrook in the second grade, sweep his feet out from under him and mash his face into the ground, shut him up for good. But I'm tired, Joshua, and I'm so scared.

Dwight opens his mouth as if to continue but is interrupted by another farting noise. He pauses, makes as if to restart again – and again somebody farts. A great rippling, squelching fart – louder this time, long, protracted and coming from the boys' section.

Dwight whirls towards the culprit. 'Who was that?'

He's answered by another noisy emission that lifts the boy in question half out of his chair, the metal legs raking the wooden floorboards. It's one of the newcomer boys, Toby S. I remember him arriving a week or so ago. He's already been confronted in one of the raps about some past incidents involving his varsity

213

football team. He's seventeen and a quarterback or halfback or fullback or something at Gunther High and they went all the way to State last year.

'Whoops, 'scuse me,' grins Toby S with a Dennis the Menace twinkle in his eye. 'Couldn't control myself.'

'Well, mister, you'd better—'

Toby farts again, cutting Dwight dead. 'Sorry, really.'

'Who cut the cheese,' you'd say. 'Whoever smelt it, dealt it,' I'd tell you. Except not in this case. In this case, it's Toby S. Everybody can see that.

Each time Dwight goes to speak, Toby farts until everyone has the giggles and can't stop. Finally, Toby gets marched off to the bathroom to relieve himself – in whatever way he needs to, says Dwight.

And the spell's broken. Ramona signals for Dwight to move on, handing him a fresh batch of report slips.

Dwight. He's another blip. He punctuates my programme days, too.

There aren't always farts to the rescue, though. And never during the punishments. They come after the ritual humiliation in front of the group. The punishments can be anything. Sometimes I have to write more in my M.I. or I have to go without lunch or I can't shower for a week because that's how dirty I am or I'm not allowed to sleep or I have to stand all day or I have to write out the Seven Steps a thousand times or I get a slap in the face.

The day after the Francis incident, while the rest of the group's running through drills, I'm punished with the stepladder. I'm ordered to climb up and down to signify the fact that I'm going nowhere in my programme. I've been on the ladder, up and down, up and down, for what must be an hour already. My legs feel like they've been filled with cement and it's so hard to lift them for the first step that I have to pull them up with my arms.

'And Two!' yells Ramona in the background.

'We accept that there is a Higher Power and decide to give our will and our lives over to it!' yells the group in response.

I'm on the stepladder in one of the far corners of the group room, half obscured by the folded-up luncheon tables, and Dwight comes to check out how I'm doing. He smirks as I grimace and place my foot on the second step, third step, second step. My back's an ache, my face wet with perspiration and my shirt sticks to me. I was given no bra this morning so I know my breasts are swinging and my nipples showing.

'You've got a lot of energy,' Dwight notes.

'And Three!'

'We make a searching and honest moral inventory of ourselves!'

He leans in closer, smells me. How do I smell, Josh?

'Tell me something, Justine,' Dwight says.

'And Four!'

'We admit to our Higher Power, ourselves and each other the exact nature of our wrongdoings!'

His eyes lock mine in seriousness. 'Are you as good in bed as your brother?'

CHAPTER THIRTY

The summer when we're ten going on eleven is an eventful one.

In the spring of that year, we move into a new house. Dad's practice has been expanding. He's hired two dental assistants and a receptionist named Zoe Eichelberger who Mom says is a spinster because she's really old, in her thirties, and still lives at home with her parents. Dad's practice is so successful that he wins an award from the local Lion's Club or something for being one of the fastest growing businesses in Carrefort, Pennsylvania, and he hangs that with his other certificates on the wall of his reception behind Zoe Eichelberger's desk. Dad brags that we're moving up in the world.

The new house is in a swanky neighbourhood that's just being built and my best friend Cindy Gregory lives three streets away though her house isn't one of the new ones. Our house is so new it sparkles. It's two storeys tall with a two-car garage, four bedrooms, a study, a separate TV lounge, living room and dining room. It has so many rooms that, for the first time, we have our own separate bedrooms.

I get a new furniture suite in my room. There are two dressers for all my clothes, and one of them has a mirror too, and there's a desk to write on and a big bed with a canopy. All matching, white with pink and yellow tulips painted on the drawers of the dressers and the headboard of the bed. You say my room looks super-girlie and that's cool.

The only problem with having our own rooms is that they're too far away from each other. Yours is downstairs and mine is upstairs. But lots of times, especially on the weekends, you sneak up to my room or I sneak down to yours to spend the night. It's better really if I come down because you've still got the rollaway so we can haul that out, taking turns sleeping in it versus the big bed, staying up until the wee hours talking and feeling our eyeballs turn bloodshot.

But the very very best bestest thing about our new house is that it has a pool. A real and proper pool, not the kind that sits above ground like a bowl but an actual concrete sunken one. It's curvy at one end like a lima bean and has a diving board at the other end. Dad buys poolside furniture with umbrellas and cushioned lounge chairs with backs that you can prop up rigid or lay flat or somewhere in between. The only thing our new pool doesn't have is a slide but Mom gets us one of those blow-up ones that's even better. We unfurl it like a runway across the back yard, one end positioned in the pool, Mom hoses it down and we run and run then fling ourselves on to it and skid the length of the yard yodelling like the Von Trapp singers off *The Sound of Music* until we plop into the water. It's great.

Once school's out, what with our new house, big back yard and new pool, it's shaping up to be one of the most excellent summers ever. We're the only kids in our class who have our own pool so we become ultra popular. Every day hordes of kids gather round our place. Cindy Gregory and Lloyd Taggart are always there but other kids come too, they travel in from all over town.

We slide on the slide, splash, shout and dunk each other, blow up rafts and beach balls, play water polo and volleyball and Marco Polo and all sorts. The diving board's a favourite too. Most of the kids can't dive worth a hill of beans. They just shimmy down the board and fall off or bellyflop on purpose or cannonball themselves to try and make the biggest splash. You practise, though, in the evenings after the other boys and girls have gone home.

You learn to dive properly. You learn to leap high and then arc into the pool so that hardly any water splashes. Then you learn to dive backwards and you teach yourself how to do all these crazy flips, twists, somersaults and handstand things. You even learn the lingo: pikes, tucks, reverses, that kind of talk. You make me score your performance. 'How was my takeoff?' you ask, and 'Did you notice my clean entry?' When the other kids are around and you talk crazy like that, everybody knows you're just showing off but no one cares much because we're letting them use our pool after all and also because it looks kinda pretty, the way you dive. I wish I could dive like that and I'm real proud of you. 'Ten out of ten,' I say.

In June, a shadow falls over our most excellent summer. Mom gets a call from Kansas and starts bawling. Then Dad takes us aside and explains that Grandpa Shirland has passed away.

'You mean he's dead,' you say and Dad says yeah, that's what he means.

We feel sad about that, but Mom is *really* sad. We try to cuddle her and make her feel better but she doesn't want to be cuddled. When she and Dad fly out for the funeral, they leave us behind in our new home and Dad arranges for his receptionist Zoe Eichelberger – who is actually Zoe Micklebaum but she isn't

called that because she hasn't met her husband-to-be Felix yet –
to house-sit and take care of us. (We don't call it baby-sitting
because we aren't babies, of course.)

We think Zoe's pretty airheaded and don't much like having
her around. She giggles a lot and tries to pretend like she's
young too and really cool and one of us.

'Imagine,' she tells us, 'if I were you guys' big sis, my name'd
be Zoe Ziegler!'

And we also don't like Zoe Eichelberger not just because she
says stupid things like that but because she's creepy and a
couple of times we find her in Mom and Dad's room rummaging
through their things.

Mom and Dad fly back home after a week or so, bringing
Grandma Shirland with them. She stays over in one of our new
guest rooms for a month. She seems real sad too, like Mom, but
she lets us cuddle her. During the day, she likes to sit out in the sun
on one of the new cushioned loungers while we swim and dive
or whatever in the pool. Dad shouts at us to keep it down but
Grandma hushes him up and says no, she likes to watch us play.

CHAPTER THIRTY-ONE

You always said I was the strong one. The joke was that the only reason you came out first was because I kicked you. You've been kicking me ever since, you used to say, meaning it in a nice way like when you called me retard because I couldn't tell the time from my Swatch. You meant I was always there for you, sticking up for you, protecting you. I think that's what you meant. 'You're strong, Justine,' you'd say when I needed a pep talk, maybe before an exam or tryouts for a school production or a big basketball game or maybe before I was going to ask Davie Kirchner to the Sadie Hawkins dance. 'You're unbeatable.'

But I don't feel so strong any more, Joshua, I don't feel unbeatable in here.

I'm not sure how or why exactly it starts, but when it starts, it doesn't stop. I have been in the programme for seventy-seven days, and I'm lying on another mattress on another floor in another host home. I start to cry and I can't stop.

The next day in the programme Dwight stands me up and asks me why I'm crying. I scan the boys' section. Rows and rows of boys. Their lily-white, clean-shaven faces. I examine each one with their stony, impassive expressions. You are not there. Your face is not in the crowd.

I tell Dwight I don't know why I'm crying.

That night I get doled out to Gwen. She screams at me to stop. She calls me a cry baby and she doesn't mean like Christy, she doesn't mean it in a nice way. I can't eat her mother's meat loaf, sloppy joes in disguise, because I can't stop crying long enough to chew and swallow. In the night, when Gwen can't sleep because of my sobbing, she leaps on my mattress and pummels me.

'I hate fucking cry babies!' she shrieks.

I feel weak for all the crying and not eating, I've got a constant headache. My nose runs and they won't give me any Kleenex to wipe it with. I've rubbed my eyes so much I mustn't have any eyelashes left, and they're raw at the corners where the salt collects and they sting. My whole face stings and burns and feels bloated with tears.

On the third day, Hilary's leading the afternoon rap with Dwight, and my crying's at the top of the agenda. Hilary decides it's a good thing.

'I'm glad you're finally getting in touch with your feelings,' she tells me. 'I think this shows real progress.'

'Real progress,' echoes Dwight, though he doesn't sound as optimistic.

'Facing up to addiction can be very emotionally debilitating, Justine, but we all have to experience it in order to come through the other side towards recovery.'

I sob.

'I think the reason you're crying is because you're in mourning for your old druggie life. You have to say goodbye to it now, let go, and that's sad.' She lowers her chin and tries to fix me with a sympathetic look. 'And hopefully, you're also beginning to grieve for the hurt and the pain you've caused, to others, like your parents, but also to yourself. Hmm?'

'I don't know,' I wail.

'Sure about that? I think deep down you do know. I believe you're starting to face up to some very tough realities, you're beginning to realise your own powerlessness. It's not a nice feeling to feel powerless, is it?'

'No.'

'But if you admit your powerlessness and understand that that's OK, understand that your situation has become too unmanageable for you to deal with on your own, you can make your First Step. Then you can yield to your Higher Power and join us all on our journey to recovery, to a better life. Let go and let God, Justine. That would be nice now, wouldn't it?'

'I don't know.'

'You don't? Well, let's think it through. Do you feel powerless?'

'Yes.'

'Do you feel that your life has become unmanageable?'

'Yes.'

'So you're admitting that you are an addict.'

'No.'

'No?' Hilary juts her bottom lip out and sighs so that her bangs ruffle round her face. 'But don't you see, Justine, powerlessness and unmanageability are the telltale traits of addiction. Don't you see?'

'This is getting us nowhere,' says Dwight.

'OK,' Hilary starts again. 'Let's try it another way, Justine. Why don't you tell us in your own words where you are with yourself?'

I sob.

'I think it would be good for you and for the group if you

shared with us what you're experiencing at this moment. Feeling words only please, not thinking ones.'

I scan the boys' rows. They're arranged in blocks today, scores of three across. I cry and shake my head.

Dwight intervenes. 'Tell us why you're crying,' he demands. 'Tell us, now.'

He leaps off his chair and starts to pace, slapping his thighs impatiently. 'Maybe I can make a few guesses – how about that? Is that what you'd like, Justine? Would you like me to guess why you're crying?'

Today Dwight is wearing a white button-down Oxford shirt and Calvin Klein jeans that fit him like a kitchen glove. Even with my blurred vision, I notice how the shirt shows off the tanning-salon brownness of his skin. I wonder if Dwight's ever shed a tear in his life.

'Now let me see, are ya crying because you miss your mommy and daddy? No? Are ya crying because you miss all your little druggie buddies? Or maybe you miss all your little high-school parties, all your little sock hops in the school gymnasium? I bet you were real popular at your school. Pretty little thing like you, you musta been real popular, especially with the boys. Did ya reckon you might be voted prom queen maybe by all those admirers of yours? Is that what it is? And now you're crying because you're not going to be wearing any crown? Is that why you're crying?'

I sob and shake my head.

'No?' Dwight steeples his fingers beneath his chin and pretends to ponder my wretched state for a moment. 'So it's nothing to do with your pathetic popularity parade. Hmm. Let me think. Now I wonder. Could it be about your *brother*? Could it be about little ole *Joshua*?'

I order myself to turn off the tears at once. I try to breathe deep, to regulate.

'I'm getting warm, aren't I? I think I may have hit a nerve. Yep, I think this here crying jag's all about that brother of yours.'

If I can just stop crying, then he won't have any need to continue with this line of questioning. But my lungs refuse to let me take in more than short, sharp gasps and my eyes won't stop streaming.

Dwight rounds in front of me, places a finger beneath my chin and lifts my face towards his. 'Now tell us, Justine, why do ya want to waste perfectly good saline on that good-for-nothing twin of yours?'

'Leave her alone!' someone shouts from the other side of the room. I wipe my eyes and train them on the row where the voice came from. It's the Gunther High football star, Toby S. The farting one.

'Leave her alone,' Toby S says again. 'Can't you see she's upset enough?'

'Toby, you need to motivate to be able to talk before the group,' Hilary cautions. The rest of the group motivates to respond to Toby S's indiscretion.

'But, she's already crying, you can't make her cry any more.'

Two fifth-phase sentries take a step towards Toby S. 'Thank you, Toby, your input is noted, but you haven't earned Talk privileges and they haven't been requested.'

'But—'

'Sit down!' growls Dwight. 'We'll deal with you later.'

Toby S retakes his seat and the group returns their gawping to me. They cease motivating and concentrate on the show at hand. I'm still crying.

'Where were we, Justine?' Dwight begins. 'Yes, we were

talking about that snivelling little brother of yours. Are ya crying about Joshua, Justine? How sweet is that? Crying over your twin? Are ya crying because he was an addict? Or maybe you were crying because he was a fairy? Is that it?'

I raise my hands like a shield.

Fairies you used to say, when you meant fireflies, which you loved to chase and catch and make palm lanterns with. Fairies you called them because you misheard what Dad said when you witnessed them lighting up the midsummer night sky and asked him what they were. Fairies, you thought, like Tinkerbell.

'We *are* getting warm, aren't we?' Dwight insists. 'You already told us you weren't ashamed to have a faggot for a brother so it's got to be something more than that. Let's see. Are ya crying because Joshua was a rent boy? Did ya even know that?'

Through a veil of tears, my eyes widen in disbelief. Don't listen, Josh, don't listen.

'Oh yes, it's true. How do ya think a teenage boy supports himself when he runs away to Florida, when he's living on the street in Miami? He gets paid by drug runners and *Cubans* for sex, that's how. He gets paid to suck them off, twenty bucks apiece for sucking off illegal immigrant dick. And thirty bucks apiece for letting them shaft him up the ass. Thirty measly dollars. Is that why you're crying, Justine? Because your saintly twin's ass is only worth thirty fucking dollars?'

Don't listen, please don't hear this any more. I close my eyes and see you in Miami where you live with your nice English boyfriend Jonathan in a pastel-coloured Art Deco apartment, where it's warm and safe and wonderful, where the sun shines 365 days a year, where nobody minds if you dress up like Audrey Hepburn. Where there are fireflies and fairies for the catching.

'But ya know what I reckon? I reckon sometimes he wouldn't even take the money, I reckon sometimes he paid those slimy Cuban cunts out of his own pocket because he loved it so much.'

'No,' I plead. 'No more.'

'*Why are you crying!?*' Dwight shouts.

'I don't know.'

'Tell us, goddammit!'

'I don't know,' I wail. 'Please, I don't know.'

Dwight launches himself at me. He slaps me hard across the cheek, backslapping me across the other cheek with the same motion, then he grabs me by my shoulders and shakes me.

'Dwight!' gasps Hilary, but he pays her no heed.

'Tell us, I said, you fucking bitch, you fucking tell me right fucking now because I can't listen to any more of your sorry, sad, fucking weeping.' He shakes me and shakes me, hard like you shake a candy machine when your Kit Kat gets stuck in the dispenser whirligig and you haven't got another fifty cents. He shakes me so hard I think my neck might snap. 'Tell us ya—'

'Leave her alone, you asshole!'

Toby S charges across the room and tackles Dwight before the sentries have clocked him. I lose my balance when Dwight goes down and I fall to the floor, too, but away from the two of them. Toby S lands a good punch or two before four or five oldcomers are on top of him, restraining him with every muscle in their bodies. Hilary blows on her whistle, blows and blows until the scuffle ceases. When they get him to his feet, Toby S is bleeding, his face resembling a vegetable, like how Dad likes to mash up tomatoes before he makes fresh juice.

Dwight jumps to his feet and makes another lunge for Toby S. One of the fifth phasers intervenes and tries to restrain him, too, and Dwight passes him a look of pure fury so that fifth phaser's in no doubt that he'll live to regret that move.

Hilary whistles again, causing Dwight to calm down some and back off. He squares his shoulders, tucks his shirt-tails into his pants and smoothes his hair.

'Leroy, take Toby S into the solitaire room to cool off,' Hilary orders and Toby S is led away. 'Justine, pick yourself up.'

I'm still on the floor with my sobs. I wobble to my feet.

'Yes,' Dwight resumes. 'Where were we?'

'I think that's enough, Dwight.'

'No, Hilary, let's continue, we're obviously very close.' He replants himself in front of me. 'Tell us, Justine. Let's just cut to the chase. The reason you're crying is quite simple.'

'Dwight, I think it's time we—'

'The reason you're crying is because that shirt-lifter brother of yours, that brother you love so very much, that brother of yours—'

'Dwight, really—'

'That brother of yours is *burning in*—'

The whistle blares loud enough to shatter crystal. Several group members jump.

'Dwight!' screams Hilary. 'That is *quite* enough!'

He shoots me a scorching look then faces her. 'But we're about to break her, Hilary.'

'That's not necessary.'

'We're so close.'

'That's not necessary, I said. That's enough for today.'

'But—'

'Dwight, *let's move on*.' There's a note of finality in her voice and her mouth is ironed out into one straight flat line. 'Justine, you may sit down.'

CHAPTER THIRTY-TWO

At twelve, we become the first kids in our class to get braces. It doesn't come as any surprise. It's to be expected really considering our dad's the town's only orthodontist, but we don't have to like it.

Dad lectures us on the importance of straight teeth. According to Dad, it's the right – nay, the duty – of all upstanding citizens to have perfect, pearly-white, straight teeth. Crooked, yellowing teeth are for people who live in trailers and don't bother to floss or pay tax.

Zoe Micklebaum greets us at the door of Dad's practice on the appointed day. She's changed from Eichelberger to Micklebaum because she's married now. Zoe tries to reassure us about the procedure. She tells us not to worry, that our dad's the best orthodontist in the world and that getting those pesky braces put on won't hurt a bit. We're not dumb enough to believe a word of it. She says that, afterwards, we can choose whatever we want out of the Treasure Chest which is just a cardboard boxful of cheap plastic toys – sliding puzzles, imitation Rubik's Cubes, leaky squirt guns and skeleton-man key rings left over from Halloween.

You go in first – or is it me? One of us goes while the other waits in reception flipping through two-year-old copies of *People* magazine and watching Zoe Micklebaum dust photos of goofball Felix in a Sly-Stallone-as-Rocky-Balboa T-shirt with the sleeves ripped off. The one in reception hears the one inside make gagging noises and strangled groans.

Then we switch places and the one of us in the dentist's chair squirms, makes noises and tries to catch Dad's eyes above his mask to get him to stop, stop please. The cementing-on of the braces isn't the hard part, it's what comes after. Dad laces the wires through the metal brackets while our lips go dry and cracked. The wire slashes at the insides of our cheeks as the vacuum sucks up all our spit. And the very worst is what comes after that. The tightening. Dad tightens and tightens the wire so much it feels like our teeth are going to shatter.

And you swear he enjoys it. You can't see his mouth behind the mask but, you whisper to me afterwards, you can tell by the way his eyes slant that Dad's smiling as he does it.

When we come out, we both have puffy eyes and cheeks and look so hateful that Zoe Micklebaum forgets to dole out miniaturised snow storms or plastic handcuffs from the Treasure Chest. We're convinced Dad didn't inject us with enough Novocaine because the pain's so excruciating. Our gums itch, our jaws ache, our teeth are splintering.

Then Dad lays down the rules for taking care of our braces. We have to wear our headgear every night for at least eight hours and he checks that ours are taut enough. We have to floss with a special loopy gizmo to ensure we reach in between the braces and behind all the wires, and we have to use the water pick religiously because he's bought it special. Seems like an awful lot of bother, and once Dad finally leaves us alone to nurse our sore mouths, we grumble in private.

You say maybe people with crooked teeth aren't so stupid after all and I laugh for the first time that day.

CHAPTER THIRTY-THREE

Dwight doesn't want to forgive me for my part in his public dressing-down and he's not about to let me forget it either. Or Toby S for that matter. Dwight lets into him as soon as he returns to the group, about a day or so after their scuffle, and he doesn't make any concessions for Toby's worse-for-wear condition.

The group falls silent when Toby's belt-looped back into the fold. He's a shuffling bruise. His skin has exploded like a fireworks display into shades of reds, purples, blacks and blues, and he has a fearsome scratch mark that runs the length of his face, from his left temple to his chin. He may have stitches above one of his eyebrows, the right one, though it's hard for me to distinguish exactly from across the room. They can't be big stitches, probably just a few of the kind that dissolve into your skin after a few days, like the ones Dad uses for gum surgeries. He's limping, too, and every move he makes is made gingerly; even when he shifts about in his chair trying to find a comfortable position, he does so with extreme care.

As soon as Toby's settled, though, Dwight pulls him back on to his feet and tears in without any consideration for Toby's condition. He starts screaming about Toby's anger management problem. He says such temper tantrums are a sign of addiction, that anger itself can be addiction, that violence is never called for in any case. He says violence is the refuge of weak minds and will not be tolerated.

He tells Toby S that, contrary to what he might like to think based on his hero image of himself, he hasn't helped me one iota. If anything, says Dwight, Toby has harmed me, maybe irreparably, that he has set back my recovery by at least a month. He says what Toby did was selfish and hurtful, mean and manipulative, not in my best interest at all. He makes Toby stand in front of the whole group and deliver a grovelling apology which he makes me stand up to receive. Only the apology's not so coherent because Toby's lip is swollen and I suspect his tongue is, too, so he can't talk so well yet.

I'm not crying any more. I want to tell Toby S to keep his empty amends and not to listen to a word of what Dwight's spouting. I want to tell him that what he did was the kindest, bravest, noblest thing anyone has done for me, maybe ever. What he did, I want to say, was the only nice thing that's happened to me since the day I woke up with my first hangover and wound up in hell. I want to skip across the room, kiss him and say, I'm the one who should be apologising to you for getting you into this mess. *I* should be thanking *you*. But all I can do is listen to Toby's garbled apology and say, apology accepted.

Dwight keeps on at Toby S nonstop after that. According to Dwight, everything Toby does and everything Toby says is a sign of his disrespect, wilfulness, self-hatred or anger problem or whatever.

He doesn't forget me, either. With me, though, Dwight watches himself more in group. Particularly when Hilary's the co-leader. He doesn't come in too close, doesn't attack me quite so ferociously. And he doesn't mention you.

But the punishments continue. More and more often, I'm told I need to carry out my atonement exercises in one of the solitaire rooms so I don't disrupt the group. My stepladdering or writing or memorising has become a distraction the rest of the group can ill afford. So they hide me away and lock the door.

Moira worries. She says it's rare for a person to be isolated from the group so much. She tells me to watch my back, I'm winning enemies. Like who?

Some of the fifth phasers don't like my attitude, she confides. They think I'm stuck-up, too big for my boots. I know she means Gwen and say as much. Moira doesn't yes or no that. 'She's desperate to be taken seriously, she wants to be a counsellor herself someday,' she observes instead. 'Gwen's fourteen going on forty.'

Fourteen. A year *younger* than me.

'Do you think they'll let her be a counsellor?'

'Sure, Gwen's got a lot going for her. She's had a bumpy ride, you know. But she's tough, and she's come a long way through her programme.'

What's Gwen's story, I ask. Moira chews her tongue, thinking, then she spells the word out like she can't even stand to say it. I – N – C – E – S – T.

I recall the small pleasurable pity I took from Gwen's expansive belly and her Franklin Mint-sized nipples. And I remember her dark and wearied father, how the men at his manufacturing plant thought he was a good-for-nothing. I think of the two of them together with the permed mother mixing her sloppy joe concoctions in the next room and little Trish sulking in front of the TV. It all seems sordid, sad, pathetic. Maybe Gwen deserves to be able to Hitler them about. And I feel a little guilty.

But then I think of the force of Gwen's tugging on my belt loop, the way she sneers at me, how she tosses her ponytail in my face, and I remember when she pummelled me to stop me crying. Incest or not, I don't like her.

'What about Hilary?' I ask Moira.

'What about her?'

'Is she an enemy too?'

Moira wheezes. 'Gosh, no. Hilary's one of the good guys.'

I tell her I'm not so sure about that.

'Believe me, she is. You can trust Hilary, all she wants to do is help.'

'I don't know what to believe any more.'

Moira squeezes my arm and tells me that what I *have* to believe is that it will get better. And it *will,* she assures me, if I would only be a little less stubborn. If I would just play along, Moira says, my life would be so much easier.

What she means is I've got to lie, pretend I'm an addict.

'Just tell them what they want to hear,' that's the way she puts it.

'I can't.'

'What harm can it do?'

'I just can't.'

'If you say you're an addict, you'll be able to see your parents,' she urges. 'If you just say it, you can get out of here one day. They're never going to release you if you don't, you know.'

Moira has a way of always sounding reasonable. Often she's right, too. I hope she's not right this time. I hope, but I still can't bring myself to say it.

'I can't say it because it's not true.'

'Who cares about the truth any more? Just say it. I. Am. An. Addict. Four words, how hard can it be to say four little words?'

But they're four words too many.

Moira throws her arms out in exasperation before offering some final advice: try and not piss Dwight off any more. 'Dwight is the last person you want as an enemy.'

CHAPTER THIRTY-FOUR

But Dwight is already an enemy and his enmity towards me grows and grows. With each confrontation, with each new round of punishment, it gets bigger and stronger.

Sometimes, during my punishments, the staff leave me in the solitaire room so long I think they've thrown away the keys and forgotten about me. Other times I hear the jailer's rattle on the other side of the door, then Dwight enters, sits himself in a corner and watches me. Just watches, hardly says a word, hardly seems to breathe. And I think I'd prefer it if they did throw away the keys.

Then one day Dwight comes in and starts talking.

It's mid-morning and I've been charged with learning the Serenity Prayer down to my bones because that's the only way I'll ever be able to achieve inner peace. I'm supposed to learn it by writing it one hundred times – or more, if they say so.

Bo installed a chalkboard in the solitaire room especially for my new penance. He gave me a handful of chalk, too, but all of the pieces are only little nub ends like the ones Melanie Heath used to collect for us to draw Hopscotch squares with during recess. I hold the chalk like a pincer with my fingernails and I'm on maybe prayer number sixty-seven by the time Dwight arrives.

Drawing his seat up, he's quiet and breathless for a while. Then he starts reading aloud what I'm writing.

'God, grant me the serenity to accept the things I cannot change, the courage to change the things I can, and the wisdom to know the difference.' He pauses. 'It's a beautiful prayer, isn't it?'

I bow my head in agreement without turning round.

Dwight comes up behind me, close. He presses against my back and I can smell his cologne. Polo, or maybe Brut or Old Spice for all I know about men's colognes. He reaches his arm under mine for the eraser.

'Ah, but Justine, you've made a mistake.' He swipes the eraser through Serenity. 'You've misspelled Serenity. Rewrite it, please.'

So I rewrite it just as it was before: S – E – R – E – N – I – T – Y.

'That's wrong,' Dwight says, 'the second "e" should be an "i".'

'No.' A slight quaver in my voice. 'I don't think so, in fact I know so. It's an "e", definitely.'

He lingers for a minute, his chin almost resting into the hollow of my shoulder bone, and it's me who doesn't breathe. Then he takes a step back and I hear the door behind me. I release the air from my lungs and keep writing.

Five minutes later, Dwight returns with a dictionary. He sidles up next to me so that I can glimpse him out of the corner of my eye. I keep writing. He flips quickly through the book until he finds his place, then snakes his finger down the page as he scans words and definitions. He slams the dictionary shut and flings it on to the floor.

His lip curls. 'You were going to college, weren't ya, Justine Z? Only a sophomore, right, and I bet you'd already picked out the school ya wanted to go to. Some Ivy League shit hole, no doubt, that Mommy and Daddy were going to pay through the nose for.

Or no, I'm wrong, you were too smart for that. Smartass little girl like you. You were probably all set to get a scholarship. Am I right?'

I lift a shoulder noncommittally and keep writing. God grant me the serenity...

He pulls over his chair and continues to address my profile. 'Me, I never once expected to go to college. Nobody else expected it either. I wasn't exactly an academic dynamo I guess ya could say. Nobody really expected anything much of me. Not until the programme anyway.'

Dwight stretches his arms above his head then folds them into the back of his neck so his elbows stick out either side of his ears like butterfly wings. 'Come Clean now has facilities in seventeen states. Did ya know that? It's the fastest growing drug treatment programme for teenagers in the whole country. That's something, isn't it?' He whistles in appreciation. 'I went through the programme down at the centre in Tennessee? Course my parents couldn't afford the fees, I was a charity case I guess. But the director down there, he never once regretted admitting me. I was his star phaser. Do ya know, to this day, I hold the record for the fastest time ever through the Seven Steps? Less than six months. One hundred and sixty-seven days.'

Dwight snorts. 'My God, in the amount of time you've been assing around in here, I was like on fourth phase already.'

Once or twice I catch the chalkboard with my fingernail and it makes that awful bleating noise. It's so impossible to write with these little chalk nubs... the courage to change...

'Then, when I graduated, I became a trainee counsellor down there. And ya know what, I was good at it. How about that? I was the best staffer they ever had at the Tennessee centre, the best they'll ever have. When I made full-fledged counsellor, I got my picture in the paper. Imagine. Little ole me, a celebrity.' He whistles again, through his teeth this time, his lips stretched thin. 'And then I came here.'

Dwight surveys the dingy room as if it were his kingdom. The dictionary's still on the floor and he stamps on its cover. 'Mark my words, within a year, I'll be the director here. A director, ya hear me. On her next visit, Nancy Just-Say-No Reagan is going to have to come and lick *my* ass. And do ya know how old I am, Miss Justine Z?'

It's not, I sense, a rhetorical question.

'Go on, guess,' he dares.

'Twenty-four?'

'I'm *twenty*.' He waits again, letting the audacity of his youth make its impression. 'Not even actually – twenty years old at my next birthday. Twenty and soon-to-be head honcho of a huge business. Not many college boys and girls could claim that, could they? Most of them wouldn't even be out of their classes and frat parties by twenty.'

I keep writing: the wisdom to know...

'Course, officially, Hilary's the programme director – *for now*,' Dwight continues. 'But that's just about in name only. Everybody knows I'm the one who really runs the show. I'm the one who keeps things on track round here. Everybody knows that.'

Dwight pushes himself to his feet and karate-chops my wrist, knocking the chalk to the floor. My eyes trail it to where it rolls to a stop next to the dictionary, its spine well and truly broken. He flicks my chin up with his thumb, like he was performing a lighter trick.

'*Everybody*,' he reiterates. 'And those who don't, oughtta. Even little college girls.'

He leaves another shoeprint on the dictionary cover on his way out, and he tells me to start my prayer penance over from one, using the 'correct' spelling of serenity: S – E – R – I – N – I – T – Y.

CHAPTER THIRTY-FIVE

One morning after a night at Moira's house when I've been tossing and turning into the small hours, Moira enquires if I might be coming down with something.

'Not coming down, just down,' I reply.

She tells me to check my M.I. notebook. 'There might be something there to change your mood,' she suggests. I hope she's not making some reference to self-knowledge or inner peace because I know there's nothing I've written in that stupid notebook worth a hill of beans.

But I flip through it as I'm told and when I flip to the back, I see a note tucked into the pages. I know straight away it's not mine because it's written in red ink and of course I recognise it's not my own handwriting anyway.

'Cheer up. I'm watching you, too.' The note's signed, 'Toby S, Your G.A.' and a doodle of a happy face.

Toby. My face hurts because I'm smiling like the doodle and I haven't smiled in so long. 'What's a G.A.?' I ask Moira, but she doesn't know.

She lets me reread the note a few times and savour it, then she says, 'You can't keep it, Justine. You've got to destroy it. Eat it or wipe your ass with it and flush it down the toilet, I don't care. But you can't keep it. If anybody finds it, we'll all be in deep shit.'

With that first note, Toby S gives me something new to think about, something nice. I'm grateful for that. Whenever images of Dwight float around in my head, I fixate on Toby even harder – his face, the slope of his handwriting, the sound of his voice.

You'd like Toby S, Josh, honest you would. Of course I don't know as much about him as I'd want to, seeing as how we've never actually spoken directly, but I gather what I can from the raps and Open Meetings.

I remember when he first arrived, a month or so ago. They brought him into the group before they buzzed him and he was sporting this spiky Billy Idol hairdo with a streak of Astroturf green in it. He was wearing an earring too, just a little stud, but I could see it clear as you like all the same, even though I was sitting on the other side of the room. Dwight whipped that out pretty damn fast and the oldcomer who searched Toby got a huge telling off. By the next day, Toby's green hair had gone the way of the earring and he was sporting the same clipped short crew cut as all the boy phasers, looking like they were assembled for a 1950s yearbook photo. They all look like throwbacks from *Back to the Future* or something and I dread to think how we girls, seated across from them, must appear.

Toby's a jock all right. Dad would talk to him about game plays or the Rose Bowl or the Pittsburgh Steelers. Toby S was on the Gunther High football team and they *did* go to State last season. And he's big and muscular, looks like he's really in shape. But you'd like Toby too because he's not your typical jock. How many jocks do you know with green hair and an earring? How

241

many jocks do you know who'd stand up for me the way Toby S did? Who'd get the shit kicked out of them like that?

He's still showing some bruises from his fight with Dwight. For the first couple of Open Meetings after that, his skin colourations were so shocking the staff made a point of seating him in the very back row of the boys' section, directly behind Fred T, one of the tallest phasers in the programme. I think they powdered his face too so the parents wouldn't notice. The bruises are mostly faded now and his skin is kind of yellowy in patches, jaundice-like, or overcooked as Mom would say, like she used to tell us we looked when we were newborn.

Toby's really not your typical stupid jock at all. He's like a cross between a jock and Simon le Bon from Duran Duran. He's a *hybrid* – that's the word for it – like we learnt in fifth grade in Miss Bedlow's botany lesson.

In addition to being a football star, Toby S was a senior at Gunther High and the word is he had a scholarship to go play ball at some Midwestern college in the fall. He'd be graduating about now if he was still back at Gunther. Can you believe that? His parents yanked him out of school and threw him into this place a month before he was going to graduate.

Toby's seventeen now but, if he should be graduating, he must be eighteen soon. He looks eighteen. I figured that once you were eighteen they wouldn't be able to keep you in here, legally they shouldn't be able to keep you once you're of age. But Moira says that's not the case. If your parents consent to admitting you while you're still a minor, they can keep you in here for as long as they like, she says. I don't understand how that can be and Moira isn't for sure either but that's the way it is. There are lots of kids in Come Clean who are eighteen, she tells me, or even older.

Toby S has a younger sister. I think she must be about our age. I don't know what her name is, but I know she's his sister because she always stands up with his parents when the mike comes round to them during Open Meetings.

I like being watched by Toby S. I can feel his eyes on me and it's not a bad thing, not like the kind of watched I feel from Dwight, Gwen, Hilary or the oldcomers. It's a nice watchfulness. Toby's watching over me, that's it. I feel protected.

He winks at me sometimes when he's watching, and he's got this smile he smiles and there's something about it that makes me know it's just for me.

Josh, you'd like Toby S. For sure you would. We could hang out and become friends, play like the Three Musketeers, watch over each other and all sorts.

CHAPTER THIRTY-SIX

Everything changes when we're thirteen.

We have our braces removed, just as everyone else in our class is getting mouths full of metal and telling us how much they despise our father. With us, Dad lays down the rules of orthodontic aftercare and impresses upon us the importance of wearing retainers.

'It takes just one week of neglecting your retainer to undo a year's worth of professional craftsmanship,' he says, and we figure he's probably exaggerating but it's not really worth testing whether or not he is. He gives us the straight teeth lecture again and even you're inclined to agree that your smile looks pretty good, when you make the effort to smile.

But the braces are just the beginning. We're changing in other ways too, radically so. It's becoming obvious, even to us – let alone doofus Wayne Westbrook who has slipped two grades behind us now – that you and I are not identical. More and more, we resemble each other less and less. My chest's filling out and you shoot up like a beanstalk, get acne and look like you don't know what to do with your arms and legs any more.

We start to behave differently, too. We like different things. I clip photographs of cute boys and Laura Ashley floral dresses out of copies of *Young Miss* and cover the walls of my room with them. And I begin to spend a lot more time with Mom and Cindy Gregory and you don't like that much. Mom takes me to have my hair cut and I get it fashioned in the style of Princess Diana. She tells me I look like a princess and that makes me feel good because I remember, when we stayed up all night to watch the royal wedding on TV, I remember how pretty Di was. I find magazine photos of her and put them on my walls too.

You spend a tot of time in your room on your own, acting miserable and grouchy. And you don't wash your hair much. When you do come out, you do stupid things like chug a can of Sprite and then burp loudly, and think it's funny.

Mom takes me shopping for make-up and new clothes. Soon, almost my entire wardrobe is Esprit or Benetton, the coolest brands on the planet, and Mom shows Cindy and me how to paint our fingernails. In private, she helps me shave my legs, too. And she says when summer comes around she'll show me how to shave other bits so I can wear my bathing suit in front of the boys and not get embarrassed.

At church one Sunday, I feel sick so I run off to the bathroom where, when I pull down my underwear, I find blood. I know it's my period because other girls in my class have already started theirs and I see them with their thick maxi-pads in PE. But I don't have any maxi-pads, I don't know what to do. The blood's already saturated my panties and soaked through my pantyhose. I'm scared if I stand up and walk about any more, it'll stain my dress too and everyone will see.

I hide in the bathroom for the duration of the service and I'm still there afterwards when the rest of the congregation has retired to the communion hall to nibble on Oreos and sip coffee from Styrofoam cups. Dad's deep in conversation with the minister or someone from the Lion's Club or whoever and Mom must be comparing recipes with Mrs Gregory, Cindy's mom. But you're kicking around bored and wondering what's become of me. After a while, you sneak into the ladies' room.

I've locked myself into one of the cubicles and am bawling.

'Just, is that you?' you call out. 'What's the matter with you?'

You sound really worried. I tell you to go away.

'Don't be like that,' you say. 'Tell me what's wrong.'

You jiggle the handle to my cubicle and I shriek not to come in here, don't even think about it, goddammit.

'I'm only trying to help.'

I tell you you can't help. I order you to go away and send Mom in.

Mom knows just what to do. We stop at the Eckhard drugstore on the way home from church to purchase feminine products and, when we get home, Mom demonstrates how to use them, then slips me a Tylenol for my cramps and tucks me in bed.

You're hurt that I sent you away and, while I'm napping, Mom attempts to pacify you. She tells you not to be so hard on me, I've had a rough day. But when you snap back that you've had a rough day, too, what makes mine so much more of a hardship, she tells you it's women's stuff and you wouldn't understand. You don't like not understanding.

The final straw comes when Davie Kirchner asks me to go steady and I say yes. You enquire if Davie is my Prince Charles and get so mad at me even though I say no he isn't and Davie and I only wind up going steady for about a month anyway. You tell me I don't care about you any more, that I'd rather hang out with Mom or Cindy or now Davie. You say I spend too much time doing 'women's stuff', scratching quote marks in the air as if it were some newfangled invention that didn't even have a proper name.

I'm going to defend myself, tell you you're being stupid and to stop complaining. But then I see how upset you are. So I apologise. I tell you there's no one in the world I'd rather hang out with than you. I say the door's open if you want to join me and Cindy when we paint our nails, curl our hair or dance around to Madonna.

But you aren't convinced. You say you don't know that and I don't mean it anyway. You gulp down Sprite and burp loudly. Then you sling the can on the kitchen floor, storm off to your room and slam the door.

CHAPTER THIRTY-SEVEN

My name's not called one evening during roll and dole call. I wait as other newcomers are picked off by their senior phasers. Toby S kicks me on his way past to the coat pile by the door. He makes it appear like an accident and nobody but me notices him wink.

It's spring now, early May I'd guess, so there aren't many coats in the pile. A few windbreakers and a wraparound shawl. Some people, including Toby, venture out into the parking lot wearing only their shirts.

I don't know what to do and am thinking perhaps someone has made a mistake. Eventually, Lois comes for me. She says I've been charged with a new penance and that, because there was no time during the afternoon rap to take me aside, I have to complete it now. She leads me into a solitaire room and hands me an *Encyclopaedia Britannica*. It's the deluxe edition with the cover that's gold and has a raised bubbly texture, like the set Dad bought for us from the door-to-door salesman when we were in the third grade. He told us we needed to expand our minds, which we did every time we had a report to write for school, before we knew what plagiarism meant. It's a thick volume, too. The letter M.

Lois instructs me to hold the encyclopaedia above my head with my arms fully extended. This is to signify that I'm holding up my receiving of knowledge. When I'm prepared to accept my own powerlessness, she says, I'll be ready to bring the book back down to my bosom and embrace knowledge.

'There's no greater gift than the gift of self-knowledge.' Until then, I must keep the encyclopaedia, volume M, up, up, up! 'And don't even think about not doing it,' Lois warns me. 'Remember, *someone* is always watching.' She points to a godsquad needlepoint hanging on the wall as she leaves, locking the door behind her. 'One Day at a Time', it reads.

Does she mean our Higher Power observes everything we do or that there's a camera behind there? It doesn't look like the kind of picture that could hide a camera. It's not a picture at all, it's needlepoint. It can't hide a camera. Then again, I didn't see any tape recorder in the room that night with our parents, though my every word was recorded. I peer round me as if someone might jump out from behind the plastic folding chair that's the only piece of furniture in the room, and once satisfied they won't, I tiptoe over to the needlepoint for a closer examination. As I suspected, there's no camera and no peepholes cut into the plasterwork either.

I take a seat. To hell with holding up the knowledge.

To hell with it, that is, until later when I hear the jailer's rattle coming down the hall outside. I bound to my feet in double-quick time and have the encyclopaedia aloft before Hilary or Lois or Bo or whoever's on the other side of the door has got round to trying and failing with their second key choice. When the door opens, though, it's Dwight of course. He struts in and sits in the chair which I stupidly haven't thought to step far enough away from. He sits not three feet from me, smiling and letting me know that he feels the seat's still warm.

If I had my Swatch I could tell you near enough how much time passes while he sits there, making vigil over me, not saying a single solitary word. It feels like it must be an hour or so, but I know my arms aren't that strong and *Britannica's* 'M's are heavy. He studies me as the blood runs out of my whole upper body, my fingertips start to tingle, my hands shake, my elbows buckle, until my shoulders start to crack and it feels like my arms are going to snap clean off and leave me with nothing but a torso. When I can't take it any more and I lower the book for a millisecond to shake away the numbness in my limbs, Dwight tells me to remove my shoe.

'Pardon?'

'Your shoe, I told you to remove your shoe. And for every time you drop the book, you'll take off another item of clothing.'

My heart skips a beat or two or three. I think about screaming, but it's late and I'm certain everyone else must have already gone home for the evening. Dwight must know they've all left or he wouldn't be here, he must have waited until the coast was clear. I think about running, but he's locked the door. Even if I bashed him in the head with the encyclopaedia, managed to get the key off him and unlock the door while my fingers are still half dead and trembling, how far would I get? He's probably locked the outer doors, too, and I don't know where the keys are for those, and even if I did, how far would I get on the outside? Who'd be around to help me in this warehouse district in the middle of the night? If I could make it to a phone and call Cindy or Lloyd, I might have a chance, but I don't think I could.

'Do you understand, Justine?'

'Yes,' I reply and I remove my left shoe.

I can't look at Dwight because if I do, he'll see the fear in my

250

eyes. So I cast my gaze down and lift my arms up and I wonder why volume M's so heavy. Why is there so much to learn beginning with the letter M? I try to remember when we used to flip through our set of *Britannicas*, if we were cribbing for a school paper or even occasionally just to pass the time, like if it was raining outside and there was nothing good on TV and we were really bored. The A's were your favourite because you liked the pictures of angels and thought aardvarks were hilarious. My favourite was volume XYZ because I couldn't believe there were enough words beginning with any of those letters to warrant inclusion in a *Britannica*, even if it was only a third of a volume and the skinniest one as well. We spent time with M, too. Malaria, that's in volume M. That's a disease you get from mosquitoes, which are also in M, in African countries like Mozambique, another M entry. Miami, Florida, is in there, too, and I know that for sure because it was only last year that I looked that one up, but Miami's a terrible place to me now, I can't think of Miami.

I'm sweating. Beads of perspiration trickle down my arms, my neck, my back, they prick at the crux of my knees, at the top of my lip, at my hairline. They tweak hairs as they move and make me itch like I've got ants crawling all over me. I may go crazy if I can't scratch myself. Madness, that must be in volume M, too, and mental disorders. I'm not crying but a rivulet of sweat forms over my brow and runs down my cheek like a tear. Dwight wipes it away for me and I recoil, drop the book and lose my second shoe.

My attempts to sustain *Britannica* aloft and steady grow briefer as I tire. I can't feel my arms any more, I can't always tell whether I'm still holding the book or not. I only know for sure that I've dropped it when Dwight informs me it's time to take something else off.

Monsters is an M entry, too, as is mythology. I quiz myself to see if I can still remember the monsters we learnt when reading the myths in Mrs Mission's English class in the fourth grade. Or was it in Mr Newhouse's history class in fifth? Or was it sixth? Well. There's the Cyclops, of course, and the centaur, those are easy ones.

I roll down one sock and kick it off towards my shoes.

Then all the scary female creatures. The Gorgons, the Furies and Harpies. The Gorgons were the extra horrible ones, like Medusa, another M, who sprouted wings and had serpents for hair. Furies had wings too and, if I recall correctly, they also had serpents for hair, the difference being that there were only three of them and they were actually goddesses. They set out to punish evildoers.

Dwight orders me to remove my second sock.

And then the Harpies. They were really slimy things and you couldn't in all honesty call them women because, although they did have women's heads, they had bird's bodies. The Sphinx also had the head of a woman but its body was a lion's. The Sphinx was the one who posed the riddle and anybody who couldn't solve the riddle keeled over and died.

I step out of my chinos.

The Minotaur, another M, was a hateful beast. It lived in the labyrinth on the island of Crete, was half man, half bull and ate human flesh, though I don't know if it ate bull flesh, too, which would only seem fair.

I unravel my hair tie and my hair that's grown too long falls down around my shoulders and into my reddened face.

M. Mythological creatures of ancient Greece. Those Greeks had lots of monsters. There was also the Hydra. That was the nine-headed water snake and every time you managed to slice off one of its grotesque heads, two more would pop up in its place.

I unbutton my shirt.

Cerberus only had three heads but it was Hades' pet, guarding the gates to hell.

I unhitch my bra, which I was lucky enough to be given this morning. I experience a surge of gratitude for the hours of support and for the extra little delay that bra allowed me. But it's gone now, and I'm left standing in nothing but my cotton granny panties. I feel horrendously fat. Why does he want to see me like this anyway?

Dwight motions for me to raise the encyclopaedia again and I struggle to do so. He's out of his chair now and standing close enough for me to hear him breathing, close enough to know he had onions on his quarter-pounder with cheese at lunch.

I swallow the lump in my throat and wonder if Dwight knows about the chimera. I bet not. But I remember that one, too. The chimera was a cross between three animals. A *hybrid*. It had the head of a lion, the body of a goat and a tail like a serpent. It breathed fire.

Dwight wipes another finger through the sweat gathering beneath my left breast. He smells his finger then puts it in his mouth. Then he shoves his nose into the place between my breasts which would be cleavage if I were bigger and still wearing my bra. He inhales deeply through his nose. Do I still smell like me, Joshua?

'You're so dirty,' Dwight says hoarsely. 'You absolutely stink.' He grins. 'Ya know, Miss Justine, you smell to me like a filthy little whore.'

I drop the book. It lands on his foot, and Dwight jumps back, yelping. He massages his toe for a millisecond, checks nothing's broken, then springs forward and slaps me. He's wearing a ring today, an Irish Claddagh one, and it reverberates against my cheekbone. I can feel the slap resounding in my inner ear.

'You finished with your tricks?'

I nod.

'I'm glad to hear it.' With his good foot, he boots the encyclopaedia across the room, which I suppose signals the conclusion of that element of my self-knowledge exercise. He starts to circle me again, dragging his finger here and there, running his hands through my hair, sniffing where he pleases.

Mathematics is also in volume M of the *Encyclopaedia Britannica*. I've never been any good at math. Social studies, history, English, government, those are the subjects I excel in. I can never keep all my calculus and trigonometry and algebra terms straight. I can't remember the difference between a quotient and a coefficient and I don't know how to calculate either.

Dwight has his lips on my cheek and he kisses me at the point where his ring made contact. 'I would love to find out how good you are, little prom queen.'

I wish I could be the strong one again, Josh. I wish I could. I search for that part of me. My eyes still glued to the carpet, I clear my throat and think of how much I hate math. 'I didn't think you liked girls, Dwight,' I say in as steady a voice as I can manage.

That makes him slap me on the other cheek, only harder and with the back of his hand this time so that the edge of his Claddagh ring catches at my skin. It stings and I can't help but gasp and let my hand fly to my face to hold back the pain. There's blood. Not much, just a drop, but blood all the same.

'I thought you said you were finished with your tricks.'

I blink in rapid fashion, like a firefly fluttering its wings. 'I – I am.'

'I won't abide any more of your foolishness.'

'I-I-I'm not... playing... tricks,' I stammer. 'I just thought you liked boys, th-that's all.'

He moves as if to slap me again and I have to rush the next words off my tongue as I stumble back. 'I – I mean, you slept with Joshua, isn't that right? So, I just thought...'

Dwight quells his hand. He makes a noise. '*Your brother.*' The noise becomes a chuckle, soft and low. 'Well, you can't really hold that against me, can ya? He was such a pretty little thing. Like you.' He pries my bowed head up and holds my gaze. 'Hardly a boy at all, I'd say. Wouldn't you?'

His fingers and hands are everywhere again. I try to back away some more but there's nowhere left to retreat. I'm up against the wall and every time I flinch or turn a cheek, his fingers pinch harder. The layer of sweat that coats my body has turned cold and clammy.

'He did have a mouth on him, though, that twin of yours. Like you. I'd say you're almost identical in that way.'

I can't keep those bizarre mathematical symbols straight either. All those squiggles, lines, eights on their sides, 'U's turned the wrong way. It's like a completely different alphabet, like another language. And I've never been much good at foreign tongues either.

Dwight unzips his pants. He's wearing those faded jeans he loves so much, the ones that look like they're older than him. It doesn't seem right that he should be allowed to wear jeans when the rest of us can't. But that's a rule I can never forget – rules don't apply to staff.

He rifles his hand through my hair again and then starts to push my head down until I'm forced on to my knees. There's nowhere else to look now so I close my eyes. And there's no strength either. It's all sapped dry. I'm like a disempowered superhero on the Saturday morning cartoons. Once proud and powerful, reduced to this, weaker than mere mortals even. Dwight is my kryptonite.

'The thing is, though, your brother never wanted to put that big mouth of his to the right use. Joshua, I used to tell him, that mouth on you would be so much better on me.' Then Dwight makes me put my mouth on him and guides my head into motion.

I don't know what I'm doing. I've never done this before and I'm so scared that if I do it wrong he'll hit me again. Did you know how, Joshua? Did you like it? I don't like it at all, and it occurs to me that if I bite down I could really hurt him, but I'm trembling too much to do that. I try to open my mouth wide, draw my teeth back and let him move my head like he seems to want to.

I remember Pythagoras' theorem, though. Or at least what it is if not exactly how it works. We were just getting to that in Mrs Henery's class before Christmas. Pythagoras' theorem is the one relating to right-angled triangles. Actually, I don't remember exactly what it is. Something to do with squares and hypotenuses and how you can derive the sums of the sides of the triangles. I don't know.

Dwight seizes my hair and yanks me to my feet. He fondles my breasts and dips in to lick my neck. I think he'd like me to lick his neck, too, but I already have the taste of him in my mouth and I don't think I can stomach any more.

'Tell me how good you are, Justine,' he rasps into my ear. 'Tell me all the things you like to do with a man.'

'I – I don't know.'

'Go on, tell me all the good whorey stuff.'

'I can't...'

Dwight grits his teeth. 'Yes. You can.'

He doesn't seem to get my meaning. 'I don't know what to do,' I try again before confessing, 'I'm a virgin.'

He chuckles, the sound churning right back in the recesses of his mouth. 'And I'm supposed to believe that?'

'I *am*.'

He pulls back to measure my seriousness. 'Oh my,' he marvels and laughs aloud more heartily. 'All the better! Tell old Dwight the dirty stuff anyway, use your imagination.'

Equation is a mathematical term and so is diameter and algorithm and quotient. Coefficient, factor, circumference, variable and tangent, they're all mathematical terms. I couldn't define what they mean though I know circumference relates to circles. I can't think of any specific mathematical terms that begin with the letter M.

'I'm on my period,' I tell Dwight and that's the truth, but he eyes me suspiciously nonetheless. He only believes it once I've pulled down my panties, my last piece of clothing, and shown him I'm wearing a tampon. He tugs on the string for conclusive proof and my uterus jerks in terror.

'Well,' says Dwight, 'I guess we don't want to make too big a mess. Don't want to leave anything behind that we can't clear up.' He smiles. 'Next time,' he promises.

Then he forces me to go down on him again.

I'm not so strong but I can just about succeed in divorcing myself from my body. Not in the sense of floating above it or anything foolish like near-death patients prattle on about. I don't want to float above and see what's going on here. I want to live inside my mind with you and the *Encyclopaedia Britannica*, volume M.

Medicine is also in there, you know. So's marketing, so's magic, so are the Middle Ages and the Mafia.

When Dwight comes in my mouth, I almost gulp it down but then, against my will, it regurgitates back up on to the carpet with half that afternoon's Happy Meal.

'I guess I was wrong,' he tells me as he zips himself up and buckles his belt. 'You aren't quite as good as your brother – yet. But then, he had so much more practice.'

He gets me a wet towel to mop up with, then switches off the lights and bolts me in for the night. I can hear him unlock and relock the double doors to the front parking lot. In the distance, I can hear him open fire his car's engine and drive off.

Volume M of the *Encyclopaedia Britannica* also contains music. You can read all about musical theory and learn what musical terms mean, words like cantata, intermezzo, arpeggio, cadence and staccato. Presto is a musical term, too, I think. But I can't remember how any songs go.

CHAPTER THIRTY-EIGHT

I have awful dreams. You're in them and they're terrible.

Sometimes, like before, we're in the swimming pool floating on our rafts, it's sunny and gorgeous, we look great and tanned, we reach out and grab hold of each other's arms and start to spin a bit, lazily, like we used to do. Only then the pool becomes an ocean, the water's dark and deep, we can't see the bottom and can't see any land, everywhere we turn there's just more ocean as far as the horizon. I remember that little kid on his raft in the opening credits of *Jaws* and how you could see his shadow beneath the water's surface and then the shark shoots up and I'm scared, Joshua. Then our rafts start to deflate. I don't know how it happens but they seem to have a leak, both of them, and we can't see where the hole is to patch it or blow the raft up. The rafts keep deflating and we're sinking. We're still holding on to each other and holding on and holding on. And then you're sinking, beneath the waves, you're falling and you're pulling me down. We can't let go of one another and you're pulling me down. 'You're strong, Justine, you're unbeatable,' you say. 'Pull me up.' But I can't. I try to scream for help but chlorinated sea water drowns my screams and there's no one to hear anyway. Then sometimes, you're not the one falling. It's me, I'm the first under the water and suddenly I don't know how to swim and all I can think about is that shark. I'm kicking and splashing about, I'm petrified and I'm sinking and it's me, I'm pulling you down, dragging you down under the surface of the waves and we can't see the bottom. I don't think there is a bottom.

Other times I dream about us and we're with Dwight. Nasty dreams. I don't know where we are, it's white, all white, but Dwight's there. I see you, Joshua, on your knees in front of him and he's got his hand in your hair. And I see you in other positions, with his hands all over you and your hands all over him and you're doing unspeakable things. I don't want to watch but I can't help myself.

In other dreams, we're in the programme, in the group room, must be during a rap. The chairs are arranged facing each other in some arbitrary formation and you're there, front and centre of the boys' section, and I'm there, front and centre of the girls' section. We're motivating like mad, snapping our wrists, elbows, finger joints. Somebody calls on us but I can't see who exactly it is, and then we're up on our feet. I'm confronting you, screaming, tearing at my hair, spitting, then you're confronting me and you're so animated they have to restrain you. We're calling each other horrible names and saying hateful things. And there are tears, there are almost always tears.

I have dreams about rules. Dwight's often in those too but sometimes it's Dad in those dreams and he's lecturing, ranting – Justine, Joshua, you must, you must follow the rules, a Ziegler is never a rule-breaker, rules are there to guide you.

Sometimes my dreams aren't so coherent. Sometimes they're just a medley of moments, outtakes from our lives except it's all a blur and there doesn't seem to be any order to them. It's mostly the bad parts or even if there are some good parts, they seem bad because they feel like they're slipping away, like they're sinking beneath the waves on our deflated rafts. We're wearing braces and Dad's tightening them and tightening them; I see us in our earliest memory on the couch served up on a plate of pears or grapes or bananas or whatever; we're being bullied by Wayne Westbrook; we're playing dress-up; we're fighting over Christy Crybaby; I see Dad grounding us; I see him making us pick up litter on the side of the road and Mom is saying 'a Ziegler is never a litter bug'; I see you in the cradle and you're crying and I see Mom place a quiet me in the cradle with you and you still won't stop crying; we're born and you come out, I kick you out, and then I follow seven and a half minutes later; we're skipping in unison; we're playing with Bunny and Funny and Teddy Kennedy; I see you running away from me, Joshua, I see you packing your bags and hitching a ride to Florida with some random stranger who idles his big bomber of a car on the highway and you're running away from me; I see us in the programme and we're both there but we're alone somehow; I see you with Chubby/Earl and those other boys sneaking out of the house in the middle of the night. I see you and you're running away from me.

There's another dream, too, a nicer one. We're little kids again, in the line at the A&P with Mom when the lady behind asks if we're twins. Mom's about to answer, but then you step forward, because you've got a mouth on you, jab your finger into the lady's collarbone and you let loose. 'Are we twins, did you say? Is the earth round? Does Santa wear a red suit? Is America the greatest country on the face of the planet? Does Dr. Seuss have a seriously demented mind? Is the White House in Washington? Does winter follow fall? Does summer follow spring? Is Chicago

261

a windy city? Does a skunk smell? Is the pope Catholic? Is Coke the real thing?'

That one's not such a bad dream at all. That's a nice dream. I try to have other nice dreams. I will myself to dream of Toby S, Cindy and you, all of us, enjoying ourselves, laughing, talking and not worrying about anything. But hard as I try to conjure them, those dreams don't come so easy or so frequently as the others.

CHAPTER THIRTY-NINE

It's a dark night and we're alone in the phaser room at her house, when Moira asks me again if I'm OK. She knows full well I'm not. I haven't been doled out to her for a while, a couple of weeks, so I haven't talked to her about what happened with Dwight but she can tell something's wrong. The dreams and the not sleeping, the fear and everything are taking their toll. Anybody could see that. Toby S, too, most likely. I can't even raise my eyes to him. I'm sullen in group, and during the raps, when I'm being confronted, I just agree with whatever the counsellors say. Almost everything they say is OK by me, everything except the addiction thing.

I consider telling Moira about Dwight. He hasn't yet made good on his 'next time' promise and I'm worried he'll collect in full soon. But what good would it do to tell Moira? What could she do? And if she knew, she'd feel awful and I might get her in trouble, too. It might make Dwight focus his solitaire attentions on her as well. I decide not to discuss it.

'I deserve to be in here,' I say instead.

She bolts upright from her mattress. 'Do you mean you think you're an addict? Are you going to do the First Step?'

'No, I know I'm not an addict, but I deserve to be in here all the same. It's like a punishment.'

'How's that?'

She wants me to look her in the face, but I won't. The room is nothing but shadows anyway so what's the point. I gaze at the ceiling where Moira's parents' constellations are up there, shining.

'Tell me what you remember about Joshua.'

'Justine, you know you're not supposed to say his name.'

'Please, Moira, tell me.'

She sighs, takes a deep breath and blows it out. 'He was nice, that's what I remember, a nice good kid.'

'Go on.'

'He was kind of quiet. All newcomers are quiet at first, but he seemed real quiet I guess. More lonesome than most.'

'Did he ever talk about me, Moira? To you or in the raps?'

'God, Justine, I don't know. That was a long time ago, I can't remember every rap.'

'You must remember something.'

I didn't realise before but, now I look, I don't think Moira's mom or dad hung the stars properly. They must have stuck them up there any old way, just thinking they'd look pretty. I don't know my astronomy so well but I know some of the star clusters, like whichever teacher taught us in elementary school, and I don't see them on the ceiling.

'Well,' says Moira, 'I knew he had a twin. I remember knowing that so he must have talked about you some.'

'What did he say about me?'

'I don't recall that.'

There's no Little Dipper on the ceiling, no Big Dipper for that matter. And no North Star.

'Do you remember what he used to get confronted about?'

'Everybody gets confronted for everything, you know that.'

'But the big ones, do you remember what his big confrontations were about?'

'No.' I think Moira does remember, she just doesn't like to say. I can imagine, though. 'Some people find it hard in the programme,' she continues. 'It's hard for everyone, sure, but some people find it particularly hard. I think Joshua found it hard.'

'Harder than it's been for me?'

'It's not the same,' she says. 'You two are different.'

Really? 'But would you say he found it harder?'

'I'd say it was harder for him, yeah.'

Cassiopeia's not up on that ceiling either.

'Tell me one more thing, Moira.' This is something I have to know. 'Do you think Joshua belonged in here? Do you think he was an addict?'

Moira's silent for a moment. We gaze at the ceiling. No Virgo, no Gemini, the Twins.

'That's not for me to judge, Justine. I'm not a counsellor. What do I know about diagnosing addiction?'

As we puzzle over the fake constellations, we also listen to the air conditioning. In Moira's house, they've got those clunky old units that attach like barnacles to windows and cool each room off individually. The window with the air-conditioning unit's just above my mattress and when the precipitation builds up it drips, cool little drip-drops fall like rain on to my forehead and my pillow gets wet. I know Moira wouldn't mind if I moved the mattress so the air conditioner didn't drip on me, but I don't feel like moving.

It was almost unbearably hot and humid late last summer when Mom and Dad decided enough was enough. Not long after our birthday, our fifteenth. We had the air conditioning on full blast then, too.

'I brought him here, you know,' I tell Moira.

'Brought who where?'

'Joshua. It was me. I helped bring him into the programme.'

We all three did – Mom and Dad and me. I didn't want any part of it, but Mom talked me round, she said they couldn't do it alone, she said you'd be calmer if I was there, not so scared. Mom tried to persuade Dad to enlist another man to help as well, one of his friends from the club, but Dad said there was no way he was going to air our family's dirty laundry in front of a golfing partner, so Mom said what about Felix Micklebaum, receptionist-Zoe's husband. Felix is no club member, he's working class, toils for a construction company and has the muscles to prove it. But Dad said no, we'd have to do it alone. Family problems, said Dad, are best handled by the family.

They came to my room first. I wasn't asleep, I couldn't sleep that night. I kept checking the batteries in the flashlight to make sure they were charged. I held the light beneath my bedspread and clicked it on, off, on, off. It glowed and flickered like the fireflies we used to chase in the back yard on a summer night like tonight. We were always so desperate to capture one and hold that glow in our sweaty little palms. Fairies you called them because you misunderstood when Dad first told you what they were. And besides, didn't Tinkerbell flit around like that, sparkling on, off, on, off? We wanted to play Peter Pan and Wendy and have our very own Tinkerbell.

Normally, the fireflies were too fast for us. Once, though, when you threw your hand up into the air, one of the little buggers smashed right into it and you clamped your fingers down before it could get away.

'I catched one,' you squealed, sprinting over to show me.

I expected the light to stream out from the cracks between your fingers like a lantern, but there was only the faintest glimmer and as soon as I got my eye to the peephole between your thumb and forefinger, it had extinguished completely. You loosened your grip for a better look.

'Darn, it's nothing but a stupid old fly.'

I followed Mom and Dad down the stairs to your room. It was three in the morning, you were sound asleep. The plan was not to turn the overhead light on right away, the plan was to use the flashlight.

'Don't wake him,' Dad ordered.

He motioned Mom to the foot of the bed and he stood at the head, then he gave me the signal and I whipped back your comforter. The sheet was tangled up beneath your arms and it twisted further as you woozily rolled away from the disturbance. I tried to pry the sheet loose but it was too knotted.

Dad said, 'Forget the sheet.' Then he started the count, 'One, two, three!'

He grabbed you by the armpits, Mom grabbed you by the feet and they lifted. Your body flopped about, loose and heavy with sleep, but as they fumbled awkwardly with your weight, you started to stir.

'Hey, what the…?'

I shone the beam in your eyes and you scrunched your lids up against it, wrinkling your nose like someone farted. Who cut the cheese? Whoever smelt it dealt it… Wake up, Joshua. Run for it.

'What the…?'

'Justine, get the door,' Dad said.

Though I didn't want to, I held the door open as Mom and

267

Dad heaved you towards it. Dad bore most of your weight but Mom still struggled with your legs. Then you started to kick. Your arms and legs scissoring madly. 'Get off!' Your heel landed solidly in Mom's stomach and she fell backwards with a thud.

'Justine, grab your brother's legs.'

I didn't want to do that either but I did and you stopped kicking. I couldn't look you in the eyes so I stared at your feet. You'd grown hair on your toes and I wondered when that had happened, why I hadn't noticed before. You kept trying to ask me what the – what the – what the heck was going on. I couldn't answer and neither could Mom, and Dad just kept talking over you. I looked at your feet because I couldn't answer. It was good really that we didn't turn the lights on. Mom took the flashlight and led us out to the garage and that's how we got you into the car.

I didn't go any further. They drove you to the programme by themselves so I didn't see you being dragged in kicking and screaming by the likes of Mark or Leroy or whoever they had manning the facility in the middle of the night when an intake was scheduled. I didn't see that. But I played my part all the same.

'I deserve to be in here,' I tell Moira and I mean it.

CHAPTER FORTY

Toby S's missives continue. They aren't long. Sometimes only a few words. Things like 'You're beautiful' or 'Keep smiling', 'You don't belong here' or 'Remember I'm watching out for you'.

Of course I remember that, I never forget. But since the Dwight incident I've been worrying about it, too, worrying what it is Toby sees when he watches me. I feel so dirty, Josh, dirty and disgusting, filthy and low-down, like something you tread in and can't scrape off the sole of your shoe. Can Toby see what's happened? Can he distinguish Dwight's fingerprints all over me?

I taste him still, you know. Sometimes the taste is so strong I can't eat my Burger King onion rings, Taco Bell enchiladas or whatever fast-food crap's for lunch. Or I have to spit it back out after one bite. It tastes like mould and salt, whole milk and chlorine all at once.

I try to catch glimpses of myself to determine whether I look as horrible as I feel. There are no mirrors anywhere, but sometimes I can sneak a peek at my reflection in the window of a host car or the door of a shower cubicle if I do it real quick before my oldcomer notices. The reflection's always blurred, though, so I can't tell much except that my hair's grown long and flyaway and my face is as big as a pumpkin.

What's more, my retainer-less teeth are a mess. When I ride my tongue over them, I'm sure gaps are opening up, amongst the incisors, the canines and molars, gaps everywhere, wide as canyons. A trailer dweller, that's me, with my crooked, gap-toothed smile. Was all the pain of braces for nothing?

And I can see with my own eyes how fat I'm getting. I glance down at my body sometimes and don't recognise it. It has folds where there never were folds before, dimples where there shouldn't be dimples. My unshaven armpits and legs make me cringe, too. I feel like a big, fat, hairy gorilla. I *am* a big, fat, hairy gorilla. And a whore, Josh, that too. Dwight's whore. This is what Toby must see with all his watching.

Though, if it is, he never lets on. His communiqués keep coming, saying 'What a pretty girl' and 'Heaven sent' and signed always 'Your G.A.'

So I learn some more things about Toby from his notes. Just by the fact that he persists in sending them, taking the risk to write them at all and then pass them to Moira somehow, I learn that he's brave, daring, courageous. And I also learn by what he writes that he's kind, warm, caring. He's a gentleman, Joshua, real and true.

Toby's notes make my day when I receive them, though that's not as often as I'd like. It can take several days for him to find an opportunity to palm one off to Moira and then awhile again before she thinks it's safe to slip it into my M.I., especially if I'm not being doled out to her regularly. But when his correspondence arrives, it's worth the wait. I'd like to write back to him and say all sorts of nice things but I don't dare. I'm not so strong as that any more.

One night, I'm doled out to Moira and I can't bear the suspense any longer so I rip open my M.I. and flick through the pages to see if she's inserted a Toby-gram. She has! I find it on a blank page in the middle. 'We can escape. Be ready. Your G.A.'

Escape?

'Close your M.I.!' Moira yaps. She seems more nervous than usual and I bet I know why. Moira swears she doesn't read Toby's notes before she delivers them, but I think she's read this one and she's frightened.

Later in the kitchen, after dinner when her parents have excused themselves, she whispers, 'You guys are passing too many notes. It's getting way too risky.' I don't say anything because if I agree she might refuse to give me any more messages and I couldn't bear that.

'Are you destroying them? Are you getting rid of them like I told you?'

'Yes.'

She whips round on me. 'I don't believe you, Justine.'

She's right not to. I mean to flush them down the toilet like she says, but sometimes, if I'm with another oldcomer, I don't have a chance to. Most of all, though, I don't want to. I like rereading them, again and again. They're the only thing that makes me smile.

'I've destroyed most of them,' I tell her.

'Give me the rest. Now!'

She snatches up my notebook, shaking it out, the notes fall like guilty autumn leaves on the floor, including the one from today. 'I'm stuffing them down the garbage disposal and that'll be the end of it.' I turn away as Moira flips the lever and the disposal makes its horrible grinding.

CHAPTER FORTY-ONE

We're fourteen and freshmen at John F Kennedy High School. Our school colours are red and blue and our mascots are presidents which are kind of hard to design a costume for. On homecoming floats and marching-band drums or whatever, the carving of the four presidents' faces on Mount Rushmore is used as an emblem, which is pretty ridiculous considering none of the four is JFK. But the student body doesn't mind, least of all us, because we love Kennedy High. We're in the big time now.

We've always dreamt about being in high school and, as we head off on our first day, we feel pretty grand, important and grown-up. Except we're not. We're only freshman and, soon enough, the seniors and juniors and the sophomores, especially, who shove us in the hall and make us drop our books, let us know the truth.

At Kennedy High, for the first time in our lives, we're also in different classes. We take all the same subjects – English, algebra, history, government and so on – but because of my grades from last year and the scores on my aptitude tests, I'm placed in advanced classes. You're not. You say that's because you're a retard and you won't believe me no matter how much I tell you that isn't so.

Our lockers are near one another and I bump into you in the hall sometimes but not so much. Usually, we don't have a chance to catch up until we get home in the afternoons when we vegetate on the sofas in the lounge and gossip and analyse the *General Hospital* shenanigans on TV. And sometimes not even then because I've started joining things, like the pep squad and the JV girls' basketball team, and often I have meetings or practice after school. But we catch up when we can.

One day during lunch, Melanie Heath plonks her tray down on the table next to me and Cindy in the cafeteria. She tells me to tell you that Mr Waldemar announced in your English class this morning that there'd be a vocabulary quiz tomorrow. I laugh and say there's no reason for me to remind you if you already heard it in class. That's just it, she says, you weren't in class. She figured you must be sick. I know very well you aren't sick, but I play along and tell Melanie Heath, whoops, that's right, Joshua's down with the flu.

All afternoon I wonder where on earth you could be. In between third and fourth periods, I nip out to the payphone in the school parking lot and call home but all I get is a busy signal. Come fifth period, I decide to skip study hall and track you down. When I unlock our front door, all seems quiet. I search in the TV room and the living room and there's no sign of you. In the kitchen, I find the phone off the hook with a cushion from the sofa fluffed over it to muffle the recording requesting the caller to please replace the handset.

Then I come to your room.

The door's shut and when I fling it open and burst in to surprise you, Lloyd Taggart nearly hits the ceiling.

'What are you doing here, Lloyd?' I start to say but it's quickly evident what Lloyd's doing here. He's naked in your bed, and you're in the bed naked too. Lloyd bails out of your bed in double-quick time, covering himself as he does so with a

273

battered Teddy Kennedy from the collection of our soft toys you still keep by your pillow. He forages on the floor for his clothes, gibbering on about how it's not what I think, this is not what it looks like, that you and he were just playing around, just experimenting and it was not at all what I must be imagining.

Lloyd puts his pants on inside out and almost zips himself into a real mess before he realises and takes them off and starts again. And the whole time, he's running at the mouth and I'm standing there at the door and you're still lying in the bed but pulling the covers up over yourself now. Lloyd begs me not to tattle, not to his parents, our parents or anybody, he makes me promise I won't breathe a word of this to Cindy or Davie or any of our friends. Not a word. It's not at all what you're thinking, he says over and over.

Then he looks at you, real embarrassed like, and he mumbles, 'Sorry, Josh.'

He gallops past me and out of the room before he has even tied his shoelaces. We hear him trip in the hallway. Then we hear him swear and pause and then gallop even faster for the front door which claps shut like a gong behind him.

'What were you thinking, Josh?' I ask, and you're just lying in the bed with the covers yanked up round your chin. 'Anybody could have walked in,' I say. 'Mom. Or Dad.' I warn you to be more careful and you ignore me. So then I tell you you've got a vocabulary quiz tomorrow in Mr Waldemar's class, you'd better study, and you keep ignoring me. You stick your head under the covers until I leave.

The next day in school, after the quiz which you fail, Lloyd Taggart asks Melanie Heath to go steady and she says yes. You don't want to talk about that or anything else over *General Hospital*. And Lloyd acts funny around both of us after that, you especially. He doesn't come round so much for a while.

CHAPTER FORTY-TWO

It's Friday lunch time and we've just straightened up all the tables. I take my seat and when I glance up, I'm surprised, oh so pleasantly, to discover that Toby S is positioned almost directly opposite me. I can't imagine how he's managed this. Maybe it's only coincidence but I doubt it. I force myself not to gaze for too long but I bow my head and grin from ear to ear to let him know how happy I am.

Burger King is on the menu and I'm served a portion of BK's version of McDonald's Chicken McNuggets which is fine by me. When I reach into the centre of the table for sauce, Toby S reaches in too and our fingers touch briefly. It's not long enough for anyone else to pay any mind but it's contact all the same, our first physical contact, and Toby's touch charges up my arm like a lightning bolt. I bow my head and grin some more.

After the meal, fifth phasers distribute pencils and blank slips and all the other phasers tent themselves over their papers to scribble. As usual, I don't know what to write. As I'm racking my brain, Toby drops his pencil. He dives beneath the table to retrieve it and while he's down there, he tickles my ankle. That lightning bolt charges up my leg just like it did my arm and it's all I can do not to titter.

I might not be able to acknowledge it out loud, but the lightning bolt inspires me. I'm feeling giddy and silly and I hunch over my report slip and write 'Malcolm X didn't finish his Happy Meal'. I think this is funny because we didn't have McDonald's today and, of course, there is no Malcolm X in the programme, but I'm willing to bet whichever idiot fifth phaser sorts through these slips doesn't know who the real Malcolm X is from a hill of beans. So I'm probably in the clear.

While I'm quietly gloating over their confusion, I hear a soft rapping. And when I raise my eyes from my paper, I see Toby S tapping the tabletop with his pencil, like you might do during an exam when you're deep in thought trying to suss out one of the questions. But then Toby puts his forefinger to the tabletop, pointing down. He wants me to look under the table.

Nervously, I scout the room. I'm sure someone is going to see. If they catch me, I'll be in big trouble. But no one seems to be watching. I take a deep breath, try to settle my nerves and then I go, let my pencil slip from between my fingers and jerk myself down to pick it up. Toby has placed another one of his notes by my foot. He's torn off a scrawny sliver of his report slip and written on it in pencil so faint it's difficult to read beneath the table where there's hardly any light. But if I strain my eyes, I can just manage to make it out.

The message reads: 'Tonight.'

I screw the paper up real quick. What should I do with it, where should I put it, what if they find it on me? I mustn't panic. I spy a leftover burger wrapper that's fallen beneath the chair of the girl sitting next to me. It's half covered in mustard and pickle. I mash the note into an extra large daub of mustard and wad the wrapper with the note inside up into a tight little ball and I leave it beneath the other girl's chair.

Just in time, I pop back up to deposit my single-folded report slip into the pillowcase for collection. I don't think anyone has witnessed my crime. The wrapper will be swept up with the rest of the lunch garbage, tied into one of those big black plastic bags and tossed into the industrial-sized dumpster at the back of the parking lot before we've even started our afternoon drills. Gone.

But that word isn't gone, it's emblazoned on my brain. *Tonight*, it said.

I know what Toby S means by that. He means that it's for real, the escape, and we're going to bust out of this place, we're going to bust out of here *tonight*. I don't know how it's going to happen and don't want to, I just want out. I trust Toby, too, and I want to believe in him.

All the same, though, I'm terrified, Joshua. An icy fist closes round my heart and my throat constricts away to nothing. I don't know if I can do it, whatever it is that's required of me for us to escape.

Still, I bow my head and grin from ear to ear to let Toby S know I received his note and know what it means, I grin to let him know how happy I am. And if my grin is a little shakier than before, a little more tremulous, he's sure not to notice.

CHAPTER FORTY-THREE

I wonder all day what form escape might take. In fact, since the day Moira gave me Toby's first note that said it was possible, I've been thinking about it. I didn't really believe it then. I thought Toby S was just writing that to cheer me up.

I haven't let myself seriously contemplate escaping from the programme in such a long time. In the beginning, I liked to tell myself that Cindy or Lloyd or whoever would be my saviour, but that hope was dashed the night I learnt I was in here for real, when Mom said all my friends thought I was in Kansas. That's when I knew no one was coming for me. Since receiving Toby S's note, though, I've been imagining it again. *Escape*. Nonstop I've been trying to picture it. In my wildest visions, I see you – brown from the Florida sun – and you're helping to spring Toby and me from here, you're coming to my rescue like how I would have done for you, Joshua, I swear, if I'd only known. I imagine how, when we're free, I'll call Cindy and Lloyd and we'll all go to the mall and hang out. I'll introduce them to Toby and they'll like him, I know they will, just like you would.

Toby S must have a plan so I try to ready myself like he told me and my muscles ache because I've been tensing them for hours now in preparation. By the time that evening's Open

Meeting gets underway, I'm fit to burst with anticipation. I see Toby S's parents and his little sister arrive and I see other familiar faces as the relatives stream in. We phasers are crooning along to the tune of *Rocky Mountain High* and I sing at the top of my lungs and punch the air I'm so nervous.

'I've got a natural hiiiiiighhh
I'm comin' clean now
An all natural hiiiiiiiiighhhh
Comin' clean now...'

Everything about this Open Meeting drags, it's interminably slow, but, more disconcertingly, nothing about it goes as normal. First off, our parents are here. I'm not expecting them. Neither has attended an Open Meeting in weeks and they haven't attended one together in much longer than that, but they're together here now. I don't spot them until they're about to sit down. Our mother actually looks up and makes eye contact with me. She smiles. I'm too shocked to smile back.

Next, there's a problem with the counsellors' microphones and it takes going on ten years for them to figure out they can't be fixed so then everything's halted while Lois runs off to find a replacement and when she can't find one she finally returns with a bullhorn. So then Dwight's circling about with a bullhorn. He resembles a moth fluttering around like that because he's dressed all in white today, with white parachute pants and white polo shirt, but he's much louder than a moth, even louder than normal with his bullhorn, and he's giving everyone a much larger than normal headache. During the parent/phaser exchange portion of the meeting, there are outrageous parent tirades when the bad news reports are heard and the staffers allow them to drone on longer than normal, and when two lucky newcomers 'go home', they seem to take a prehistoric age to sprint the length of the room and then the hugs and the tears and the cheers go on for longer than normal, too.

I feel a pinch of fiercer-than-normal anxiety as the mike wends its way down my row. When I stand up, Hilary announces my status and that's one thing not out of the ordinary at all. 'Justine Z remains in denial,' Hilary decrees.

I haven't seen our parents since before my crying jag and I want them – our mother in particular – to know that I've wept, bawled my eyes out, but Hilary doesn't mention that. Ramona hands Mom the microphone for her reaction and Mom's mouth forms into this sad small pout; I can tell she's holding back her own tears.

'I miss my babies, Justine.'

She passes the mike to Dad and I brace myself for his look-what-you're-doing-to-your-mother onslaught, but Dad looks sad, too. His shoulders droop. 'I miss you, too, Justine,' he says. 'We know you can do it. Just pull yourself together, OK?'

'I love you, Mom and Dad,' I shout as per the script.

Finally, the fifth phaser testimonials roll around and I can't concentrate in the least. Eric H recites his testimonial and I've heard it at least three times already, about the LSD, the pushing, the nark. I glance in Toby S's direction to see if maybe he'll give me a signal somehow. But I can only see him in profile, can't make out his expression.

My ears perk up when Hilary introduces Moira. Come to think of it, I don't recall ever having heard Moira's testimonial. I'm sure I must have after all this time, but if she's presented the Open Meeting testimonial since I've been in the programme, it must have been one of the weeks when I was just plain out of it because I don't remember a word. I listen up now: the girl she describes doesn't sound anything like the Moira I know.

I hear about how Moira met her druggie boyfriend at a nightclub one night and she wasn't supposed to be there in the first place because she was underage but she managed to get in because her druggie friend loaned her a fake ID, and the bouncer knew it wasn't Moira because the picture of the girl in the ID didn't look anything like her but the bouncer was willing to overlook that fact if Moira made out with him, which she did, right there on the doorstep of the club, and he did overlook it and then she went home that night with him when she was supposed to be spending the night with her druggie friend and she had sex with the bouncer and it wasn't even her first time even though she was only fourteen. The bouncer became her druggie boyfriend and Moira didn't tell her parents about him because they wouldn't approve as he was more than ten years older and had a prison record though he never revealed for what.

Moira's bouncer boyfriend was into all sorts of drugs and though he wasn't a serious pusher, he did sometimes sell them on the door of the nightclub to the right people if they were in the know, like, but he dished them out to Moira for free. She'd already smoked pot and stuff, but her new druggie boyfriend turned Moira on to cocaine, magic mushrooms, Benzedrine, uppers, downers, all sorts, and she developed a taste for them. She liked how she could use a drug to pick and choose a mood like if she wanted to feel up, up, up she could take something to feel up and if she wanted to level off, she could take something to bring her down, or if she wanted to just feel normal she could take something for that too.

Thing was, Moira started having to take more and more drugs to get the same effect and the highs became shorter and the lows became longer and then Moira's druggie boyfriend said she was becoming too expensive, he said he didn't earn enough at the nightclub and from his little deals on the side to support both their habits and that she was going to have to start pulling her weight. For her first contribution, Moira stole some money out of her mom's purse, but that didn't go very far so pretty soon she was stealing bracelets from her mom's jewellery box and other silly things she hoped her parents wouldn't miss straightaway, like her father's fishing tackle that was packed up on a shelf in the garage and Christmas presents that were hidden in the attic already wrapped, and then those didn't go very far either so Moira and her druggie boyfriend concocted a plan to stage a fake robbery at her parents' house. They made it look like somebody had broken in and they got away with two TVs, a VCR, the microwave and all the remaining contents from her mom's jewellery box.

Once they'd sniffed and snorted their way through that, Moira's druggie boyfriend said they could run the same drill on other houses, so they picked off some of the houses in Moira's neighbourhood, starting with ones where she used to baby-sit or water the plants for old folks who lived there. They'd only enter when they were certain nobody was home and they'd set themselves flying high before every job; but that's where they started to get sloppy because they got too high and forgot to be careful, and one night they were in a house and they opened one of the homeowner's drawers looking for cash and found a gun and it was loaded. Moira's druggie boyfriend started horsing around with it and going, hee hee, look at me, I'm Butch Cassidy and you're the Sundance Kid, and then while he was horsing around, the homeowner, a retired guy, ambled in on them and they hadn't even heard him approach so when the druggie boyfriend spotted him over Moira's shoulder he was so startled, addled, high, he didn't even think, he just shot the retired guy dead. And Moira got blood on her shirt.

The police found Moira the next day at her druggie boyfriend's apartment. They knew exactly where to look because her and her boyfriend's fingerprints were all over everything and Moira was half dead from the shitload of drugs she'd pumped into her body and the druggie boyfriend had run off. The police caught him later and shipped him back to prison. Moira got off lighter because she was a minor and the police figured out she hadn't been party to the shooting even though the druggie boyfriend said she had, so Moira ended up in juvenile detention where they gave her hell, let her detox for a few months and then the authorities allowed her parents to take her out of the detention centre because they promised to admit her into Come Clean under strict surveillance. Once she was in the programme, though she denied her addiction for months, Moira finally accepted her own powerlessness, gave herself over to her Higher Power, and joined those who'd gone before her on the road to recovery, and she'd like to thank them for helping her get clean and most of all she'd like to thank her parents for saving her life. One day at a time.

Moira's testimonial is by far the longest I've ever heard at an Open Meeting, but no one begrudges her the overrun. The audience is spellbound. I search the crowd for Moira's parents. Both of them have tears in their eyes and Moira's dad holds up a fist of victory; they look so proud. I can't believe they've been through all that, can't believe Moira has. I look at the three of them anew and I feel proud too. And confused.

With the testimonials over and the final announcements made, Dwight says it's time to break off into individual rap sessions. Ramona rallies the siblings to follow her and, as they collect their belongings, that's when it hits, the first sign that Toby S's escape plan might be for honest-to-goodness real.

CHAPTER FORTY-FOUR

The tail end of the Open Meeting is disrupted by an almighty explosion from the direction of the parking lot. Bang! And then another one. Bang!

Some siblings make a dash for the double doors. They fling them open and peer out into the night. Bang! Several smaller ones plug their ears and start to cry. Then one of the siblings gasps. 'Ooooh, pretty!' she says. She must be about nine or so; she's got pigtails, a cute smile and her face's bathed in a purplish light. Everybody cranes their neck to see and so do I and I catch a corner of the night sky and – bang! – it's awash with the colour, fizz, crackle of fireworks. 'Aaaah,' goes the crowd.

Then something comes sailing through the open doors over the head of the pigtailed girl. It's sizzling and smelling bad and is tracked close behind by another projectile. Both land in the midst of the group and – Bang! Bang! – they explode and the room is filled with smoke. I don't see any flames but someone does or thinks they do because I hear one of the mom's yell 'Fiiirre!' and then a male voice screams 'Run for it!' and the building's fire alarm starts wailing. Parents and siblings stampede both exits and phasers upend their chairs and charge for the door to the parking lot, which is the closest one to us. Dwight has the bullhorn and he's bellowing for everyone to please fucking control themselves. I can hear Hilary's voice as well, appealing for calm and telling oldcomers to escort newcomers out of the building in an orderly fashion.

Everybody's racing around now, though, coughing, spluttering, screaming and you can't tell phasers from siblings from parents from staffers. Through the haze, I see one of the male fifth phasers try and belt-loop Ramona by mistake and she slaps him silly. Someone grabs hold of me, they wrench me up so hard by the seat of my pants it feels like I might slice in two. There's a bottleneck at the door and lots of pushing, shoving, stamping on feet, and I hope that little pigtailed girl's OK. Whoever it is who's behind me loses their grip and, I can't believe it, because as I slip through into the parking lot, I'm free, I'm out in the open air and no one's holding on to me, no one at all.

The chaos continues outside, though, and my brief elation is soon overtaken by disorientation. Fireworks go off overhead and smoke bombs are exploding all over the place and the air's hot and stinking of cordite, oil grease, sweat and God-knows-what, and people are running around, coughing, spluttering, screaming. What looks like a football player zips past me. A weird-looking football player. His face is smeared with grease and he's dressed all in black except for his shoulder pads which are flopping around on the outside of his shirt, and except for his helmet which is white with a mascot painted on it in green which seems to be a grizzly bear. Like the *Gunther High* Grizzlies.

I'm running around with the rest of the crowd and I'm searching for Toby, but it's hard to tell phasers from siblings from parents from staffers, especially from the back, especially with the boy phasers who all look exactly the same from the back with their crew cuts. I try to remember what shirt Toby was wearing but can't remember if it was blue or green and I can't really distinguish colours very clearly anyway with the fireworks bathing everything in eerie shades of light. I grab somebody by the shoulder and hope it's Toby but it's not, it's Jack F, and he's gone before I can ask if he's seen Toby.

I hear people running for cars, glass smashing, engines revving but then there's a lot of screeching and more smoke, burning smells, and none of the cars are moving and I can't find Toby anywhere. There are more football players now. They're zipping about all over the place and they start tackling people. They seem to target anyone wearing keys or whistles, anyone who looks to be in a position of authority. Dwight's a dead easy target, what with being dressed all in white, like he's some beacon, and bellowing into that bullhorn ordering people to fucking get back inside now. Four blackened football players bring him down with a thud and from some corner I hear a cheer go up as Dwight's face hits the ground. I start running again and searching and searching and I can't find Toby anywhere.

I spy some phasers darting round the sides of the building and I'm about to hightail it after them when someone loops me again from behind. 'Stop right there, you little cunt!' It's Gwen and her face looks like one of the Gorgons' out of Greek mythology from the *Encyclopaedia Britannica*, like a face shot up from Hades itself. 'This is all your doing. *I know*, I saw you, you and your boyfriend.'

'You don't know what you're talking about.'

'I know, I know!' she shrieks and her ponytail spins round the crown of her head like a top. 'I saw you, just today, flirting with that Toby S, flirting like the slut you are. You planned it. All of this.'

'Shut up!' I'm fighting to break away from her and I'm searching and searching. Where is Toby?

'I know! I cleaned up at lunch. *I cleaned up!*'

'Let go of me, witch!' I'm fighting and hunting the faces of passers-by for Toby's face.

'You're not going anywhere. You most certainly are fucking not!'

But smoke bombs are exploding all over the place and people are running, coughing, spluttering, screaming – it's chaos and, when I reel round on Gwen, she's caught off guard. I hook my foot behind hers and shove. She holds on damn tight, I'll give her that, but these are a cheap pair of Kmart specials; that overstrained belt loop rips off in her hand and before she can even catch her breath, me and the rest of my pants are out of there.

I bolt round the side of the building, into the visitors' and staff parking lot in the front and then out on to the service road. There are other phasers ahead of me and none of them are Toby, but I follow them anyway. Francis is ahead of me and I just about catch up with him. He's running faster than I'd ever give him credit for. Last I remember from the roll call, Francis had been in the programme for 680 days, nearly two years and he had been started over four times and is still only on third phase. Francis has plenty to run for. He picks up the pace again and so do I as we pass the corrugated iron warehouses, the Caterpillar tractor warehouse, Billy's Printing Supplies warehouse, the Dutch Tulips. If I can get as far as the Harvey's Shrimp Shack I'll be OK, I tell myself. I'm sure Harvey's is open all night and I'm sure there's a payphone there: if I can just get there, I can call for help. Harvey's, with its rickety neon sign. All You Can Eat Shrimp – $5.97. That's the marker, that's my escape.

My chest's hurting and I'm out of breath but it's not far now, I've got to keep going. Harvey's, I tell myself.

Near the highway, long before Harvey's, there's more chaos. I hear sirens and see lights, flashing red, and a crowd's forming at the junction where the service road meets the highway. They must have called the police already, told them to blockade us in. People are screaming, crying, running around and I'm searching faces but I can't see Toby anywhere. I'm scared, Joshua, so scared. If I get arrested, that's all they'll need. They'll throw me back into the programme with Dwight and Gwen or somewhere worse and they'll throw away the key.

Francis keeps running but I peel off at the Dutch Tulips warehouse, shimmy round the back and turn right again towards the highway, but there at the back of the Tulips lot where I thought I could get out, it's sealed off with a tall fence topped with barbed wire. The service road is the only way out and the police are there. I can't get arrested, I can't.

There's nothing else to do. I double back on myself, head towards the programme building via the warehouse parking lots. Things have calmed down some by the time I return. The fireworks have stopped, the smoke's clearing and there are no blacked-up football players zipping about. Most people seem to have gone back inside. I skulk about amongst the cars that still haven't gone anywhere until I find Mom and Dad's. One of the rear windows has been smashed so I unlock the door and climb in.

I sit on the back seat for a while and I don't know what to do. I'm all alone and scared, I twist myself up into a ball and squeeze into the hollow behind Dad's driver's seat like we used to do when we were little and making the long vacation drive to

Rehoboth Beach or wherever and we were sick of playing stupid roadside alphabet games with Mommy. I'm too big to fit in the space really but I can manage if I stick my legs out behind Mommy's seat. I'm cold and shivering even though it's a balmy June evening and I almost feel safe with my head against Daddy's chair where the map books are. I don't ever want to come out.

CHAPTER FORTY-FIVE

We're going on fifteen and you're acting more and more peculiar.

You don't hang out with Cindy or Lloyd or Davie or Richie or any of our friends any more. You don't even seem to like to hang out with me. On the days when I rush home to watch Luke and Laura and Scotty and weird weather conspiracies on *General Hospital*, I'm usually watching on my own, and even when you're there, you're so out of the loop you can't keep up with the plot lines.

You have a whole new set of friends and I don't know most of them. Some don't even go to Kennedy. I think some of them don't go to school at all. I know for a fact one of your friends is a dropout and he has a job at the A&P stacking shelves.

Increasingly, you skip school yourself and kids get so used to it they don't even bother to ask me if you're sick any more. They stop telling me to pass on assignments, too, because you never thank them, or me. And you certainly don't do the work, you don't seem to pay any mind whatsoever. By the end of the school year, you're close to flunking three of your classes and it's a miracle you pass the ninth grade at all.

That summer you fall into a pattern of sneaking out at night and sleeping in real late. During the day, you stay holed up in your room all morning and afternoon with the door shut and the curtains drawn and I can't even lure you out to the pool for a swim, not even if I tell you I'm desperate to learn one of those dives you do so well and won't you please teach me, Joshua. Sometimes when I knock on your door, it's locked and I hear you whispering and I'm sure you've got somebody in there with you and not Lloyd Taggart. Other times the door's locked even when you're not in the house.

One day when I know you're out, I pick the lock and steal into your room. It's a mess and it smells and I know Dad's going to get on to you soon about cleaning it up, but that still doesn't seem reason enough to lock the door. Then I take a peek under the bed and there, between the rollaway mattress and the box frame, I find bottles. Lots of bottles, some empty, some still half-full. Not piddly wine cooler bottles either or Mickey's Light beer, but hard stuff. Vodka, gin, rum and such.

I start to worry about you and I tell you as much. And you tell me, well don't, nobody asked for my concern.

Then I follow you that night on your joyride, tagging along with you and your greasy dropouts in the trash-heap car driven by the guy with cotton ball sideburns. I sit in the back next to Chubby/Earl while your friends laugh at me and I smoke my one puff of marijuana. And I wonder what you're doing with that driver guy down by the river – though I pretty much know.

After that night, I confide in my best friend Cindy Gregory. I tell her you're acting crazy and not yourself and I ask her what should I do. I want to know if she thinks I should tell our parents. No way, she says, absolutely not. So I don't, of course. I could never tattle on you.

But Mom and Dad aren't deaf, dumb or blind. They suss it out themselves soon enough. They receive your report card from JFK, then Dad uncovers your retainer in the bathroom and it's obvious you haven't been wearing it at all in probably months and that sends him into a rage. All the time, you keep sneaking out nights, locking your door during the days and I keep not saying anything. One night, you sneak out and you aren't home in the morning when Mom and Dad leave for work. They ground you for two weeks. Not a week later, when you're still supposed to be grounded, you stay out all night again. Dad grounds you for a month and you tell him to go to hell.

CHAPTER FORTY-SIX

Back in the Come Clean parking lot, I must have passed out because next thing I know Mom's hovering over me, enfolding me in her arms, hugging me and crying, telling me how worried they were, what happened to you, sweetie, and thank heavens you're all right. She calls me her baby and says everything's OK now. I hug our mother back. She's sitting on the back seat of the car and she lifts me into her lap. I coil myself up, tuck my feet behind her knees and breathe in her Chanel perfume, revel in the warmth of her breast, the gentle rising and falling of her ribcage. I feel small again and I wish she'd read me Dr. Seuss. I feel safe.

Then I start to cry.

'You're crying,' our mother says, surprised, because she doesn't know how many tears I've built up inside. And maybe she doesn't know what to do but she does fine. She clucks reassuringly and tells me everything's OK now, not to worry, little one. She unsnaps her pocketbook, produces a shredded Kleenex and wipes my cheeks free of tears, bits of broken glass and droplets of blood. Then she offers me a Tic Tac.

'I was so worried about my baby,' our mother whispers as she rocks me. 'So worried. I thought that was my baby out there on the highway. They wouldn't tell us who it was, Justine, and I thought it might be you. I couldn't bear that, sweetie, I couldn't bear to lose the both of you, just couldn't bear it. You're my only babies, my little monkeys, you'll always be my only babies.'

I don't really understand what Mom's saying. In my mind what I'm hearing is 'Sam I am eats green eggs and ham' and I hear you asserting your right to eat green eggs and ham too and who wouldn't eat green eggs and ham if Dr. Seuss would write a whole book about you.

That's how our father finds us when he ventures out into the dead firework- and smoke-bomb-strewn parking lot looking for Mom who was only meant to be getting some wet wipes out of the glove compartment. We're sitting curled up on the back seat, rocking, sucking on Tic Tacs, tasting green eggs and ham and listening to Mom singsonging for me to stop crying, stop crying now. Hush baby.

Our father acts glad to see me, too, at first. His eyes mist over and he embraces me, tells me how worried they were and I must never, ever, please honey, worry them that way again. But then he steps back. He holds the car door open and balances himself gingerly against the window, the sliver that isn't broken, smudging his fingerprints on the glass like he'd never do if he was thinking straight.

He takes a deep breath, and then tells me I have to go back. He can't be rock-solid serious; Mom doesn't think so in any case. Our mother disagrees, she almost never disagrees with Dad. 'No, Jeff,' she says softly but firmly. 'I think our baby should come home with us. Let's bring her home, 'kay?'

'Now, Helen, you know that's not right.'

'Yes. It is.'

'It's not for us to decide. The professionals know what's best for Justine now.'

295

'Don't think so. Mommy knows best.' She wraps her arms around me tighter and we're rocking and rocking. I bury my face in her chest and rise and fall, faster and faster, with her ribcage.

'Let go of her, Helen.'

'No.'

'Let go, this isn't helping.'

Dad wrestles me out of Mom's lap and out of the car, glass tinkling. He tries to stand me up but I lock my legs beneath me and won't stand. I'm on the ground and our mother is crying, she's saying 'Don't cry baby, don't cry' and then she's screaming to 'stop, Jeff, stop'.

'Quiet!' Our dad grapples with me and tries to pen our mother into the car. 'Enough is *enough*! Now, Justine. I know you don't want to hear this, but it is for your own good. You're going to march back into that programme there and you're going to put some backbone into it and re-emerge for the better, you are going to come out of this shining. I'm not going to hear another word about it.'

'Dad, you don't understand what it's like—'

'I understand perfectly well, and what you need to understand is that a Ziegler is never a quitter. And what's more, a Ziegler is never, *never* a rule-breaker.'

'Dad—'

'I know you like to bend them or forget them when they're inconvenient. But rules are rules, Justine, and they are there for a reason.'

'I don't belong here, Dad! And neither did Joshua. He should never have been in this place. *You* should never have put him here!'

'Young lady, you don't know what you're talking about.'

'I *do* know, I—'

'Joshua had a problem, Justine.'

'No, Daddy!'

'Yes, Justine, he did. You don't know the half of it, we've tried to shield you from the worst.'

'No.'

'Justine Amanda Ziegler, I recognise it's hard for you to accept. But your brother *did* have a problem, a very serious one.'

I wag my head ferociously and our father nods just as ferociously, as if his counter gesture will negate mine.

'Yes, yes, he did. Joshua was an addict.'

'No, Dad,' I scream. 'No! *Joshua was gay!*'

Dad rears down and comes up swinging. His right fist connects with my left cheek like a two-ton magnet drawn to an army tank. He punches me with such force I think for a millisecond it must have been Dwight who hit me. Mom howls in pain. Baby, baby, don't you hurt my baby. I hold my cheek with my hand and then reach up to press the prism point between my eyes. I need clarity. This will all make sense in a minute. My mouth's open, yawning wide open and I'm crying. Dad wants to apologise, I know that. Really Joshua. And I'm crying, open-mouthed and crying.

Our father stares down at me. His hand, the one he struck me with, quivers like neither it nor he can believe what the two of them have done. Then Dad's eyes fix and harden in my direction.

'Justine Ziegler,' he says, and there's a tremor in his voice, not normally there, that he's trying to subdue. 'This is just what I'm talking about. I cannot believe this,' he slaps the palm of his hand hard against his thigh and shoots darts into my open mouth. 'Where the hell is your retainer? What have you done with it?'

My retainer? In a flash, I remember Gwen taking it off me during the strip-search after my initial intake. So long ago now – more than three and a half months. I run my tongue up to my gums. Are there gaps? Have my teeth shifted after all that time? They're chattering too much to tell for sure.

'Expensive orthodontic equipment,' Dad rumbles, gathering momentum. New moulds would need to be made. How could I have been so careless?

'But Dad—'

'No buts,' he roars. 'I am sick to death of your buts. You have no respect for your teeth just like you have no respect for yourself or your mother or me or authority of any kind, or the sheer necessity of perseverance, of discipline, of *rules*. So. What you're going to do, young lady, is march back in there and face the music! That's what you're going to do. *Right now!* And if there's punishment due you for your breaking of the programme rules tonight, well, so be it.'

'But the rules are *destroying* us!!' I scream through my tears.

'Not another word,' says our dad, still trying to contain Mom.

He's about to alert the troops and turn me in, but there's no need. They've heard us and are gathering at the double doors. I hear a whistle and somebody shouts 'Found another one!'

Our mother's rocking, crying, squealing, 'Don't cry, baby,' and 'Stop, Jeff,' and she's tearing at the open window even though there's glass everywhere and her Kleenex is shredded and stained red. And I'm bawling and pleading, 'No, Daddy, no Daddy, no.' My legs lock beneath me, I'm on the ground and can't stand up.

'It's Justine Zeeee!' somebody calls out.

Fifth phasers surround the car and grab hold of our mother to

298

restrain her even though Dad tells them that's not necessary and to take their cotton-picking hands off his wife. They lay their hands on me, too, and I'm kicking, screaming, spitting, pleading, not standing and he doesn't tell them to unhand me. Our father yells at me that this is all for my own good, he tells me not to struggle, that I'll make it easier on myself if I don't struggle.

It's for your own good. Dad looks sad, his voice textures with resignation, his face sags with disappointment. And I remember that night when I helped to bring you into this place and you were kicking, screaming, pleading, not standing. That night with the flashlight, the sheet and you stuttering, 'What the – what the –' Too confused to even form a sentence. Those are the very words that Dad kept saying over and over again, over you, over everything. 'It's for your own good, Joshua.'

I'm kicking and screaming, hearing Mom crying and you stuttering, blinking against the flashlight in your eyes, struggling against the sheets tangled tight around your torso, smelling the faintest whiff of Mom's perfume and dreaming of Dr. Seuss spinning echoes.

Then Mark or Leroy or whoever assists me into the building and the last words I hear our mother screaming are: 'Give my baby a glass of water. Please...'

CHAPTER FORTY-SEVEN

Sentries spray water in my face with a hose to calm me down and then take me back into the group. All phasers have been moved to one of the smaller rooms, the one where the sibling raps are usually held, because the families are still milling about in the main hall as they wait for mechanics to come fix their cars. In addition to the smashed windows, there are parts of engines missing, tennis balls shoved into tailpipes, tires slashed, all sorts of automotive havoc, and there probably aren't enough mechanics in the county.

The sibling room's maybe a third of the size of the main hall and the phasers are jammed in shoulder to shoulder, boys' and girls' chairs situated much closer than they ought to be. I'm shaking and not just because of my wet hair which drips all over my already drenched shirt. I've got that clammy sweat coating my whole body. Mark or Leroy ties me to the chair with a pair of socks and I bet they're not even clean and I'm shaking real bad and the chair starts to rattle.

I scan the faces of the boys' section but you're not there and neither is Toby S. Along with Toby, Francis, Shaun N and sweet-sixteen Emily are also missing. Three or four others attempted to run off too but, like me, they've been rounded up and are sitting strapped to chairs.

Dwight's not all-white any more. He's smeared with dirt, black stuff, and his parachute pants are ripped below both knees. He's flapping about the group in a fury. I don't see Hilary anywhere. Dwight says Emily's in the hospital. He says she was struck by a car as she was dashing about the highway where she had no business being, heading up towards Harvey's Shrimp Shack. There was a pile-up and Emily's in a very serious condition.

Under her breath, a girl to my right dissents. 'Emily was run over by three different cars,' she says, 'Emily's dead.'

'No fucking side-talking!' Dwight blasts.

Ramona tiptoes in. She's dressed in a denim top, prairie skirt and cowboy boots. She's laden with a big pile of paper slips, which she distributes, along with pencils. She tells us we've all got to report in detail what we saw and heard about who did what and when and how tonight, we've got to say if we know anything at all that might explain what happened. Everybody casts their eyes about the group and then they hunch over their papers, using their thighs or the seats of their chairs as desktops.

Leroy unties my hand so I can fill in my report slip but I'm still shaking so bad I can't write anything and I don't intend to write anything anyway so I just make a squiggle and fold the paper over.

Ramona collects the ragged little slips in the pillowcase and presents it to Dwight. He twists the pillowcase like he was wringing a chicken's neck and then waves it over his head. 'I hope that ya'll have been truthful,' he says. 'I hope none of ya'll are holding anything back because if ya are, we will find out about it. We'll stay here all night, all weekend if we have to, until we find out who's responsible.'

He summons the fifth phasers to accompany him and help sort the reports. Ramona and Bo are left in charge and they order the fourth phasers to stand up and assume the vacant sentry positions around the perimeters. Ramona leads us in some Seven Step drills without much success. Everybody's antsy, including her; she loses count of the Steps, the phasers keep getting the words wrong and no one's in unison.

We wait for Dwight to return and it feels like an election, like the fifth phasers are counting secret ballots. The suspense is nerve-racking and I'm still shaking.

They're gone for maybe an hour and when they return, the room's graveyard silent. The phasers hold their breaths, their eyes dart about the room and the ones tied up with socks strain against them. Gwen comes to the centre of the group and my name is the name she calls.

CHAPTER FORTY-EIGHT

I'm escorted into a solitaire room, the one where Dwight taught me things about self-knowledge and the *Encyclopaedia Britannica*; he and Hilary are in there already with a few extra folding chairs. Gwen leads me in with Leroy and once they get me seated, they tie my hands again. Then Dwight nods and Leroy leaves but Gwen loiters at the door until Hilary thanks and dismisses her too. Gwen sneers and, as she pivots on her heel to go, she flicks me the finger, gripping it low against the expanse of her tracksuited belly, so only I can see.

There are no tables in this room but piles of report slips and other papers line the floor along one of the walls. I eye them with apprehension.

Hilary raises her clipboard. 'OK, Justine. I'm going to come straight to the point. We know Toby S was the main instigator of this evening's…' She searches for the right word. '…*escapades*. And we know you were involved, too. So let's keep things simple, shall we? I'd like you to tell us in your own words how we got here.'

I'm shaking and keeping shtoom.

'Tell us what you know, Justine. Come on now.'

'I don't know anything.'

'I think you do.' Hilary waits for me to say something, the pause becomes a lull, the lull grows and all that's audible is my chair's rattling.

'Enough of this bullshit,' Dwight fumes. 'We've got the note, you silly, stupid girl.' He snatches a plastic document wallet from a pile. The scrap of paper Toby S left under my foot at lunch time is in it, stained with mustard and crumpled but ironed out now, still legible. *Tonight*, it says.

'How do you explain this?'

I shrug.

'Were the others in on it, too? What was Emily's part? And Francis? And Shaun N?'

'You'd better just come on out and tell us now, Justine,' says Hilary as she jots something on her clipboard.

'They'll be caught, ya know,' Dwight assures me. 'All of them will be caught just like you've been caught. And when we get them back in here, they'll find out what difficulty is, compared to how easy they had it before. Just like you're going to find out, Miss Justine Z.' His eyes are all over me, on my skin, familiar as fingerprints. I want to squeeze my eyes shut and blacken out this scene, blot it out of existence, make it stop dead in its tracks.

But instead the interrogation spirals on and on. Dwight and Hilary tell me again and again I was one of the plotters. They say they know we had a grand scheme, that we were trying to burn the building down, that we were planning to destroy the programme altogether, we didn't care if people got hurt, we hoped some parents and siblings and staffers would get killed. They say all kinds of nonsense, Hilary writes things down, and my chair rattles.

Despite Hilary's efforts to rein him in, Dwight keeps circling me and getting in my face and, once or twice, he slaps me. I want to fend him off but my hands are tied and when I kick out my folding

304

chair topples over. Hilary has to unfold me and set me right again and she orders Dwight to sit down too.

'Give it up, Justine!' Dwight yells. 'This is your chance to confess before it's too late to make any amends. We know you're guilty. You've been planning this for weeks, you've been passing notes and scheming. We know; you've been reported on for fuck's sake.'

'Gwen doesn't know what she's talking about,' I say.

This amuses Dwight. 'Oh ho,' he chortles and stretches back in his seat. 'You think it was Gwen who reported you, do ya?'

'Dwight, you know reporting is confidential.'

'Come on, Hil,' Dwight says, adopting one of his all-too reasonable tones. 'I think this will be a valuable lesson for Justine. She thinks it was our young Gwen who reported her...' And he's talking about me as if I'm not here. '...which is quite right of course.'

'Dwight,' Hilary chides.

'But what she doesn't know is that it wasn't only Gwen.'

'That's enough, Dwight.'

'OK right, I'm not naming any names, but the point is that what Justine doesn't know is that two people reported her, *not one but two*.' He enjoys the look of shock on my face. 'You're trying to figure out who it was, aren't ya, Justine? Trying to figure out who turned you in, who *betrayed* you.' Dwight grins. 'I can't name any names of course...' He waves an acquiescent hand in Hilary's direction. '...but, gee, I sure don't like to see ya tussling so. Maybe I can help you sort your thoughts out.'

He's on his feet again. 'Let's see now. I wonder. Maybe it was one of your co-conspirators sitting tied up over there in group. Or maybe it was someone else. One of your other little phaser friends. Hell, maybe it was even your little boyfriend. Maybe Toby S dished the dirt on ya before he lit out of here himself.'

'Don't be ridiculous.'

A shadow passes over Dwight's face. 'Ridiculous? I think you probably know better than to call me that.' I can almost read his thoughts for a millisecond or two and he's thinking, *you've got a mouth on you missy and it should be on me*. I can taste the cum and chlorine on my tongue.

I choose my words more carefully. 'Toby didn't report me.'

'I didn't say he did, I said *maybe* he did.'

'But he couldn't.' *Could he*, Joshua?

'No? You don't think so? Well, I'd have to disagree with ya there.' Dwight rummages through the piles on the floor. 'He left his M.I., ya know. Lord, that boy got through a lot of pages in the short time he was here. Could be lots to implicate a person in there, lots.' He fans through the notebook in front of me like it was a deck of cards and I recognise the handwriting and the ink, red as hearts and diamonds.

I'm struck by a feeling of *déjà vu*. I scan the piles on the floor for copies of my long-lost journal.

'No,' I say.

'No! No?' Dwight chucks Toby's M.I. back on to the floor. 'Ya know there's even this crazy rumour going round that Toby S was a plant. That we planted him in here to stage a break-out and help us catch would-be escapees. The weakest links.' Dwight snorts. 'Can you credit that? Just so far-fetched it might be true, eh Justine?'

'No.'

'No? Hmm. But you're not sure, I bet.'

'I'm sure. Toby wasn't a plant. He didn't turn anyone in.'

'Well, then, Justine, you're stupider than ya look. Haven't you learnt yet that everybody watches everybody?'

'Not everybody.'

Dwight's wearing his Irish Claddagh ring on the middle finger of his left hand today. I'm sure it's not usually on his left hand but that's where it is now. He gives it a half turn in one direction and then twists it back. 'OK, you name me one person, just one, who you reckon would never turn you in if it meant making their life easier? Wouldn't say a word against you even if it was you or them?'

'Toby wouldn't,' I say. 'He didn't.'

'No proof. Try again.'

I don't have to think twice, of course. I tell him the one person I know would never betray me, I tell him my soul mate, my twin. You.

Dwight bursts out laughing. 'Don't make me laugh!' he says and laughs again. 'Joshua! Ha! That brother of yours was the worst offender. He'd squeal as soon as blink.'

I appeal to Hilary with my eyes, but she's fingering her key necklace and chewing on the cap of her pen. 'No he wouldn't. I don't believe you.'

'That brother of yours went through more pencils than any phaser in the history of Come Clean. He'd ask for *extra* reporting slips. *Every day.* That brother of yours would report on anyone.'

'Dwight,' Hilary pipes in, 'reporting is confidential!'

'Oh please. Like there's any reason to protect Joshua Ziegler's confidentiality!'

'No,' I say and I'm shaking so much my chair rattles. 'Not me, Joshua wouldn't report on me.'

His laughter rings in my ears, it fills the room. The air's bloated with the sound of Dwight's ha-ha-haaaing. 'You dumb, foolish girl,' he says fitfully. 'How do ya think you got here? That brother of yours reported on you *before you even arrived*!'

If my hands were loose, I could reach the prism point between by eyes, could press down hard and everything would make sense, and I could cover my eyes, my face, my ears, block all of this out, I could not hear what this man's saying or witness the delight on his face as he says it.

'That's not true.' Please let that not be true, Josh. *Please*.

'How do you think we knew about your doped-out nights down by the river?'

It was only one night. 'That was Chubby,' I say and I'm sure of it. I have to be sure of that. 'I mean Earl, that was Earl.'

'It wasn't Earl. Earl didn't even remember your name before you showed up here. And what about that diary of yours? How do ya think we got that?'

'No.' My eyes dart back to the piles on the floor. Are there more copies, more pages on the floor? What else will they bring out?

'I suppose you thought that was your parents. You probably thought your mother or father raided your room.' *Of course* it was Dad. It had to have been. Dad found the journal, Zoe Micklebaum photocopied it – that's how I imagined it. I mean, why would *you*... how... when... no! You couldn't have. It was Dad. That's what I tell myself as Dwight continues. 'Well, your parents didn't turn you in; it wasn't them at all.'

It's like in those old goofy comedy sketches on the Carol Burnett show. Carol goes, 'Doctor, I've got an ache in my stomach,' and the mad physician goes, 'Show me the ache, Miss,' and while Carol shows him, he slams a hammer down on her fingers, and when she screams about the pain in her hand, he says, 'Ya-ha, but you're not worried about your stomach any more, are you? Fifty dollars, please.' I don't like this, Joshua, I don't like this place, and I wish Carol would bring me a glass of water.

'No, Justine,' Dwight continues, mashing the hammer down into my knuckles like they're nothing but dust. 'You wouldn't have even been a candidate for Come Clean if Joshua hadn't brought you to our attention. And with no small thanks to yourself, of course. Going out and getting wasted and then bringing it home, flaunting it in your parents' faces. After everything they'd been through. That just confirmed their suspicions, their worst fears. What did you expect them to think? What did you expect them to do?'

It can't be true, it can't. I'm shaking and my heart's going to stop or burst out of my chest or something.

'It's true, Justine Z, all true. *Everybody* reports on *everybody*.'

Dwight hurls one of the document wallets at me. It's stuffed like a piñata and it breaks open as it hits the wall above my head. Slips flutter in the air then settle to the carpet at my feet. Dozens and dozens and dozens of slips of paper, some in pencil, some in blue ink, some black ink. And some in *red*.

I just want it to stop now, Josh. And what does the truth matter any more? The actual truth. Did you care about the truth? Or love? Or loyalty? Does any of that matter to anyone in here? So I tell them what they want to hear. That's the only way to make them stop. The only thing that passes for hope any more. The only thing that brings some relief, however temporary. They aren't satisfied with the little I actually know so I elaborate. I tell them Toby was the ringleader, that he organised everything on the outside though I didn't know how, and I tell them Shaun N, Francis and Emily helped plan it, I tell them those other phasers tied to their chairs in the sibling room were in on it, too. Maybe they were… somehow. That could be the truth. We're all guilty, I say. And in some way, we are. I know that now. That's certainly true.

Dwight nods smugly, Hilary takes notes and taps on her clipboard.

CHAPTER FORTY-NINE

It's the morning after Toby S's escape and my 136th day in the programme. I'm still here and I'm tired of feeling scared so I decide not to feel anything any more.

The final parents depart just before daybreak, which is when the fifth phasers shepherd us back into the main hall again. Entering the room, I glimpse the backs of an exhausted mom and dad as they exit to the parking lot littered with the detritus of fireworks, smoke bombs and vandalised cars, and over their heads, before the doors are locked tight behind them, I see the sky, that early morning colour of slate grey.

We've been here all night with drills, interrogations, confrontations and, seeing as how another morning has already broken, the staff must figure they might as well keep us here and get on with it. So they do. With everyone tired and half asleep, my 136th day in Come Clean proceeds in surreal fashion. Like it's being unveiled in slow motion. Ramona trips through the roll call and when she calls my name, I say, 'Still here and 136 days clean,' and I don't feel anything any more.

Everyone else's confronting everyone else for the smallest of infractions from last night. Rachel B didn't belt-loop her newcomers firmly enough, Rick didn't move back inside the building fast enough, Jennifer J gravitated towards her parents in all the chaos and she hadn't earned Talk privileges yet, Gino tried to restrain Ramona by mistake and none of us were paying proper attention to Dwight's commands over the bullhorn and all of us were responsible for allowing Toby S, Francis, Emily and Shaun N to escape because we obviously didn't do enough to stop them. So look what happened to Emily.

As a consequence, there are new rules, lots of 'em. First off, from now on, the doors to the parking lot are to remain locked during Open Meetings, just as they do at all other times. And there's a new fire-drill procedure according to which every first through third phaser must be properly accounted for and looped before anyone evacuates the building. An engineer has been called in to disconnect the smoke-alarm system so that nobody is tempted to panic if it goes off again unexpectedly which it won't any more. Because from now on, it's only a fire if a staff member says it is and not a moment sooner. Anybody who disobeys any of these rules will be set back, and not just a phase or two either; their entire programme will be immediately nullified and restarted.

About mid-morning, they drag Francis in. He's dirty, dishevelled, and has two black eyes and looks even more exhausted than the rest of us. And Francis who is, he declares, 681 days clean today, is immediately started over.

Not long after that, they untie us runners from our chairs and prop us up in the centre of the group. There are six of us, including Francis. The rest of the phasers scream at us from all sides, their insults and condemnations pelting us like hailstones, and Ramona takes her Ping-Pong paddle to us. And I don't feel anything any more.

Then the other runners sit down and it's just me left standing in the bear pit. Dwight announces to the group that I'm the worst offender, I was Toby S's main co-conspirator, that we'd been carrying on an illicit relationship under all their noses for weeks, that we'd wilfully set out to damage the programme and jeopardise the recovery of each and every one of them. I'm to blame, says Dwight, and they must vent the worst of their anger, their disappointment, frustration, hurt, bitterness and resentment, all their bad feelings towards me directly, with the fullness of their conviction.

It just doesn't seem real any more, not real at all. When my head lolls, that's what I tell myself. It can't possibly be real. It's just one long practical joke. We're on *Candid Camera*, that's it. They've hidden the miniature camera behind one of the needlepoints. I'm so certain, I can hear the whirring of the film, spinning round in its canister, recording every last indignity. Any minute now, you'll come loping out, smirking, trying not to burst. You'll hug me and call me a sucker for falling for it. 'Hey, Just, can't you take a joke?' 'Sure, I'll say, I love jokes.' Only when I try to laugh, that all stops. Freeze-frame. I want to laugh to make you standing there in front of me real as flesh and bone, only I can't. The dormant laughter chokes in my throat and the harder I try to get it out, the more I gag. The studio audience fades away, the cameras fall silent, and you disappear into the wings. We are not on *Candid Camera*.

Dwight and Ramona marshal all the phasers out of their seats and one by one they approach me to scream and call me names, they scratch at my face and tear at my hair, they slap, shake and punch me, boys included. They spit in my face, that too.

When the last phaser has sat down, Dwight proclaims that, also as part of my retribution to the group, I'll be required to stay late at the building each night for at least the next two weeks in order to carry out special penance exercises of his bidding.

I'm not on my period now and the bastard knows it. And I don't feel anything any more.

By lunch time, everyone's dizzy from no sleep and no food. Everyone, that is, except for the fifth phasers who've been napping in turns in the infirmary and the staffers who got to run themselves home for naps, shaves and showers. The rest of us are reeling and ravenous, and when they set out our course of Hardee's chilli dogs in front of us, we devour every last morsel, including the condiments, in next to no time.

Then the reporting slips are passed round again and some people burp or sneeze, some actually groan, because they've had their fill of reporting. After last night and this morning they're reported out. Not me. I accept my slip gladly and submit a real and proper account for the first time.

I report on Gwen.

I write about how she didn't check my bra for underwires when I first arrived and she strip-searched me, I write about how she threw my belongings out the window to cover up, and how she flicked me the birdie. I'm about to make up some stuff, too, but the pillowcase comes before I have a chance.

That afternoon, Gwen gets hauled up. It's unusual for such a senior phaser to be confronted in a rap so everybody perks up slightly when Gwen steps forward, startled. As confrontations go, it's pretty mild and Lois and Bo, who're on duty at the time, don't rile Gwen much, but a few other newcomer girls motivate to give feedback. They pounce up and say Gwen didn't check their bras either, their heels, shoelaces or whatever. Bo deals her a penance and says he'll discuss with Dwight just what it should be. She and her ponytail squirm deliciously as she glowers in my direction. And, though it's a minor confrontation by normal standards, I relish the moment.

CHAPTER FIFTY

We're going on fifteen and our annual family vacation is booked for the end of the summer. Dad announces that we're spending it in Ocean City again. We'll head out on our birthday itself so Mom acts like it's a special birthday treat. You mutter that it's hardly a treat when you don't want to go anyway and we'll just be staying in the same crap beach house as usual, so what's so special about that. Ocean Shitty, you call it.

Dad corrects you. 'We're not going to rent the beach house; this year, we're staying in the Hilton.'

We've never stayed in a five-star hotel before and I have to admit I'm pretty excited. The Hilton has its own private beach not two shakes from the boardwalk, not to mention two pools, a water slide and a nightly disco just for teens. Plus, you and I will have our own room; Mom says we can even order room service if we like.

The night before our birthday and our Hilton vacation, we're packing and I keep jogging down to say, this'll be fun, don't you think. And you actually seem excited too. You're packing tons and I make a joke that you must be packing enough to change your outfit three times a day.

You smile, a twinkle in your eyes for the first time in ages. 'I reckon there'll be some hot, rich guys staying at the Hilton. I want to look my best.'

I giggle and tell you to hush about that in front of Dad, but I'm so relieved to have you acting halfway normal again, I don't care what you say.

In the morning, Dad rises early to load the car. My suitcase is ready to go so I hop in the shower and when I hop out again, I hear banging. Downstairs, Mom bangs your locked door. 'Why's Joshua locked the door?' she asks when I come down, a towel wrapped around me. 'I don't think he can hear me, he must be sound asleep.'

The commotion brings Dad down next and he starts banging and shouting, too, ordering you to open up. The pair of them do that for maybe twenty minutes until Dad decides to break down the door. I don't tell him that I know how to pick the lock because that would be as good as admitting I knew you'd been locking your door for some time already, as good as saying I knew you had something to hide. Dad rams the door and it gives on the fourth go. Your room's dark, the curtains shut tight, but even by just the light of your old Mickey Mouse night-light, it's plain to see you're gone.

Two days later, the police find you, hiding out across town, living with the cotton-ball-side-burned driver, in a trailer park set next to a cemetery for a Seventh Day Adventist church. The driver's name is Vinny, he's twenty-three years old and he's arrested for harbouring a minor or some such and the police bring you home.

It's too late to go to Ocean City. Dad cancels the reservation at the Hilton and I overhear him railing at Mom late into the night. He grounds you indefinitely, you tell him to go to hell on a hockey stick then storm off to your room. I wonder what'll happen to driver Vinny and I wonder if he has crooked teeth, seeing as how he lives in a trailer and must never have been to an orthodontist like Dad. I mean to ask you whether you noticed, thinking that might tease a smile out of you. But when I sneak down to your room that night, the door's locked and you don't open up when I knock. 'Josh, it's just me. Let me in please.' You tell me to scram.

In the morning, it's you who's scrammed. Again. That second time, you're gone longer and you go much further than Vinny's trailer park. It's two weeks before we hear anything and then it's from police again down in Miami, Florida. They say you hitched all the way down I-95. They say some other things to Mom and Dad on the telephone, things I can't hear and they won't tell me about. Dad's face turns like stone and Mom weeps.

I look up Miami in our *Encyclopaedia Britannica*, and I find out that it sits in a part of Florida called the Gold Coast, that it has a subtropical climate, its Art Deco district is famous and so is its citrus fruit and it has a very nice aquarium. I reckon Miami probably isn't such a bad place.

The police in Miami have trouble apprehending you and getting you back home and Mom and Dad argue all the time. Dad says we oughta just give up on you. He says, if Miami's what Josh wants, let him have it. Joshua is no son of his. Mom calls Grandma Shirland and cries down the phone, and she pleads with Dad. Miami's no place for our baby, she tells him, and eventually she talks him round.

But later, when they think I'm out of the room and earshot, I hear Dad say, 'He's become too much for us, Helen. We can't handle him any more.'

Mom sniffles and maybe she agrees.

'He needs professional help,' Dad concludes.

CHAPTER FIFTY-ONE

The evening of my 136th day in the programme, I'm not doled out with the rest of the phasers. As Hilary, who's back on duty, unlocks the doors to the parking lot to release oldcomers and newcomers to moms, dads and newly serviced automobiles, Dwight towers over my chair and tells me it's time to retire to the solitaire room, time to make my amends. He's towering over me, mouthing the words, *you dirty little whore*, and I don't feel anything any more.

But a hand on Dwight's shoulder stops him. It's Hilary, who says not tonight. 'Everybody's tired. Justine can start her penance exercises tomorrow.'

Hilary doles me out to Moira as she leads Dwight away, and he casts me a look back over his shoulder that's pure wrath. It lets me know tomorrow night will be that much worse.

Outside, it's raining. Moira and I hustle ourselves over the wet, crunching gravel. By the time we reach the green station wagon with wood-effect side-panelling, my overgrown hair is matting to my brow and the crown of my head. Moira's dad's behind the wheel as usual. 'Hi, darlin',' he chimes. Moira tickles the back of his neck and asks him if he's had a good day.

'Had worse, I guess,' says Dad and then cautions us to be careful of the glass because he's not one hundred per cent sure they cleared it all up. He makes a joke about how his car was long overdue for a service anyway so no harm done last night really, as far as he's concerned. Then he goes quiet, yawning, driving, thinking to himself.

In the back seat, Moira and I listen to the windshield wipers, and the patter of raindrops on the car's roof. Then, out of nowhere, Moira starts small-talking me. Animatedly, she explains how Hilary isn't so awful, how Hilary had a younger brother, did I know that, and Hilary was the one who turned him on to drugs but then he got hooked real bad, he OD'd at the age of fifteen. Moira squeezes my knee for emphasis and tells how Hilary went straight after that and helped found the programme. She means well, really and truly, and she works so hard because she doesn't want what happened to her brother to happen to any other kids, not if she can help it. Hilary would keep the whole world off drugs if she could.

'Which isn't such a terrible aim, now is it?' My knee aches from her vice-like clutch. 'It isn't so awful.'

And I don't give a damn. I watch the raindrops dry on my forearm, goosebumps springing up. I'm feeling nothing any more so what's the point but I've got to know. No more screwing around. I turn to Moira and just come right out and ask. 'Did you turn me and Toby in?'

Off comes the hand from the knee. She makes a noise in the back of her throat and looks aghast or hurt or something. 'Everybody knew Toby was behind last night. They were wearing Gunther High football helmets for heaven's sake.'

'What about *me*?' I say. 'Did you turn *me* in?'

'Oh come on.' She widens her eyes and mouth around that expression of hers as she edges away. 'That was Gwen. She found your note under the lunch table. I warned you about that, Justine. I said you were passing too many notes, I told you to destroy them. Gwen was bragging to everybody in the fifth phaser rap last night about how she nailed you.'

'The fifth phasers left the room *after* the reports were submitted,' I recollect.

'So?'

'So Dwight told me *two* people reported me – which would have been *before* the fifth phasers left.'

Moira drops her eyes, bites her lip. She's edged so far away she's practically adhered to her passenger door like a fixture. She fiddles with the hole where the lighter goes except the lighters have all been removed because they're against the rules. 'It could have been anybody. How should I know who it was? Anybody could have seen you, it was getting too risky, you were careless.'

'I don't think anybody else saw anything.'

She fingers the lighter cavity, inspecting it like maybe there's a fault with the car. When she finally looks up, her eyes have darkened. She glares at me like she's found the mechanical glitch and I'm it. 'Why do you have to make everything so difficult, Justine? I tried and tried to help you, but you made it so difficult. Too stubborn, just like your brother. If you'd only told them what they wanted to hear. I mean, you're a smart girl, you could have been halfway through now. Other girls not half as bright as you, they started later and some of them are already on second phase. But you, you just won't play—'

'Why should I play along? Why should I lie and say I'm an addict? I'm *not* an addict.'

'You might be, you never know, Justine. You could have addictive tendencies. You—'

'No,' I cry. 'You said yourself, that first night I stayed at your house, you said I didn't have an addiction. You said there were others, too, people in the programme who shouldn't be here.'

'Ah hell, what do I know? I'm not the professional. Hilary's the professional. Hilary knows. She's trying to help. She just wants you to come clean.'

'I don't need to come clean. *I am not an addict!*'

Moira motions for me to keep my voice down lest her father intervene. 'Look!' she hisses, her eyes narrowing. 'Whether you are or you aren't, that's really not the issue any more. *My God*, you're so selfish.' She scowls and shakes her head. 'Gwen always said you were and I defended you. But now I can see you for what you really are. You think the programme is so terrible, you think it's such a hellish place. Well, let me tell you something. That hellish place back there saved my life. And it saved lots of other kids' lives, too.'

The back of my shirt's damp, especially between my shoulder blades where my wet hair has been dripping. It wouldn't be so bad on a summer night except that all the windows are wound shut and Moira's dad has the air conditioning cranked up. The treated air gusts straight down my spine. I shiver then remind myself I can't feel anything any more.

'What about Joshua?' I ask her, my voice flat as a French pancake. 'Did it save my brother's life?'

'*Fuck* Joshua!' she spits back. 'Fuck Joshua, Justine, and *fuck you* too. You are both selfish brats, only thinking of yourselves and what's best for you. There are lots of other people, lots more than just you and your twin brother, kids who *need* that place, who *need* recovery, and you, you're jeopardising that for all of us.'

320

'That's not true.'

'It is. Don't you listen to people in the raps, don't you hear the stories, what they've been through, what they've overcome?'

'I hear them, but so what? I don't know what to believe any more.'

'You can believe every word in every story. These are real people, real lives. They're opening up their hearts in that group, they're getting honest, just like you ought to.'

I don't recognise this person any more, this girl I once confided in. 'Moira, they've brainwashed you. Don't you see, people aren't honest in that place. They're terrified.'

'You kids OK back there?' Moira's dad calls out. Moira makes a shush signal in my direction, her forefinger to her lips, then tells him yeah, we're fine.

We listen to the windshield wipers and the sound of the rain on the rooftop – I love the sound of the rain – and I'm arguing but what's the point really because I don't feel much of anything any more. Still, I've got to know.

'So did you?' I ask again.

'Did I what?' It's more a challenge than a question; she knows exactly what's what.

'Turn me in.'

'Oh please.' Her eyes roll back into her head.

'I just want to hear you say it.' And that's the truth because I know now, I knew really back during the interrogation when Dwight held up the piñata of evidence, when I saw Toby's notes in with all the others. Dwight had me confused for a while. But it wouldn't have been Toby. And who else could it have been? Toby's red-inked notes, written just for me, were the proof. The ones Moira confiscated and played like a hand of poker, the ones she claimed she stuffed down the garbage disposal. I never actually saw her do that. Never saw it because it never happened. She was so right – I should have flushed them all as soon as I'd read them.

'I need you to admit it,' I tell her, and Moira growls, 'Drop it!' just as we come to an intersection.

That's when Moira's dad slams on the brakes at the red light and we all jerk forward in our seats. 'What on earth!' he exclaims and Moira tells me to buckle my seat belt.

A horn blares and the inside of the station wagon is pulsing off on off on with a piercing light. 'What on earth!' says Moira's dad and he flips his rear-view mirror down because it's bouncing the light directly into his eyes. Moira tells her dad to check the automatic safety locks are on.

I twist in my seat towards a red blur behind us. The windows have fogged over some but I make out a van and it's honking its horn, flashing its high beams off, on, off, on, off, on. I squint because I can't actually see much of anything when they're flashing directly into my eyes like that. I hear the red van revving its engine, honking and blaring, and there's loud music blasting out of the van's stereo, some heavy metal band and there are voices shouting that aren't part of the music.

The van judders forward and nudges the station wagon. Moira's dad swears and says he's not going to take this. He revs his engine, too, to get an early jump on the traffic light so he can speed us away from these damn crazy people. Then he lurches forward and rams right into the back of a VW Beetle, trying to speed through the intersection before the light turned red, coming the other way.

We all jerk forward in our seats, feel grateful for seat belts and swallow our hearts back down our throats.

The accident isn't too bad. Moira's dad is OK although his newly serviced station wagon's now belching smoke from under its hood. It looks like everyone's OK in the VW too, although its backside is mangled up like from a can opener, and the Beetle driver's going crazy. He shakes his fists, runs up to our car and screams at Moira's dad to get the fuck out you moron.

Meanwhile, the red van's still behind us, honking and flashing its high beams. Suddenly, there are more people running up to our car, swarming all around, shouting, screaming, singing along to the heavy metal music.

'What on earth!' exclaims Moira's dad.

The swarming people bang on the station wagon's smoking hood, on the roof, splashing in the puddles forming on the tarmac, dancing around with the rain slanting into their faces and flattening their hair. They start chanting next. I can't quite understand the words at first and then I realise. They're chanting my name.

'Just-tine! Just-tine! Just-tine!'

Then there's a face plastered up against my window, startling me. Through the window's fog, the face is just a distortion of shapes and colours. I drag my sleeve across the glass to clear it and I see the face is grinning, friendly and very familiar. It's Toby! He's at the window! He's chanting for me! Toby S has come to my rescue, just like he said he would.

I claw at the handle but the child-safety lock's on and I can't open the door. I put my hand to the window where Toby's face is pressed up against the other side and smudge my fingers all over the glass.

'Let me go,' I tell Moira.

'You shouldn't, Justine. Don't go. It's not right.' Her voice sounds shrill and strangled. 'You should stay and work through the hard stuff, stick it out. You'll be glad for it later.'

I think of Dwight, I think of you, Joshua, and all the others and I could scratch this girl's condescending do-good eyes out. 'Let me go.'

'You said yourself you belong here.'

'No, I didn't.'

'What did you say then?'

'I said I deserved it.'

'So?'

'I don't believe that any more.' I'm sorry, Joshua, sorry for everything. I'm sorry Francis, Shaun; I'm so sorry, Emily. But I don't deserve this. 'Nobody deserves this' and I mean that. Then I scream at Moira, at the top of my lungs. 'Let me go!!!'

Toby and his friends bang the windows now, harder and harder, and they chant my name and bounce footballs off the windshield. It's an order this time, not a plea or a request or a prayer. I'm through with this shit.

'Just-tine! Just-tine!'

Via the rear-view mirror, her dad beseeches Moira for instruction and she tells him to unlock the doors. 'They'll just break the windows again if you don't.'

I claw at the handle and it gives this time.

'They'll catch you, you know,' Moira says. 'Somebody will turn you in and they'll put you back in the programme for a long, long time. You can't trust anybody. Somebody will turn you in. They always do – eventually.'

But I'm not listening to her any more because now the door's open and I'm leaping into the street, into the rain, into Toby S's arms. I'm in Toby's arms and he speaks to me, directly to me, for the very first time.

'I hope you didn't think I'd forgotten about you,' he says.

CHAPTER FIFTY-TWO

You killed yourself. Of course you did. And I found you. It was New Year's Eve and we were fifteen years, four months and six days old.

You'd only come home the week before. Mom, Dad and I were all at the Open Meeting when you made your victory dash. None of us had been expecting it and we were ecstatic, more ecstatic still when they said you could stay with us for a whole week. Normally, coming home privileges only lasted one weekend, after which the phaser was supposed to return to the programme, living in host homes again until phase four. That's when they came home for good, assuming they didn't suffer any setbacks, and when they themselves became oldcomer hosts to new newcomers.

But because you earned your first home privileges on Christmas Eve and the programme facility was shutting for a few days over the holidays, they made an exception. There were conditions, of course, lots of rules, and we had to drive you back for raps on the days that weren't public holidays, but the important thing was you were at home.

We had a quiet Christmas because, with you in the house, we weren't allowed to play any music, not even traditional carols, and we weren't allowed to give you any presents so we agreed to forego all gift-giving. And you were quiet too, very quiet. We asked what you'd been learning in the programme but you didn't want to talk about it and we weren't supposed to talk about friends, music, TV shows, current affairs or whatever so there wasn't much to say at all. But what a meal we had! Turkey and cranberry sauce, stuffing and rolls, ham, pies, fruit salad and everything – all the trimmings.

At night, I'd creep downstairs to sleep in your room with you. It was amazing to be near you again and though we hadn't slept in the same room for years, it felt so right. We brought out the rollaway and took turns sleeping on it versus the proper bed, just like we used to do when we were little and would fight over who got to have Christy Crybaby or Teddy Kennedy or whoever tucked in beside them. We didn't fight any more. We didn't gab into the wee hours like we used to either because there was nothing to say, but I listened to you breathe and it soothed me. Once or twice during the night when I was sure you were asleep, I snuggled, placed my nose at your neck and took a whiff. You still smelled like you, Joshua, and it was wonderful.

One night when I came into my room, I discovered you there. I thought, happily, that you'd at last taken the initiative to be near me again. But you didn't stick around. Instead, you asked me not to come downstairs later. You told me you never had a chance to sleep alone and it would be nice to for a night or two. 'You understand, don't you, Justine?' you said and I swore I did even though I didn't and I felt wounded to my soul.

On New Year's Eve, your last night at home, Mom and Dad were invited to a party. They promised they wouldn't be late and in the morning we'd go out for a special New Year's Day family brunch at ChiChi's before we drove you back. I'd been invited to a New Year's Eve party, too, with Cindy and Lloyd and the gang, but we weren't supposed to leave you alone so I declined. You thought I was staying in because I had to watch you, like I was on baby-sitting duty, even though I said that wasn't true and I wanted to stay home and be with you.

Once alone, I suggested we flick on Dick Clark. You said it was against the rules and I said, ah heck, who's to know. When the ball dropped in Times Square, we toasted the new year in with wine glasses filled with apple juice and munched Entenmann's gourmet cookies.

At about twelve thirty, the doorbell rang and it was Cindy and Lloyd. If Mohammed couldn't come to the mountain, the mountain would come to Mohammed, they chirped. They came armed with silly hats, noisemakers and party horns that rolled out like tongues. They knew you were home and wanted to see you. They'd been missing you, too. Although they were kind of tipsy from wine coolers and imitation champagne, they weren't totally wasted or anything. I told them to hang on while I checked.

When I returned to the lounge, the TV and Dick Clark were zapped off and you were just sitting there. I asked if you were feeling OK and you said sure. I said Cindy and Lloyd were at the door and you grunted.

'Shall I let them in?'

'I can't mix with druggie contacts,' you told me.

'They're not druggie contacts, it's Cindy and Lloyd, for God's sake. We've known them since we were eight.'

'Whatever. But I can't say their names and I can't see them. It's against the rules. In fact, no one but family is supposed to be in

327

the house at all,' you said, your speech accelerating, your hands bunching into tight balls. 'That's against the rules. And Mom and Dad shouldn't be gone either because there should always be at least one parent in the house, and we shouldn't be watching TV because that's against the rules, too.'

I got annoyed with you then. 'Your rules are a pain in the ass.'

'They're not my rules, Justine.'

'Yeah, well, they stink anyway.' I stomped out of the room, trying to fabricate some excuse for why Cindy and Lloyd couldn't come in. As it was, I just told them the truth and we sat outside shivering on the steps for half an hour or so kind of laughing about you, Joshua, and all those stupid rules. We didn't mean to be nasty, but it seemed so silly.

When they left and I came back inside, you weren't in the lounge any more. I looked in your bedroom, in both beds, and you weren't there. You weren't in the bathroom either or the kitchen or my room or the master bedroom. You weren't in the guest room, the living room, Dad's study or the garage. I started to panic. You weren't in the basement either and you weren't in the attic. If you ran away again when I was supposed to be watching you, I'd be in so much trouble. You were probably halfway to Florida by now and Dad would have to telephone the police again and all that shit and Mom would have a breakdown. Anything but that, I prayed, anything.

And then I found you in the back yard.

Mom likes to think it was an accident. I'd like to believe that, too, but for the longest time I couldn't believe anything. I wouldn't believe you were gone at all.

The truth is, it was no accident, was it, Josh? A person does not take a running leap off a diving board into an empty pool by accident. They said later you must have bounced on the board several times, got some serious height, and you must have done one of those fancy forward dives you liked to do when you were showing off, because you plummeted head first into that pool and struck the bottom of the deep end so hard it cracked your skull open like it was no sturdier than an eggshell. Even so, that wasn't what killed you. It knocked you out good and probably would have killed you or left you a vegetable, but what killed you in the end was about two inches of water. A puddle of four-month-old chlorinated pool water that hadn't drained away completely and was half iced over, filled with leaves, dirt and God-knows-what. You drowned in that.

They told our mother I was in shock and maybe so because I don't remember what happened afterwards. I must have known it was no use calling anybody. They say I lay down beside you and I imagine I was trying to smell you though the smell of the chlorine, though the blood and ice probably masked that lovely aroma of yours. They say our parents had to hold me down when the coroners came to take you away. They say I stayed there at the bottom of the pool for two full days, until Grandma Shirland arrived and coaxed me up the ladder from the deep end.

CHAPTER FIFTY-THREE

Toby and I both know we can't go home. And we can't stay with Cindy or Lloyd or whoever of his friends because they'll surely come looking for us there. We've got to go somewhere far away and quick. I suggest Kansas.

'Like with those little singing munchkins?' Toby jibes.

That was Oz, I say, where the wizard lived, the wicked witch and the flying monkeys. 'Kansas was safe, the place Dorothy and Toto were trying to get back to.'

'The black and white bit?' Toby asks and I say yeah.

One of his friends lends us some money to catch a Greyhound and we leave that very night after Toby rescues me from the green station wagon and Moira. The Greyhound drives through the night and somewhere around Pittsburgh it stops raining and we stay up talking. I don't think we close our eyes for one single solitary second. I ask Toby how he ended up in the programme. He says he and his football buddies used to raise some hell and I can believe that, but that was acceptable to his parents because, after all, the team had gone all the way to State. After the football season, Toby kept raising hell and his parents weren't so enthusiastic any more, but it was acceptable because by that time Toby had sewn up his scholarship. It was only for a

330

small private school in Illinois, River Oaks College – 'Hey,' says Toby, 'I was a good quarterback but I wasn't that good.' – but that was acceptable because it was a full-tuition scholarship and you couldn't look a gift horse in the mouth. What wasn't acceptable was when Toby told his parents a couple of months before graduation that he was thinking about postponing college and the all-paid-for scholarship because he and some of his buddies wanted to travel round Europe for a year. Toby's parents freaked. They had visions of him and his friends raising hell in London or Paris or Madrid or wherever and that was most certainly not acceptable. They told him he was ruining his life and Toby said, 'It's my life,' but they weren't prepared to accept that. Next thing he knew he was in Come Clean.

Toby tells me more details about the escape, too. In fact, he didn't organise any of it because how could he from the inside. It was his little sister – whose name is Stephanie and he's certain I'd like her – who orchestrated the evening. She thought the very idea of her big brother being a drug addict was totally bogus so she rounded up his hell-raising football friends and planned it all. They just had to wait until after final exams and graduation, but his friends were up for it. And then Stephanie tipped Toby off in the Open Meeting the week before.

'We have some secret hand signals, Stephanie and I,' Toby explains. 'You know, from when we were kids.'

It's pitch black outside the bus and we're the only passengers with our reading lamps still lit. Somebody hisses at us to turn our lights out and let us all get some sleep already. So we douse them and we mustn't be near any towns because it's absolutely pitch black outside. But neither of us are the least bit tired, we don't want to give in to sleep so we carry on in whispers.

I can't believe it's only been twenty-four hours or so since the interrogation when Dwight got me so twisted in my thinking that I resorted to turning Toby in. I want to apologise to him but I can't talk about that, and I can't bear to think about the others I betrayed. So instead I tell Toby how much his notes meant to me on the darkest days in the programme. 'There's just one thing that puzzles me. What does G.A. stand for?'

And he tells me: it stands for Guardian Angel. That makes me well up and think of you, which is what I tell Toby. So then he asks me about you and I tell him a little, but not too much. I don't feel ready to talk about a lot of things yet, though I do tell Toby 'yeah' when he asks me if I think you would have liked him and really honestly, Josh, you would.

We stare out the windows and maybe I am feeling just the teensiest bit tired. It's pitch black outside and I don't know what time it is because I never did get my Swatch back. There are no house lights, streetlights or neon signs, only the reflection from the stars and with our lamps off, it feels like we're in a spaceship and we're flying.

It occurs to me that I still don't know Toby's full name.

'Toby Louis Sheridan,' he tells me. 'And you?'

'Justine Amanda Ziegler.'

'Damn pleased to meet you, Justine Amanda Ziegler,' he says and I say I'm damn pleased to meet him too. Then he shakes my hand and doesn't let go. He grips it all night, tight like a lifeline.

CHAPTER FIFTY-FOUR

We arrive in Edmiston, Kansas, in the morning, turfing up at Grandma Shirland's house with nothing but the clothes on our backs. She hugs me hard, hugs Toby even though she's just met him and tells him she's damn pleased to meet him too. Then she whips up some pancakes, takes us clothes shopping at the local Kmart – which is fine by me – and installs us in the guest rooms at opposite ends of the hall from one another and that's fine too.

Mom's the first to call. Toby and I listen as Grandma says, 'No I didn't know… you don't say… no.' Her eyebrows twist into slugs of concern, she swears blind to Mom – and then to Dad, then Dwight, then Hilary when they call – that she hasn't seen hide nor hair of us.

But our mom knows her own mom well enough, I guess, and she twigs before long. One day in early July, Mom arrives on the doorstep, unannounced just like Toby and I had except she's carrying a suitcase. Assuming Dad must be with her, Toby and I run and hide behind the rusting shed in Grandma's vegetable garden. But after a little while, Grandma Shirland pokes her head round the corner of the shed. Mom's on her own, she tells us.

Once Toby and I are cajoled back into the house, Mom gathers us both in a perfumed embrace and presents us Tic Tacs from her pocketbook. Then, tearing at the plies of a man-sized Kleenex, she informs us that she's left our father. She doesn't know if they'll divorce – she dreads to think of having to pay for good dental care – but she knows they need a break. She says she thinks Dad might be having an affair. She blames herself.

'I was in an awful state after we put you in the programme, Justine. The house was so empty. I wept around the clock. Your father simply didn't know what to do, and Lord how he hated attending those interminable Friday meetings. Then his work became extremely busy – or so he said – and he missed one meeting, then another and another. Some nights, even when it wasn't a Friday, he'd come home so late I'd already be asleep. Then, when he made you go back in after that awful night with the bombs and rockets in the parking lot… Well, I know he felt terribly guilty, but I couldn't forgive him even still. I couldn't bear the thought of losing both you and Joshua for ever, my two little monkeys. Your father couldn't look at me – he stayed gone for nearly two days after that. He was the only person I had left and I was losing him, too.'

When I ask Mom who she thinks Dad's mistress is and she tells me his dental receptionist – 'You remember Zoe Micklebaum, don't you?' – it almost makes me laugh. If Mom and Dad did get divorced and Zoe left muscle-bound Felix and married Dad, then her initials really would be ZZ.

It's a nice summer and the four of us fall into a routine pretty quickly. We sleep in, shop at the Kmart or the new mall outside town, visit the library to leaf through magazines and check out escapist novels (Harlequin romances for me, Mom and Grandma, sci-fi thrillers for Toby), we go to half-price matinees in the middle of the afternoon or stay at home and overdose on soap operas and reruns of sitcoms.

Toby says he needs to get back in shape so he exercises a lot, jogs every evening around dusk, spends hours at the YMCA, does push-ups and sit-ups, pumps hand weights the size of barrels before he goes to bed.

Often, while Toby's exercising, Mom, Grandma Shirland and I indulge in girlie things. We become regulars at the Edmiston Ladies' Beauty Salon. I change my hairstyle every week or so, Mom tries out highlights and a new shade called Sierra Gold, Grandma has a facial and we all sign up for a Colour Me Beautiful makeover. The colour consultant decides I'm a Deep Winter and should wear primary colours, black eyeliner and terracotta blush. Grandma, meanwhile, is a Cool Summer, best suited to greys, violets and blue-based reds, and Mom's a Warm Spring who should avoid pure whites in favour of browns and beiges. With our colour charts in hand, we attack the mall afresh and come home laden with new wardrobes and weird and wonderful nail polishes for daily manicures.

In the evenings, Mom and Grandma Shirland teach Toby and me how to cook and we eat altogether at the dining room table, chattering in between bites about whatever we want or nothing at all and listening instead to the radio or the music of crickets on the warm cross breeze that blows through the house's open windows. After the place settings are cleared, we watch a movie from Blockbuster or we madeover ladies give Toby a fashion show or we play Trivial Pursuit or Grandma brings out photo albums and talks us through the yellowing images of her wedding day or the life stages of a little-girl Mom with curls and buck teeth ('Long before I knew any orthodontists,' Mom sighs).

Then, when we retire to bed, we leave our bedroom doors unlocked, swinging wide open, and the bathroom light stays on all night.

We do all of those things. What we don't do is talk about Come Clean. Toby says he just wants to forget and that suits me, because I'm sure if he knew everything, he'd never look at me the same way again. Not him, or Grandma or Mom, who seem happy enough to pretend too.

CHAPTER FIFTY-FIVE

So all of our routines for forgetting and pretending make for a nice summer all right, and – despite the fact that neither you nor Dad are with us and that whenever Dad calls, every few days, Mom bats the receiver away and retreats by herself to the porch – life in Kansas starts to feel almost normal. Until one evening about four weeks after Mom's arrival.

Toby's gone out for his regular jog, Mom and Grandma are in the kitchen preparing stroganoff for supper, the aroma of warming garlic bread just gathering force, and I'm in the front room relaxing in front of the TV and an episode of the *Brady Bunch* so oft-watched that I can recite the lines. It's the one where the Brady boys knock Carol's vase over and break it and then try to fix it with glue. The scene where the basketball comes hurtling down the stairs is being replayed for about the 555th time.

I hear the screen door open and thwack shut behind me and glance at my new watch to check that Toby has time for his post-jog shower before dinner. I hear Bobby Brady's echo of 'Mom always said, don't play ball in the house,' and then another voice, not from the TV and not Toby's, says to me, 'See what happens when you don't follow the rules, Miss Justine Z.'

I go rigid for a millisecond or two until a hand reaches over my shoulder and hits the remote on the armchair. The television images snap away to a pinprick and I whirl round to face Dwight.

'Surprised?'

He looks the same, all fanged grin and slick blond hair. 'I reckon you didn't expect to meet old Dwight again, did ya? You certainly don't seem too happy to see me,' he remarks and pulls an exaggerated frown as if he's hurt by the rejection. 'But I'm happy to see you, Justine, very happy.'

The screen door creaks and thwacks again as Hilary enters carrying a briefcase and twirling a Hertz rental-car key chain around her finger. She looks taller than I remember, positively Amazonian. Dwight licks his lips greedily before Hilary draws level with him, and I realise I've been holding my breath. I exhale as I back away from them, bumping a side table as I do so. The table's lamp teeters and then tumbles to the floor. It smashes into awkward-shaped pieces just like the Brady vase.

'OK out there, Justine?' Mom calls from the kitchen.

'Mrs Ziegler?' Hilary calls back.

Mom might recognise Hilary's voice but Grandma doesn't. 'Honey, if that's the Avon lady, tell her we already ordered at the salon,' Grandma shouts.

But when she enters the room, wiping her hands on a paper towel, Grandma Shirland must sense that Dwight and Hilary are not from Avon. Mom, on Grandma's heels, knows them at once and stops short.

'Mrs Ziegler, you're aware why we're here,' says Hilary. 'I'm glad you're on hand to help.'

'Help with what?' Grandma wants to know. 'What's all this about?'

'Mrs Shirland, correct?' says Hilary, offering her hand in

338

introduction. 'We're staff from the Come Clean rehabilitation centre in Pennsylvania.'

Grandma makes no move to shake Hilary's hand, just stares at it stubbornly until Hilary lets it drop.

'We've come to ensure that Justine here has a chance to complete her recovery,' Hilary continues. 'We've come to take her back to the programme.'

'The hell you are!' Grandma steps in front of me defensively. She wads up her paper towel and pitches it at Dwight's feet. 'Now get out of my house. Nobody asked you here, you've got no right.'

Hilary props her briefcase up on to her thigh. 'In fact, we do have a right to be here,' she says, clicking open the case and pulling out a sheaf of official-looking papers, rubber-banded in the middle. 'We've been given parental permission.'

My eyes fly to our mother and so do Grandma Shirland's but shock has registered on Mom's face too. She tips her head from side to side. 'I – I – I gave no such thing.'

'No,' agrees Hilary, 'you didn't, Mrs Ziegler, but *Mr* Ziegler did.'

Our father, Joshua. *Believe in Him.*

Mom starts to argue, then dissolves into customary tears. 'Don't you hurt my baby again,' she wails. And Grandma Shirland gets angry. She grabs a broom and tries to shoo Dwight and Hilary out of her house as if they were misguided flies. All along, I stand there, wanting to do something, but only able to keep standing, mute and frozen, like when we used to play statues.

Hilary continues to speak calmly, saying how we shouldn't make this more difficult than it need be, this is for Justine's own good, she'll thank us all one day. Besides there's no point in fighting, she contends, holding up the briefcase papers, it's been legally authorised. Then she says, 'I took the precaution of calling the local police for backup before we arrived. They'll be here any minute.'

Police. I can't get arrested, Joshua. If they take me back into the programme now, I know I'll never get out in one piece again. They really will throw away the keys this time and every night will be like our worst nightmares with Dwight in the solitaire room or else something worse. I can't get arrested, I can't. And Mom can't stop them, Grandma can't stop them. Terror rises within me and I've got to get out of here, we've got to get out, got to run and run, keep running and never stop.

I lift my frozen feet and make a dash for the kitchen, the back door and the vegetable garden. But Dwight's too fast, he captures me before I even reach the dining room and shoves me back roughly against the wall where Grandma's watercolour paintings hang. One painting falls to the floor and the wooden frame splinters, the glass breaking into more jagged pieces like the lamp and the Brady vase.

'Don't you hurt my baby!' screams Mom.

'Now, Justine,' Hilary reasons, 'this will be so much easier if you don't resist. Mrs Ziegler, Mrs Shirland, I know this must seem heavy-handed, but let's not focus on the means, let's focus on the ends. We need to keep in mind what's best for Justine.'

I cling to the wall while Hilary tells our mother and grandmother that I'm sick, just like you were sick. Addiction's an illness, she says. You were an addict and now I'm an addict. Co-dependency is an illness, too. You and I were co-dependent. She explains the signs, symptoms and consequences of co-dependency. She says I need help, they must help me.

I squeeze my eyes shut.

Mom weeps, Grandma throws in a 'Hogwash!' or two and Dwight paces in the background, opening his mouth every so often, then reconsidering, and biting his tongue. And the panic's in me, Josh. In my mind, I retrace the route to the back door, I wonder whether the bathroom window's unlocked, I try to remember if there's a baseball bat in the hall closet where the winter coats are kept. I measure the distance to the front door. If I hit Dwight over the head with the bat and rammed my way past Hilary, I might – just might – be able to get away.

I'm so distracted imagining what could happen that I almost miss it when Toby appears, sweaty and out of breath, on the front porch. But I see him before anyone else does and I see, as he peers inside, the look of horror, mutating into anger, then fury, that sweeps across his face.

Hilary and Dwight, their backs to the door, don't notice Toby until they hear the screen thwack and then he's charging across the entryway and, just like in the rap when Dwight tried to make me ashamed of you, he's tackling Dwight. There are no fifth phasers to restrain Toby, but Dwight doesn't seem to need much help this time. The two men wrestle on the floor for a few minutes, another lamp topples and shatters, Mom screams and Grandma tries to jab her broom in to separate them. Then Dwight lands a well-placed blow and another, a kick in Toby's groin and then, as Toby crouches over in pain, Dwight elbows him in the back of the head. Toby collapses into an unconscious heap.

Mom gasps, Grandma drops the broom and the three of us fall silent, listening to the sound of Dwight's panting. The garlic bread is burning out in the kitchen now and the stench is horrible.

Hilary clears her throat. 'I don't really think that kind of force was necessary.'

Dwight wheels on her, incredulous. 'Didn't ya see him attack me?'

'Yes, but—'

'Come on! Didn't ya see him come charging out of nowhere?' Dwight's voice rises a notch or two as he jabs his finger towards the floor where Toby lies. 'Besides, this is better, much better. Now we can take them both in. We were always going to get her...' He grabs my arm and jerks me into his chest. '...but he would have been more difficult. That one was always going to put up a fight. Now he'll come along quietly enough.'

'Don't touch her,' our mother screeches.

'Right,' says Hilary, 'let's all just calm down. Let go of Justine, OK?' She waits a beat. 'Dwight. I said, let go of her.'

His grip tightens around my wrist, then twists, tearing at the little hairs. Reluctantly, Dwight releases me. I stagger backwards, trip over Toby's foot and break my fall awkwardly with a squat. 'Sure,' Dwight says, his teeth gritted. 'I can lay off. No problem.' He spreads out his fingers like a magician trying to prove he's not hiding the quarter up his sleeves. 'Whatever you say, Hil. You're the boss.'

I steady myself against the back of the sofa. My ankle hurts, the room's spinning and not even the prisms I keep hammering into my brain can keep it still. They're going to take me away again, Joshua, and there's nothing I can do to stop them. I grasp the sofa, struggle to find my balance and my voice.

'He doesn't mean that,' I manage to whisper.

Hilary settles her attention on me. 'What's that?'

'He doesn't think you're the boss, he thinks *he's* the boss, the real boss.'

Dwight laughs and Hilary nervously follows suit.

'It's true, he told me so. And he doesn't mean it either when he says he'll lay off. He's only backing down now in front of you and Mom and Grandma. It's different when you're not here. Once you're gone, he'll do more than that.'

Dwight flaps his hand in dismissal. 'Give it a rest, Justine, no one wants to hear what you've got to say.'

'I wanna hear it,' says Grandma Shirland.

Hilary considers then nods for me to go on. So I do go on. I spill the beans about Dwight and the threats, the confrontations, the Ping-Pong paddles, the special penances. Her eyes flash at mention of the solitaire room. Is something dawning there? Maybe not. Before I can glean any meaning, she erases all expression from her face.

Oh, but I've got a mouth on me, Dwight, and I know how to use it. I keep talking though he tries to interrupt and out-yell me. He breaks into a sweat, his brow glistening as the room fills with smoke from the burning garlic bread. Maybe if the alarm goes off, it would distract them and I could make it out the front door and down the drive. They'd still get Toby, but I might be able to find some way to come back for him later. Does Grandma even have a smoke detector?

I stop to catch my breath, and Dwight intones sternly, 'I think we've heard enough of this.'

'No! No one's heard nearly enough yet.' I go on and tell them about the *Encyclopaedia Britannica*, volume M; about his undressing me. When I describe myself on the floor on my knees, my mother faints and joins Toby on the floor in an unconscious heap.

'Is this true?' Hilary asks Dwight. 'Any of it?'

He snorts and half spins his eyes in response. Grandma Shirland takes a cushion from the sofa to prop up Mom's head and I go on. I tell them what Dwight had in store for me next, what he's promised will happen once he corners me into solitary again.

'She's lying!' Dwight's sweating, grunting in feigned disbelief, pacing the floor behind Hilary who stands positioned between us now like a wall. 'It's nothing but lies. It's so sad how all addicts lie like they do. Pathetic.'

'I'm not the only one either,' I persist. 'I don't know how many others there have been, but I know my brother was one of them.'

Grandma shakes her head and holds her arm up like a shield to keep from hearing any more, but I go on still, avoiding the look in her eyes.

'Dwight tormented him,' I say, and I can't imagine the half of it, I know that Josh. What must have happened, especially in those final days, when even being promoted to second phase and coming home didn't alleviate your despair? What did he do to you that drove you into my bedroom that night at Christmas – that's when it must have been – searching for my journal, for ammunition, some kind of temporary protection? What did he do that made you want to... I can't even begin to put it into the right words. 'He probably drove Josh to do what he did,' I announce.

'Don't be fucking ridiculous!'

'OK, OK,' says Hilary, 'let's all take a breath and try to calm down now.'

'Shut the fuck up, will ya!' Dwight snaps in her startled face.

'You did, you son of a bitch, you did. You *raped* him and – and... I don't know what... He got away from you the only way he could!' On the diving board, on New Year's Eve, on a frost-bitten night.

Dwight pushes past Hilary and launches himself at me. 'Shut

your dirty, fucking mouth!' He blasts, grabbing me by the throat with one hand, slapping me across the cheek with the other, Claddagh-ringed one. 'I did not rape that little faggot. I *told* you. He wanted it, he was begging for it.'

I can't breathe. Like you in the water, Joshua, all two inches of it. Dwight has me by the throat, he's shaking me and I can't breathe. I try to focus on Grandma Shirland's watercolours, Impressionist imitations, pond lilies, boating parties, ballerinas floating by.

He unhands me at last and there's nothing more to say. I gulp for air, and Grandma Shirland and Hilary stare at Dwight with dark expressions. I should run now, make a break for it, but I have no energy for running.

'Lies,' Dwight mutters, taking a step back, then two. He tucks in the tails of his now dishevelled polo shirt, smoothes down his hair, squares his shoulders. 'Don't ya worry about a thing, Hil. We'll straighten this all out once we're back at the programme. These two will be back on the road to recovery before you can snap your fingers. I'll see to that.'

He's talking in that aw-shucks voice of his now, while shifting his weight from foot to foot. 'Hey, did I ever tell you that I own the record for the fastest time ever through the Seven Steps? That was down at the Tennessee centre. Less than six months, that was my Step time. One hundred and sixty-seven days.' He whistles long and high at the sweetness of the memory. 'Lordy, they loved me down there. When I made counsellor, they took a picture of me and it got printed in the local newspaper. A credit to the rehabilitation process, that's what the caption said. Boy, if there's anybody you can count on to get a kid back on track, it's me, don't ya worry about that.'

There's a rap at the door while Dwight reminisces. Two

uniformed policemen tip their caps, and Hilary motions for them to come in. One of the policemen looks younger than Toby, he has a faint peach-fuzz moustache trembling over his top lip and teeth the colour of milk, but the other cop's older and broader and has his hand poised over his gun holster as if that was the only place for it. *I can't get arrested, Josh.*

'You Miss Navarre?' the older cop asks. Hilary nods and this is the first time I've heard a person address her by her last name. Hilary Navarre. It sounds more foreign than I ever imagined.

The cop squints at the four of us standing and then at Toby and Mom sprawled out on the floor. His young, milk-toothed partner fans his face. The air's thick now with smoke from the charred garlic bread. Grandma Shirland mustn't have a smoke detector.

'You requested help in apprehending somebody?' the older cop sputters.

'Yes,' reply Hilary and Dwight simultaneously.

'Yes,' Hilary says, louder, firmer, holding up a hand to silence Dwight.

The two officers don't look like unreasonable men. Maybe I could talk to them, get them on my side. Maybe, I tell myself, but I know Dwight and Hilary have that piece of paper Dad signed, I know it's wishful thinking. Nothing can stop them.

Hilary fixes her eyes on me, and I can't read the meaning of her look. I wonder if that kid brother of hers, the one who overdosed, had eyes like that, small, grey, widely set. I wonder if he could ever tell what she was thinking or feeling.

'Yes,' she repeats, and those eyes follow her extended arm, her hand, her fingers. And then her stop sign gesture turns into an arrow and it's pointing straight at Dwight. 'Please apprehend that man there, Officers.'

CHAPTER FIFTY-SIX

Summer resumes but the season's lost its lazy lustre. Toby, Mom, Grandma Shirland and I sleep in, shop, rent videos, check out novels and whatever else like before but without enthusiasm. Dorothy and Toto notwithstanding, Kansas doesn't feel safe, sound or black and white now, and none of us is quite sure what we've escaped from or why or if we really have.

Before long, Toby turns eighteen and no one can put him anywhere he doesn't want to be any more – and that's something he is sure about. Gunther High lets him finish his coursework by correspondence, his diploma arrives in the mail, and after all that, he decides to go ahead and enrol at River Oaks College for the fall. I guess, like Kansas and summer, maybe Europe has lost its lustre too. Toby buys a map at the Texaco and shows me where River Oaks is. Only a couple of hours by Greyhound, he says, even closer once I get my driver's licence, which won't be long now.

The night before he departs, Toby and I climb the fence at the back of Grandma's vegetable garden and trespass on to the farmland that borders her property. The field there has been rotated and left fallow and the grass reaches up past our shins, tickling the soft spots at the back of my knees as we walk.

We spread out the afghan we swiped from Grandma's day bed and lie down with a picnic of corn dogs, apple juice and Peanut M&Ms.

Gazing up at the stars, we munch, sigh, digest. I think of the stickers Moira's parents pasted on the ceiling of their phaser room and they definitely got the constellations all wrong. Toby knows some of the ones I don't recall so well from the lectures of Miss Fawcett or Mrs Wolf or Mr Newhouse or whoever it was, and he points them out to me – Cassiopeia, Orion's Belt and some others. I show him Gemini, the Twins, which is one I do remember. It makes me think of you and the stars look much like the fireflies you loved to catch, flickering up there in the sky just out of reach. I tell Toby about how you used to think those wily little bugs were called fairies, as in Tinkerbell with her pixie dust.

'Hmmm,' says Toby dreamily and we both imagine what it would be like to fly the way Peter Pan could.

Long minutes pass before either of us finds anything more we want to say and then it's me who breaks the silence. I stumble over the words a bit, but I finally get them out. I thank Toby for rescuing me, which causes him to chuckle. 'Who ever said you needed rescuing, Justine Ziegler?' he asks. Then he grips my hand and doesn't let go. Maybe, after all, Toby needed rescuing too, just like you, Mom and Dad, and all of us.

The next morning, mid-August, Toby kisses Mom, Grandma and me, promises to write and waves us goodbye, hanging out the window of the Illinois-bound Greyhound, en route to football practice and college registration.

Our birthday rolls around after Toby's departure. I turn sweet sixteen on my own and tell Mom and Grandma I don't want a cake or any presents. We treat ourselves to an expensive meal at an Italian restaurant instead, and the waistcoated waiter frets and dispenses grated parmesan as we all weep into our pasta. Grandma Shirland massages the small of Mom's back, little circular motions interspersed with pat-pats, says 'there-there', and calls Mom her baby.

'Your mother never did know how to cope with twins,' Grandma muses across the restaurant candlelight after Mom sniffles away to the bathroom. 'She tried, of course, she meant well, but she always felt so left out around the two of you.' I can't think how to respond, Joshua, so I just wait for Mom to come back and volunteer some loose change for the tip.

Sometimes when we're at home or in the car or at the Kmart, Mom musters up the nerve to ask more about you and me and what happened to us in the programme, about those things she started to hear the day Dwight and Hilary came. Mom believes she wants to know the details; she can take it, she says. So I tell her little snatches of incidents, not even the worst bits, until she brakes the car and jumps out, dashes away to the porch or hunches over blubbering and apologising.

'Your father and I really did believe it was for your own good,' she tells me.

Grandma, on the other hand, never asks about the programme or if I'm OK or how I'm feeling. Maybe that's why it's easier with her. I don't like to with Mom in the room, but when she's not around, I often find myself talking to Grandma about you. Sometimes we just talk about the old days, before everything changed. Other times, we talk about now.

Grandma says it's OK for me to still communicate with you the way I do. She admits that, though Grandpa Shirland, God rest his soul, has been dead for five years, she still says goodnight to him each and every night. I tell her I don't only say goodnight to you. I tell her we have whole conversations with one another, reliving moments from our childhood, when we dressed the same and thought the same and were the same, and all sorts. Grandma says that's perfectly understandable. And then I confess that, actually, that's not all either.

'Every thought,' I tell her one afternoon as we sit at the Edmiston Ladies' Beauty Salon waiting for our toenails to dry, 'every single thought that passes through my mind… It's like it's not my thought at all. It's like Joshua's in my head, and I'm talking to him all the time.'

Grandma Shirland says that's OK, too. 'Joshua will always be in your head, Justine,' she tells me. 'And in your heart.'

She rests her fingers against my cheek. The manicurist painted our fingernails first and Grandma's have dried into perfect Violently Violet moons. The pads of her aged fingers, behind the gloss, are dry and rough like sandpaper, but they're warm and I incline my head towards her touch.

'Did you know, Justine, that your Grandpa and I were married for fifty-four years?'

'I didn't know it was that long.'

'It was. Fifty-four good years. We were high school sweethearts – your grandfather was the only boy I ever kissed.' Grandma dabs at the corner of her eye, but she's beaming at the memory all the same. 'So when Grandpa died, I thought I was going to die, too. It felt like God had reached down from on high and cut my living-breathing heart out.' She says she imagines it must have felt somewhat the same for me, even worse maybe.

'Remember, Grandma, that story you used to tell us about how Grandpa thought at first, when he saw us in the hospital, he thought we were a two-headed baby?'

Grandma chuckles. 'Wasn't that funny? He thought you were Siamese twins, conjoined-like.'

'I think we were in a way, conjoined. And when Josh left, it felt like… it felt like I'd lost my head and my heart and half my body. Half my everything.'

I try to picture you and to picture Grandpa. And I picture me and Grandma right there with you, and nobody's missing any limbs or organs or whatever. We're happy and whole. Grandma dabs at her eyes and smiles, I wriggle my feet and fan my toenails with a three-month-old copy of *Good Housekeeping*.

'So what did you do?' I ask. 'After you lost Grandpa?'

And she says, as if it were just that simple: 'I didn't die.' Then she massages the small of my back the way she does with Mom and it feels good and she calls me baby too.

Another time when Grandma and I are having one of our talks, she tells me something else. She says that, though I probably won't believe it, it will get easier for me, Joshua. She says I'll go on, I'll have a life of my own and more loves like Toby – plenty of 'em, she predicts – and experiences that are all mine and mine alone. Even my own thoughts, and she says that'll be OK too.

Grandma says I have to trust her on that.

EPILOGUE

This much I accept: Joshua had some problems.

They tried to tell me I had a problem, too, and that's also true. My problem is my brother is dead, my twin, my soul mate, my Joshua. And I miss him.

I miss you, Joshua. I will always miss you.